Havoc

Acknowledgements

To Anne Buhrmann, Mary Young and Rosemary Bowe for
their editing, proof-reading and pertinent comments.
A special thanks to Frank McClendon in Nevada for his support
and keeping me abreast of events on his side of the pond.

To Gregor,
All the best!.

Paul Hunter

Havoc

Prologue

His passport described him as a reporter. When pressed, George C. Clarke *also* described himself as a reporter. The truth was, he hadn't reported much in over a year. In fact he had been sliding down the totem pole for nearly a decade now. And at fifty-five he had few places left to go. Which was why he'd accepted this latest assignment to Egypt. His editor back in New York had made it clear – either go to Africa or clear his desk. So he'd gone. Now here he was in a crummy bar in Cairo, drinking too much aquavit and beer chasers.

He could trace his slide from grace to exactly eight years ago. *Happy Anniversary*, he toasted himself in the dirty mirror lining the bar. Getting home from the Moscow trip early and finding his wife in bed with another man had been a shock. Breaking his jaw had been satisfying but expensive. She'd got the house, the kids, and the portfolio of investments. He'd been lucky not to go to jail for assault.

Alcohol cured his despondency for a while. He'd started drinking. Only in the evenings at first. Within a year it had been lunchtime. Now lunchtime started around eleven o'clock and frequently finished twelve hours later. His hand shook as he raised the shot glass of clear liquid to his lips. He threw it down in one smooth gesture and followed it with a mouthful of beer. The shaking stopped.

He took stock of the dump he was in. The room held about fifty scarred and battered tables, arranged to face the small stage. A fat belly-dancer was lethargically going through her routine.

1

The place was half full or half empty, depending on your outlook. For him, like his glass, it was half empty. He knew he needed to get back to the conference centre to cover the afternoon's session, but what the hell. He'd get what he needed from one of the others. Hacks stuck together, usually.

Electric fans turned slowly, re-distributing the smoke-filled and oppressive air. He signalled the barman for a refill and watched hungrily as the liquor was poured. To delay the moment of drinking, he turned his back on the bar and surveyed the room. The clientele consisted mainly of men, with a few prostitutes adding colour here and there. One table in the corner caught his interest. There was something vaguely familiar about the man sitting with his back to the door. It would come to him if he gave it long enough.

Clarke turned back to his drink. He stared it like it was his enemy, before wrapping a clammy hand around the glass. His was the action of the practised drunk and he drank it greedily. Lighting a cigarette, he leaned back against the bar and tried to stop thinking about the next shot. The gyrating woman did nothing for him and he lost interest as soon as he looked at her. The occupants of the other tables showed the same lack of interest. He glanced again at the corner table. Two Europeans and two Arabs, in deep discussion. His reporter's instincts twitched. It was a feeling he hadn't had for many years.

With beer glass in hand he moved to an empty table for a better look. He definitely knew the man. But who was he? His memory, befuddled by years of alcohol abuse, was working slowly. Even one of the ragheads appeared familiar.

What the hell, there was no harm in it. The thought had barely formed when he found himself at the table, looking at the four men. 'Say, don't I know you?' The reporter held his hand out to one of the Europeans, a silver-haired man about his own age.

'I don't think so. This is a private conversation. Please go.'

'Sure I do,' Clarke withdrew his hand, too drunk to notice the consternation he'd caused. 'It'll come to me in a moment.'

The man he had addressed said something to one of the Arabs. The man nodded and quickly rose.

'Hey,' Clarke protested as he was hustled towards the back door.

Another man crossed the room to help. Clarke found himself in a filthy alleyway at the back of the club. The Arab slipped a stiletto through the base of Clarke's skull and into his brain in a flash of agony. He didn't die for three seconds. Time enough to make the connection, *Charles Gustav*.

1

Know your enemy. Hunter had been studying his prey for several minutes. Watching the palm spider weave its delicate track across his arm. Tenacious, a survivor, it scurried into the bed of rotting leaves as soon as Hunter made a minuscule movement of his fingers. Hunter closed his eyes, allowing the sensations of the jungle to pour over him. Instinctively he filtered the noises. Directly above was the hiss of a tree-rat. The TIFAT operative hoped the rodent would stay until nightfall, when the other, larger mammals went marauding.

Hunter had been in the jungle on three previous occasions and had hated each one. His love was the sea, his passion was diving and sailing. Being in a hide in Suriname was not his idea of fun. He and his team had been there for four days. The smallest country in South America, Suriname in recent years had become a major route for the transhipment of drugs destined for Europe. According to intelligence reports, the heavily escorted mule train of cocaine that they were waiting to ambush was worth in the region of half a billion dollars. The sums of money involved were astronomical.

There were ten of them in the team and most of them lived on an income of less than £32,000 per annum, which included special services pay, and here they were yet again putting their lives on the line. He grinned mirthlessly. Neither he nor the rest of the team would have it any other way.

Their ingress into the country had been secret. Official permission for the operation would never have been forthcoming. For eight of the last twenty-two years the military had been in power. Suriname was trying to strike a fine balancing act between the civilian and military rulers. No permission and no official recognition. It was too easy to be betrayed by a corrupt pen pusher. There were many hands greased by the huge bribes that oiled the trade.

They had parachuted in from a Hercules W2, normally used for weather reconnaissance and operated by the Meteorological Research Flight based at Boscombe Down, in England. The aircraft had a white and grey fuselage, and long pointed nose and operated mainly in the northern hemisphere. A special visit to Brazil had been arranged at short notice and the plane despatched. They had refuelled from Hercules tankers twice before arriving in Suriname airspace. The team had bailed out high, at night, aiming for a clear spot in the jungle. Not long ago the jump would have been considered suicidal. But using satellites and mobile positioning gear they could leap out at 25,000ft with pin-point accuracy. They had landed safely with all their equipment, bivouacked for what was left of the night and at dawn began a forced route march through the interior. Two of their number had taken the opposite direction. They had the heaviest loads to carry but had only five kilometres to cover. They would make the journey four times ferrying the back-up equipment. Hunter hoped they wouldn't need it.

The remainder of the team had twenty klicks to travel. Thanks to up-to-date satellite mapping, they were steered along existing paths, past impressive waterfalls, to the track they wanted. The trip had taken under five hours. It had seldom been necessary to cut back the encroaching jungle. Each man carried 65lbs on his back, carefully packed into his bergen. The going was tough, with the temperature in the nineties and the humidity over eighty. Sweat poured out of them as if they were under a shower. They chewed salt tablets, sipping their specially prepared water – doctored with much needed chemicals – at regular intervals. Rests were taken five minutes every hour. No one complained. It was what they had signed up for.

The nine men and one woman in the TIFAT patrol were

hand-picked special services operatives from the world's best. Hunter would have trusted any of them with his life and often had. Their skills and tenacity had carried the team through countless extreme situations. A mine and bomb-disposal diving specialist in the Royal Navy, Hunter led the team. His second-in-command was Joshua Clements, an American on secondment from Delta force. In the party were Jan Badonovitch, a Russian Spetsnaz, Claude Masson, a French Commando, Doug Tanner – the only African American, was a SEAL from Louisiana. Frank Hales – a New Yorker seconded from the Green Berets – was the other American on the team. All the others, REME sergeant Don Masters, a quietly spoken, tough Scotsman, David Hughes, an SAS sergeant from Wales, and Douglas Napier, a lieutenant with the British Special Boats Service, were British. The tenth person – Ruth Golightly, the only woman in the team – was on loan from the Israeli Mossad. Bringing her along on the mission had been a difficult decision for Hunter. They had been lovers for some time and his instinct was to protect her, not expose her to the dangers of the South American jungle. But Ruth was as committed to the eradication of the drug runners as any member of the team and he had no justifiable reason to leave her out.

In recognition of her sex, Ruth's pack weighed merely 45lbs, the only concession offered or accepted. They had yomped in single file, with Hughes half a klick ahead, and Frank Hales the same behind. Intel updates were transmitted every hour, on the hour, from TIFAT HQ in Scotland.

They had set up the ambush along a well-worn path, wide enough to allow two donkeys to pass without touching. Hughes continued on point, ready to warn of the smugglers' arrival. Frank Hales went back half a klick along the path to mop up the advance guard they knew would be leading the donkey train.

When it wasn't raining it was steaming hot. On arrival, each of them had dug a hole waist deep and long enough to lay down in. The hides were carefully camouflaged. Nobody moved outside their hole to ensure that there was no disruption to the area. After only a few days it looked like a natural part of the landscape.

One give-away in these situations was the sense of smell. Rotting vegetation was one thing, cigarette smoke and the minty tang of toothpaste another. None of the team were smokers but they all missed brushing their teeth. Hunter used small pieces of twig to clean his, chewing fern tips he knew to be safe.

The other major problem of being in a hide had been taken care of. Prior to arriving in Suriname they had spent four days eating special rations. By the second day their systems had been cleansed. They would not need to go to the toilet until after the operation. Apart from urinating. Even that was an art form, as their urine passed through a personal purifier for re-use. They had tried a group purifier but the consensus of opinion was they would rather die of thirst than drink it.

Each of them heard the Intel updates on their personal sat-nav phone and were assured that the narco-traffickers were finally coming. Only their time of arrival was unknown. The smugglers were using a trail that was over a thousand kilometres long. A combination of dense rain forest and vast quantities of camouflage netting kept the smugglers hidden from the spy-satellites. Infra-red seekers were almost useless. The temperature difference between the surrounding jungle and the bodies walking the route was insufficient to register properly.

Three days they had been in situ. The hours had dragged slowly, sapping their energy. It was too dangerous to walk through the jungle at night and so there had been no fear that the smugglers would have arrived while it was dark. Day and night the jungle was never silent. Small animals and reptiles roamed freely amongst the ferns and spiky palms that made up the undergrowth. The odourless insect repellent the team was using was ineffective. They were tormented by mosquitoes at dawn and dusk.

They had two escape routes once the job was over. The one Hunter favoured was a helicopter ride into Brazil. The second meant a trip down the River Maroni, fifty klicks to the east. The two-man escape team was already there and waiting, just in case.

The radios picked up a signal a few minutes before 3pm. No voice, just three clicks then a pause, followed by three more clicks. There was a further delay while Hughes counted the advance patrol as they passed him. He sent five clicks. Five armed men in front. The team waited, nervous sweat mixing with the perspiration caused by the heat and humidity.

Five men came into sight, dressed in army fatigues and carrying rifles slung over their shoulders. They were speaking loudly in a Portuguese patois that was incomprehensible even to the two Portuguese speakers in the team.

More clicks. Two this time, as Hunter and his team watched the five men vanish around a corner in the trail. The main body of the caravan was half a klick behind. They waited with coldeyed determination. Half a billion dollars worth of coke would cause untold suffering in the West. It had to be stopped.

'Boss,' Hughes broke radio silence with a whisper. 'I don't like it. I count eighteen armed guards and here's the bad news, they're all either European or American and highly alert.'

'Roger that,' whispered Hunter. 'Any tail-end Charlies?'

'Negative. There are twelve donkeys being led by one peasant with another bringing up the rear. The guards are either side.'

Hunter and his men were armed with silenced Steyr Tactical Machine Pistol submachine guns. Constructed entirely in synthetic material, the TMP was so tough that steel inserts to guide the bolt were not required. It fired in single or automatic bursts and the magazine held up to twenty-five rounds of 9mm Parabellum cartridges. The sound suppressers they had fitted reduced the noise of the gun to a burp in a high wind. Yet their primary weapon remained surprise.

They could hear the caravan approaching. Two soldiers came into sight, unshaven, their wary eyes roaming back and forth. They spared only a glance for the positions where the team were hiding. The first soldier had already passed Hunter when a click in his ear piece told him that the last smuggler had reached Badonovitch at the furthest end. It was the signal to begin. Hunter aimed upwards from a distance of about three metres, firing through a slit in the foliage. He fired twice, aiming at the third man in the file. Both shots hit home – one through the heart, the other through the throat. His second target screamed as he smashed onto the track, struck by Hunter's bullets. The man in front spun around with an oath but he was far too late. Hunter's next two shots killed him instantly.

Pushing back the camouflage, Hunter leapt out of the hole. The jungle air was filled with yells and curses. The donkeys began to bray and kick as automatic gunfire rent the air. Hunter took a snap shot at one of the peasants but he was already vanishing into the jungle and the bullet missed. One guard lying on the ground brought his gun to bear and pulled the trigger. It was on fully automatic and the bullets stitched a pattern across the track and into one of the foxholes. Hunter killed the man with a double tap, both shots to the body.

The other members of the team were climbing out and finishing off the job. Because they had been so well hidden none of the team were shot at directly. Most of the smugglers had died before they even knew what was happening. The peasant at the end of the donkey train had turned and fled. Hunter sent out a radio message which Hughes acknowledged. He would wait until the man arrived at his position.

Frank Hales reported in. 'All five down. No problems.'

'Roger that. Stay where you are in case of unexpected visitors.'

The team began cutting open the sacks tied across the donkeys' backs. They contained pure white cocaine, refined to the highest quality. They hacked the sacks to pieces, scattering the fortune in coke across the jungle floor. Already the slight breeze was dispersing it, wiping out half a billion dollars. The rain began again and helped the process. The donkeys had settled down and stood placidly, snorting, shifting a leg, unperturbed amidst the clouds of white dust.

Napier had been rifling the pockets of the dead men. 'Boss, you'd better take a look.'

Hunter took the offered document and recognised it as a French passport. He compared the picture. It was him all right.

The wounded smuggler groaned. Hunter knelt by his side. 'What's your name?'

The man looked at Hunter with hatred and spat out a mouthful of insults, his French vowels identifying him as a native of the

Midi. Hunter asked the question again, in the same language. He was given another mouthful of abuse.

The remainder of the team had been ready to move at a moment's notice and were already pulling their bergens from their holes and strapping them to their backs.

Hughes radioed in. 'Boss, we've got problems. A patrol has just rushed past me, moving fast. I counted twenty in all. They're on foot and heavily armed.'

'Roger that. Time to go.' Hunter was preparing to put a bullet in the head of the injured man when the Frenchman arched his back and exhaled for the last time.

Standing up Hunter grabbed his bergen, searching Ruth out automatically. 'Are you okay?' he asked her.

'Sure. No problems. You?'

He looked into her brown eyes and grinned. The shower had already passed and the sunlight filtering through the treetops reflected on her smooth, lightly tanned skin. The shadows from the leaves made geometric patterns across her beautiful face. 'Listen up,' he called. 'You heard Dave. We need to move fast. All set?'

They moved out at a rapid pace. Hunter had already prepared a number of booby-traps while he had been in the foxhole. He quickly set them.

'Dave, are you following?' Hunter transmitted.

'Affirmative. They're coming fast as they're travelling light. Between me and them are three donkeys, each with a minder, with packs. Another man has just joined them.'

'He was probably the one who ran up the track. They'll slow down now, if they know what's happened. Can you take out those four and ditch their supplies?'

'Will do. They've stopped. Some of them don't look too happy about following. They're arguing. Hang on.' The radio went silent for a few seconds. 'They're coming this way. They're heading back up the trail.'

'In that case leave them. As soon as they're out of sight follow us. Frank?'

'Here, boss.'

'Stay hidden. As soon as we're past, set the explosives. When Dave reaches you follow behind. We'll have whoever is chasing us between a rock and a hard place.'

'Roger that.'

Hunter surveyed his handiwork. The green thread was impossible to spot. He hurried after the others, opening out his stride. At six-foot two he had a long reach. The traps he had just set were, according to international agreements, illegal. Classed as an anti-personnel mine they were a variation on the Claymore. He had set four of them. Any of eight tripwires would set them off. When they did, C-4 plastic explosive would fire seven hundred steel balls in a forward sixty degrees pattern that grew to six feet and killed anybody within one hundred and seventy feet.

They passed Chief Petty Officer Frank Hales who had set a similar trap before dropping back into his hide.

The team had travelled nearly three klicks when they heard the explosions, remarkably faint in the distance. They continued on, moving fast, returning along the path they had followed three days earlier. It was twenty minutes before Hughes called in.

'The Clays took out three and wounded one. He was shot through the head by his own people. One of the men went berserk, screaming orders at the top of his voice. They radioed in somewhere but I've no idea where or to whom.'

'Roger that. I'll ask HQ. Isobel's listening to all frequencies in this area. When you reach Frank follow – fast and carefully.'

Hunter broke the connection. Like the others he was breathing heavily as they kept up their killing pace. Plan Alpha was the cushy option – a helicopter ride out. They were meant to return to the drop point and await the arrival of the helo. If they couldn't stop their pursuers there was no chance. They would have to use plan Bravo. They were nearly forty minutes from Hales when he radioed.

'The trap took two. They're well strung out now, taking fewer risks. I count fourteen.'

'Roger that. Follow with Dave but don't get seen.'

'He's here now. We're moving out.'

They had a lead of about forty-five minutes. Too small a margin to sit waiting for a helicopter to arrive, so there was no choice. The odds now were almost even. An ambush would turn the situation to their advantage. Hunter was already planning ahead, remembering the terrain they had crossed. One piece of ground sprang to mind. He knew the track passed through a defile, with walls as high as twenty or thirty metres in some places. At one time it had been the bed of a stream but the water had long since dried up.

Explosives each end and an ambush from above would soon settle matters.

Between gasps he briefed everyone over their personal radios.

He had just finished when the sat-nav phone warbled.

'Nick? Isobel.' Hunter recognised the voice of TIFAT's IT expert. 'You've got a big problem. We intercepted a radio message from the scene of the ambush to somebody in the capital, Paramaribo. They called for helo backup. Three have been scrambled.'

'Hell! We've nothing to take out a helo. Are they attack 'copters or just bringing in reinforcements?'

'We don't know at this stage. But from the transmissions we've intercepted you've kicked over a hornets' nest. Somebody is going berserk over the loss of the shipment – over the half a billion profit, more like. The men chasing you have been told if they fail they needn't bother returning.'

'Any chance of back-up?'

'The General is working on that right now.'

Hunter was thinking furiously. They had about eight klicks to the ambush site. He was gasping when he asked, 'Are those enemy helos airborne yet?'

'Negative. I'll let you know as soon as they are. You can cross into French Guiana at the River Maroni.'

'What's the chance of hot pursuit?'

'Inevitable, I should think. They could scream murderers and thieves and demand free access.'

'That's what I figure. All right, I need to go.'

Breaking the connection, Hunter knew that if they were to survive they had to make the river.

Hunter checked the sat-nav picture and broadcast to the others. 'Three klicks. Let's step on it.'

They increased their speed, the pace murderous to all but the fittest. It became a brutal race. They needed cover, they needed time to prepare and they needed luck, and not necessarily in that order.

The team got to work as soon as they reached the narrow gorge. Each member knew what was required without being told. Hunter left them to get on with it while he climbed the steep slope to the top. From the jungle plain the hill he had climbed sprang up like a carbuncle. It had been cut in two by eons of water erosion, though the stream running through had dried leaving a rocky defile. Steep-sided, a hundred feet high in the middle, it was surrounded by impenetrable jungle on all sides. It was the only way through and a good place for an ambush. A fact their pursuers would surely recognise as well.

Staying low he crawled over the top and lay behind a boulder, focusing binoculars on the path they had just run. He called Hughes and Hales for a sitrep.

'Boss, we're about five klicks away. About half a klick behind the enemy.'

'Roger that. Close up when you're one klick away. When I give the word launch an all out attack.'

They broke the connection. The sat-nav phone warbled softly and Hunter answered it. General Malcolm Macnair, head of TIFAT, his gruff voice slightly distorted by space and distance, coming all the way from Rosyth, still managed to instil Hunter with a sense of power and authority.

'Hullo, sir. Any good news?'

'Yes. The *Ark Royal* is on exercise in the Atlantic. She's steaming at full speed towards Suriname. According to the Captain, he can launch in five minutes.'

'What's he sending?'

'Harriers, Foxtrot Alpha Twos.'

Hunter knew the Sea Harrier named was used in the twin roles of combat air support and battlefield interdiction. They carried Sidewinders, AMRAAM missiles and cannons.

'How did you manage it, sir?'

'Friends in low places,' joked the General. 'They know the picture. They'll be coming up country following the river Maroni, staying on the border between Suriname and French Guiana.'

'How long will they stay?'

'No more than five minutes. The enemy helos have launched and we reckon they'll be on site in thirty to thirty-five minutes.'

'Roger that, sir. Thanks and thank the *Ark* for us.'

'Will do.' The General paused and then added, 'Good luck, Nick.'

The connection was broken and Hunter turned his attention back to surviving the next forty minutes.

The team had already deployed. If they were tired after their yomp through the jungle they didn't show it. Hunter shucked down by Ruth.

'You okay?' He respected her professionalism too much to compromise her with anything more.

Their eyes met, conveying emotions which could not be articulated just then.

'Sure, Nick, quit worrying.'

At that second, he wished fervently that they had told the General about their plans. Maybe Ruth could have gone home and told her parents. Her father had been the Deputy Prime Minister of Israel and was about to start fighting a general election. He was a man Hunter greatly respected.

As if reading his mind, Ruth smiled. 'Once this is over we can make the announcement and celebrate in style.' She eased her bergen and lifted out a couple of hand-grenades.

Hunter tapped her shoulder, smiled and moved to his position ten yards away. The team checked in. All preparations were complete. They lay silently in the baking heat. The sun was hidden by a thick layer of cloud and as they looked across the top of the jungle they could see isolated storms. Jagged flashes of lightning streaked across the sky. There was no rain as yet, just a heavy, hot and humid atmosphere.

Hughes radioed in. 'One klick and closing fast.'

'Okay. Close up and when I give the word hit them with everything you've got.'

It was another five minutes before Masters broke the silence. 'Here they come. They're at the edge of the jungle.'

'I see them,' replied Hunter.

One man was edging along the path, cautious now without the cover of the jungle. He stopped and spoke to another, who was still out of sight. There was more movement and the second man appeared. He put a pair of binoculars to his eyes and began to slowly scan the defile. Nobody in the team moved, hardly breathing. Another two men came equally cautiously into view.

Hunter spoke softly into his microphone. 'Dave, Frank, hit them . . . now.'

From inside the green jungle screen came the unmistakable sound of machine-guns opening fire followed by the loud bangs of detonating grenades. Hughes and Hales were certainly doing as they had been instructed. Across the two hundred metres of open ground came the yells and curses of soldiers being attacked.

The man with the binoculars pointed and bellowed an order. All his men came streaming out of the jungle and along the path towards the defile. Hunter and the team waited patiently. Twelve men in total, so the attack had whittled down another two of their number.

The lead man was already at the gorge and turning to give covering fire to his colleagues. They quickly entered what they considered to be the relative safety of the defile and fanned out, ready to fend off whoever was behind them. They could afford to wait. With attack helos and reinforcements arriving soon they had nothing to lose and everything to gain.

Masters set off the first explosion.

The plastic had been carefully laid at the entrance to the defile. When it detonated tons of rock were dislodged, raining down on the men in the gorge. Two were killed outright and three were seriously wounded. The remainder turned as one and ran along the path. The first man was almost at the midway point when a second explosion erupted at his feet. He was blown to pieces, as was the man close behind. The third man was shielded and stayed on his feet but a rock the size of a football landed on his head and crushed it like a ripe tomato. Other rocks rained down maiming and injuring others.

Before the dust had settled hand grenades were lobbed down. Any screams and yells ended abruptly. The team stayed where they were, listening intently. So far it had not been necessary to show themselves and risk getting shot. A wounded man could easily be waiting below, determined to get revenge before he died.

After a few minutes Hunter cautiously looked over the edge. He saw nothing except fallen rocks and body parts. He scanned the area closely. Nothing moved. Over his radio he said, 'Take a careful look.'

Along the edge of the defile the team moved slowly, inching forward, taking a snap look. The gunshot was loud in the aftermath of the battle. A bullet struck a rock next to Napier's head and a chip of stone cut deeply across his cheek. In order to fire at his target, the man had stood up suddenly. Before he could drop back down out of sight Doug Tanner put a bullet in his brain.

Hughes and Hales arrived at the entrance to the defile and were working their way along, looking for live bodies. They reached the spot where the second explosion had occurred and gave the all clear.

'Prepare for the helicopters arriving,' Hunter ordered. He called TIFAT HQ and gave a sitrep.

'Excellent, Nick,' said the General. 'But you're not out of trouble yet. Their helicopters are five minutes out. Our Harriers are fully ten minutes behind them.'

'Roger that, sir. We'd better get ready.' At the bottom of the defile the team were checking the bodies of the dead men, searching for papers.

Claude Masson joined him. 'Boss, I recognise one of these scumbags.'

'Who is he?'

'Used to be a paratrooper with the Legion. Tough son of a bitch. One thing I remember about him, he was ultra right-wing.'

'How do you mean?'

'You know, the usual crap. France for the French, provided they're white. I'm sure he was thrown out for killing an Algerian in a brawl in a bar in Toulon.'

'Did he go to prison?'

Masson shrugged. 'Sorry, I can't remember.'

On impulse Hunter thrust a handful of passports at him. 'Take a look at these and see if you recognise anyone else.'

The sergeant quickly looked through them and looked at Hunter in puzzlement. 'I'm positive about one other and I'm almost sure I recognise a third.'

'Who are they?'

'Special forces. Or ex, anyway. You know what a small world we inhabit.'

Hunter nodded. He knew people all over the globe who were in special forces. Theirs was a close-knit world.

He'd just buttoned the passports into his top pocket when the first helicopter screamed into sight.

They were AS565s, known as Panthers. Built in France by Aérospatiale the Panther carried various externally mounted weapons, including air to ground missiles. The lead helo pilot made a grave error almost immediately. He flew in close to determine the identity of the men on the ground. Unfortunately for him, the TIFAT operatives he targeted were Badonovitch and Weir, the latter an Olympics standard rifleman. They already had their sniper rifles out and loaded with a specially constructed explosive bullet. They fired simultaneously and both men hit the helicopter. The bullets exploded on impact, killing the pilot outright. Out of control, the helo began to spin before crashing and erupting into flame less than a hundred metres from where the team stood. The other two 'copters swung down and away before the riflemen could take aim.

'Incoming!' Badonovitch yelled, seconds before a missile slammed into the side of the gorge. The explosion was huge. Tons of rocks were blown into the air, landing amongst the team, causing some minor injuries.

The helicopters hovered out of range and a second missile was launched at the team. It landed between Ruth and Frank Hales who were lying on the ground behind large boulders. The explosion sent a rock flying through the air striking Hales on the temple, killing him instantly. A second rock flew high and landed with a sickening crunch on Ruth's leg. She screamed in agony as her knee was crushed.

2

Men began to rappel out of the helicopters. Before the first touched the ground a Sidewinder missile flew into the side of the helicopter and blew it to smithereens. Debris and burning fuel tumbled out of the sky, killing the soldiers who were deploying underneath, preparing to attack. The cavalry, in the form of the two Harriers, had arrived just in time.

The other helicopter met the same end. When the second missile hit it, two of the soldiers had already reached the ground and were running in the direction of the defile. They had been expecting the helicopters to supply massive covering fire in the form of missiles and cannons. When the helicopters blew apart the two men stopped in shock. The first was killed by Badonovitch and the second wounded by Tanner.

The two Harriers flew over, waggled their wings and streaked north again, out of the country. They would be back on board the *Ark Royal* in time for tea.

Hunter had not waited to watch the action. Within seconds of hearing Ruth scream he was beside her, tearing open a first aid kit, frantically searching for an injection of morphine to give her. Don Masters was with him, rapidly undoing a bandage to wrap around the badly bleeding wound. Ruth was moaning, only semi-conscious, from the pain and shock of her injury.

Hunter injected a powerful pain-killer into her left thigh and calf. Within a few moments Ruth stopped moaning and passed out completely.

Apart from bruises and cuts none of the remainder were hurt.

A bodybag was opened and Frank Hales placed inside. Special Services never left the bodies of their own behind. Folding stretchers were quickly assembled. Hunter meanwhile was reporting to TIFAT.

Macnair acknowledged the report. 'The extraction helo won't get to you before tomorrow and then it'll take you to Brazil.'

'I know, sir. We're going to run for the river. We'll take the inflatables and head downstream as fast as we can. Please ask *Ark* for a helo to casevac Ruth. The doctors on board may be able to help.'

'How bad is she?'

Already the team were preparing to move out. Unable to trust his voice for a second, Hunter looked around him. It would be fast and furious to the river and all unwanted equipment was being abandoned. Guns and water were about all they would be carrying. Along with the two stretchers.

'Bad, sir. The knee is completely crushed. Bones right through the flesh.' He didn't say it but he didn't think Ruth would ever walk on that leg again. She would be lucky not to lose it from above the knee.

'Roger that. Get moving. We'll be tracking you. I'll let you know when the helo is on its way.' The General didn't bother telling Hunter that he was already embroiled in a diplomatic row for sending in the jets. To Macnair his people came first and diplomacy a very poor second. The helo would be sent in as soon as possible.

The team moved out while Hunter joined David Hughes next to the wounded mercenary. The bullet had hit him in the right shoulder and passed through, smashing the collar bone and leaving a gaping exit wound.

'Leave him,' said Hunter callously, 'and let's go.'

'I know him, boss,' was Hughes' startling reply.

At that moment the wounded man opened his eyes and said, 'Hullo, Taff. Fancy seeing your ugly mug here.'

'Save it, Fletcher! What outfit are you working for?'

The man looked at Hughes through narrowed eyes before replying. 'Fix my shoulder first and I'll tell you.'

Hunter placed his gun to the man's temple and said harshly, 'Answer the question or, by God, you'll regret it.'

'You wouldn't dare,' Fletcher gasped, the barrel digging into his skin.

Hunter could feel the adrenaline pumping around his body, making him giddy. 'Thanks to your mob one of my men has been killed and a woman seriously injured, you little piece of excrement. Personally, I'm more than willing to end your pathetic life. So I suggest you start naming names.'

The man could see that he meant it. Hunter's face was set as if it was carved from stone, his dark blue eyes almost black in their anger and hatred.

'I left Hereford last year and joined a mob who wanted heavy muscle. That's all there is to it.'

'Wait up,' said Hughes. 'I've been trying to remember. You were thrown out for attacking a black soldier. Another SAS man. A few of you were named as members of some sort of right-wing organisation connected to Le Pen in France.'

Hunter took the man's passport and checked it. It was genuine. 'So what were you doing in Suriname?'

'We were sent in to kill you after you stopped the drug shipment.'

'Who sent you?'

'No way – I've said enough. I know my rights. I'm a soldier and under the Geneva Convention . . .'

He got no further as Hunter hit him across the mouth with the barrel of his gun, breaking three of the man's teeth. Fletcher screamed loudly.

'Who sent you?'

'I swear I don't know.' The mercenary spat out blood and jagged pieces of tooth. 'We were hired by an outfit in Britain and sent here to cover the shipment of coke. I swear, that's all I know.'

Hunter could see he wouldn't learn anymore and he had neither the time nor the inclination to make him talk. He stood up. 'Let's go, Dave.'

Hughes nodded and the two men turned to leave.

'What about me?' Fletcher said.

'You can live or die for all I care,' Hunter said calmly, picking up the man's machine-gun.

'You can't leave me.'

'Your gun will be by the path,' replied Hunter. He and Hughes broke into a jog. As they ran, Hunter checked the weapon. When he dropped it near the jungle path there was only one bullet left. Hunter threw the rest away. He doubted Fletcher would live long as the wound was a nasty one and still bleeding. If a big cat or other predator chanced upon him he had a choice. Kill the cat or kill himself.

The team were well ahead and Hunter and Hughes opened up their pace. Hunter ran on automatic, his fear for Ruth all-pervading. He knew that the two team members at the river would be getting ready to move out, having been briefed by Macnair. One of the two, Matt Dunston, was a trained medic. More than that, he was a friend. He would have a drip ready and anything else he could think of. Thinking of Ruth made Hunter speed up again. Hughes didn't complain but kept alongside. The pace was crippling.

They caught up with the remainder of the team near the drop zone. Hunter ran alongside Ruth, who was still unconscious on the stretcher. The team changed carriers every fifteen minutes without breaking stride, eating up the kilometres to the river. They knew that once they got there they could rest.

Hunter checked their position. 'Two klicks, keep it up,' he called.

The knowledge put new heart into them and they picked up their flagging speed. Each man was drenched in sweat. Luckily they would be at their destination before dehydration became a problem.

Ahead of them they suddenly heard the deep-throated roar of an outboard motor bursting into life. Rounding a bend they found themselves at the edge of the jungle, the brown, sluggish water of the river in front of them. Tethered to the bank were two large inflatables, each powered by an Evinrude 120hp engine.

They quickly climbed on board. Ruth was handed over to Matt

Dunston's care. Hunter sat at the boat's console while Dunston was already feeling for a vein in Ruth's arm to feed a drip into her.

Hunter engaged the gears in reverse and backed away from the bank. The other inflatable followed, driven by Weir. They turned in unison and headed downstream. The river was a hundred metres wide and over three metres deep in the middle. On either side, the jungle formed a wall of green hiding the eyes of predators as they streaked past.

Dunston worked silently on Ruth's leg, muttering a prayer as he tried to reset pieces of the bone. But he knew it was hopeless. Eye contact and a grimace to Hunter spoke volumes.

Whenever the boat passed a low bank or shallows, alligators could be seen. They watched in total disinterest as the two boats flashed past, pushing 25 to 30 knots. Hunter's boat led. In the bows lay two lookouts watching for hidden obstacles in the water. Utmost vigilance was called for. The river had many branches and logs floating on or just under the surface. The remainder of the team were eating and drinking, each man with his weapon close at hand. The second boat followed in the wake, ten metres behind. The deep-veed hull of the inflatables ate up the distance. On land they dealt in kilometres, now they were on the water, as at sea, they dealt in miles. A hundred and twenty remained until they reached the coast.

Occasionally they passed an isolated building, sitting forlornly at the water's edge. There was other river traffic, going both ways. Mostly slow and cumbersome shallow draft boats carrying people and livestock. The people on the boats saw the armed soldiers and watched stony-faced.

Hunter passed a sitrep to Macnair using his sat-nav.

'We're following your beacons on the screen,' said the General. 'The *Ark* is heading towards the coast at flank speed. As soon as a helo is en-route I'll give you an ETA. How's Ruth?'

'Not good,' replied Hunter, his tone flat.

'I'm arranging to have a surgeon flown down to *Ark Royal*. He works at San Diego hospital but has a reserve job with the SEALs at Coronado. Specialises in bones.'

'Thanks, sir.' Hope flared in Hunter. He should have known that Macnair would do all in his power to help. 'Any unusual activity around the river?'

'Not that we can see. It appears clear all the way to the coast but of course that can change at any time. I'm playing Suriname off against French Guiana and hoping they'll let you fall between the cracks.' He didn't tell Hunter he had already been on the phone to the Foreign Office to get the Foreign Secretary to threaten both governments if they tried to interfere. The FS was tough and enjoyed throwing his weight around when he could. He had let both governments know in no uncertain terms that any attempt to stop the team would have the direst consequences. He hadn't specified what, but had invoked the anti-terrorism mantra that had arisen since 9/11. *The enemy of terrorism is our friend; a supporter is our enemy; there are no bystanders.*

Of course that did not cover rogue elements in the armed forces of either country. Or even a general with too much pride who took it as a personal affront that the TIFAT team was in his country without permission.

Hunter began weaving the boat around a ferry that was crossing left to right, its decks packed with people looking and pointing. The diverse cultural mix of the Suriname population was evident – the people on board were of Asian and African extraction, as well as South American.

On each side of the river stood a motley group of houses, wooden and ramshackle. Flags hung in the still air announcing a customs post, although there were no signs of any officials.

Hunter checked their position. Eighty miles to go to the coast. Glancing back he saw that Weir had been relieved at the wheel of the second boat and Josh Clements was now driving. He indicated to Napier to take his place. Kneeling by Ruth, Hunter took her hand. She was in a deep sleep and looked peaceful enough.

'How is she?' he shouted to Dunston above the noise of the engine.

His friend shrugged and pulled a face. 'It's not looking good, Nick.'

Hunter nodded. He was totally helpless and that was a feeling he hated. To occupy himself he collected the passports they had lifted from the dead men and went through them. There were eleven in total, two British, two Dutch, one Austrian, two German, three French and an Italian. The names and faces meant nothing to Hunter, but they all had one thing in common. They all looked like tough sons of bitches.

Taking out the sat-phone stowed in the boat he put on earphones and face mask. Without them, struggling against the noise of the engine, it was impossible to have a conversation without yelling and asking for repeats.

'Isobel? Hunter. Can I speak to the General?'

'He's right here.'

'Nick? You seem to be making good progress. The helo is launching in five. It'll be with you in an hour.'

'Just the one?'

'Yes. For Ruth only. A paramedic is on board. He'll take care of her. As soon as you're in the open sea we'll lift the rest of you. There isn't time to take anybody else. We're beginning to get signal noise around your area. Nothing specific yet but something is stirring.'

'Understood. The reason I called is that the dead men are all Europeans. Matt is scanning in the passport details now and will transmit them as soon as he's finished. Get Isobel to do a trace. As far as we can gather, they're all ex-special forces. I suggest Isobel checks their reasons for leaving the services and more especially their political leanings.'

'Specifically?'

'Right wing, fascist, the usual garbage.'

'Will do. I'll also get Isobel tracking the money, their bank accounts, see what they throw up. Who their paymaster is.'

'Good idea, sir.'

'Good luck and be careful.'

'I will.' But Hunter was talking to a disconnected phone.

The closer to the coast they got the more traffic there was on the river. They were eventually forced to slow down to about half speed. According to the readout on the console they were still thirty-three miles from the coast when they heard the clatter of a helicopter. A second later they saw a Sea King Mk 6, the roundels of the Royal Air Force painted on its side.

Napier throttled back to 10 knots and the helo hovered over them. Radio contact was kept to a minimum. With a maximum speed of 150 knots and a range of 450 nautical miles, the helo was being flown to its limits.

A hook reeled down and was touched by an earthing pole to remove the static electricity that had built up during flight. Matt grabbed the hook and snatched it on to a harness. The stretcher was whisked away in seconds. Ruth vanished in board and the hook reappeared. This time the bag containing Frank Hales' body was lifted away. With a lump in his throat Hunter watched the helicopter increase speed and head north, weaving around the bends, following the border between the two countries. Ruth would soon be in good hands.

Napier was already increasing speed back up to 15 and then 20 knots. Checking their position Hunter saw that they were only minutes away from the towns of St Laurent on the right bank and Albina on the left. He signalled to the boats to slow down as now the river was seriously crowded with everything from bum-boats to large ferries crossing in both directions.

The river was widening to the estuary and the raucous call of sea birds could be heard as they scavenged for food. The inflatables were down to 5 or 6 knots, weaving amongst the other traffic. The team was wary, keeping a sharp lookout for trouble. Their weapons were held close at hand but out of sight. They had stripped off their camouflaged jackets and trousers and now wore T-shirts and jeans, courtesy of the escape party. Every scenario had been addressed – the plan refined endlessly until finally Macnair announced it was time to go with it. Heads of departments had agreed. But they also knew that for all the planning, double-guessing and forethought there was no way they could foresee the unexpected. All plans were set in clay, not stone, to be recast at any moment.

The houses on each side of the river were drab and in need of repair. The atmosphere of the villages was strangely Asian, the women wearing sarongs, their cooking smells wafting down to the riverside. Men thronged the waterfront on both sides and the noise of street vendors mingled with the sound of vehicles belching smoke through cracked silencers. The water was filthy and stank of open sewage. Dead animals floated on the surface, the ebbing tide taking them slowly to the sea. They were about half-a-mile from the river entrance and the open sea when a black and white customs boat pulled out from the left bank and headed directly towards them. On board were a dozen armed soldiers. They appeared to be natives.

An official waving a bullhorn ordered them to stop in the water.

Napier looked at Hunter who nodded. The boat slowed but was kept in gear.

'Put up your hands so I can see them.' The accent was heavy but the English was intelligible.

None of the team moved a muscle but sat looking at the approaching boat. The second inflatable had drifted to one side – far enough away to cause the soldiers to have to split their attention. From their scruffy uniforms it was immediately obvious to the team that they were dealing with poorly trained troops. The advantage could however also create a huge problem. Bad training resulted in poor discipline.

The boat was old, about forty feet long with a machine gun mounted on the bows. One man stood swinging the gun between the inflatables while a second nervously fingered its bandoleer of bullets.

Hunter assumed that the man standing on the open bridge with the bullhorn was an officer although it was difficult to tell from that range.

'What's the problem?' Hunter yelled up.

'You are in Suriname territory. I demand you come ashore for questioning.'

'We're in Guiana waters,' Hunter replied, 'and demand safe passage.'

'No demands *Inglês*!' Feedback on the horn caused a high-pitched squeal that would have been comical under other circumstances.

By now Hunter's inflatable was within fifty yards of the Suriname boat. All eyes were on him, just as he wanted. Bad discipline was working in the team's favour.

Hunter gave a hand signal and the team in the other inflatable grabbed their weapons. A single silenced shot hit the bullhorn and sent it flying into the water. The officer screamed loudly, cursing in the local lingua franca. Before the troops realised what had happened five guns were pointed at them from the other inflatable.

'Look behind you,' Hunter called. 'I think we have what the Americans call a Mexican stand-off. We'll cut you to pieces although you may get one or two of us.' He made another hand signal. A second silenced shot hit the windscreen of the boat and shattered it.

The distraction was enough. The troops turned to look at the other inflatable, allowing Hunter's men time to grab their guns. The sound of bolts being worked was ominous, making the Suriname troops more nervous than ever.

Hunter knew that he had to diffuse the situation quickly. One nervous finger on a trigger and all hell would break loose. Some of the team could be injured or even killed.

'Captain, I beg you, let us pass. Pride is not worth dying for and you would be the first. Tell your men to slowly put down their weapons. We don't want any trouble. We just want to get out of here.'

Hunter's inflatable had motored slowly towards the customs boat. Now they were less than twenty yards apart. Hunter could see the nervous perspiration on the officer's face, his unshaved cheeks and thick moustache black against a deeply tanned face. His troops looked to be no more than teenagers.

Hunter used psychology, a face-saving gesture. 'Captain, I will happily pay a customs toll to let us pass. Five hundred dollars. Your choice. You can go into town to-night and have a good time or . . . you can die on this stinking water. What's it to be?'

The officer hesitated for only a second. The money would be most welcome. Theirs, after all, was a poorly paid and thankless profession.

'I take the money.'

'Good. Tell your men I'm coming closer. Tell them to put up their rifles.'

'No! I do not trust you. Advance *Inglês*.'

Hunter knew he had no choice. 'If they look like making a move, open fire,' he said softly.

Reaching into his pocket he removed five one hundred dollar bills and held them up for the soldiers to see. The troops, most of them unsure what was going on, relaxed when they saw what he was holding.

The officer was nervously licking his lips as he climbed down the ladder and onto the deck. His boat was three feet above the water line and he stood at the guard-rail as the inflatable nudged closer.

Hunter stood, feet astride for balance, his pistol in one hand, the money in the other. He took a gamble. Placing his weapon on the seat next to him, he used his free hand to hold the inflatable steady next to the boat. He held the money up to the man.

'No tricks, Captain. Or you will surely die.'

The man nodded. He'd had enough. This was meant to have been an easy task – arrest the men in the inflatables and hold them until further orders. These men looked like bandits – heavily armed, tough, unshaven, unwashed. He took the money, glanced at it and slipped it into his pocket.

'I suggest you reverse away while we move slowly towards the sea.' The nod Hunter received was sufficient. Like dogs bristling at each other they slowly disengaged, both sides ready for trouble. Napier turned the inflatable and moved slowly downstream, following the others who had drifted ahead. The customs boat moved back towards the shore, the gap rapidly opening between them. The Suriname soldiers gave not so much as a backward glance. With the thinning of boat traffic and an opening of the estuary, the inflatables picked up speed. Within seconds they were flying along, pushing 40 knots.

They skirted around a couple of freighters that were coming into the river, passed two more that were also heading for sea and then they were out. The muddy, filthy water began to change colour and a mile from the entrance the blue of the sea greeted them.

The team exchanged rueful looks, thinking of Hales in his body bag. The operation was nearly over. The trouble was, there was always a price to pay.

Hunter reported to Macnair.

'Good work, Nick. That was money well spent. A Sea King will be taking off in ten. It'll be with you in an hour at the most. From the looks of things around you there doesn't appear to be any boats taking an interest.'

'What about aircraft?'

'Nothing on the usual radio channels. That doesn't mean you shouldn't be prepared, just in case. I've got two CAPS watching. They're at the twelve mile limit, Harriers.'

'Thanks, sir. That's a relief.'

'They're on the guard frequency. Anything comes near you and they'll be warned off. But only once. Ruth's ETA on *Ark* is six minutes.'

'Roger that. Any word on the names we passed you?'

'Yes. I'll have a full report forwarded to the *Ark* when you get there.'

'Roger that.'

The connection was broken and Hunter sat, deep in thought. Now they were away from the land the sky had cleared and a hot sun burned down. Canvas shelters had already been erected for shade and the breeze across the bows was pleasant on their faces. Most of the team had fallen asleep, the past few hours having caught up with them.

Hunter relieved Napier at the helm, pleased to have something to do. Dunston sat beside him, talking about Ruth's condition. Sipping from a bottle of water Hunter unburdened himself.

'I think she's crippled, Matt.'

Dunston looked hard at his friend. 'How do you feel about that?'

'We haven't tied the knot yet but my feelings and commitment are still the same. For better or worse, Matt . . .'

Dunston smiled although he wasn't surprised by the answer.

'She'll need help and support, love and understanding. But no pity. Ruth couldn't stand that.'

Hunter nodded. 'You're right. What's the worst case scenario? She loses her leg. Hell, that's nothing compared to what a lot of people have to put up with.' He sighed. 'It helps, talking.'

Dunston tapped his shoulder. 'It always does, my friend. It always does. Prayer helps as well.'

Hunter smiled. 'I'll leave that to you.'

Dunston took no offence but smiled back. 'God listens, you know.'

Hunter said nothing. Their friendship went deep and wide with neither man trying to cram his beliefs, or lack of them, down the other's throat.

'Incoming helos,' said Hunter. 'Ten minutes out.' He raised his voice, 'Stand to, lads.'

They came alert and prepared to be lifted. They struck down the awning, and secured all loose gear. Lastly, they put on their security harnesses and waited patiently.

Two Sea Kings came into sight. Way was taken off the inflatables and the helos hovered above each of them. The winch was lowered, the hook earthed and then fixed to the eight-strand lifting strop. The inflatables lifted cleanly out of the water and even as they were being winched up the helicopters were turning and picking up speed. The inflatables went straight up to their locking positions on the starboard side of the 'copter. Each member of the team undid his safety harness and climbed inside the fuselage. When the last man was in and the doors shut the helos accelerated. Most of the team settled down to sleep. For Hunter it was a time for introspection. As the adrenaline subsided his thoughts turned to his past and his future.

He had wanted to be a naval officer ever since he could remember. Much to the amusement of the family he had spurned a business degree at an Oxbridge university and gone to Dartmouth instead. There he had elected to specialise in what was considered one of the toughest courses in the military – underwater bomb and mine disposal. He'd gone on to command minehunters before volunteering to join TIFAT. There had been no regrets. But now? With Ruth in her present condition, wasn't it time to re-consider his options? A top job in the family business almost anywhere in the world was his for the asking. He sighed. Somehow, it wasn't him. The truth was, he enjoyed what he did. With that thought he fell asleep, exhaustion finally taking its toll.

3

Intelsat and Inmarsat satellites which moved in geo-stationary orbit around the earth accounted for the vast majority of phone and fax communications traffic between countries and continents. Within countries, old-fashioned land lines, fibre optic lines and mobile communications systems carried billions of messages each and every day. ECHELON, the huge network of land-based intercept stations, intelligence ships and top-secret military satellites whirling twenty thousand miles overhead, hoovered up everything that was transmitted. It fed the information to the massive computer banks of the National Security Agency. There the advanced voice recognition and optical character recognition programs did their work. Using the Echelon 'Dictionary', key words and phrases were identified. The message was flagged and recorded and then transcribed for future analysis by highly-trained operators. Messages intercepted were automatically forwarded to the agency most likely to be interested in their contents. This process continued twenty-four-seven, all year round. Amongst the billions of words analysed, some phrase or sentence could help the world's security agencies prevent a terrorist outrage.

Following the horrendous events of 9/11 this type of surveillance had been stepped up as high as possible. Nothing was too trivial to be ignored.

The most important complex in Europe was at Menwith Hill near Harrogate in North Yorkshire. There were eight satellite dishes with names such as STEEPLECHASE, MOONPENNY and SILKWORTH. No transmission however small was missed or ignored no matter how it was sent. This collection of data would have been useless due to the overwhelming amount flooding in every minute if it was not for the highly advanced and incredibly sophisticated computer software that worked the recognition programs. Voice recognition software converted conversations into text messages for further analysis whenever a key word or phrase was identified. One system, code named VOICECAST, could identify an individual's voice pattern and automatically flag, transcribe and forward the conversation. When the relevant agency dealing with the subject was identified, the information was automatically disseminated by use of a prefix. If the information was for GCHQ, the UK Government Communications Headquarters at Cheltenham, it was given the prefix ALPHA – ALPHA. If the information was top secret the word UMBRA was added.

'Eyes-only' information for TIFAT, the relatively new International Force Against Terrorism, based at Rosyth in Scotland, was given the prefix YANKEE – YANKEE. During the last three months a vast amount of information had been passed to Isobel Sweeney, the information technology boss at the special services complex. Her task was to filter the information and pass it to her commanding officer, Lieutenant General Malcolm Macnair.

They called it morning prayers. Promptly each morning at 08.05 Isobel began an intelligence briefing in the auditorium, attended by heads of departments, deputies and all team leaders. The room had the latest and most sophisticated anti-listening devices in existence. Any agency or person attempting to eavesdrop would only hear loud white noise. Equipment used to try and listen in would be detected and tracked. The outcome was guaranteed to be very unpleasant for the eavesdroppers.

This Monday morning the auditorium was less busy than usual. Isobel's normally calm demeanour was absent. She had a great deal of bad news to impart. 'Gentlemen,' she waited for her audience to settle down and pay attention. 'It appears that the disturbing racist attacks experienced in recent weeks have been a mere prelude to something far worse. There have been literally dozens of race-based incidents in the past forty-eight hours. Seemingly random events – street fighting, clashes with the police, demonstrations with no apparent pattern and several very serious acts of terrorism with no prior warning to the authorities. The Intel we've downloaded is truly frightening.' Her plain face was now looking positively glum. 'We've never seen anything like it, ever.' She pressed a button on her remote control and a map of Europe appeared, filling the wall. 'Each star represents a recent terrorist act of one sort or another. I tried colour coding them but it was too complex. Leo is handing out detailed notes of each incident.' Leo was Isobel's right-hand man in the department and one of the first people to join when TIFAT was originally set-up. His expertise was primarily in hacking but he had also proved to be very adept at covering his tracks once he had broken into a computer system. Isobel often joked that if he had not been working for the organisation Leo would be in jail. Leo's riposte was always the same – they'd never catch him.

'I believe these attacks now represent a wave of terrorism – part of a pre-planned movement, rather than activity by individual terrorist cells. There have been over two hundred attacks in three months. Every single one has been carried out by known or recently identified Islamic terrorists. They are, beyond doubt, a part of the Al-Qaeda network but . . .' Isobel paused, unsure whether to voice what she really thought.

'Please go on, Isobel,' Macnair prompted.

Isobel shook her head. 'These incidents are definitely being carried out by Islamic fundamentalists and Muslims. There is no question about that. The proof is overwhelming.'

'So what's the problem? We're certain Al-Qaeda is involved, so presumably the dead hand of Osama bin Laden is still on the tiller?'

'I'm not so sure. You know my rule. If in doubt, follow the money.'

'And?'

Isobel shrugged. 'The trail isn't leading where it should.'

'Where should it lead?'

'To Saudi, sir. It usually does. But not in this case.'

Sensing Isobel's reluctance to commit herself further, Macnair moved on. 'All right. We'll follow up on that later. What about the latest incidents?'

'Thirty-three over the weekend. Leo will give you the details.' She handed over the remote control and Leo began a run-through of shootings, bombings, stabbings, riots, robberies, car-jackings and muggings.

Macnair asked the important question. 'How many incidents did we have prior knowledge of?'

'Thanks to the new software,' Isobel replied, 'we knew prob-abilities but we had no details. Because we hadn't cracked the codes we were unable to act. But now, by marrying incidents to recorded messages, we're better able to identify what's going to happen.'

'I take it the software used was POLITICIAN?' the General asked.

'Yes, sir. As you know, we helped to develop it and now its incorporated in the ECHELON system.' Registering the confused expressions on junior officers' faces, she explained. 'It identifies nonsensical chat. For example, one person says something like – *It's nice weather* and gets the reply – *Especially since it rains in Spain*. That was actually one conversation we identified and tied in to the recent riot in Barcelona. We have managed to identify code words and statements that fit every incident. This means we can be ready for the next event that occurs and possibly pre-empt it, provided we get co-operation.'

'I don't doubt we'll get plenty from all the agencies,' Macnair said heavily. It had been a long time coming but, finally, territorial wars between the different security agencies world-wide were becoming a thing of the past. At the military level co-operation had, for a long time, been excellent. But between Britain's MI5 and MI6, America's CIA and FBI, France's DGSE and SGDN, Israel's Mossad and Shin Bet, and amongst the hundreds of other organisations, co-operation had been non-existent. Vital informa-tion that could have often saved countless lives and hundreds of millions of pounds in damage had been withheld. Thanks to the influence of TIFAT and the example set by Macnair, co-operation was much improved and, more importantly, more effective. The American President was also prepared to knock heads together to achieve co-operation, which helped greatly.

'Where does this new found knowledge leave us?' Macnair asked.

Isobel frowned, pursed her lips and decided to go for it. 'The scale of the attacks has climbed dramatically. We believe further attacks will take place in these areas over the coming week. They are graded one to five in order of likelihood. Five being the most certain.' Isobel proceeded to show a series of slides with probable places and dates.

'Good grief,' said Macnair. 'That many?'

'I'm afraid so, sir. They stretch from Ireland in the west to Greece in the east. And from Spain as far north as Norway and Sweden. Not a single EU country will be unaffected.' Isobel's careful preparation allowed a terrifying insight into the sheer range and scope of recent European terrorist activity and its numbingly fast momentum.

'Our political masters aren't going to like this one little bit,' said Major Jim Carter, TIFAT's Quartermaster and Macnair's right-hand man for logistics.

Several pairs of eyes honed in on a particular listing. 'What's that item in the Gulf of Mexico?' Colonel Hiram B. Walsh asked in a deceptive drawl. Late of the American Delta Force, he was TIFAT's second-in-command. In his late thirties, Walsh stood six-five in his bare feet and was as tough as he looked. With thinning fair hair swept back from a high forehead, he had a hooked nose that had been broken at least twice. His brown eyes had a perpetual laugh in them, unless he was riled, then they turned as hard as agates.

'We're working on it right now. All we know is that something big is being planned but we have no idea what. As soon as we get anything, I'll let you know.'

The briefing finished shortly after. The men filed out leaving Macnair, Walsh, Carter and Isobel alone.

'Why the hesitation over the money trail, Isobel?' Carter asked.

'Nothing matches with previous al-Qaeda patterns, Jim. We've been tracking currencies moving across the world for weeks now. The information sent in by Nick from Suriname appears to be a breakthrough.'

Macnair frowned. 'How can that be? What's the connection? We've established that the Suriname smugglers were all ex-special forces. All of them had been involved with extreme right-wing groups. Many had been dismissed from the services due to their white supremacy politics.'

'But here's the strange thing, sir,' said Isobel. 'The money leads in the same direction for both the Islamic fundamentalists and the white extremists. They're both being funded from the same source.'

'Are you sure?' Macnair saw the look on Isobel's face and held up his hand. 'Sorry. Any ideas?'

'None that make sense,' she said slowly.

'But?' Macnair prompted her.

'We need to find the ultimate source of the funds but I do have a theory based on what we've learnt so far.' To give herself time to think, Isobel stood up and poured coffees for all four of them. The others didn't rush her, knowing she would tell them in her own time. Sitting back down, she sipped her coffee and asked, 'What's the biggest problem facing Europe now?'

'In what way? Old nuclear weapons from the former Soviet Union?' Carter suggested. 'Iraq? The Middle East? India and Pakistan? Hell, the list is endless. Drugs, immigrants, Northern Ireland blowing up again? Need I go on?'

There were cynical smiles around the table.

'I meant *within* Europe,' said Isobel. The men nodded and she continued. 'We all know and understand the issues but the right-wing is really playing on the phobias of the electorate. The problem of immigrants is becoming serious. Elections are coming up in Denmark, Germany and France. In a year's time it will be Italy and Spain. What are the polls showing?'

There were sighs from the three men. There was no doubt

that the terrorist attacks taking place all across Europe were feeding the existing natural xenophobia of its people. A backlash was already taking place. Mosques had been attacked and fireballed, Muslims were routinely beaten up and women wearing the veil were being spat on and harassed. Muslim women no longer went out of doors unless protected by their menfolk. Gangs of youths armed with sticks and metal bars attacked immigrants en masse. Appeals to the police resulted in shrugs and token enquiries. Few, if any, arrests were being made.

'Clashes with immigrants are the ugly face of a broader dissatisfaction amongst Europeans. Ideological differences and terrorist threats are opening up a huge divide – people want to safeguard their way of life. The extreme right are either going to get into power or at least attain positions of significant influence across the continent. Here in Britain we're seeing serious trouble too. There were riots last night in Leeds, Bradford and Oldham.'

'And a mosque was destroyed in south London,' said Walsh, leaning back in his chair, his coffee forgotten on the table in front of him.

'If things continue as they are we will be forced into creating a fortress Europe,' said Macnair. 'We know what that will mean. The entire world will polarise. The rich West will pull up its collective drawbridges and the rest of the planet can go hang. Poverty and ignorance will inflame the masses who already live on next to nothing. Without Western aid they'll have even less to lose. War will be inevitable. The have-nots against the haves. Us against the Muslims. Countries such as India will side with the Muslim states as they will have nothing to lose. It's a nightmare scenario which some of our politicians understand only too well.'

'But the more clear-sighted politicos are fast becoming a minority,' said Carter. 'If things continue as they are for another year then fortress Europe could become a reality. The British government will be forced to go along, because if they don't they will definitely lose the next election. But people aren't fools. Europe's governments have been lying to us for years. We know that Al-Qaeda operatives have been coming into Europe along with the other illegal immigrants and the genuine asylum seekers. It is they who are now causing all the trouble.'

Isobel nodded. 'I agree al-Qaeda are responsible.' Isobel paused before she dropped her bombshell, 'But what if the terrorism was being *financed and orchestrated by Europe's right-wing*?'

The three officers looked at her in shock.

'Now there's a thought,' said Macnair slowly. 'Expand.'

'White extremists as the puppet masters? That would create exactly the atmosphere, the panic, we are witnessing now. Look at the lessons of history. Hitler's rise to power was achieved with a few well-placed bombs, lots of political posturing that placed the blame for Germany's woes firmly on the Jews and other minorities. A classic strategy that I know you've studied at staff college.'

Isobel knew the military was adept at learning from history in an attempt to prevent mistakes from being repeated. It was a shame, it was often said, that politicians didn't learn the same valuable lessons.

Isobel tapped into her computer and projected a new image onto the wall. 'You can see the way money has moved from banks in the Cayman Islands, British Honduras and Gibraltar to accounts in the cities on the left of the screen.' The list held almost every major city in western Europe. 'There are thirty cities each with several major banks holding accounts that we now *know* belong to the terrorists who committed the outrages of the past few months. By following the paper trail we've come back to the three banks you see here.' She flashed to the next screen. 'It comes as no surprise to find the Caymans and Honduras involved but Gib is too close to home for comfort.'

'Where does the trail lead from there?' Macnair asked.

'We're working on that now, sir. If I was to guess I would think a mainland, mainstream bank, probably more than one. The work we did that sent Nick and his team to South America also led us to the same banks. The DEA in the States helped us out there. It's thanks mainly to them that we found out about the Suriname operation. And that's only because the American Aluminium

Company have such a big stake in the country. As always,' she gave a little shrug, 'luck played a big part in identifying the banks involved. The men killed in Suriname all had bank accounts in those banks. *The same banks financing terrorism in Europe.*'

'Coincidence?' Walsh suggested.

'Perhaps, but I doubt it. There are tens of thousands of banks all over the world who would and do handle secret transactions. They know the money is dirty but couldn't care less. Whether it's stolen aid or drug money, the world's awash with dirty cash.'

'You think it's too much of a coincidence?'

'I do, General,' said Isobel, with a firm nod.

'So do I. We must learn where the trail leads. Put everything you've got onto it.'

There was a knock on the door and a rating appeared. 'Sir, call for you. I told them you were in a meeting but they said it was urgent.'

'Who is it?'

'The Pentagon.'

Chantelle Suchard removed a red, peaked cap to reveal long blond hair tied in a pony tail. She smiled at the immigration officer who quickly stamped her passport and wished her a pleasant stay in the United States. She thanked him and walked out to the taxi rank. She was twenty-nine years old, an engineering graduate from the University of Rheims and held a private pilot's licence with over five hundred hours on twin-engined aircraft. However, her passion was the sea. She had been involved in diving and exploration since she was a teenager. It was while diving off Greece that she had been introduced to her current employer. One night, over dinner, she had shown her true political colours and they had become friends but not lovers. Since then she had done many and varied jobs for her boss, travelling the world, seeking excitement but always with an end goal in sight. She shivered with anticipation and pleasure. Soon, she thought, soon it will all have been worth it. The tantalising question was what she would do with all that lovely money. She salivated in anticipation.

* * *

'Malcolm, it's Colin Stafford.'

'Colin, I take it this isn't a social call.' A four-star general at the Pentagon did not make contact without good reason. Especially when Macnair realised it was the middle of the night in Washington.

'I wanted to bring you up to speed on an incident in the Gulf of Mexico.'

Macnair's grip tightened on the receiver and he pressed the loudspeaker button. 'You're on loudspeaker, Colin, with my heads of departments listening. We anticipated activity in the Gulf but have no specifics.'

'A liner has been hijacked. One of the Silver Star line.'

Macnair nodded to Isobel who was heading out the door. There was a lot of information she needed to pull.

'We'll get to work on it right away,' said Macnair. 'What can you tell us?'

'We received a radio message from the company's head office in Oslo. About four hours ago an automatic alarm was sent from the ship, the *SS Silver Beech*. Although it's rare for one to go off by mistake they didn't panic and began a series of checks. Each one panned out. There's no doubt that the ship's been taken over. Approximately ninety minutes ago they had the first direct contact with the hijackers. Somebody claiming to be a part of the al-Qaeda network radioed and told the owners to stand by for a list of demands to be forwarded to, listen to this baloney, the "decadent governments of a corrupt West".'

'That was all?'

'That's the lot. Oslo tried calling back but there was no reply on any channel. We've tried to contact the ship but every frequency is being jammed, including satellite connections and radio frequencies. It's a blanket blackout.'

'What are your plans?'

'We're sending a task force from Pensacola to investigate. Hell, it's hardly that. Two Coastguard cutters are getting up steam as we speak.'

'What role do you see for TIFAT?'

'You know there can be no negotiation with terrorists. If they give us the slightest cause I want to send in a team to take out the perps. You're the only outfit suited to this sort of thing.'

America could not go it alone. TIFAT had an international base and a mandate to operate without political interference. True, Macnair was accountable, but usually after the event, not before or during.

Macnair sucked his teeth. 'We've no assets available but I'll see what I can do.'

'None?'

'Sorry, Colin. Every team we have is out. You know what we're up against here in Europe. We're helping the internal security forces of practically every EU nation counteract terrorist attacks.'

There was a heavy pause. 'Okay. Get back to me as soon as possible, will you? If I have to, I'll send in a SEAL team from Coronado but the President isn't going to like it one little bit.'

'When will the Coastguard reach the liner?'

'In about ten hours.'

'Their orders?'

'Tell the ship to heave to and prepare for boarding. They'll send across a boarding party and find out what's what.'

'I shouldn't,' said Macnair.

'It's SOPs.'

'Colin, it may be standing operational procedure but it's highly dangerous. We've been monitoring signal traffic in the area because we knew something was being planned. Let us try and find out more before you go in at full charge.'

'I hear you, but as of now we've no choice.'

'How many terrorists are there on board?'

'We don't know. Apart from the one radio message we've heard nothing. We're re-routing all possible satellite assets to take a look. You can log in to everything we find.'

'PACER SKY?'

'It's being reprogrammed even as we speak. The whole kit and caboodle is over Afghanistan and monitoring the India Pakistan stand-off. It'll be in place in about thirty minutes.'

PACER SKY provided real time reconnaissance information

using radar, visual and infra-red detection equipment. The system's accuracy was phenomenal and still classified under the heading of top-secret.

'Is there anything else at the moment?'

'Nope, I don't think so. I heard about our man in Suriname.'

'Yes, we're really sorry. Hales' body is on board the *Ark Royal*. The Captain's making the necessary arrangements to ship him home. Who'll tell his next of kin?'

'We're doing that. He has parents living in New York.'

'All right. I'll speak to you later.' The two Generals broke their connection. 'Hiram, have Isobel make the necessary arrangements, will you? If his people don't need the money tell them to give it to a charity of their choice.'

Since its formation TIFAT had waged war against terrorists, drug dealers and criminal gangs. A war with rich pickings. Thanks to the skills of Isobel's department, hundreds of millions of pounds, dollars, yen and euros had been taken from the criminals' bank accounts and channelled into TIFAT's coffers. The funds had been used to good effect, buying state-of-the-art equipment from around the world to be used in the war against terrorism. If anyone was killed while on active service with TIFAT their next-of-kin received one million pounds. They were told it was the proceeds of a life insurance policy.

The meeting broke up and they each went about their duties. As in any modern organisation, paperwork was the bane of the General's existence and he was wading through his correspondence and action files when Isobel cornered him in his office.

'We've tried everything to contact the *Silver Beech* but it's no use. Whoever is on board has a very sophisticated and powerful jamming device. We've received information from the owners, including details of the ship and the crew. We're looking through it now.'

'Good. Anything else?'

'PACER SKY is on station and tracking. The liner is moving at a sedate four or five knots and will reach the USA in six days at their current speed.'

'Why so slow?'

Isobel shrugged. 'I've no idea.'

There was a knock on the door and Leo entered. 'Oslo has faxed through the *Silver Beech*'s passenger list.'

'Anyone of interest?' Macnair asked.

'Not yet, General. There are two hundred and forty-seven passengers and two hundred and twelve crew. We're cross-referencing every name right now. It shouldn't take too long.'

'All right, please let us know what you find. Have the lists been forwarded to other agencies?'

Leo smiled. 'Just about everyone I could think of. Would you like to see?'

Macnair waved him away with a 'No thanks'. He had complete faith in his men and women to do their jobs properly. If he didn't, they would no longer be working at TIFAT.

The General's direct line rang and he lifted the receiver. 'Macnair.'

'General, I have the PM for you. He's on loudspeaker in the COBRA office.' The Cabinet Office Briefing Room was where the most sensitive of political subjects were discussed. Briefings were usually attended by the majority, if not all, of the Cabinet, as well as their political advisers.

'Good morning, General.'

'Good morning, Prime Minister.'

The PM cut straight to the chase. 'What's your take on the situation in the Gulf of Mexico?'

'All we know is that a liner has been hijacked.'

'Are there any British subjects on board?'

Typical, thought Macnair. 'We don't know yet. We've received the lists of passengers and crew. Odds are they'll be mostly Americans and Europeans and so I expect some British are bound to be amongst them.'

'What do you intend doing?'

'I'm still assessing the situation. The Americans are sending in two Coastguard cutters to stop and board. Personally, I consider it foolhardy. The men who have taken the liner are not going to give up just because the USA Coastguard arrive on the scene. They may use it as an excuse to start trouble.'

'What exactly?'

Instead of saying how the hell do I know, Macnair kept his tone reasonable. 'I've no idea, Prime Minister, but somebody will be killed.'

'Are TIFAT getting involved?'

The mandate that Macnair held was, in effect, open warfare on terrorism. TIFAT's mantle often sat uneasily on the shoulders of the democratic governments of the West.

'Not directly, Prime Minister. We are currently co-ordinating the intelligence gathering and disseminating information to all interested parties. I have no operatives available at this juncture as they are all out on operations.'

'Right. Good. Thank you for that. Please keep me posted.'

The connection was broken.

'There is one team available,' said Isobel softly.

Macnair nodded. 'I know, Hunter's lot.'

4

The *Ark Royal*, 206m long, displacing 20,600 tonnes and capable of a speed in excess of 30 knots was the biggest ship in the Royal Navy. With the air squadrons embarked there were over a thousand men and women on board. As a consequence, the galleys ran night and day, cafeteria style.

Hunter had showered and dressed in clean shorts and T-shirt. The team had been kitted out in the NAAFI once Hunter had established a line of credit with the manager. Cabins had been allocated and the men were now taking a well-earned rest. He sat picking at a meal of steak and baked potato but hardly noticed what he was eating, his thoughts on Ruth.

A surgeon had arrived from San Diego shortly after Ruth had landed and had gone straight to work.

The ship carried a fully-equipped operating theatre, manned by highly competent doctors used to dealing with serious wounds. Some of the best people in the world were working on Ruth's knee.

Waiting was so frustrating – the outcome so far beyond his control. He was worried and he didn't care who knew it. Hunter pushed his plate away and went and prowled the corridors outside the sick-bay.

After a while a junior doctor came out of a door and approached him. 'You're with the troops who flew in today, aren't you?'

'Yes. I'm the boss of the team. Hunter. Nick Hunter. Lieutenant Commander.'

'Ah! Right, sir. I didn't know.'

'That's all right. I work with an informal lot. What's happening to Ruth?'

'She's being well taken care of. Look, I've come out to get a cup of coffee. Come with me. There's nothing you can do here. They'll be hours yet.'

Hunter nodded, grateful for the distraction and the chance to learn more about Ruth's condition. The *Ark* was large enough to get lost in and strategically placed maps showing 'You are here' directed them. Enroute, the doctor introduced herself as Margaret Murray. She was in her mid-twenties and not long qualified. After a year at a shore establishment she was on her first sea assignment. She had removed her operating greens and was dressed immaculately in uniform. The gold braid on her shoulder boards with the red stripe in between gleamed, not yet tarnished by the salty air of sea time.

They went into the aircrews' mess. There were men and women seated at tables, eating, drinking and smoking, going about their duties and their lives as usual. Hunter found the air of normality surreal, when Ruth was lying on the surgeon's table, in danger of losing her leg. 'Any idea when I'll be able to see her?'

'No. They've been working on her for three hours and I expect they'll be another ten or twelve . . .'

Hunter nodded gloomily. 'So long?'

'I'm afraid so. Look, the rock smashed not only her patella, her kneecap, but the surrounding bones and joints. They are taking out tiny slithers of bone and cartilage, cleaning the wound, fixing arteries and veins, and then rebuilding her bones. I've never seen anything like it. Believe me, if she was in a civilian hospital right now they would have amputated above the knee and had done with it.'

Hunter somehow managed not to blanch. 'I see.'

'This operation is pioneering stuff.' Margaret gulped her coffee. 'I need to get back. Will you be all right?'

He nodded, watching her go, sipping his coffee for a few minutes longer, thinking of the future. Ruth was such a strong, independent woman, how would the injury affect her? There was no way of telling. Finally, he stood up. He had work to do and brooding wasn't helping Ruth one iota.

He found Clements and Napier in a corner of the lower hangar, checking the gear they had brought back with them. Their weapons had been stowed in the ship's armoury and the inflatables collapsed and stowed.

Clements asked, 'How's Ruth?'

Hunter shrugged. 'They're working on her. We won't know anything for hours.'

'What's the score, Nick?' Napier was fixing one of the outboards to a tank of fresh water to flush out the seawater. 'Are we along for the cruise or are we being shipped home?'

'I've no idea, Doug. I'll go and see the Captain. He may know something. Have you seen Matt?'

'He's in the operating theatre, I think,' replied Napier.

Somehow Hunter wasn't surprised. Matt's paramedic experience would give him access. Knowing he was watching over Ruth made Hunter feel slightly better. 'Once the lads have had a decent sleep and something to eat tell them to take it easy.' Hunter stood in the hangar for a few seconds, looking around him. The ship was moving more slowly than he would normally expect and no fixed-wing operations were taking place, which was unusual. A moment later he arrived on the flight deck where a soccer game was being played. He saw that both Masters and Hughes were taking part. He grinned in spite of his worry.

Hunter ran up the stairs to the bridge. He attracted the attention of the Officer of the Watch. 'Permission to come on the bridge.'

'Granted.' The OOW held out his hand. 'Nick! Good to see you.'

'Hello, Jeremy. I hadn't realised you were on board.'

'Yep. I'm second ops. Let me introduce you to the Captain. Sir,' he turned to the grey haired man sitting in the captain's chair on the starboard side of the bridge, 'may I introduce Lt Cdr Hunter? Nick, this is Captain O'Neill.'

The Captain slid to the deck and offered his hand. 'Welcome aboard, Commander.'

'Thank you, sir. And thank you very much for your help. We wouldn't have made it otherwise.'

'All part of the service.' Holding up a signal clipboard O'Neill motioned for Hunter to follow him. 'I need to talk to you. You'd better come below.'

Stepping across the bridge he opened the door to the lift and gestured for Hunter to enter. Only the Captain used the lift and it was always on the floor where he was. It took him from his cabin up to the bridge or down to the operations room.

Once in his day cabin O'Neill said, 'Please, take a seat.' He sat at his desk. 'Do you know anything about the liner hijacked in the Gulf of Mexico?'

'No, sir. When did this happen?'

'A few hours ago. We're steaming towards the area, albeit rather slowly.'

'I noticed the ship wasn't moving at your usual speed. What are we doing? Eight knots?'

'Seven. At the surgeons' request, to give them the most stable platform while they operate on the woman.'

'Ah! Right. I see. Thanks, sir.'

The Captain shrugged. In his mid-fifties this was to be his last job in the Royal Navy. He was retiring in six months and looking forward to it. His craggy, narrow features and beetling eyebrows hid a keen sense of humour which, as a younger officer, had often got him into trouble. 'I received a signal a short while ago. Eyes-only-Captain. You're on notice to prepare to board the ship and take out the terrorists. That's all.' Shrewd eyes looked at Hunter. 'What do you need?'

If he was surprised by the announcement Hunter didn't show it. 'Secure communications to TIFAT, sir. My operators only.'

'Not a problem. I'll send for the Communications Officer. He can arrange it. What else?'

'I'll have my men check all the stores you have, sir, to see if there's anything we can use. I'll need permission to help ourselves.'

'No problem. The Supply Officer will sort it out. He'll give you anything you want.' The Captain smiled before adding the caveat, 'Provided you sign for it.'

O'Neill snatched a phone from a wall bracket behind him and

issued instructions. 'At this speed we won't be in the Gulf for days. Even if we increase to launch speed it would take too long to get you near enough to be of any assistance.'

Hunter nodded. 'I'm aware of that, sir. Is there a room I can use to brief my team?'

'Certainly. The aircrew briefing room is ideal. There's no flying for three days so you won't be disturbed. If there's anybody in there send them packing.'

'Thank you, sir.' Hunter stood up to leave.

'Good luck. Anything else, just ask.'

Hunter found Clements and Napier where he had left them. The soccer match was still in full swing. Hunter signalled Masters and Hughes that they were needed. They apologised to their team mates and joined the three officers.

'What's up, boss?'

'I'll tell you later. Round up the team and meet me in the aircrew briefing room in thirty minutes. Josh, Douglas, we need to find the communications centre.'

The *Ark's* Comms Centre was state-of-the-art, enabling communication with anyone in the world, anywhere and at anytime. Messages were automatically encrypted and, depending on how highly classified the message, were designed to withstand cracking by a sophisticated eavesdropper from eight hours to eight days. After that there were no guarantees. The power of computers was simply too great.

The *Ark Royal* was part of a task force and never travelled alone. Around her was a screen of three anti-submarine frigates and two anti-air destroyers. There had been so much interchanging of equipment in recent years that both classes of ship were now highly effective in either role. Hunter wondered if one could be detached.

The Communications Officer gave them a private cubicle and ran through the equipment with them. Hunter nodded his thanks and was soon talking to Isobel. She patched him through to the General. Ideas and information were exchanged and the contact broken. The TIFAT operatives sat in silent contemplation of their instructions for a few seconds.

'He's not asking much, is he?' Napier ventured finally.

'You could say that. I'd better go and talk to the Captain. You start briefing the lads. If we're to go, it'll be tomorrow night. And you'd better get a weather forecast.'

Hunter's meeting with the Captain was brief and to the point. Signals were already flying through the ether, giving orders, re-tasking the naval force. At the same time the President of the United States had issued his instructions and the logistical might of the biggest and best-equipped armed forces in the world was swinging into action.

Hunter went down to the briefing room. Detailed drawings of the liner had been sent, loaded into a computer and were already being projected onto a screen. The hijacked *SS Silver Beech* was 19,000 tonnes. It had five decks in total, four for the passengers' use. There were casinos, restaurants, a ballroom, cinemas, a range of shops, a theatre and on the top-most deck, two swimming pools. A golf range allowed fanatics the opportunity to hit golf balls made from a substance that dissolved harmlessly in seawater. Now the passengers' pleasure palace had become their prison.

'Since the hijacking nobody has been seen on the upper decks. There are no reports of casualties and to the best of our knowledge the ship is undamaged. We don't know how the terrorists got on board, whether they're fare paying passengers or were picked up at sea. The *Silver Beech* may have responded to a fake distress call. Isobel's lot are analysing the passenger and crew lists as we speak. Make lists of the gear we need. Brainstorm in pairs.'

At that moment the door opened and Captain O'Neill appeared. 'I've had a signal from TIFAT. I've brought it down to see if there's anything more you need.'

'We ought to get a move on, sir. I think we need to disembark to one of the escort vessels and head north as fast as possible.'

The Captain nodded. 'I came to the same conclusion after speaking to General Macnair. The *York* is the fastest ship in the task force. I've already detached her. She's steaming full ahead now. You'll transfer by helo.'

'Thank you, sir.'

'I gather a Lockheed C130 is being sent from San Diego.'

'Correct. There's specialist equipment which only Coronado or ourselves have.' Coronado was the base of SEAL Team 6, a source of highly-trained men to TIFAT.

'Well, rather you than me.' He looked at the tough individuals standing or sitting before him and nodded. 'Good luck to you.'

A chorus of thanks followed him from the room.

Throwing himself into the job of planning the operation enabled Hunter to put thoughts of Ruth to the back of his mind for much of the time. He was continually checking equipment, revising lists, talking to Macnair, or discussing the operation with the team. The job they were contemplating was highly dangerous. To drop from 25,000ft, at night, attempting to land on a moving target in the middle of the sea against unknown and armed terrorists was verging on the suicidal. The team had stealth, modern equipment and superb training in their favour. Hunter hoped it was enough to give them the edge they needed.

'Sir, the Pentagon's on the line.'

Macnair picked up the receiver. 'What's the news, Colin?'

'Bad. The cutters caught up with the liner and told them to heave to.' The American General paused, hating what he had to say next.

'How did the hijackers react?'

'The *Silver Beech* ignored the Coastguard until one of them put a shot across the liner's bows. At that moment passengers and masked gunmen appeared on the promenade deck. They opened communications on channel sixteen.' General Stafford paused again. This time Macnair did not prompt him. He had a sick feeling in the pit of his stomach.

'The bastards lined up men, women and children and shot them. Thirty innocent lives. Just like that. Then the bastards called on channel sixteen and told the cutters that if they were still within sight in fifteen minutes another thirty people would be shot.'

'What have the Coastguard done?'

'High-tailed it out of there.'

Macnair nodded. There had been no other option open to them. 'Any demands yet?'

'No, but the hijackers claim to have set a ring of explosives around the hull of the ship. Any trouble and they'll send the ship to the bottom with all lives.'

'Including their own.'

'Since when has that mattered to people like these?'

Macnair sighed heavily. 'You know this leaves us no option?'

'I know. We won't negotiate with terrorists under any circumstances. With the death of those passengers we have no choice. How are your team's preparations coming along?'

'It's all in hand. Their biggest problem is fatigue. They've been in the field for nearly a week and you know what happened in Suriname.'

'Tired or not, they're still the best we've got for this sort of operation. Are you in touch with Coronado?'

'Yes. All the special gear is being loaded. The C130 should be airborne soon. Hunter's team are transferring to HMS *York*. The ship will detach and make best speed for Trinidad. They'll helo ashore and be picked up by the Hercules.'

'Do you think this has anything to do with nine-eleven?'

'It would account for the slow passage of the liner. They would arrive in the US of A in time for some sort of commemorative attack. If that's their intention then I expect they'll be planning something pretty spectacular.'

The privately owned submarine had a crew of eight and could stay submerged for only ten hours. Designed and built by an Italian company, it was originally intended to take sightseers in comfort and safety down to depths of one hundred metres. It had a top speed of 8 knots submerged and each of the fifty seats, twenty five down either side, had a large port hole, for passengers to admire the wonders of the deep. For only two million dollars it had been a bargain.

Most of the seats had been removed and storage space created

The original colour, a bright yellow, had been changed to a drab green. It was being transferred on the back of a pipe-laying ship, the SS *Goliath*, that was normally on charter to *Elf Nationale*, the French oil company.

The *Goliath* had departed Galveston in Texas twenty-four hours previously and was steaming at full speed towards the hijacked vessel. Already an exclusion zone had been set up around the liner and other Coastguard and United States Naval units had joined in the screen to keep away intruders. Nothing was being allowed within twenty miles of the *Silver Beech*.

Because of the electronic blackout created around the hijacked ship, the sub's rendezvous position had been established in advance. The crew was now working to a strict timetable.

Charles Gustav sat in the captain's quarters of the *Goliath* and looked at his assistant with narrowed eyes.

'You remain certain that all TIFAT teams are fully occupied?'

'We have accounted for all operatives. They are deployed in practically every country in Europe in one counter-terrorism operation or another. The exception,' he hesitated momentarily, 'is the team which wiped out our people in Suriname.'

'And cost me half a billion dollars.' Suppressed fury was betrayed only by the tell-tale white spots on Gustav's cheeks. He controlled his anger. Revenge would be all the more gratifying for the waiting.

Although Swedish by birth, Gustav was French by adoption, having moved to France in the late seventies. There he had begun to build his business empire. Now it spread around the globe like the tentacles of an octopus, encompassing everything from off-shore construction for the oil industry to huge media and publishing concerns. Known to be a billionaire many times over, Gustav was careful to hide his true worth from prying eyes, be they tax officials, governments or nosy reporters. He now used his wealth to finance his obsession – Europe inhabited only by white Christians and forced repatriation of all minorities. Second, third or fourth generation immigrants would be returned to the land of their ancestors. Whether it was Africa, India or any Muslim state, Gustav wanted them out of Europe.

The restoration of a white's only Europe would be a fitting tribute to the memory of his sister.

For ten years he had been working towards his goal and now it was within sight. Whilst Europe's politicians wrestled with strategic myopia, moral hypocrisy and futile wrangling for power, he, Gustav, was fuelling the tension between white and black. The anarchy building in the streets needed strong leadership to counteract it. Both political and military strength were called for and he, Charles Gustav, was the man to supply both. Over the years he had carefully nurtured politicians and military officers who had shown any sign of sharing his ideology. There had been mistakes over the decade but the challenges had served only to affirm his vision. The end of the Cold War meant that America's commitment to Europe was waning – she had her own battles to wage. Once American bases were shut down and all USA military personnel had returned to the States he would have greater freedom to act. Europe stood at a new dawn. There was wide disenchantment with conventional politics across the continent. Using his vast media empire, Gustav had continuously highlighted rising crime, threats to national security, rising unemployment, feeding on the electorate's paranoid fear of outsiders. He prided himself on the xenophobic reactions his red-top newspapers generated, increasing the sense of insecurity on both sides of the divide. Carefully plotting the rise in tension, his beautifully orchestrated flashpoints of conflict had led to a reawakening of extreme nationalism on a scale unprecedented since the Second World War.

Enlisting groups of skinheads and other fascist groups, and establishing networks of 'white-power' enthusiasts had given him particular pleasure. A complicated web of willing activists organised overt and covert attacks. Gustav had become adept at using his television and radio stations and newspapers to spread the message. And it was working. The disenchanted left were now voting for the right wing parties he surreptitiously helped to fund and establish.

His secretary, Duval, ever the observer, watched as Gustav stood up and paced the wood-panelled room, ten paces one way, ten the other. Lean and fit, an avid tennis player, Gustav had taken good care of himself. Now in his late fifties, he was a non-smoker and non-drinker. In all the time Duval had known him the Swede had never shown any interest in sex. His focus in life had been to make money, money to fund his dream of a whites-only Europe. At six feet three, he stooped slightly as though to listen more closely to what was being said to him. Those big, strong hands Duval knew had been used more than once to kill. Despite his shock of white hair Gustav's features were only saved from mediocrity by his eyes – a curious light grey which had a tendency to darken when angry. His tan was deep and even and owed nothing to the sunlamp. Gustav spent his time outdoors. He was a keen big game hunter, loved skiing and spent August on his yacht in the Mediterranean. There he dived for treasures from lost civilisations which he ceremoniously handed over to the Department of Antiquities in France. Let the French government argue ownership, particularly of those artefacts found in Egyptian or other African waters.

Ronald Duval had been his secretary for over twenty years. American by birth, Duval was of medium height and average weight. Behind immobile features was a first class mathematical brain which oversaw all of Gustav's business interests, allowing Gustav the time, energy and most importantly, the money, to pursue his objective.

Unknown to the Western authorities, one of the satellites which formed part of Gustav's media business also contained highly sophisticated eavesdropping equipment targeted at the security forces. He lacked the computer systems to break the codes as quickly or as accurately as Western governments but he enjoyed a great deal of success in interpreting them. It was imperative he knew TIFAT's movements.

The whereabouts of Hunter and his team was still a mystery, as all signals had been sent encrypted at the highest classification.

'Is everything ready?'

Duval nodded. 'We launch in two hours.'

'What's the shipping situation?'

'Nothing too close at the moment. We'll be well outside the exclusion zone when we put the submarine into the water.'

'And our Arab friends?'

'Have stayed in their cabins as ordered. They won't be any trouble.'

Gustav grimaced. 'They're Arabs. Excitable morons who through a quirk of nature own so much of the world's oil. If it wasn't for the West . . .'

Duval had heard the arguments before, many times. Over the years he had become inured to Gustav's rants. Twenty years ago Duval had been enthralled by the fierce intellectual arguments on race brought to bear by Gustav. But it was becoming increasingly clear that the man's senses were now totally warped, his former genius misdirected to the point that he was incapable of living in reality. Psychologists understood that such an obsession usually had its roots in childhood. In Gustav's case the root cause was found in the childhood of another – his sister. Duval thought about the file he had recently found. It's contents shocking and explicit, it explained Gustav's obsession.

Gustav's mother had died when he was young. A few years later his father had remarried. Unusually, Gustav and his stepmother had got on well together. She'd given birth to a daughter, named Katrina. A blonde, blue-eyed bundle of mischief. Charles had doted on her in spite of being seventeen years older. When Katrina was thirteen she had gone on a school holiday with her classroom friends to France. At the time, Charles had still been living and working in Sweden, attempting to buy his first local newspaper.

Negotiations had been at a crucial stage when he received the phone call from his distressed father. His beloved sister had been gang-raped and murdered.

It had taken nearly a week for the full story to be put together. The girls had been staying in a hostel near Royan in Western France. During visits to town they had been harassed by a group of youths. A gang of immigrants with little money and too much time on their hands. One evening the girls had become frightened and run away. Katrina had somehow become isolated from the rest. Her naked body had been found in a local park.

At first the pathologist refused to give Charles the details of the traumatic end of Katrina's short life. Finally he had relented when Gustav pointed out that the details would become known in court. Katrina had been raped by an estimated ten men. No orifice had been spared. She had bled to death. The information sent Charles Gustav over the edge of sanity for a short while.

No trial took place. DNA testing was still unavailable. Witnesses were too frightened to come forward even though the police were convinced of the identities of the ten youths responsible. A wall of silence protected them and the asylum seeking community closed ranks. The rapists varied in age from eleven to nineteen. Six were Algerian, two were Iraqis and two were Albanians. All were Muslim.

Charles' step-mother committed suicide exactly a year after Katrina's death. His father never recovered and spent the next three years vilifying all things Islamic, speaking out against immigrants at every opportunity. Most significantly, he gave Charles the money to buy his first newspaper on condition it reflected his xenophobic views. It did.

Charles bought another small paper and a commercial radio station. Just over three years after Katrina's death, his father was killed in a road accident. He had become a heavy drinker, looking for escape and solace in a bottle of schnapps. One winter's night he had been drinking. Driving too fast he had hit a tree. He had died on reaching hospital. Charles blamed the loss of his father on the immigrants who had killed his sister.

The money he inherited allowed him to expand more quickly. That was about the time he, Duval, had come on the scene. Duval had been auditing one of Charles' companies. Charles had made him an offer and he had accepted. They shared an intense dislike of non-white races although his own feelings were not as passionate as Charles'.

Since the death of Katrina, Charles had used his growing wealth to keep track of the youths who had abused and killed his sister. Much to Charles' chagrin one of the Iraqis died from a heroin overdose three years after Katrina's death. This prompted him to make his move.

In the course of the next three years, starting with the eldest, Charles had each man abducted. They died horrible deaths at the hands of a group of men who shared Charles' views. The men were paid handsomely for the work. There was only one condition attached. Before each man died he had to know *why*. The last to die had been eleven at the time Katrina had been killed. He was seventeen when he bled to death from internal injuries inflicted by a pick-axe handle inserted into his rectum. It had taken him nearly twenty agonising hours to die. Charles had been there to watch, indeed to participate. Of the nine murdered, he had personally killed two of them.

Still Charles wasn't satisfied. He started a campaign against the families of the dead men, who had kept silent at the time of Katrina's murder. Houses were burnt down and people continually harassed. Two families, having received warnings that their children's lives were at stake, left France and returned to Algeria. It had been the beginning. From there it had been only a few steps to where they were today.

But a recent development had Duval truly worried. Using Arab fundamentalists to perpetrate these crimes in Europe – financing Islamic terrorism in order to turn the people of Europe against Islam itself – beggared belief.

Duval had made up his mind. After this, he was retiring. He had amassed a personal fortune of over fifty million dollars in various bank accounts around the world and he wanted to enjoy his wealth. Still the right side of fifty, he had so many things he wanted to see and do. And with that much money he could indulge his fantasies with the world's most beautiful women. This latest and most terrible act of terrorism was one step too far. America would never rest until they caught those responsible. And for the kind of reward that would be on offer, someone would betray him.

Duval's antennae picked up the question and he tuned back in.

'Are copies of the newspapers in yet?'

'No, sir. As soon as they are we'll get them. As requested, I spoke with the anchorman for *24 Hours*.' The current affairs magazine was one of Gustav's flagship programmes and had been Duval's idea. Broadcast from 7pm to 8pm every day in every major European country, it was anti-immigrant, highly racist and right-wing. Frequently *24 Hours* was in trouble with the broadcasting standards authorities. Whenever there was a problem or complaint Gustav's print empire of newspapers swung into action, screaming that the minority interests of the immigrants were undermining the rights of the majority. The drip-feed of bigotry had led the people of Europe almost to the point of no return. Job losses were blamed on immigration. Poor housing? Blame the immigrants. No social security payments? Spent on the immigrants. Bad schooling? Overcrowded hospitals? Too much crime? Too many drugs on our streets? Judicial system too slow? Police stretched to breaking point? Everyone knew who was to blame, the immigrants.

The counter arguments, diversity of culture, much needed skills, highly intelligent, hard-working people prepared to do low paid, menial tasks, the backbone of health services across Europe, and so on, were lost in the clamour of perceived woes. Immigrants of all generations were finding it increasingly difficult to defend themselves. And now, with atrocities being committed across Europe by Islamic fundamentalists, the ideals of the right were being justified.

The cost of supporting the terrorists was huge though Gustav considered it money well spent. Funding Muslims to create their own ultimate destruction was a master stroke of genius. But even he could not afford the outlay for much longer. The loss of the Suriname shipment had been a terrible blow. Although his every instinct screamed for revenge against TIFAT, he knew it must be used as a major prop for the new regime he envisaged, its officers replaced by his own people. The possibilities were endless.

Gustav stopped pacing and looked at Duval for a moment before nodding. 'Check everything is as it should be and please let me know when the submarine is to be launched.'

Duval, dismissed, left the room and went up to the bridge. The Captain was sitting in his chair monitoring the dials arrayed in front of him. He looked up as Duval entered but said nothing. There was no love lost between the two men although they had only met the day before.

'How long to go?'

'Four and a half hours. I'll let you know when the sub's going in.'

'Good. Are the crew all right?'

'Why shouldn't they be? We may be short-handed but for a ten thousand dollar bonus they can manage.' His cut was twenty thousand and he was enjoying thinking about what he would spend it on while he sat on his bridge.

'Let's keep it that way.'

The ship had sailed with only a skeleton crew of six men. It was far too few for safety, in fact downright illegal, but the money on offer for a few days work was too great to resist. Apart from the captain and engineer there were four deckhands whose main task was to launch the submarine.

The *Goliath* was pitching into a long, low swell. Above, the sky was clear, the stars shining and a new moon was creeping over the horizon. The bridge-wing doors were open and Duval stood in the warm breeze for a few seconds, savouring the night. Thankfully the weather was in their favour. If there had been a high wind or a storm then the launch would have been next to impossible. As it was, everything was running to schedule.

A teleprinter clattered and the Captain heaved his bulk out of his chair and stepped across the bridge to take a look. It was the weather forecast. He scanned the map, read the information and grunted in satisfaction. A weak front was gathering in the north and would be sweeping across the Gulf in about twenty-four hours. Taking a file from the shelf above his head he put the report away. Perfect.

Duval was looking at him enquiringly.

'Weather forecast. Nothing to concern us.'

'Good. I'm going to check the sub,' replied Duval.

Aft of the bridge and accommodation, the deck was a large

flat area about a quarter of the size of a football field. Normally it was packed with pipes being transported to the oilfields but now lay empty, except for the submarine looking small and insignificant by comparison.

A tarpaulin covered the area and two people in overalls were walking around the outside of the sub, making last minute checks.

'Everything okay?'

'Yes, Mr Duval.'

Duval nodded. A pity, he thought. She was such a beautiful woman. It was a waste but unavoidable.

'All systems are go. The batteries are fully charged and the air scrubber has been tested.' Chantelle Suchard smiled, hiding her nervousness at what lay ahead.

'Excellent. We'll load in another two hours.' Duval left her to her preparations and returned to the bridge. It was his job, amongst many, to check and double check all arrangements. Nothing was left to chance.

The radar showed a few contacts and he questioned the Captain about them. They would pass well clear. So far everything was looking good.

Returning below decks he found Gustav reading copies of newspaper articles in English, French and Swedish, transmitted via satellite from his media empire. Gustav smiled with satisfaction. Governments were beginning to panic as Europe's citizens demanded action. In the previous twenty-four hours there had been nine incidents involving the deaths of white Europeans. The articles pointed the finger of blame squarely at Islamic fundamentalists. If it was untrue, who cared? A retraction of a story meant a small paragraph buried on page nine. The story itself made front page headlines.

'Excellent. By next week, the clamour will be overwhelming. With America under siege the President will have no choice but to withdraw his troops. That will leave the road clear for us.'

Duval nodded. It was impossible to have a whites-only Europe if American troops were stationed there. Too many of them were black. With the event Gustav planned for the anniversary of 9/11, the Americans wouldn't hesitate to fall back and protect their borders.

The phone rang and Duval answered it. 'We're at the drop-off point.'

'Good. Time to open the safe.' From inside the safe Gustav gingerly removed a round object about the size of a football. Hard, dark-brown and seamless, the sphere appeared to be made of plastic. In fact its whole surface was an aerial. Inside was a small detonating device that could be set off by a signal from a satellite or a transmitter. With one explosion, two litres of nerve agent would be released into the atmosphere. Contact meant death within three to four minutes – a horrible and painful death, with no available antidote. The toxic gas had a life of eight hours after which it was rendered harmless by oxygen in the atmosphere. From computer analysis Gustav estimated between 100,000 and 250,000 people would die in the targeted area – Houston, Texas.

Handing the sphere to his secretary he said, 'No mistakes, Duval.'

Back on the pipe deck Duval watched eight al-Qaeda operatives climb into the sub. The last man, a machine gun slung over his shoulder, waited for him. In his early thirties, Abu Al-Adil had a pathological hatred for all non-Muslims. He was a Saudi by birth and a fanatical follower of bin Laden by choice. Alive or dead, bin Laden continued to exert a huge influence across the Islamic world.

'Here is the toxin.'

Abu Al-Adil took the proffered sphere with breathtaking nonchalance and dropped it into a string-bag.

'You know what you must do?'

'Of course. We attack those whom Allah the All-knowing has cursed. Judgement is his alone but this deed will be a glorious tribute to his name.'

Duval kept a straight face. Their fanaticism appalled him. Once again he marvelled at Gustav's manipulation of their commitment to God. It was a master stroke.

Waving casually to Chantelle sitting in the pilot's position in the front of the sub, he stood and watched as the ladder up to the conning tower was removed. The hatch was closed and Duval ducked under the hull and paused for a second. Placing a high explosive onto the hull he pressed the micro-electric switch. The magnetic bond would be impossible to break without first removing the battery. He signalled the crane driver, the strops were raised until they took the weight and then the sub was raised into the air and swung gently outboard.

As the submarine dropped below deck level, Duval waved one last time to Chantelle. Reaching the water, the engine was started and, as the weight came off the lifting strops, the gears were engaged. The sub inched slowly backwards clear of the strop and away from the ship's side. There were no lights showing and almost immediately the sub sank from view.

Duval returned to Gustav who was nervously pacing the cabin.

'All done?'

'They are on their way to the *Silver Beech*.'

Something in Duval's inflection caused Gustav to step directly in front of his assistant. As always, he knew what was bothering him. 'Chantelle has been a very useful ally. She is also greedy and unscrupulous. The temptation to tell the Americans of my involvement would have proven too great.'

Duval nodded. But that also applied to himself. Did Gustav have similar plans for him?

5

The operation on Ruth's knee was still in progress. Hunter was shocked to realise that the surgeons had been working on her for nearly fourteen hours. Finally, Matt Dunston appeared, looking exhausted.

'All I did was stand and watch and occasionally fetch cold water for the doctors. What they're doing is amazing, pioneering stuff. They've rebuilt all the shattered bits of bone and literally glued them back together.'

'How much longer will they be?'

'Not long. They've almost finished.'

'What's the prognosis?' The briefest eye-contact betrayed the anxiety behind Hunter's question.

'No idea. She won't be running the marathon for a long time, if ever, but it looks as though she'll keep her leg.'

'Thank God,' said Hunter, feeling a terrible weight leave him.

Dunston nodded. 'Amen to that. Praying was all I was good for.'

'Well, it looks as if your prayers are needed again. I've a lot to tell you. Come on.'

In the briefing room Hunter went over the operation in detail. As soon as he heard the plan, Dunston said, 'I'm coming.'

Hunter nodded. He wasn't surprised. 'I figured you'd want to.'

Just then, Masters appeared with a wide smile, waving something in his hand. 'Look what I've found, boss. An ex-torch.'

Hunter grinned back. 'Excellent. That'll make searching for any explosives far easier.'

The ex-torch was an explosives detector, the size of a torch-light and powered by four ordinary batteries. Instead of a beam of light, it emitted an x-ray that also carried an explosive sensor beam. The unique, unstable atoms of an explosive could be detected by the ex-torch through walls and even steel up to an inch thick. If any explosives were found the green light on the base of the torch would change to amber or red depending on the power of the signal. The ex-torch was new on the market and although TIFAT had tested them, Hunter was surprised Masters had found one on board.

'The Petty Officer Jack Dusty ordered it by mistake. It was slotted for return as soon as they got back to Pompey.'

'His mistake is our good fortune. Have you tried it out?'

'Yes, boss. Works like a charm. You'd better take it.'

'Thanks.' The torch was a godsend in the circumstances. Placing it on the desk, Hunter then thought better of it. In any sea it could roll off and be damaged. He packed it with his other kit, ready to go.

The phone rang and Hunter answered. The Officer of the Watch on the bridge informed him that the helicopter was ready to move the team to the destroyer, HMS *York*.

Hunter had one call to make before he left. He found Ruth in the sickbay, her face pale and wan, the pain she had suffered etched deeply into her face. A sickbay attendant sat next to her, thumbing through the day's newspaper produced by the ship.

'How is she?' Hunter asked him. 'Do you know how successful the operation was?'

'I can't say, sir, but here's someone who can.'

A tall, distinguished-looking man entered.

'Are you the surgeon who operated on Ruth?'

'Yes. How do you do?' He extended a long, slim hand that had a surprisingly strong grip. 'Surgeon Commander Fred Stewart.'

'My name's Hunter, Lieutenant Commander Hunter. Pleased to meet you, sir. Ruth's a member of my team.' He did not elaborate on his personal relationship with her. 'How is she?'

The surgeon shrugged and pulled an expressive face. He ran a tired hand through his greying hair. 'It's too soon to tell.'

'She will be able to walk again?'

'Oh, I should think so. Impossible to say yet how mobile the joint will be. It will, however, never be as good as it was. I fear her days in the front line are over. I understand from Matt Dunston that she's at TIFAT.'

'Yes.' If Hunter was dismayed by the news he didn't show it.

'Sorry I can't be more specific, but the reconstruction still comes very much under the heading of pioneering medicine. I've only performed it twice with our own people at Coronado.'

'Were those operations successful?'

'It depends on how you define success. One of the men had his foot shattered when a terrorist bomb went off in Bosnia. I put it back together again and he has maybe fifty, sixty percent articulation of the ankle. He's teaching with the SEALs and has just been promoted to Chief Petty Officer.' The surgeon paused, glancing at his sleeping patient.

'And the second one?' Hunter prompted him.

'Ah. Not so good, I'm afraid. A young man who had his heart set on becoming a SEAL. He was flying through the course. He even enjoyed Hell Week!'

Hunter nodded. He knew how tough the course was. Even after very careful selection, fewer than half the men passed. 'What happened?'

'A stupid accident. He was abseiling when his rope snagged and he took a bad fall. His left leg was shattered. I worked hard on that young man and he got about seventy percent use of his leg back.' Pausing again, he shook his head in sorrow. 'It meant he was out of the SEALs of course.'

'What happened to him?'

'He committed suicide. Decided there was nothing to live for. None of us had an inkling until we found his note. One of my failures.'

'And you can't be more accurate about Ruth's prognosis?'

The surgeon rubbed his bristled chin, fatigue evident in his kindly, brown eyes. 'If you mean, what's the worse case scenario,

I think she could have only partial movement of the knee. Even so, it should be enough so that she can walk without a limp. Sitting will be awkward, though not impossible. She'll have discomfort, twinges of pain, for a very long time, even after the bones have knit. In later life she will probably suffer from rheumatism in her knee but anti-inflammatory drugs will help. She'll be able to dance but probably not run. If I said any more, I'd be guessing.'

'Thanks for your honesty. I appreciate it.'

The surgeon looked at him shrewdly. 'Something tells me there's more to your relationship than just her being a member of your team.'

Hunter grinned wryly. 'We're planning to get married.'

'Well, congratulations. With the right support she'll come through her ordeal. Now, if you'll excuse me. I'd like to examine my patient and then get some sleep.'

Hunter nodded and the two men shook hands again. 'Thanks, Doc. Thanks very much.' With a final glance, Hunter left. Things were not as they were, but they could have been much worse.

Minutes later he was on board the helicopter and he and the team were being whisked across to HMS *York*. Now that Ruth's operation was over the task force was running at its more usual 15 knots with the *York* already twenty miles ahead with full speed rung-on. The destroyer turned to put the wind across her deck at green four-five, forty-five degrees over her starboard bow, and prepared to receive the Lynx Mk 8 she had despatched to pick up the TIFAT team. Hunter could clearly see her pennant number, D98, on the ship's port side and stern.

The helicopter made three trips back and forth to the aircraft carrier, ferrying the team and their equipment. Hunter was on the first flight and as soon as it landed he quickly made his way to the bridge.

Hunter asked permission to enter and stepped forward with a smile. Captain Brian Matthews returned the smile and the two men shook hands. 'Nick, what a pleasant surprise! I had no idea it was you who was coming. We'll go below and you can brief me.

Officer of the Watch, I'll be in my day cabin. Let me know when the Lynx is returning.'

'Aye, aye, sir,' the Officer of the Watch acknowledged.

The last time Hunter and Matthews had served together had been on board *HMS Antrim*. Hunter had been a sub-lieutenant trying to earn his watch-keeping certificate, while Matthews had just been promoted to lieutenant commander and was the ship's navigating officer. Hunter had been his assistant for nearly two years.

With a welcome cup of coffee at his elbow, Hunter brought Matthews up to speed on what was happening.

'My orders were simply to detach and head at full speed towards Trinidad and that the team leader would brief me. You'll be sent ashore by helo the minute we're within range. As soon as you're disembarked we're to join the exclusion zone around the liner.'

'I would have thought the Yanks had sufficient ships for the job.'

'We make it an international affair, politically preferable, don't you know?'

Hunter nodded. 'Makes sense. As soon as the remainder of my men arrive we'll bunk down and get some sleep.'

'I'm afraid all we can offer are camp beds. Three of you can sleep in the sick-bay.'

'We'll manage. Thanks, sir. After nearly a week in the jungle this will be luxury. First though, I need to contact TIFAT and find out if they've any Intel for me.'

'I'll take you to the Comms Centre and then I had better get to the Ops Room. I'll also brief the crew. How much can I tell them?'

Hunter shrugged. 'The minimum.'

Matthews nodded. 'Pretty much what I expected.'

The submarine settled on its course at a depth of fifty metres. Usually, when taking passengers for a night trip, her powerful searchlights shone in all directions. Now she sailed in darkness, using sonar and cameras only. The monitor in front of Chantelle

Suchard showed a sea alive with all kinds of fish. Many of them were unknown to her but she had no difficulty recognising a tiger shark and a shoal of barracuda.

Chantelle piloted the boat in silence. She had nothing in common with the man in the co-pilot's seat. From the moment they had met she had loathed him almost as much as he disliked her. Arabs, their habits and rituals repulsed her.

Her eyes checked the instruments and she made a minute alteration of the dial for the automatic pilot. The electric motors ran silently, with only the faintest of vibrations indicating that they were operating. Outside, the sea was black, apart from the flashes of phosphorescent plankton which swept past the window. Three TV screens gave her a view ahead of 180 degrees. The small amount of light that did exist, even when the world seemed dark, was enhanced by computers which also added colour. The resulting pictures were almost as clear as daylight out as far as three or four cables.

Taking a sip of water from the bottle in the holder in front of her, she allowed herself to day-dream. The two million euros promised by Gustav would be very useful. She could pay off the mortgage on her apartment in the South of France and possibly buy a ski chalet. Or maybe a yacht? Something sleek. She could keep it in the marina at Golfe Juan near Cannes. Automatically, she registered the battery dials, the oil pressure, the atmospheric sensors analysing the air. Everything was working correctly. This had to be the easiest money she had ever earned. Meeting Charles had turned her life around. He had been generous in the extreme. Initially she had expected him to make a pass, but it never happened. Part of her was disappointed, but on the whole she was relieved. She liked keeping her business and private life separate.

She shared his dream, his goal. A whites-only Europe was something her parents had often talked about. Thinking of them, Chantelle's fists clenched involuntarily on the arms of her chair. Their car had been involved in a head-on collision on a mountain road in Bavaria. They had been killed outright. The occupants of the other car, two Kurds seeking political asylum from

Saddam Hussein's regime, had been driving a beaten up wreck, uninsured and without valid driving licences. One of the men had died and the other had walked away. He had not even been prosecuted. Bile erupted in her stomach. Six months later she had met Gustav. His rhetoric had been balm to her grieving soul. Chantelle forced herself to relax and checked the navigation data. They would be with the liner in three hours and ten minutes. She informed her co-pilot, Al-Adil, who merely grunted in acknowledgement. *Loathsome swine.*

Abu Al-Adil was busy with his own thoughts. He was looking forward to seeing his younger brother again, although their meeting would be brief. But they would have all of eternity together in paradise, God willing. His heart pounded in excitement. The name of Abu Al-Adil would go down in Arab history. He would become as famous as their exalted leader, Osama bin Laden, whose name was spoken with such reverence across the Islamic world. He had only one task, to get the *Silver Beech* to Texas. In order to do so every man, woman and child on the liner were to be used. If the Americans tried to stop them, he would kill the passengers and crew indiscriminately. It would keep the Americans away until it was too late. His eyes glinted with anticipation as he looked out of the darkened window, oblivious to the beauty of the sea around him.

As the submarine approached the rendezvous position, Chantelle took them up to five metres and raised a thin periscope above the surface of the sea. She had no need to look through old fashioned eyepieces. Instead an all-round picture appeared on screens in front of her. It was still dark, although dawn was not far away. She adjusted the magnification and there she was, gleaming white, at a distance of four miles. Chantelle plotted a course to intercept the *Silver Beech*.

The liner was travelling due north at a speed of 4 knots and Chantelle brought the submarine expertly to the ship's port side, paralleling the course and speed of the large vessel, before surfacing.

Al-Adil had gone back to join his men, and when she gave the signal, he opened the hatch. The sea was calm and the sub moved sedately alongside. Chantelle switched the power to diesel and began to recharge the batteries while the men passed up their equipment to others on board the liner.

Al-Adil did not even say goodbye. After a few minutes Chantelle realised there was no sound behind her and when she looked, she saw the lounge was empty. Angrily she climbed from her seat, closed the outer and inner hatches and sat back at her control console. Without a glance at the liner she turned the sub away and began to submerge. Once she was clear she sent a signal to Gustav. *Mission accomplished*.

Duval heard the insistent beeping and snapped awake. He checked the signal from Chantelle and went to find Gustav.

'Good. You know what's required now. Send for the helicopter. I want to get back to Europe as quickly as possible.'

Minutes later Duval appeared on the bridge with a mug of coffee and a sandwich. 'I brought you these, Captain. We should call the crew – the sub will be back soon.' After the submarine had been despatched the men had hit their bunks in anticipation of an early start.

In order to facilitate such a small crew, the only cooked food aboard the *Goliath* was a large pot of stew kept warm on the range in the galley. It was topped up from time to time by a tin of soup or casserole. Otherwise the crew ate bread, biscuits and fresh fruit. An urn of boiling water for hot drinks was also provided and it was into this that Duval had placed a powerful sleeping draught. As an afterthought he had added it to the stew and a flask of orange juice.

If he was surprised by the offer of the food and drink the Captain did not show it. Nodding his thanks, he wolfed down the sandwich and washed it down with the coffee. It wasn't as hot as he liked and he drained the mug in three swift gulps.

'Thanks.' He seated himself back in his chair and reached for the microphone to the tannoy system. He announced it was time to 'rise and shine', and to be ready to receive the submarine alongside in half an hour.

The crew arrived in the galley one after the other, tired,

yawning, keen to get the recovery over with. They helped themselves to juice, tea or coffee and a sandwich. None of them bothered with the stew. They were sick of the sight of it.

Satisfied that the men had drunk enough of the drug to put a
horse to sleep, Duval went back to the bridge. He found the
Captain fast asleep in his chair. Lifting the microphone he broadcast, 'Do you hear there? There's been a change of plan. The sub
will not be returning for another three hours. I suggest you all
return to your cabins and get some more sleep.'

The men, already feeling the effects of the drug, returned to
their bunks. Gustav appeared on the bridge.

'I see the drug worked as expected. Have you contacted the
helicopter yet?'

'Yes, sir. It'll be here in one hour.'

'Sufficient time for you to set the charges.' An accomplished
sailor, Gustav ensured there was no shipping in the vicinity and
altered course to the east. Increasing speed, he watched with
satisfaction as the bow wave grew. He set the cruise control to
18 knots. Glancing at the bridge clock, he saw the time had
come. The radio at the back of the bridge had been modified and
carried a very-ultra high frequency signal on the back of a high
frequency pulse. Its signal was picked up by a thin wire trailing
from the submarine.

Chantelle, in accordance with her instructions, was at a depth
of ten metres and had released the antennae buoy which now
trailed behind the sub. In one minute Gustav would call her to
confirm everything was in order and that the rendezvous point
remained as originally planned. She checked the battery power.
All systems were working correctly and in less than three hours
she would be able to have a hot shower and a few hours sleep.
She yawned happily at the prospect.

The submarine shuddered and suddenly she was wide awake,
thoughts of a shower and sleep wiped from her mind. Coolly she
ran her eyes over the gauges in front of her. What the hell
had happened?

The engines were running smoothly, the life support system

was functioning, the sub was moving at 4 knots through the water and . . . and the depth was fifteen metres and increasing. She checked the gauge again, aghast. It was impossible. She checked the trim and the levels of water ballast and knew that she should have been on a level keel. Her hands flew across the console as she opened valves to dump water. The depth gauge was now showing nineteen, twenty, twenty-one metres and still going down. Finally it stabilised. The needle trembled at twenty metres and began to unwind back up. Nineteen, eighteen . . . *Come on, you bitch. Come on*, Chantelle prayed. Fifteen, fourteen . . . Yes! It looked like she was going to make it!

The needle stopped moving. For a heart-wrenching moment it was static, then it began to wind down once more. Chantelle sat frozen for a second and then checked the echo sounder. The sea floor was over two hundred metres away. If she hit there she would never escape alive. The submarine lurched, now at fifteen degrees to the horizontal and sinking faster all the time. She could hear cracking noises all around; the outer hull was breached and the inner one was feeling the strain. Grabbing the release valves she began to pressurise the submarine with air.

In the event of an emergency there were numerous means of escape. The sub was intended to carry fare-paying passengers and as such had fail-safe systems incorporated into the design. The rupturing of the outer hull was unheard of. Only an explosion could do that. An explosion! Cold certainty swept through her with the thought. Gustav was trying to kill her!

Her brain still struggling to grasp this betrayal, Chantelle moved quickly. If she were to escape the vessel whilst under the surface she needed to equalise the pressure inside and out. Then the escape hatches could be opened and she could swim to the surface using the emergency breathing masks. She cracked open the bottle valves as far as they would go, feeling the pressure increasing rapidly. Thank God she dived regularly, as otherwise she doubted her eardrums would have been able to take the pressure change.

In the passengers' lounge she whipped open the wheel above her head and let the hatch drop inwards. Frantically she pulled down the emergency ladder and climbed the few rungs she needed to reach the outer hatch. She turned the wheel and pushed with all her strength. It wouldn't move. The sea pressure outside was too great.

Glancing at the repeat depth gauge on the bulkhead panic flared in her. The sub was at forty-eight metres and still dropping. She pulled open a tool box and grabbed the heaviest wrench. Grunting with effort she attacked the air bottle bank. Her hands and arms jarred as she smashed at the connecting pipes and valves. Leaks appeared and the air escaped into the submarine faster than ever. The pain in her ears was excruciating. She swallowed and tried holding her nose, blowing hard, trying to clear them. Suddenly the pain vanished and she knew her eardrums had burst. The gauge was at sixty metres when she dropped the wrench and climbed back up to the hatch. Escape hood and air bottle slung over her shoulder, she put her back to the hatch and pushed until her eyeballs popped and her muscles ached with the strain. Finally the seal cracked and water poured in but she couldn't sustain the pressure and the hatch closed again. Taking a deep breath she readied herself mentally and pushed again. With a gut-wrenching, back-breaking effort she raised the hatch an inch. Water poured in and the pressure in the submarine suddenly equalised. The hatch opened and Chantelle, trembling, climbed out.

Slipping the mouthpiece between her teeth and the hood over her head, she began to swim to the surface. She knew that she was 70 maybe 80 metres beneath the surface. She needed decompression stops but she had no idea how many, at what depth or for how long. Briefly she contemplated what faced her when she reached the surface, rising from that depth. For a second she almost spat out the mouthpiece, but something forced her on. The deepest she had ever been was 40 metres and that for less than ten minutes.

Even as Chantelle had been desperately trying to escape, hatches on the side of the sub had blown open and self-inflating life-rafts had popped to the surface. As soon as they hit, automatic beacons started broadcasting and could be heard by ships and aircraft many miles away. The United States Coastguard, on station around the liner, fixed the location of the beacons within seconds. Five minutes later a helicopter was airborne and heading towards her.

Swimming upwards through twenty, fifteen, ten metres, Chantelle watched the sharks begin to gather. She was trailing blood from a cut in her hand. The prehistoric predators were already circling. She had intended to hang in the water at ten metres until her air ran out, to help with her decompression. That was no longer an option. Fear clawed at her. Should she survive Charles Gustav would regret his treachery.

As she watched, one of the sharks, from the mottled appearance of its skin a tiger, came closer and almost touched her. Chantelle knew there was no escape. The sharks would be on her within seconds of reaching the surface. Again she considered spitting out the tit and breathing in water but she had a perverse, overwhelming desire to feel the sun on her face once more. Looking up she saw the yellow bottom of a life-raft, then a second and a third. Suddenly hope flared within her.

Hitting the surface she swam frantically for the nearest inflatable. A black fin appeared, bearing down on her even as she grabbed the side of the raft. Kicking frantically she pulled herself inside the canopy and lay there gasping, tears in her eyes. After a few moments rest she gathered her wits and sat up to take stock. She found glucose sweets, water and a Very pistol. She drank a pint of water. As she lay quietly, gathering her strength, the pain struck. Her body convulsed as though an electric shock had coursed through her nervous system and she knew she had the bends. It passed but she knew another spasm would occur any second, then another, each worse than the last, until the pain was continuous and agonising. The solution was to grab the escape bottle and dive down until the pain ceased. But below the surface, the sharks were waiting. Gathering her wits, she ripped open the first aid kit and frantically searched through it. The hypodermic carried a warning. Use only in extreme emergency. Moaning, she broke the seal and rammed the needle into her biceps. She pushed the plunger steadily, emptying the narcotic into her system. Taking a second hypodermic she injected her thigh. Another spasm hit, worse than the first and she screamed in agony. When the third spasm came she was unconscious.

Chantelle didn't hear the helicopter, nor did she see the crewman being lowered and checking each raft. Hers was the third and final raft. As she was lifted into the helicopter and flown back to the ship, her condition worsened, the bubbles boiling in her blood causing irreparable damage to her nerve ends. She remained unconscious, unable to tell her rescuers the harm they were doing.

With 32 knots rung on, HMS *York* heeled sharply whenever the ship altered course. A warning pipe was made over the tannoy system to give the ship's company time to brace but even so a few bruises were inevitable. Hunter had spent most of his time on board talking with TIFAT HQ, planning, refining the operation, discussing options. As always, they were looking for a backdoor.

Reaching the liner safely was the most dangerous part of the mission. Once on board the team had at least some control over their destinies. Every precaution would be taken but the initial stage of the operation was risky in the extreme.

Macnair finally had a back-up solution. 'I've learnt that the nuclear submarine USS *Swordfish* is steaming at full speed for the area. It will arrive around midnight and take up station about half a mile astern of the liner. Its task is to watch and follow. The SEALs have emergency transponders which they're supplying with the other kit. If you fail to land on the liner, set off the alarm and the *Swordfish* will pick you up. Apparently they're accurate to within a few feet so there shouldn't be any difficulties. What's the weather forecast, Nick?'

'There's a weak front coming down from the north. Gusts are fifteen, twenty knots. It shouldn't be a problem, unless they hit at the wrong time.'

'Have you received a full list of the equipment Coronado are sending?'

'Yes, thanks, sir. It's as comprehensive as you'd expect. They're pulling out all the stops to help.'

'When the chips are down we know who our friends are. When are you leaving the *York*?'

'In approximately two hours. The C130 will be waiting at Trinidad when we arrive. Has Isobel learnt any more?'

'Some. The money trail definitely links Al-Qaeda terrorist acts in Europe and the smugglers in Suriname. Leo has managed to trace the cash to an account in a Jamaican bank which is actually fed from Paris. The sums involved are staggering.'

'Isobel's instincts were spot on as usual. I saw on the news bulletin that Seville's cathedral has been damaged.'

'The attacks are unrelenting now. Al-Qaeda have admitted responsibility for the bomb. The cathedral was built in the fifteen century on the site of a mosque, apparently. It's full of priceless art treasures. Now the Muslims are claiming the site for themselves; they're demanding a mosque be rebuilt there.'

'That's ludicrous, sir.'

'Of course it is. Islamic leaders all over the world reject the demands of these fundamentalist madmen. They've even said that Israel must cease to exist and all Jews must return to their countries of origin. They know none of it is possible. It's getting totally out of hand, Nick. We now have armed men guarding cathedrals and churches all over Europe. As many as a dozen people have been accidentally killed by armed police. The rightwing are in a feeding frenzy. There's a police presence at all major tourist sites, department stores, subways, airports, railway stations. It's even been suggested we deploy the military. Over two dozen mosques have been torched. In Germany a mosque was shown being set on fire on TV and the police stood and watched it happen. The situation's even worse in France. The gutter press are stirring it for all they're worth. The EU is talking about implementing legislation which will play into the hands of the bigots. Enough politics, Nick. You concentrate on the operation in hand and leave the big picture to me.'

'Roger that. Can you confirm that the hijackers have planted explosives on the ship?'

'That was the information given to the US Coastguard and I've no reason to doubt it. PACER SKY has been tracking and watching the liner for hours now. The only people we have seen on the upperdeck have been carrying weapons. Isobel is forwarding some of the images we've received. See what you make of them. They should be with you by now. There's also an interesting clip that Isobel cut out and sent. See what you make of it.'

'I'll go and have a look now, sir. Thanks.' Breaking the connection, Hunter walked thoughtfully up to the Operations Room. The *York* was in defence watches and half the ship was closed up and on duty. The helicopter was returning from its final trip from the aircraft carrier and would be arriving in ten minutes. The ship had been called to flying stations to receive it. Hunter stopped by the surface plot to see how busy the sea was around them. The marked contacts exceeded forty and he decided to stay away from the bridge which had been his next port of call. They would be busy dodging shipping and recovering the helo. He felt the ship slow down for the landing and made his way aft to greet the rest of the team.

They sat in an annexe of the Operations Room and looked at the pictures of the *Silver Beech* beamed in from PACER SKY. As always, the clarity was startling. Four terrorists could be clearly seen patrolling the upper deck with guns slung over their shoulders. Two were on the topmost deck while another two were on the main promenade deck, three decks down.

'Why are the men outside?' Hunter asked the group. 'Are they guarding against somebody trying to make a bolt for it, or an attack by us?'

Clements voiced his thoughts. 'Travelling at such a slow speed the ship's crew must know that they can launch lifeboats and life-rafts. I think it's to stop people escaping.'

Jan Badonovitch clicked his fingers and pointed at the screen. 'That's true boss, but I think they're looking out for submarines. See how they're leaning on the rail and looking at the sea. They fear a sub sending in special forces.'

'You could be right,' said Hunter. 'It's encouraging that nobody appears to be looking at the sky.' Hunter pressed a button on the console in front of him. 'The General suggested we look at the next bit of film and see what we make of it.'

They watched as the port lifeboats were slung out and lowered halfway to the sea. White awnings were thrown over the boats and fitted from one to the other, creating a canopy running a third of the length of the ship and projecting about twenty feet out. The screen split, the left half showing video, the right showing infra-red images.

A hot-spot appeared under the canopy. It was large and tracked alongside the ship. Smaller hot-spots appeared, evidently people. Probably passing items inboard. They quickly finished and the bigger hot-spot vanished.

'They've just been reinforced,' said Don Masters. 'I counted seven extra.'

'I counted eight,' frowned David Hughes. 'Though it was difficult to tell.'

'Makes no difference,' said Hunter. 'We've no idea how many were there in the first place.'

'That was definitely a submarine alongside,' said Claude Masson. 'But whose?'

'Good question, Claude,' said Hunter. 'We need to find out in a hurry. A submarine suggests an enemy government. And it also begs the question, what gear was taken on board? What nasty surprises do they have in store for us?' He let the thought hang in the air.

A rating knocked on the door and put his head round. 'Sir, the Captain wants you on the bridge.'

'Thanks. I'll be right there.'

Matthews, seated in his chair, was leafing through his signal pad when Hunter arrived. 'You sent for me, sir?'

'Yes, Nick. Two things. One, we'll be within range in an hour for the first sortie and two, take a look at this.'

Hunter took the proffered signal pad. It was a general message from the Coastguard to all ships relating the rescue of a survivor from a sunken vessel. They had located three large life-rafts in the area but nobody else was found. 'Where exactly is this, sir?'

'I need to plot the position but I think it's relatively near the liner. At least within fifty miles of it.' Sliding off his seat, Matthews added, 'Let's take a look.'

In the chart room the captain identified the correct folio and slid it from its drawer. Consulting the list on the front, he took out the appropriate chart, spreading it on the table. Using a parallel ruler and pencil he established the position of the liner and the life-raft.

'It's too close to be a coincidence as far as I'm concerned,' said Hunter.

'Me too. The signal says the survivor was a young woman. But where did she come from?'

'No idea. Have we pictures of the area prior to her being found?'

'Not yet. I've asked for them.' The phone went and Matthews lifted the receiver. 'Captain.' He listened for a moment and said, 'I'll be right there.' Replacing the phone he smiled at Hunter. 'The satellite pictures have just arrived. Let's go to the ops room and take a look.'

By superimposing a latitude and longitude lattice over the screen they were able to watch the movement of ships and small craft in the area for an hour prior to the appearance of the rafts. The film, in fast frame, took only seven minutes to view.

'There they are,' said Hunter. 'They appear literally out of the blue.'

'Obviously a submarine,' said the Captain.

'And I think I know which one.' Briefly Hunter described the film footage of the sub going alongside the *Silver Beech*.

'It makes sense but why and how?'

'I'd better radio the General. If I'm right then the sooner the woman talks the better.'

6

Chantelle groaned in her sleep. The bubbles of nitrogen in her bloodstream had grown to a devastating size and were trapped in her joints and spine. Nerve ends were being irreparably damaged. The effects of the powerful narcotic she had taken were wearing off and the pain was beginning to penetrate. Suddenly she snapped awake and screamed.

A medical orderly ran to her side. Chantelle writhed and groaned, tears streaming down her face. In a panic, he took another ampoule of a powerful painkiller and injected her with it. In a few seconds she lay quiet again, her screams reduced to a whimper. Immediately the medic telephoned the captain.

'What the hell is causing it?'

'I've no idea, sir. There's no obvious cause of pain – no broken bones, nothing. She could have ingested something, but . . .' he paused.

'What?' his captain prompted him.

'There's only one thing that fits, sir,' the medic said dubiously. 'But it don't make no sense. I think she's got decompression sickness. The bends.'

After a few seconds of thought the Captain said, 'It could be. But how did she come by the bends in the middle of the Gulf?'

'I've no idea, but it's the only thing that fits.'

'We've no chamber. She needs to be sent ashore. Good work, Hudson. I'll send the helo.'

Chantelle was airlifted to Galveston where a special unit dealt with diving accidents. She was pressurised in a diving chamber by a doctor who saw her pain easing almost immediately. However, he knew that it was too late. The damage would be permanent. Such a beautiful girl too.

Gustav checked the ropes securing the ship's master to his seat before he poured himself a cup of fresh coffee. Checking the radar, there were no other vessels inside fifteen miles. The radio burst into life and he heard the ship's call sign. Answering it, he established that the helicopter would be with them in fifteen minutes. He nodded with satisfaction. Everything was going according to plan. With the submersible and Chantelle gone and the ship and its crew following soon after, his tracks were being well covered. The helicopter crew would have no idea what was happening and would never make the connection between the events on the liner and him. After all, the world press knew the hijackers were Arabs.

Duval appeared on the bridge. 'I've taken our bags down to the deck.'

'Good. Here's the helicopter.' Stepping outside he waved to the pilot who waved back as he lined up to land on the huge open deck. 'Let's go.'

The two men hurried aft in time to see the helo hover over the deck prior to touchdown. Gustav took a transmitter from his pocket, flicked a switch to arm it and pressed a button. Under their feet the two men felt a series of small explosions. They crossed to the helicopter and climbed on board, closing the door behind them.

'Let's go,' yelled Gustav at the pilot.

'Yes, sir.' The helicopter lifted off the deck and swung clear, the pilot heading east.

Gustav sat with Duval in the passengers' section and looked back. Already the ship was settling by the bow, the engines still working, the propellers driving the ship forward and down. Gustav quickly scanned the sea. There were no ships in sight, no witnesses.

* * *

'Sir,' Hunter advised Macnair, 'we're leaving in ten minutes. Somebody needs to question the girl urgently.'

'I've spoken to the Pentagon and they're informing the FBI. We need to leave it to them. Back to the job in hand. Once you're on board the liner, it's imperative you find the device that's jamming communications.'

'Will do. Anything from the passenger and crew lists?'

'The passengers appear clean. Nothing obvious. But the crew are a different kettle of fish. So far we've identified twelve members who are non-Christian, using false papers and references. Isobel received photographs from the shipping company a few minutes ago and is forwarding them now. You had better take a look, although I doubt they'll be much use.'

Matt Dunston entered the room and handed a sheaf of papers to Hunter. The photographs were passport size, obviously from job applications. Macnair was right. 'It's hard to tell one from the other, the photos are so bad, sir.'

'That's what we thought. Still, they may help. There's also an anomaly with one of the entertainers. A woman singer whose father was a Palestinian. She's never been in trouble but you never know. Trust nobody, Nick, apart from the master and his immediate officers.'

'Right, sir. And definitely nothing on the passengers' side?'

'No. If there is we won't be able to tell you unless you stop the jamming.'

'I appreciate that, sir, over.'

'Good luck to all of you. Out.'

Hunter said his farewells to Captain Matthews and soon afterwards was airborne and heading for Trinidad with half the team. The Lynx Mk 8 helicopter had a cruise speed of 125 knots and a range of 330 miles. Everything that could be stripped from the helo had been taken out or off. It carried no missiles, no torpedoes and no guns. Neither did it carry any seats. The five members of the team sat on the floor, along with some of their equipment. With all flying profiles laid down by the manufacturers, there was margin for error. On this flight most of that margin had been used up.

The flight took 2hrs 30mins and their air speed was a record breaking 139 knots. By the time they landed the engines were practically sucking air. It was still a couple of hours short of midnight and the main airport had closed for the night. A Hercules C130 had arrived earlier and the equipment that it had brought had been laid out in a hangar. Armed marines protected the area. Diplomatic egos had been stroked and promises of favours made and accepted. The US had *carte blanche* for the operation. Although Trinidad had the kind of aviation fuel used by helicopters, for speed of turn-round the Americans had brought their gas with them. The Lynx was quickly refuelled and sent back to the *York*, which was already eighty miles closer.

Hunter was introduced to a Lt Cdr O'Connell, the boss of Seal Team 6, based at Coronado, San Diego. At 6ft 6ins he was taller than Hunter, with shoulders to match. His cauliflower ear and broken nose suggested an interest in boxing. The American greeted CPO Doug Tanner like a long-lost friend.

'So, how's it going with the limeys?'

'Not bad, sir. I just wish they spoke English.'

The two men laughed at the shared joke before O'Connell turned to Hunter. 'I've brought everything you asked for and some. I had my guys brainstorm the operation as well to see what we could come up with. There are one or two items we thought of that might come in useful, like flash-bangs. Also we brought two ex-torches.'

'Thanks. We've actually got one.'

O'Connell nodded. 'But they break easily. Have you used one of these before?'

'What is it?' Hunter looked curiously at the oddly-shaped weapon.

'Let me show you.' It was a peculiar looking gun, about the size of a .45 pistol, with an iron rod sticking out of the barrel. 'It attaches to your body using this harness. The bolt is fired via a powerful compressed air cartridge, attached to a thin line with a breaking strain of over eight hundred pounds. The line is contained inside the hollow butt. It will travel one hundred feet. When it reaches the end, the line pulls the bottom of the bolt, releasing a three pronged hook. If you pull the trigger a second time the line reels in and takes you with it. We developed it for exactly the kind of job you're going on now. I've got one for each of the team if you'd like to try them. We call them a hook-gun.'

'I appreciate it. They could come in useful. Anything we need to know about the wings?'

'Pretty much as standard. You've used the mark five?'

'Yeah. Okay, let's start working our way through this lot.' Hunter turned to his team.

But O'Connell wasn't finished. 'I also brought a consignment of Calico M-960As. Ever use one?'

Hunter shook his head as he hefted the machine gun in his hand. 'Nice. Light and well balanced.'

'It's the best the US of A has to offer. I brought fifty-round and one hundred-round mags. This is the concealable model where the barrel doesn't go past the fore-end. The helical feed mags are guaranteed not to jam. They're incredibly accurate and with this babe fitted,' O'Connell picked up a silencer, 'it's like a sheep farting in a high wind.'

'Okay. I'll try one, 'said Hunter. 'We'll let the rest of the lads decide for themselves.' As in Special Forces units the world over, the men had, and often stuck with, a favourite gun.

Although they had brought their weapons from the operation in Suriname, most of the team took the opportunity to try the American gun. Each man also carried a silenced handgun strapped to his side, either a Swiss SIG or a German Heckler & Koch.

The team began to sort out the remainder of the equipment. O'Connell had two of his men with him and they helped. Beacon frequencies were set and locators married up to orbiting satellites.

'Can you send Morse?' O'Connell asked.

'I'm a bit rusty but I reckon I can manage seven or eight words per minute,' Hunter replied.

'Good. I've got this as well.' The American handed over a small torch with a signalling trigger. 'The SSN following you are keeping a lookout from the time you jump. You can signal them with this. They can reply using the periscope. If you send, the most they'll do is a single flash in acknowledgement.'

'Okay. Though I doubt we'll need it.'

'You never know. Take it just in case.'

The remainder of the team had now arrived. Hunter asked the pilot of the Herky Bird for a weather update. The printout showed the weak front was deepening and that the wind for the area of the drop was now gusting 18–28 knots.

'Not exactly ideal jumping conditions,' said Dunston.

Hunter shrugged at his friend. 'No use worrying. Into the valley of death and all that.'

Dunston nodded.

Every precaution possible had been taken.

At midnight there was nothing left to do but depart. Once they were in the air Hunter established communications with TIFAT HQ and spoke to the General.

'Any information about the woman they rescued from the liferaft?'

'She appears to have the bends. She's being treated right now but it looks pretty bad. She needed help a lot sooner but they had no way of telling it was decompression sickness. She's still unconscious but we had a stroke of luck. The Coastguard sent a vessel to recover the life-rafts. We're trying to trace them now and it looks promising. We ought to be able to tell from the inflatables where they came from.'

'Good. Is *Swordfish* on station?'

'Affirmative. The ship has not changed her pattern of zigzagging or altered her speed. There's no doubt that at this rate the *Silver Beech* will be arriving in Houston on the eleventh – the anniversary.'

'Precisely. If they're aiming to top nine eleven by an even greater atrocity then they must have something spectacular planned. Maybe a nuclear device.'

'Possibly, but we've put pressure on practically everybody in the world who could know anything about such a weapon and we've drawn a blank.'

'That doesn't mean to say they don't have one.'

'True. But you've no idea how hard we're shaking the trees and nothing's fallen out yet. No, I think it's something else.'

Hunter cleared his throat. 'Any news about Ruth, sir?'

'She woke up briefly and asked for you. But I gather she's sleeping off the anaesthetic still.'

'Thanks for what you did. Flying in the surgeon for her.'

'Forget it, Nick. We look after our own. You know the objectives.'

'Roger. Thanks.' Hunter broke the connection. How could he forget? Save the passengers and crew, take out the hijackers and last but not least, save the ship. A piece of cake.

Leaving the flight deck he joined the team as they were putting on their dark grey combat suits. Having slung their folded aerofoils over their shoulders they secured the straps. Each man checked a buddy, carefully. Their night-vision goggles were computer-chip controlled. They reacted fast enough in the event of a sudden bright light that the wearer wasn't blinded, unlike with previous models. Weapons were checked and secured. Flashbang grenades were distributed. The three ex-torches were tested by aiming them at a piece of plastic explosive. All three worked. The team split into five pairs. Hunter would be jumping with Matt Dunston. They would leave the aircraft at one minute intervals, each pair jumping together. Beacons were checked once more, frequencies locked on again and personal communications tested. Then came the hardest part – waiting.

Gustav and Duval were ensconced in the first class lounge at Kingston airport, Jamaica. Their Air France flight had been called and they made their way to the plane. They had left the room before CNN reported the rescue of a woman from a liferaft in the Gulf of Mexico. The report was merely a foot note of local news and would not be broadcast again. Events in Europe and on board the liner were gripping the world to the exclusion of all other news coverage.

Gustav refused a glass of champagne, sipping a mango juice instead. He avidly scanned the newspapers for the latest information on Europe. He needed to read the response of the liberal masses. The reports were gratifying. Support for the right was growing while the threat to security was escalating daily. Extremist terror was no longer a brief intrusion into the life of the average European.

'Most satisfying.' Draining his mango juice he pressed the call button for the stewardess. She arrived with alacrity and he ordered a coffee. The plane began to taxi for take-off just as she arrived with the hot drink. In her haste to serve Gustav and return to her seat she spilt it over his left knee, staining his trousers. She was immediately very apologetic.

'Accidents happen,' said Gustav containing his anger with difficulty. White spots of fury lightened his cheeks and Duval placed a hand on his arm to calm him.

'Leave it,' said Duval to the stewardess, 'and go and sit down.' The young woman fled to the front of the cabin. 'Don't get upset, Charles. Everything is working perfectly. Focus on what's happening in Europe right now. Savour the taste of victory – your goal is only weeks away.'

'The stupid black bitch. She and her kind won't be working for our national airlines in the future. She'll be lucky to get a job cleaning toilets.' Unclenching his fists the anger drained from him as quickly as it had risen.

Duval pointed to the two items in the German paper, *Die Welt*.

'Let me see.' Gustav snatched the paper and read the articles quickly. 'Excellent. The Austrian police shot dead a dozen rioters, all foreigners. Ah, look at this. The Germans are pointing the blame for the riot in Paris on the Algerians. Five were killed, including a gendarme. Kill five, terrify fifty thousand. Excellent.'

'Not so loud, Gustav, we don't want to be overheard.'

Gustav looked around him, his mouth twisted in disdain. Five seats had black occupants and he dropped his eyelids to conceal his hatred. Settling back he closed his eyes. 'I shall doze for a while. Wake me when dinner is served.'

Macnair had briefed General Stafford at the Pentagon on the planned operation to retake the liner. As soon as the team was on board they were to go below to find the explosives. Once

91

they had been made safe the team would clear the upper decks of the guards, take out those who were watching the passengers and get the hostages to the lifeboats. While the passengers and crew abandoned ship the team would track down the remaining hijackers and deal with them. Macnair acknowledged the high risk nature of the plan, but nobody knew what the consequences of the liner reaching America would be. This way at least there was a chance that many of the passengers and crew would live to tell the tale.

Macnair voiced his fears to Stafford. 'What if the team fails?'

'The President has given *Swordfish* orders. In the event of failure the submarine is to sink the liner. It must not reach America. We believe the hijackers have some sort of weapon of mass destruction on board. All the *Swordfish* needs is the hit signal.'

'What did the Captain of the sub say to that?'

'Nothing. He verified the order, but he'll carry it out.'

'The loss of life could be appalling.'

'But imagine the consequences should the ship dock. We know that Islamic fundamentalist groups have been working for years to get their hands on some sort of nuclear or biological weapon. Maybe this is it. Right now the National Security Adviser is recommending we bring our troops back to protect America. She's saying it's time Europe looked after itself.'

'And what do you say, Colin?'

There was a pause. 'I guess she's not far wrong. It's certainly a sentiment that most Americans share. Hell, we've pulled Europe's chestnuts out of the fire twice last century and a third time in Yugoslavia. It's time you stood on your own two feet.'

'You'd better have your President tell my Prime Minister.'

'He has, in no uncertain terms, about an hour ago.'

On that note the connection was broken. Macnair knew that the day was coming when the Americans would say enough is enough. While Europe supported welfare programs America was prepared to back its military. The States spent twice as much of their gross national product as Europe on defence. It was time European governments woke up to their responsibilities and shouldered their fair share of the burden.

Macnair picked up the telephone to Downing Street. He needed to brief the Prime Minister.

The C130 was at 25,000ft and circling. The waiting was almost over. Hunter stood in the cockpit behind the pilot's seat and looked at the picture on the screen. A down-link with PACER SKY showed the liner clearly. Cloud was beginning to build up and the picture fluctuated between video and infra-red. Four guards were still clearly discernible on the upper deck, one either side on the bridge wing, and one either side on the lower prom-enade deck about half way between the bow and the stern. They appeared to be lounging on the rails, looking out to sea, their guns slung over their shoulders.

'They look relaxed enough,' said the pilot.

'Let's hope they stay that way,' replied Hunter. 'What's the weather doing?'

'There are gusts pushing thirty to thirty-five knots. Cloud base is ten thousand feet, thin and scattered but building.'

'Time to go?'

'Whenever you're ready.'

'Okay. Let's do it. The longer we wait the worse the weather may get. I'd prefer to go in about two hours when their alert threshold is even lower but now is good enough.'

'A green in ten?'

'Fine. And thanks.'

'Good luck, buddy. We're rooting for you.'

Hunter nodded and went back into the cavernous hold. The team were at the farthest end and already getting into line. The jump lights changed from red to amber. With a last word to each of the men Hunter went all the way aft and stood next to Matt Dunston. A quick last check and they were ready. The rear doors stood open and the wind whistled around the cabin, making Hunter shiver. He adjusted his night-vision goggles, pulled on thin cotton gloves, ran a hand over the equipment he was carrying and waited. His mouth was dry in anticipation, more from excite-ment than fear. His tiredness sloughed off him like a shed skin as his adrenaline began to pump. He thought fleetingly of Ruth, saw the amber glow in the corner of his eye turn to green, felt the thump on his shoulder and he was walking off the ramp, throwing himself to his right, to port, while Dunston went left. Accelerating at 32ft/sec/sec he settled at a fall rate of 110mph, passing through 1,000ft every six seconds.

The wind whistled past his head and as he fell he looked at the readout on the electronic gauge he carried. The feet were unwinding fast and he looked up and back to see Dunston about a second behind him. They were both in the classic stabilised position for free fall – bellies down, arms and legs outstretched, legs slightly bent at the knees. From the height they had launched at they could see the dots of lights belonging to ships outside the exclusion zone around the *Silver Beech* but these were quickly vanishing under the horizon as their view of the world shrank rapidly.

The liner was steaming without lights but could be seen easily. The night-vision goggles gave a faint bluish tinge that was no more distracting than wearing sun glasses at noon. Down they arrowed towards the target which grew larger by the second. The faint buzz on his wrist told him he was at the correct height and the wing on his back deployed automatically. It opened with a snap, bit into the air and Hunter's feet dropped below him as he suddenly stood upright. He was at eight thousand feet and coasting gently downwards. Now he could feel the wind buffeting his body, causing the wing to rise and fall while he manoeuvred around the liner still over six thousand feet below.

Looking up he saw the black wings of the team, like huge bats, scattered across the sky. The wing they were using could be inflated using helium. The gas was contained in small high pressure bottles sewn into the lining, and controlled by two buttons on the small panel in front of each man, one to inflate, the other to dump as required. As the liner moved through the water a satellite picture of the ship was changed into latitude and longitude and relayed to each jumper. The wing automatically corrected its heading, taking into account wind speed and direction. It was only when they were within a hundred yards or so of the target that each man would take responsibility for his height, speed and the distance to travel.

Hunter eased the Calico gun on his chest and touched the safety. He would be landing any minute and he needed to be ready. Each member of the team knew where they were to land. The objective was to avoid the lookouts at all costs or, if that became impossible, to kill them before they gave the alarm. It was a tall order.

The wind suddenly gusted from the west, veered about thirty degrees and swung back again. Hunter swerved off course, corrected his bearing and added height by increasing the helium in the wing. He repositioned himself to land on the aft top deck of the liner, astern of the swimming pool. The ship was a hundred feet below him and about the same ahead. He gained a bit more height, corrected his course and aimed straight at the deck. At about fifteen feet he saw it was clear and turned to land. A gust of wind came along the bows, lifted him and sent him over the stern rail. He had missed the ship altogether and would land in the sea any moment. Frantically he pumped in helium and felt the wing lift. The air around him, deflected by the ship's superstructure, had no pattern to it. It was coming from all directions and he couldn't control the wing. One second the lowest deck was under him and then it was past. The ship was sailing on without him and the helium lift was not enough to give him another opportunity.

The hijacker, urinating over the side, froze in mid-arc as Hunter passed him under the stern.

7

Hunter fired the hook-gun straight at the hijacker. It missed, blossomed open and snagged on the middle of the guard-rails. Hunter threw the quick release switch on the wing's harness and the wing sailed away, vanishing into the night. The hijacker was reaching to unsling his gun from his shoulder when Hunter hit the water. He was pressing the trigger on the hook-gun even as he did so. Holding his feet in front of him, he swung in towards the stern of the ship. The line tightened and the harness around his upper torso pulled him in, like a fish being landed. His head broke the surface and he came out of the sea, his feet slamming into the hull. Shaking his head, he looked up in time to see the hijacker point his gun at him.

Matt Dunston had watched the drama unfolding and had changed direction. He was still about twenty feet above the deck when he released his wing. Plummeting down he landed with a sickening crunch on the terrorist's back, breaking the hijacker's neck on the safety rail. Crouching over the stern he saw Hunter walking up the side of the ship as the hook-gun reeled him in.

'Are you all right?' Dunston called in a loud whisper.

Hunter raised his hand, his thumb and forefinger forming in a circle. Okay. He climbed, dripping wet, onto the deck and stood there for a few seconds getting his breath back.

He tested his communications system with Dunston who answered immediately. 'Now we're inside the jamming device comms appear to be working.'

Bending down, Hunter turned over the body of the hijacker

and had a look at the face. He could not be sure but he thought he recognised one of the men in the photographs Macnair had sent. Checking the corpse's pockets, he searched for ID but found none. Heaving the body over the stern he stood up.

'Let's get the team together.'

Dunston grabbed his arm and pointed. Hunter stood in horror as two wings hit the water astern of the ship. Then a third. It looked as if the whole team was coming down into the sea. He counted them. There was one missing. He tried the radio but got no reply. He tried again.

'Boss,' a voice whispered in his ear, 'I'm on the top deck. One of the guards is pretty close.' Hunter recognised the voice of Jan Badonovitch, the Russian Spetsnaz.

Looking out to sea, Hunter saw the dark heads of his team bobbing on the surface. It looked like Macnair's backdoor was going to be needed after all. Ripping off his NVGs, he removed the signal torch from his pocket, pointed it aft and began flashing. Dash, dot, dot dash, dash . . . Laboriously he continued sending – Team missed. In water. Please rescue – he sent a single letter, kilo – dash dot dash – over. He was rewarded with a single, faint spark of light. He hoped the USS *Swordfish* picked them up all right. What in hell was he going to achieve with just three of them on board?

'Jan, don't speak. Click if you get my message.'

Click.

'The team missed the ship.'

Click.

'Can you come aft without being spotted? Two clicks for yes.'

Click, click.

'We're on the lowest deck at the taffrail. We'll wait here.'

Click.

Hunter and Dunston had pulled off their hoods and ditched the wings' harnesses. The night was warm and Hunter's clothes were already beginning to dry as the two men took stock of their equipment.

Badonovitch appeared a few minutes later.

'What happened?'

'The wind came out of nowhere, boss. I was lucky. When I realised I was missing the side I released my harness. I only just made it. Josh was right behind me one second and gone the next. He was about twenty, maybe thirty feet higher and that made all the difference.'

'Only one ex-torch, then,' said Hunter, testing it on a piece of plastic explosive. 'It works, thank goodness. 'Two flash-bangs and our personal weapons.'

'Plus PE and dets,' Dunston whispered.

'Damnation,' Hunter spoke with feeling. 'Well, the operation continues. We need to get between decks and down to the engine room.'

The team had memorised maps of the liner. The door behind them marked 'Crew Only' led to a flight of stairs.

Hunter cracked open the door and carefully looked inside. It was empty. A short corridor had two doors leading off either side and ahead lay the stairwell. Stepping inside, Hunter used the butt of his gun to smash the nearest light bulb and fitting. He destroyed the other two he passed, plunging the area into darkness.

The second door on the right was locked and bore a warning sign, declaring 'Danger – Electricity' printed in bold with a red forked lightning motif.

'The secondary electric switchboard for this part of the ship,' said Hunter. 'If we take it out, a third of the ship will be darkened.'

'Dawn is still four hours away. The darkness would help us,' said Dunston.

'I agree but I don't want to waste any plastic on it.'

'Not necessary, boss,' said Badonovitch, walking back from the stairwell, hefting a fire-axe in his hands. He took aim and smashed the curved point into the door before heaving on the handle. The door flew open and would have crashed into the bulkhead if Dunston hadn't caught it.

'Good work,' said Hunter. 'Keep a lookout, both of you, while I take care of this.'

Inside was an electrical switchboard with a master handle on the right-hand side. Along the board were rows of fuses, each one representing a compartment or other part of the ship. The schematic on the wall showed clearly that the board controlled all five decks and a third of the ship. Hunter pulled every fuse as quickly as he could and passed each handful out to Dunston who threw them overboard.

Having gained the advantage of darkness, they went down the stairs, Hunter leading, Badonovitch covering their rear. As they passed the emergency lamps fitted in the corridor they smashed each one.

Two decks down they came to a passageway that ran the length of the ship and was broken up by doors every ten paces or so. They knew that the cabins on either side were crew's quarters. In sharp contrast to the passengers' parts of the ship, the corridor was bare and lined with tiles. They checked a couple of the cabins and found them empty. As expected, the crew was probably held with the remainder of the passengers in one of the large lounges or dining rooms.

A third of the way along, they found the door marked 'Engine Room'. There were bound to be watchkeepers on duty and they would be guarded by hijackers. The engine room was the logical place to put explosives, so they had no choice but to go inside. They knew from the plans that the area stretched about a third of the ship. There were two huge diesel engines. In the event of a breakdown, they could be mechanically crossed over, enabling one to drive both shafts. Four generators created sufficient electricity to power a small town, but only two were ever in use at any one time. The watchkeepers occupied a sound-proofed office on the starboard side, near the middle. From there they monitored the myriad dials which ensured the ship's safety and the passengers' comfort.

Hunter cracked open the door and was immediately hit by a wall of noise. He took out a small mirror on the end of a telescopic handle and pushed it through, meticulously searching the space. There was nobody in sight and he eased the door open wide enough to slip through. The others followed. They found themselves on a platform, high above the space.

From their vantage point they could see inside the control room where two armed men were sitting. Three other men in overalls were evidently engineers. One of the crew spoke and pointed through the window. A gunman nodded, and the engineer, adjusting ear-protectors, entered the engine room. Hunter, looking down from three decks above, watched the engineer making his rounds. Even if the man happened to look up, it was doubtful the team would be seen. They were standing on a metal grill, in shadow. As the engineer finished and re-entered the control room, they descended the stairs. In seconds they were hidden from sight by the bulk of one of the main engines.

While Dunston kept guard, Badonovitch and Hunter walked slowly along the deck, Hunter aiming the ex-torch. Its green light turned amber and then red. Simultaneously, Badonovitch pointed out the missing deck-plate screws. With his knife, the Spetsnaz prised the plate up an inch while Hunter dropped to his stomach to took a closer look. It looked clear of booby-traps and Badonovitch lifted the plate.

The explosive was sitting against the hull. No effort had been made to hide it. Hunter lay for a few moments examining it and decided it was a bog-standard set-up. The plastic had one detonator which was sticking out about an inch. He recognised the type. American made, it could be set off either by a radio signal or by pulling out a percussion pin. Depending on the delay on the fuse, the detonator would explode anything from ten seconds to ten minutes later. Removing the detonator, he handed it to Badonovitch before lifting the plastic explosive clear. As they moved further along the deck, the torch changed again to amber and then red. Again, the screws were missing. It took only a few seconds to see that the set-up was identical to the first and to remove the detonator and explosives. They had removed a fourth lot when Dunston signalled. They just managed to duck down behind a generator before one of the ship's engineers appeared.

He walked straight up to where Badonovitch was hiding then stepped back in shock when he saw the Russian crouching there. Before the man could react, Hunter clamped a hand over his mouth and Badonovitch rose, putting a finger to his lips. The engineer nodded and pointed at a door. The four men hustled through it and found themselves in a sound-proofed secondary control room. For the team, the relief on entering the comparative silence was considerable.

'Who are you?' The engineer asked, excitedly, with a strong Dublin accent.

Hunter replied, 'Special forces. We need you to answer some questions. What's your name?'

'Mick O'Flynn. Second engineer.'

'How many hijackers are there?'

The Irishman was in his late forties, small, balding, with the sallow complexion of people who don't see too much sun. He screwed up his face and considered the question. 'I'm not sure, but there must be fifteen or so.'

If the team were dismayed at the number they didn't show it.

'Where are they positioned?'

'Here, the bridge and in the main dining room. Oh, and the galley,' he added as an afterthought.

'Are the passengers and the crew being held in the dining room?'

'Except for us three in the engine room. Do you know they put bombs under the deck plates?'

Hunter nodded. 'We found them. Are they only in the engine room? Or did they put them anywhere else?'

'I think only in here. Though I can't be sure.'

'Fair enough. We'll double check.' Hunter looked at his watch. 'How much longer have you got before the guards come looking for you?'

O'Flynn shrugged. 'I dunno. I've been out before and nobody's come after me. I don't think they like the noise.'

'I don't blame them,' said Dunston with feeling.

'Are the lights on or off in the dining room?'

'All on. It lets the hijackers keep a closer eye on them.'

'That figures,' said Hunter. 'All right, here's what I want you to do.'

* * *

The SSN picked up the remainder of Hunter's team about fifteen minutes after they hit the water. The men had collected together and waited patiently, treading water, shucking their gear, lightening their load. The submarine surfaced only yards away and they had swum across to it, quickly climbing on board. They had all been in and out of submarines so often it took only seconds to embark. The sub sunk quickly beneath the water again.

Clements reported to the Captain in the conning tower. 'Permission to come aboard, sir?' He saluted, dripping water onto the deck.

'Permission granted. What happened?'

'A hell of a wind came out of nowhere, sir, and we missed the target. I think my boss and two of the others made it okay. At least, there was no sign of them in the sea.'

'What do you want to do?'

'I'd like to contact my CO, sir, and tell him what's happened.'

'I see no problem with that. I'll get CPO Jones to show you the way to the radio shack.' The Captain, Henry Cabot, newly promoted and tipped for the top, was on his first patrol. His thin face was pensive. Shrewd brown eyes stared at Clements. 'How many of you are there?'

'Seven, sir.'

'We'll get you kitted out in dry clothes. What rank are you?'

'A Captain with Delta, sir, now seconded to TIFAT.'

'Any other officers?'

'One, sir. The rest are NCOs.'

'Okay. I don't suppose this'll be for long. The Exec can sort out bunks.'

'Thanks, sir.' Clements was shown the radio room and was soon patched through to Macnair.

'There's nothing to be done about it,' said the General. 'Knowing Lt Cdr Hunter he'll carry on with the operation.'

'I concur, sir. Is there any way we can get back there? We could take an inflatable from the sub.'

'Too noisy. They'll hear the engine. You'll either be shot to pieces or run down by the ship. Either way, the hijackers will shoot more innocent people. Our only hope is they get the passengers off before the shooting starts.'

Chantelle Suchard finally woke up. The pain had gone away although she felt discomfort through her whole body. She tried to move but couldn't. Immediately a hand touched her shoulder.

'Take it easy. You need to rest.'

'Where am I?'

'In a hospital in Galveston. In a decompression chamber.'

Tears welled up. 'I'm crippled, aren't I?'

The doctor was young. He still had to learn the art of speaking to a badly injured or sick patient. He hesitated.

'Please tell me the truth. I've been diving for long enough to know what a bad case of the bends will do to you.'

'Then in that case, yes, I think you will be crippled. We can't be one hundred percent certain. The bends affect people in different ways. It's a question of time. Your nerve ends have been harmed by the pressure of the nitrogen bubbles on them. Damaged nerves cannot be repaired. But the amount of damage depends on how long the bubbles were trapped in your joints. They will dissolve slowly out of your blood now, as we decompress you. We'll have to wait and see.'

Thoughts were hurtling around her head. Gustav, Duval, Al-Adil, the submarine. The outcome of the mission, justifying the target in her mind. Blaming herself for her stupidity. The terrible realisation of Gustav's betrayal. Above all was the knowledge that her life had changed irrevocably, forever. And Gustav was to blame . . .

Chantelle nodded. 'I must speak to someone. I have important information.'

'Calm yourself. You must rest.'

'Please. You must send for the police or the FBI or somebody.'

'I can't just send for the Feds,' the doctor almost smiled. 'I need a reason.'

'Is the death of a quarter of a million Americans good enough reason?'

'What?' His jaw dropped and he stared at her for a second before he realised his mouth was open and he shut it. 'What on earth are you talking about?'

'You know about the ship in the Gulf? The one that's been hijacked?'

'Sure. It's on all the news.'

'I know who did it and what they plan to do. You must get me somebody to talk to.'

'How do I know you're telling the truth?'

Chantelle thought for a few moments before answering. 'What do you know about me? I mean, how did you come to have me here?'

'A naval helicopter brought you in. They'd picked you up in the Gulf.'

'Precisely. And there was no ship I could have come from because I escaped from a sinking submarine. A privately owned one. The hijacked liner is carrying a nerve gas that the terrorists plan to let loose in Houston. It's lethal. The lives of hundreds of thousands of people are at stake.'

'How do you know?'

'I . . .' she was about to admit her part in the scheme when she had second thoughts about what she should say. She needed to think of a story that at least gave her a chance of going free. If the Americans knew of her involvement she could end up in the gas chamber. 'I can't say. Please, try and get the FBI to come and speak to me.'

'I'll see what I can do. First I need to take some blood and then I need to get out of here. I've been in the chamber long enough and I don't want to have to go into stop time. How's your hearing?'

'I've a buzzing in my head.'

'That's because you've burst your ear-drums.'

The doctor drew a syringe of blood, went through to the exit chamber and was decompressed back to the surface. The blood was taken for analysis while he went to find a telephone. He asked directory enquiries for the number of the nearest FBI office. He was surprised to learn that there was one in Galveston.

It was the middle of the night and all he got was an answering machine. Non-plussed he replaced the receiver without leaving a message. He hesitated for a moment and decided he could not leave the matter there even for a few hours until the local office opened. The girl might be lying, but the risk was too great to take. This time when he called directory enquiries he asked for the FBI in Washington DC.

Dialling the number the phone was answered immediately. 'FBI.'

'I . . . I'd like to speak to somebody, please. I have some information I need to pass on.'

The FBI took thousands of calls a day, many from hoax or crank callers. The female operator kept her voice steady. 'What is your name please, sir.'

'Sydney Carmichael.'

'Occupation?'

'Doctor.'

'Where are you calling from?'

'A hospital in Galveston. A patient has given me information which I think is important.'

The telephonist had already been tracing the call and the screen in front of her confirmed that the caller was telephoning from Galveston. 'Wait one second, sir. I am transferring you to an agent.'

'Smith.'

The doctor wondered for a brief second if that was really the man's name.

'Mr Smith, my name is Sydney Carmichael. I am a doctor at a hospital in Galveston.'

'How can I help you, Dr Carmichael?'

'I am treating a patient, a woman, who was picked up out of the sea with decompression sickness. She says she has information concerning the hijacked ship in the Gulf. She says it's very important that it's passed on to the appropriate authorities.'

'What information?'

'She wouldn't tell me the details. But I think she's genuine She says that hundreds of thousands of lives are at risk.'

'Where is the woman?'

'In a decompression chamber. She has a bad case of the bends. She says she got them coming up from a submarine.'

'Right, sir. You can leave it with us, now. Just one thing. I'd appreciate it if you told no one about this. I'll have two agents with you ASAP. On behalf of the Bureau, sir, I thank you for calling.'

Replacing the receiver the doctor wondered if the man had been serious or whether he had been humouring him. What the hell! It was no longer his problem. He had patients to look after. Fifty minutes later Dr Carmichael was visited by two agents who flashed their badges at him, identified themselves and immediately asked to speak to the woman.

Outside the decompression chamber he explained, 'You can talk to her via a speaker or you can go inside.'

'Inside?' Gail Gabonne looked askance at the idea. A striking woman in her late thirties, she looked as though she had been awoken early from a deep sleep.

'Yes. I'll show you.' Carmichael led the way into the room that contained the huge chamber, capable of holding half a dozen patients in comfort, as well as staff to treat them. 'You go through this door. We pressurise you, the inside door's opened and through you go.'

'No thanks,' said Gabonne. 'What about you, Barney? You going?'

Barney Sullivan shook his head. 'We'll speak to her from here.' He was older than his companion, grey haired and turning to fat.

The doctor demonstrated the microphone and loudspeaker. 'Press this switch and you can talk to her. Let it go and you can hear her. She only needs to speak and a microphone in the chamber picks up her words. If you listen carefully you can hear her breathing.' On the monitor they could see Chantelle lying on a mattress, covered by a thin sheet.

'Let me just check the time and pressure.' The doctor looked at the gauges and nodded. 'In fifteen minutes I bring her up another ten feet.'

'How long will she be in there?' the woman asked.

'Thirteen more hours. It's a slow process bringing somebody up from a bad bend. But she'll have to get used to waiting. She'll probably be in a wheelchair for the rest of her life.'

'Okay. Thanks.'

The two agents waited until the doctor had left the room. The woman pressed the switch to the microphone. 'Miss, can you hear me?'

Chantelle nodded and said, 'Yes. Who are you?'

'FBI.'

'I need to see some ID.'

'You can see my badge if you come to the little window.' The woman held her badge to the small, round port-hole.

'I can't. I can't move,' said Chantelle. 'I'm . . . I'm probably crippled.' The statement, expressed for the first time, was made less harrowing by the hope that it would gain her some sympathy. She had spent the last hour going over the possibilities in her mind. How to save herself from prosecution and yet nail Gustav? How to wreak her revenge and yet protect herself? She needed guarantees.

'We're sorry to hear that, miss. Please believe me when I tell you that we're FBI.'

Chantelle sighed. 'I believe you. Look,' there was urgency in her voice, 'that liner, *Silver Beech*, the one that's been hijacked, I know who's behind it. But I want a guarantee. If I give you the information, I walk free . . .' Chantelle seemed oblivious to the irony of her request.

'Why should we want to prosecute you?' Gabonne was genuinely puzzled.

'Because I know what they're planning to do.'

'And what might that be?'

'You must give me your guarantee first.'

'I'm sorry, miss. I'm not authorised to make deals.'

'Then get me somebody who is.'

'Why don't you tell me what it's all about first and let us decide.'

'No guarantees, no information.'

Gabonne turned to Sullivan. 'What do you think?'

'She's not the normal nutcase. I'd better call Jerry. He can call the shots from here on.'

Jerry Stapizki was the Senior Agent at their office. He was not at his own apartment but, unknown to the two agents, staying with a new girlfriend. The battery in his mobile phone had discharged and he was uncontactable. Sullivan gave up trying to get hold of him.

'What now?' he asked his partner.

Mick O'Flynn refused the offer of a gun. Instead he hefted a large wrench in his hand and said, 'They're sloppy bastards. They think because they've got the guns they've nothing to be afraid of. We'll take care of them.' He slipped the wrench into the long pocket in the side of his trouser leg.

'Okay, remember, lights out at precisely three-forty.' Hunter double checked with the engineer.

'Don't worry. You can count on Mick O'Flynn.'

'You'd better go back to the control room. And listen, Mick, don't look too happy. Remember there's a lot can go wrong.'

O'Flynn wiped the smile off his face but said, 'Aye, but not with you guys here. If there's three of you I figure there's thirty. But you ain't saying. It's okay.' He held up his hand, 'I understand – need to know. I've read enough books in me time.' Slipping out the door he left the TIFAT operatives to exchange wry glances.

They continued searching and found four more explosive devices each side of the hull. The amount of PE the hijackers had used would have taken the bottom of the hull clean away. The ship would have sunk in minutes. Hunter figured there were at least five maybe six kilograms of plastic, which made for one hell of an explosion. They left the engine room as unobtrusively as they had arrived. In one of the crew's cabins, Hunter opened a porthole and threw the detonators and PE into the sea.

For the next half an hour they searched the ship, looking for more explosives. Without the ex-torch it would have been a fruitless task. By the time they had finished, they were as sure as they could be that all the explosives had been removed.

The crew's quarters were empty. Not a soul to be found anywhere. At least not alive. They discovered six bodies, two of which were young women.

In the main galley, just as Mick O'Flynn had told them, they saw two armed guards overseeing the chefs. Keeping hostages fed and watered was easier than having to control hostages who were hungry, thirsty and ready to rebel.

The main dining room was full. People sat in chairs, at tables or on the floor with their backs to the bulkheads. They looked exhausted, woebegone. Many of them were trying to sleep as the long night dragged on. Standing at the round observation window in the door at the back of the room Hunter counted the terrorists, relaying to Dunston and Badonovitch in a whisper where each one was situated.

'Head count?' Hunter asked.

'Nine,' replied Dunston.

'I agree, boss,' said the Spetsnaz.

'Okay. Let's go and take a look on the bridge.'

Climbing the outside ladders used by the crew, on the upperdeck they paused. There was nobody there. The bridge was perched right forward with windows all round, giving the officers on watch a three hundred and sixty degree panoramic view.

Keeping low, Hunter darted up to the port, aft window and used his mirror to check the inside. He was slow and methodical, changing places five times before he rejoined the other two. 'I counted six hijackers and only two crew. One looks like he could be the Captain.'

'Why so many gunmen?' Dunston asked.

'They appear to be having a discussion.'

'What do we do, boss?' Badonovitch asked. 'Take them out?'

Hunter nodded. 'Jan, you and Matt take the port door. I'll take the starboard. Hold it! Someone's coming!'

The team crept like ghosts further along the deck and hid behind a lifejacket container. A further three gunmen appeared and joined the others on the bridge. The odds were now distinctly against the team and Hunter indicated they should go below. They descended two decks before they spoke again.

'There are too many on the bridge,' said Hunter. 'We couldn't kill them all before they started shooting the ship's officers.' He looked at his watch. 'Damn! The lights go out in five minutes if Mick is on the ball. We'd better be ready. You know which doors to go to?'

The two TIFAT operatives nodded.

'We'll have to clear the upper decks of guards later. Okay, let's go.'

8

Mick O'Flynn looked at the clock on the wall above the console. The other two engineers, with no knowledge of the TIFAT presence, were checking dials and making notes in their log books. The two gunmen sat nonchalantly, their machine guns across their knees, barely taking any notice. There were three chairs in the room, two facing the main console and one opposite the switchboard. From the switchboard the engineers controlled power throughout the ship.

O'Flynn turned to one of the gunmen. 'I need to check the ancillary pump.'

The Arab was about twenty, perhaps younger. He nodded his head and played with the butt of his gun, his hand never still as he nervously caressed the metal stock. Translating quickly for his fellow guard, an older, squatter man with a squint, he gestured towards the exit.

'All right. Go!'

O'Flynn nodded and opened the sound-proof door. Immediately, the noise in the control room was ear damaging. Leaving the door ajar, he stepped over to a tool box and lifted out the first and second layer of tools. The guards were now less than six feet away. He rummaged in the bottom. The two guards watched him for a second and then turned away.

Suddenly O'Flynn was very nervous. In the next minute he could be dead. Mustering his courage he slipped the heavy wrench from his pocket and took the two paces needed to reach the English-speaking hijacker. He raised the wrench and slammed it down on the gunman's head with brutal force. The Arab's skull caved in and he died instantly. The noise from the engine room had muffled the sound. The second hijacker wouldn't have known what had happened if he hadn't happened to look across at his friend now sliding to the deck, blood soaking his kaffiyeh and white shirt. The gunman sat in shock for a full second, not believing what he was seeing. Before O'Flynn could attack he sprang to his feet and started to bring his gun round on the engineer.

The other two engineers reacted quickly. The chief engineer, a bear of a man, threw himself on the other gunman, wrapping his arms around him. He didn't know or care what O'Flynn was up to but this was better than waiting for some stinking Arab to shoot him.

O'Flynn's first swipe with the wrench missed the second gunman's head but hit his shoulder, breaking it. The hijacker screamed in pain. O'Flynn changed his grip and his aim and this time hit the man on the temple. He went out like a light.

The third engineer closed the door. He was ashen-faced, shaking. 'What have you done? You fool, O'Flynn, they'll kill us for this.'

O'Flynn smiled. 'Special Forces are on board and are about to retake the ship.'

'What? What yer on about?' asked the chief engineer, his Glaswegian accent thickened by the rush of action.

'I'm telling you. I met them on me last lot of rounds. They want us to cut all power to the ship in,' he glanced at the clock, 'four minutes. That's when they're going to attack. There's a whole regiment of them. It'll all be over soon.'

The other two men smiled.

'Well done, Mick, you Irish git,' said the chief, clapping the smaller man on the back. 'I'll buy you as much whisky as you can drink when this is all over.'

'As long as it's Irish then I'll take you up on that kind offer. After we've switched off the lights we wait ten minutes and then put the engines out of action. They're going to launch the lifeboats and get the passengers and crew off.'

'Why would they need to do that if there's a bleeding regiment of them? They'll retake the ship and kill the swine.'

O'Flynn shrugged. 'I dunno. The man also said that we should be ready in case there's any trouble.'

'What sort of trouble?' the third engineer asked.

'How the hell should I know? He said trust nothing and nobody until we hear from him.'

The chief engineer picked up one of the machine guns from the deck. The gun was ready to fire with the safety off. He flicked it back on. Having been a marine during the Falklands war he knew, as he put it, one end of a frigging gun from the other. 'Okay. Cover the door. If anybody puts so much as his head through it we shoot it off.

The Senior Agent in Charge of the Galveston office was driving home a happy man and looking forward to a hearty breakfast of waffles, bacon and eggs, over-easy. He was salivating at the prospect. Jerry Stapizki, now in his mid-thirties, had trained as a lawyer before joining the FBI. Behind the wise-cracking and flippant manner was a clever and ambitious brain. He somehow managed to be popular with both his subordinates and his bosses, a feat almost unique in the history of the FBI. He was a serial womaniser, never staying long enough to have a meaningful or deep relationship. It suited his temperament and his ambitions. He was ready to move to any FBI office in the country if it furthered his career. Six feet tall, darkly handsome, he worked out regularly, drank only moderately, and had never smoked. If the FBI were to print a thumb-nail sketch of the ideal agent then Jerry Stapizki would be the role-model.

The first thing he saw when he entered his apartment was the flashing message light on his answering machine. He listened and phoned the hospital. Barney Sullivan brought him up to date with events.

All thoughts of breakfast were gone. 'I'll be there in thirty.' Replacing the receiver he hurried into his bedroom, shedding yesterday's clothes. Showered, shaved and dressed in a dark suit he was on his way in fifteen minutes, heading downtown. At that time in the morning traffic was light and he had no need to use his siren or lights. He stopped in the emergency parking bay, put the FBI Agent on-call sign in the window and hurried from his car.

Marching into the room containing the decompression chamber he introduced himself to the doctor. 'How long before she gets to the surface?'

'Seven hours and some minutes.'

'That's too long. I need to go in and talk to her.'

'You been in one before?'

'Sure. My hobby is scuba. I've never had an accident but we use a small chamber for training.'

'Good. If you take off your shoes and jacket, make sure you don't have any pens or anything with you. Oh, and I'd leave the gun if I were you.'

Stapizki nodded. 'You think she's on the level?' he asked his agents while he removed his shoulder holster and handed it to Barney Sullivan.

The agent shrugged. 'It's hard to be sure but if she isn't I don't see what she's got to gain from all this. I think,' he said slowly, 'she is. But how can you give her a guarantee that she won't be arrested? If she's mixed up in something serious?'

Stapizki shrugged. 'I can't. But like everyone else she's entitled to a fair trial.' He climbed into the outer chamber, the door was closed and the pressure began to increase. He took hold of his nose from time to time and blew down his nostrils, clearing the slight pressure in his ear drums and the twinge in his sinuses caused by lack of practice. The pressure equalised and he entered the main chamber. His first thought was that Chantelle Suchard was one of the most beautiful women he had ever seen.

She was watching him warily.

'My name is Special Agent Jerry Stapizki. FBI. Here's my ID.' He showed his badge and she looked at it carefully.

Handing it back to him she said, 'Thank you.'

'I gather you have some information to tell us.'

She looked at the agent for a few moments. 'I will tell you only if I am given immunity against prosecution.'

'That will be very hard to do.'

'Then it's no deal.'

Stapizki nodded as though that was perfectly reasonable. Then he said, 'I understand that whatever you know has something to do with the hijacked liner.'

'That's true.'

'Why don't you tell me what you know and let me judge the value of what you say. I'll then do my best for you in court. If it ever comes to that. It may not, of course.'

'Who makes that decision?'

'That's above my pay-grade. I just file the report.'

'But your recommendations will count for something?'

'I guess. Look, if you're in some sort of trouble then I may be able to help. I promise I will, if I can.' Stapizki had known many attractive women in his time and he could see past Chantelle's beauty to the manipulative creature behind.

She bit her lower lip. This was harder than she'd thought. Her confidence in Gustav had been so great, she had given no thought to the consequences should she be called to account for her actions. She had simply expected to get away with it. Her thoughts on how to handle her situation since regaining consciousness had been confused, vague. She was also doped to the eyeballs with painkillers which didn't help her to think clearly. How much did the authorities already know? Had they made the connection between the submarine and the liner? She would have to downplay her roll, but Gustav . . . She wanted him caught and tried. Vilified by the world. Crucified for what he'd done to her!

Her thoughts contorted her face. Stapizki thought the grimaces were caused by pain. 'Are you all right, miss?'

Chantelle took a grip on her emotions and gave a brief nod, her face a hard mask. She made herself relax. Now as never before she needed a cool head if she was to get out of this. The thought of prison caused fear to shudder through her. How much should she tell him? If she admitted knowing about the nerve gas she would go to prison for the rest of her life.

Slowly she shook her head. 'I must have the guarantee.'

'Look, miss, let me explain something to you. If the liner is going to be used in some way to cause the deaths of more innocent people then you're what is known as an accessory before the fact. You'll be charged as if you were responsible and believe me, if the crime is big enough you'll either go to prison for a very long time or you'll get the death penalty. We still have it in this state and we use it with monotonous regularity.'

Chantelle closed her eyes to hide the horror there. Dr Carmichael's voice came over the loudspeaker, informing them that he was reducing the pressure. For a few seconds the chamber was silent, apart from the hiss of escaping air. It gave Chantelle time to think.

'The men who took over the liner initially were joined by eight others. I was forced to take them out to the liner in a small submarine.'

'Forced? By whom?'

She shrugged. 'I didn't ask their names.'

'What nationality were they?'

'The men I took out to the liner were all Arabs.'

'How do you know?'

'They prayed on their knees four or five times a day.'

'Fair enough. And the men who you say forced you to take the sub?'

'I'm not sure.' Wanting to divert Stapizki away from that line of questioning, Chantelle added, 'I overheard them talking. They plan to hit Houston on September the eleventh – with an anniversary present.'

Stapizki looked at her steadily. 'What sort of present?'

Chantelle bit her lower lip, her mask slipping. 'I'm . . . I'm not sure.'

'What do you mean you aren't sure?' Exasperation made his voice hard.

'Look, I think they have some sort of nerve agent or gas. They have a ball which they treated very carefully. And,' she paused wondering what to say to convey the importance of her information while at the same time not letting them know *how* she really knew the facts. 'It was something the men said and the way they handled the ball. They talked of it killing hundreds of thousands of people.'

Shocked to the core, Stapizki kept his voice level. 'What nationality were these men?'

'I told you, they were Arabs.'

'That covers a lot of people. Were they Palestinians? Or Iraqis? Or Jordanians? What?'

'How the hell should I know? All Arabs are the same to me.'

'Ain't that the truth. Do you speak Arabic?'

Startled, Chantelle replied, 'No. Of course not.'

'Then how do you know what they said?'

Without thinking she replied, 'They spoke English.'

'I see.' Which made no sense to Stapizki. Whoever these men were they'd use their own language. So she was hiding something, only what was it? Whatever it was, he'd find out soon enough. Now he had to deal with the threat to Houston.

'Are you sure about the nerve gas?'

Now she had to be careful. 'As sure as I can be.'

Damn! 'Barney, you copy?'

'Yes, Jerry. I'll phone it in now.'

'Let's get back to the men who forced you to take the sub. Who were they?'

She shook her head.

'Does that mean you don't know or aren't willing to tell me?'

Chantelle licked her suddenly dry lips. She realised the more she said the bigger the hole she was digging for herself. 'I need to think.'

'Why don't you just tell me the facts? Everything?'

'I can't. I told you. I need to think.'

'About what?'

Again she shook her head, but then made a serious mistake. 'Not now. I want to use something to bargain with.'

'Why would you need to bargain if you were *coerced* into taking them to the ship?'

Realising her error, Chantelle replied, 'I don't trust you, that's all.'

'Miss, need I remind you that it was you who sent for us? As far as we know this could all be some elaborate hoax.'

'Why on earth would I do that?'

Stapizki shrugged. 'We don't know. But people do crazy things for crazy reasons.'

'I'm telling the truth.'

'Maybe. How did you come to be driving the sub?'

'I've said enough for now.'

'Where were you when you were apparently abducted?'

Chantelle said nothing. Normally intelligent and quick-witted, she knew she was getting into deep water. One lie would lead to another. *Was* leading to another. She shook her head.

'Does that mean you won't say or you can't?'

'It means I'm . . . I'm having difficulty keeping the facts straight in my head. I was unconscious for hours. I'm trying to help. You're wasting time. Please, I need rest. I'm exhausted.'

'This will do for now. I strongly recommend that you get a lawyer. If necessary we can appoint one.' Stapizki hadn't bothered taking notes. He knew the conversation was being recorded. Entering the outer chamber, he closed the door and waited for the pressure to return to atmospheric. Climbing out he took his shoulder holster offered to him by Barney and as he strapped it on he asked, 'Well?'

'She's lying through her teeth.'

He looked at the woman agent. 'Gail?'

'I agree. A great deal of what she said doesn't add up.'

'That's what I thought. But I do think she was telling the truth about the nerve gas.'

Gail nodded. 'So do I. I think the lack of co-operation is all about saving her skin.'

It was breakfast time at the White House, and the President was enjoying his grapefruit and black coffee. He treasured these few quiet moments, and was irritated when his phone rang. He grabbed the offending article, placed it to his ear and said, 'This had better be important.'

'It is, sir,' said his Chief of Staff. 'I have information on the hijacked liner. From the FBI in Galveston.' He quickly briefed the President, the only man who could make the necessary decisions.

'Jesus Christ! Then they have to be stopped now.'

'I agree, sir. We are in the situation room waiting for you. We have a specialist on nerve gas coming in who'll be here any minute.'

The President sighed. More often than not nowadays he wondered what lunatic urge had made him run for the job. It was bigger than any one man. The decisions he was called on to make every day were enough to last any normal person a lifetime. And it never stopped. Slipping on his jacket, he went down from his private quarters.

In the situation room everybody stood up as he entered. He indicated for them to sit and said, 'Let's get started.'

It took twenty minutes for the President to realise that he had no choice. The liner had to be stopped. He didn't dare wait for the TIFAT team to do its job. And anyway, what could three men accomplish? The ship could not be allowed to get any closer to the continent of the United States of America.

'Send the signal to the *Swordfish*. And tell the Captain he is not to surface under any circumstances in case the nerve gas is released. If people make it to the lifeboats and get away all well and good. If not . . .' he shrugged sadly. 'All right, people, let's get to it.'

The three of them were in position. Dunston said a short prayer for the men who were about to die and adjusted his night-vision goggles. On cue the lights throughout the ship went out. Automatically the emergency lamps fixed to the bulkheads came on. They cast a faint glow around the edge of the room but left most of it in darkness.

Consternation swept through the prisoners but the majority of them had the sense to stay where they were. Hunter stepped through the door, right behind one of the hijackers. The man must have felt a draught or perhaps sensed Hunter's presence because he began to turn. Hunter shot him with his silenced

119

Calico, twice. Once in the chest and the second time in the head. For no reason, consternation was turning to panic and one or two passengers suddenly stood up. Hunter shot another hijacker who was standing about thirty feet away. Another double tap ensured the gunman would never get up again.

Somebody screamed from further inside the room and now people began to move.

'Stay still,' Hunter yelled. 'Don't move or you could get hurt.'

Someone began to yell and curse. Hunter's third target had been cradling a machine gun across his chest and now he raised it as if to open fire. The man was backing towards the door behind him when Hunter took a snap shot. The bullet hit him in the shoulder and he fell backwards, his gun flying from his hand. He screamed something in a language that Hunter could not understand. A machine gun started firing, the noise devastating in the confined space. There were more screams as panic gripped the passengers and crew and they started getting to their feet. The gun suddenly stopped firing.

'Stay where you are!' Hunter yelled again. 'We've come to rescue you!'

Those people who were on their feet threw themselves back onto the deck, while some were pulled down by those who hadn't moved. Hunter dodged around inert bodies as he tried to reach the terrorist he had just shot. The man was frantically feeling around for his gun.

Hunter heard Dunston say through his earpiece, 'He's out, Jan, through the door behind you.'

'I'm after him,' replied the Spetsnaz.

Hunter saw the downed gunman touch the barrel of his machine-gun but was too far away for a clear shot at him. Innocent lives were in danger. He had wanted to keep things quiet for a lot longer but that was now impossible. He grabbed a grenade, pulled the pin and threw it at the terrorist.

'Flash-bang coming now,' he announced over his radio, warning the other two.

The grenade had a two-second fuse and blew up in the gunman's face. The noise and light were horrendous and people began to scream again. Hunter had closed his eyes tightly and put his hands over his ears. He opened them to see the hijacker, who had scrambled to his knees, falling back, his hands to his face. At ten paces Hunter put another two bullets into the man. This time he would not be getting up.

'Matt, you okay?'

'Affirmative. My three are down. Jan got two but the third went through the furthest door. Jan's gone after him.'

'Jan? Do you copy?'

'Yes, boss. He got away. He'll warn the others.'

'If they haven't heard already. Come back here and cover the door. Matt, you cover the entrance behind you.' He stopped transmitting and raised his voice. 'Listen up, everybody. Quiet, I said!'

Gradually silence descended over the room.

'Now listen to me. We're special forces . . .' he got no further as a ragged but heartfelt cheer went up. 'Please listen. The effects of the grenade will wear off soon. So sit quietly. We have to get out of here. There are still twelve or more hijackers to deal with.'

'Surely you can take care of them?' A man's voice queried.

'There are only three of us. Open the curtains. Dawn isn't far away. The lights will stay off but you should be able to see enough. Is there anybody here who's used a gun before?'

A dozen hands went up. Most of the male passengers were well into their sixties or seventies, although one or two appeared younger.

Kneeling next to one man he asked, 'Where did you learn to shoot, sir?'

'Vietnam. Colonel in a light infantry regiment. Kenyon's the name.' He held out his hand and Hunter shook it.

'Hunter. You out rank me, sir, but I'd appreciate it if you did what I told you.'

The old man smiled. 'Heck, son, that was a long time ago. You just tell me what you want me to do.'

Hunter had picked up the hijacker's machine gun and handed it to the ex-Colonel. Placing it into Kenyon's hands he said, 'This is the safety. Push it forward to off, back and it's safe. Take that door over there and keep a sharp lookout. Anybody comes, shoot first and ask questions afterwards. Okay?'

'No problem.' The Colonel turned to the woman on the floor beside him. 'Mary-Beth, you stay here.'

Matt Dunston and Jan Badonovitch were busy doing the same, distributing the terrorists' weapons. Three crew members had fought in the Gulf War and they quickly took up positions around the room. When they had the entrances covered Hunter identified the ship's officers.

'I'm the First Officer,' said a tall, blonde woman. She was strikingly good-looking with an air of authority about her.

'The ship will be slowing down in a few minutes and I want you to start getting the passengers off the ship. I've no idea how much fire power the hijackers have but it could easily be enough to turn the tables on us.'

'They have guards on the upper deck.'

'We know. We're going to take care of them right now. Jan, let's go. Matt, you stay here.' Hunter could see that the dawn was a sliver in the sky and the darkness of the room was already fading. Shadows were becoming more substantial. 'As soon as we send for you, come up in the order your lifeboat is called.' He looked at the First Officer. 'I take it they all know where to go?'

'Of course.'

'Good. I'll leave it to you to organise them. In the meantime, please wait for Matt over there to give you the nod. I'll radio him when it's time to move.'

'What happens when we're in the boats?' The First Officer demanded. 'We'll be very vulnerable. The ship could plough over us or they could use us for target practice.'

Hunter nodded. 'Don't worry. The engines will be stopped permanently. Let's go, Jan.'

The two men hurried across the room to the door leading aft and carefully opened it. The hail of bullets which smashed around the door sent them both diving for cover.

Moments earlier, Abu Al-Adil had been standing on the bridge and looking out at the faint hint of dawn with a great deal of satisfaction. So far everything had gone according to plan. In a few days the world would see that the Great Satan was as vulnerable as any other country. The infidels would pay for their crimes against Islam and for defiling the Holy Land. The events of 9/11 would fade by comparison. If the Americans tried to prevent the liner from entering port he would shoot the women and children. They didn't have the stomach to watch their people dying. Not, he thought, as we have had to do.

Unexpectedly all power to the equipment on the bridge went out. The radar stopped, the background hiss of the radio faded away, and the automatic pilot ceased functioning. The master of the ship instinctively grabbed the telephone and rang the engine room. There was no answer. He tried again. Still nothing, though he could hear it ringing.

'What is it? What's happened?' Al-Adil's voice was shrill. He fingered the machine gun slung across his chest, flicking the safety on and off.

'There's no answer from the engine room.' The ship's master, Johann Ericksen, looked at the terrorist with loathing. 'If my crew have been harmed . . .' He got no further. Al-Adil struck him across the mouth with the barrel of his gun, breaking his two front teeth.

'Shut up, you fool, or I'll kill you.' He turned to his men and said in Arabic, 'Saif, go to the engine room and see what has happened. Sulaiman, you go with him.'

The two men nodded and rushed away.

The ship's master lay on the deck, spitting blood from his injured mouth. Right then he would have given his soul to get his hands on a gun.

The ship began to yaw to port as the automatic steering gear disengaged. Without it the liner would continue in circles until her fuel was expended. Because of its battery back-up, the compass in the binnacle still pointed to true north. In the quiet of the bridge only the master heard it ticking as the ship's heading changed, each tick representing one degree. Honed by years of experience at sea he also felt the slight change as the ship slowed down even further. Whatever was going on, he hoped it was good news.

Al-Adil gestured with his gun. 'You! Get up!'

Laboriously, Ericksen climbed to his feet. He was a big man of fifty-eight and overweight from too much time on luxury liners where he was expected to mingle with and entertain the passengers.

Abu Al-Adil's skin was crawling. Something was happening and he had no control over it. The drugs he and his men had taken to keep themselves awake were making him edgy. As he prepared to deal Ericksen another blow, there was the faint sound of an explosion. Al-Adil rushed out onto the bridge wing to see what was happening. He heard the unmistakable sound of gunfire.

Who was attacking? None of the passengers or crew had guns. How had they risen up against his men? 'Mohammed, Ayman, go and see what is going on. If there is any trouble shoot some of the hostages. Go. Go!' He screamed the word a second time. 'Akmir,' he turned to his brother, 'stay here and guard these two.'

Al-Adil's younger brother nodded with relief. He was ready to die for the cause but not yet. Akmir envied his brother's courage, his willingness to sacrifice his life for Allah. Akmir hoped he would be able to equal him when the time came.

He looked nervously at the round plastic sphere sitting at the back of the bridge. He knew it contained the deadly nerve agent and it terrified him. Death from a bullet was one thing, death from the contents of the sphere was another.

By now Al-Adil noticed the ship's swinging compass. 'Captain! Get this ship back on course, immediately!'

Ericksen disengaged the autopilot and moved the joystick. The liner slowly turned back to starboard.

One of the hijackers burst onto the bridge, calling Al-Adil's name. There was a furious exchange of words. Al-Adil shrieked an order and the man scurried out again.

Composing himself with difficulty, he said, 'It appears that armed attackers have shot my men and are hiding in the diningroom with the passengers. No matter. We will kill them and then kill more passengers as a warning to any others.'

'You filthy swine,' began the master but stopped when AlAdil pushed the barrel of his gun into the side of his face.

'Silence! Or I will kill you.'

'You need me to take the ship into harbour, you fool.'

'Your First Officer will do just as well.'

It was true but Ericksen wasn't going to let Al-Adil know that. Instead he played on his prejudices. 'You have met her. A woman! What does a woman know? We give them the positions and the titles to keep them quiet. She would make a mess of it.'

Al-Adil saw the sense in what Ericksen said and nodded. Flicking the safety switch on his gun he nonchalantly pointed the weapon at the back of the junior officer who had been keeping the watch and pulled the trigger. Bullets stitched up the young man's back and his white shirt was instantly saturated with blood. 'A warning, Captain, keep this ship on course. I will return directly. Watch him carefully, Akmir.' Al-Adil disappeared through the bridge doors.

Sickened to his stomach, Ericksen bent down, lifted the body by the shoulders and dragged it behind a curtain, into the chart room. He lay the dead man on the deck and went back to the bridge. The ship was again paying off to port and he corrected the movement. Anger and hatred seethed through him. There would be a moment, he promised himself, when he'd get his hands on the bastard.

Hiding on top of the control room, only a metre or so lower than the platform by the door, O'Flynn nudged the Chief Engineer who nodded. He had seen it too. The lights in the engine room, like the rest of the ship, were reduced to the emergency lamps. The one by the door cast a sufficient glow to show the movement of a silver handle and the door opening.

After a few seconds an armed hijacker appeared at the door. The wall of sound that hit him was mind-numbing, distracting to those who weren't used to it. The engineers waited nervously. The terrorist looked over his shoulder and appeared to be talking to somebody behind him. Then he came inside, stepping onto the grill. He looked down at the control room but could see no one in the darkness.

The man came on alone, his gun held out in front of him, his eyes darting back and forth. The two engineers waited no longer. Both started firing with their machine guns on fully automatic. The man died in a hail of bullets. Even over the racket of the engines the sound of the shooting could be heard. The second hijacker peered through the door. O'Flynn caught a glimpse of movement and altered his aim. His bullets ricocheted around the door, flattening on the steel, flying through the entrance. One bullet, bent out of shape, hit the terrorist in the arm and he flew backwards, his gun dropping from his nerveless grasp. The bullet had severed the muscle and smashed the bones, leaving the arm hanging by shreds of flesh and skin. The hijacker lurched away, blood pumping from the stump, his right hand gripping the wound. He was halfway along the passageway when he collapsed and died from loss of blood.

9

Macnair looked at the message from the Pentagon, originated by the FBI, and the blood drained from his face. Questions seethed through his mind. 'A nerve agent, Isobel! From where? How?' Isobel shook her head. She had been sitting but now, in her agitation, she got to her feet and paced the office. 'How on earth did they get hold of a nerve agent?'

'Saddam?' The General ventured. 'Before the war?'

'I'm not so sure. We looked at the region very, very carefully. There's been not so much as a hint. Remember when we thought he was up to something?'

Macnair nodded. The West had been sure that Saddam Hussein was close to perfecting a nerve agent of a particularly virulent type. Although there was no proof, their suspicion was a near certainty. The King of Jordan had received a phone call from the President of the United States. As a result, a very nervous King had telephoned the Iraqi President. He made it absolutely clear that unless all production stopped within twenty-four hours and the Americans saw proof that it had stopped then Saddam's palaces were going to be wiped off the face of the earth. Saddam had tried bluster but without any success. He had received further calls from Iran, Saudi Arabia, Syria and even the Lebanon. Each leader made it clear that this was no bluff. Saddam had backed down gradually. He had been a past master at tweaking the tail of the American tiger but finally he had gone too far. Now he was history.

'If not Saddam, then who?'

Isobel shook her head despondently. 'We need to look else-where. But I've no clue where to even start. What about Europe?'

Macnair shrugged. 'Possibly. Do what you can. Have you seen the latest PACER SKY pictures?'

'No. They'll be in shortly.'

'Let me know when they arrive. I want to see what Hunter's up to if we can.'

Aboard the *Swordfish*, the SSN Captain, Henry Cabot, looked at the signal in resigned horror. He had been dreading receiving it and here it was. He sent an authentication signal which was immediately answered. He knew that the paper in his hands spelt the end of his career, whatever decision he took. He was damned if he acted on it and damned if he didn't. The fact was, the signal was a direct order from his Commander-in-Chief, and one he couldn't ignore.

'Exec, come round to a heading of zero four five. Increase speed to ten knots.' He lifted the receiver off the bulkhead next to the plot table. 'Forward torpedoes? Load numbers one and two with forty-eights. Yes, dammit! Live!'

'What's happening, sir?' his Executive Officer asked.

'We've been ordered to sink the liner.'

'What! We can't do that, sir! What about the passengers?'

'I know, Exec. I don't need reminding.'

'Why two torpedoes, sir? Why not one? One would give them more time to get off. We could save a lot of lives if we surface and help. Hell, we should send for the Coastguard to be ready to give assistance.'

'Nope. We stay submerged. If the ship sinks fast, so be it. If it stays afloat we are to stay away until a special team arrives by helicopter. Survivors in the lifeboats are to be left alone. The Coastguard are to stay clear.'

'In God's name, why?'

Cabot looked at the younger man for a few moments and considered telling him to obey orders. Instead he said, 'My best guess, Number One, is that the ship has some sort of weapon of mass destruction on board. There can be no other reason for such an order. The signal emphasises that the ship must *not* reach America. It's something we've feared for a long time and it looks as though it's finally come. So we stop it. And we stop it here. Understood?'

'Aye, aye, sir. I'll have a resolution for firing whenever you need it.'

'Let's get to work. Up scope.'

Hunter and Badonovitch were outside. There was no more gunfire. Slowly they climbed a set of stairs, the Russian guarding their backs. Hunter cast a wary eye over the edge of the deck and paused. It all looked quiet. Taking another step took his head above the protection of the top stair and all hell broke loose. A machine gun opened fire and a swarm of bullets splattered into the metal stairwell, bouncing into the night, winging past Hunter's head as he dropped below the skyline. A swift glance had located two gunmen. One to the left behind a ventilation shaft, a second behind a life-jacket stowage container.

'You okay, boss?' Badonovitch whispered.

'Yes. There are two of them.' Hunter slipped a grenade from a pouch, pulled the pin, counted three and lobbed it into the air between the two gunmen. It erupted at knee height. Hunter dived over the edge of the deck and rolled behind the container. He could hear nothing. Cautiously he inched forward. Both men had disappeared. He signalled the Spetsnaz who quickly joined him. They continued to make their way along the deck towards the stern. In order for the passengers to escape safely they needed the lifeboat decks cleared of terrorists. Halfway along Hunter heard a noise, a faint scuffle, more imagined than real. He signalled and both men froze, listening. They heard it again. Cloth on cloth. Somebody easing cramped muscles. There was a faint clunk, metal hitting a solid object, from the other side of the lifeboat davit nearest to them.

Hunter slithered slowly on his belly across the deck. Stopping, he listened and sniffed. Now he could smell the man's scent, a mixture of tobacco smoke and sweat. Another couple of feet and he glimpsed a red and white checked kaffiyeh. Hunter slid out the knife he carried in his right legging and moved cautiously forward. The terrorist had his back to him, leaning on the railing, looking back and forth at the deck below. Some instinct must have warned him. As Hunter rose to his feet a pace behind, the Arab turned his head. Instead of clamping his hand over the man's mouth and shoving the knife under his ribs and up into the heart, Hunter found himself looking into the gunman's eyes. Swinging the knife from knee height, Hunter rammed the blade into the man's throat and up into his brain. The gunman collapsed onto the knife, the razor-sharp, serrated edge sawing into the jaw bone. Quickly he lowered the body to the deck. The snicker of a safety catch had Hunter throwing himself flat onto the deck with a bone jarring, breath taking thud.

Hunter turned onto his back in time to see Badonovitch shoot the second Arab through the head with two silenced shots.

'Thanks, Jan.'

'Anytime, boss. Always a pleasure,' the Russian grinned.

Quickly now, as time was running out, they scoured the remainder of the decks. They found nobody else. Hunter looked at his watch. It was time to abandon ship.

It had been O'Flynn's idea. He had wracked his brain trying to think of an easy way to put the engines beyond use. Their instinct was to fix machinery, not wreck it. It went against the grain but it had to be done. The Chief Engineer had reluctantly nodded. At the agreed time they stopped the water cooling pumps. Quickly the engines began to overheat and the room filled with the cloying stench of burning oil. In minutes the engines began to growl and grate as metal rubbed on metal. The temperature gauges shot up and warning bells began to clamour. O'Flynn grinned humourlessly; the noise would be repeated on the bridge. He hoped it was sowing panic amongst the Arabs.

After a few minutes O'Flynn hit the emergency stop buttons and the noise ceased. Blessed silence descended and the men removed their ear protectors. The ship began to lose speed and steerageway. Without forward movement, the stabilisers became useless and the liner settled beam onto the swell, rocking gently.

'They won't be started again in a hurry,' O'Flynn said sadly. 'Time to go, so it is.'

The three engineers made their way up the steps and into the corridor. They hurried aft and stopped at the door to the outside deck. Cautiously they opened the door. The dawn was as silent as a crypt. Stepping onto the upper deck O'Flynn went to the taffrail and looked down. The ship was dead in the water.

With the lightening of the day came rain squalls and an increase in the wind. The *Silver Beech* was now rocking a few degrees either way, with a steady list to port as she drifted broadside on to the wind.

The engineers stood quietly in the dark, terrified of a confrontation with the hijackers, while at the same time relishing the opportunity to shoot the bastards. A door opened slowly. They couldn't see who it was and so they waited. A figure appeared and took a hesitant step over the combing. In the strengthening light they saw it was the First Officer.

'Ma'am,' whispered O'Flynn, 'over here.'

The passengers were leaving the dining room, one behind the other in order of their lifeboat numbers, to avoid confusion once they reached the upperdecks and began to launch the boats. Doorways along the route were covered by armed passengers, with Dunston and Kenyon bringing up the rear. It was the excolonel who noticed the nervous young woman passenger reach into her handbag and take out what looked like a revolver. In the half-light he wasn't sure at first, but as she began to raise and point it at Matt Dunston he knew. Kenyon threw himself into Dunston and knocked him to the deck as the woman opened fire. The bullet sailed harmlessly between them, missing the TIFAT man by a hair's breadth. Before she could shoot again Kenyon fired a short burst of his machine-gun. The last round hit her in the middle of the forehead, creating a third eye.

People began to yell and scream. More shots were fired. Passengers and crew dropped in terror, some dead, others injured. Dunston scrambled to his feet and lurched along the corridor, stepping over and around the casualties. Although it was growing light the corridor was still gloomy. Dunston, wearing his goggles, could see as clearly as if it were broad daylight. Two men who had been amongst the passengers were firing revolvers indiscriminately at the cowering crowd. One of the armed crew shot the furthest gunman, killing him. The second man turned his gun on the crew member. Dunston yelled loudly and the man looked over his shoulder at him. Dunston shot him in the back, between the shoulder blades. The bullet severed the man's spinal cord and smashed him to the floor. An elderly male passenger leapt on top of him and ripped the gun from his hand.

The hijacker turned his head and said in English, 'God is great.'

'Mine is, not yours,' said the man. He put the end of the barrel to the hijacker's forehead and pulled the trigger. There was an empty click, the hijacker smiled at him and died. 'Rot in hell,' said the silver-haired grandfather with feeling.

The liner's medical staff administered first aid to the wounded and shook their heads over the bodies of three of the passengers. Distraught relatives were crying while others were cursing. 'We need to keep going,' said Dunston. 'The sooner you're all off the ship the better.'

The words were hardly out of his mouth when a machine gun started firing and bullets flew along the corridor, thudding into the bulkheads on both sides. Running back, he yelled, 'Close the door!'

The order was superfluous as Kenyon and another man were already doing just that. The bullets suddenly ceased but could be heard hitting the metal watertight door like angry bees. Miraculously no one had been hit. They hammered the door clips home as tight as they could.

'That should hold them for a few seconds,' said Dunston. 'Follow the others and get off the ship.'

'What'll you be doing?' asked Kenyon.

'Helping the other two. We'll keep the hijackers away while you escape.'

'No, son, I don't think so. William Kenyon never ran from a fight in his life and he isn't about to this time.'

'Sir, we don't have time to argue,' Dunston began . . . '

Then don't, you're just wasting your breath. Come on, we'll close each door as we move back.'

By now the passengers were milling around the stern of the liner, fearful of other terrorists appearing. A figure suddenly popped up on the higher deck and gestured. 'Time to go! Man the lifeboats!' Hunter gave an encouraging wave and then was lost to sight as he darted back towards the bow where the sound of gunfire suddenly rent the morning air.

'Sir, firing solution. Locked on.'

'Thank you, Ben,' Cabot said to his executive officer. 'Fire one.'

'Fire one, aye, aye, sir.'

The submarine gave the slightest of shudders as a mark forty-eight torpedo left the tube.

'Fire two.'

The second torpedo started on its way.

'Time to impact?' Cabot asked, checking the stop-watch hanging around his neck.

'Twenty-six seconds, sir,' his XO answered immediately.

'Agreed.'

'Something strange is going on, sir,' a sonar operator reported. 'The ship is slowing down. And I'm no longer hearing any engine noises.'

'Up scope.' Cabot twisted his gold-leafed, baseball cap backwards and bent to meet the periscope. He adroitly adjusted the lens and lined up on the *Silver Beech*. 'What the hell . . .'

'What is it, sir?' The Executive Officer asked, praying for a miracle, a reason to halt the firing.

'They're abandoning ship. The lifeboats are being lowered to the water.'

'Sir, we must abort! If a torpedo hits while they're alongside we'll blow up the lifeboats and kill hundreds.'

Cabot, white-faced, had already reached the same conclusion. Turning to the Fire Control Officer he ordered, 'Stop both weapons!'

'Stop both weapons, aye, aye, sir.'

The order was passed along the wire to the torpedoes and both engines ceased. The torpedoes slowly sank to the seabed, automatic switches cutting out the firing sequence, isolating the explosives and the firing mechanism. Cabot looked at his stopwatch. There had been less than two seconds to impact. He took another look through the scope.

'The boats are at sea level. Some are disengaging and moving away. They're staying close to the side and heading towards the ship's stern.' Adjusting the magnification he took a closer look, focusing on the figures he could see on the deck. 'There's a firefight going on. One of the men on the bridge wing is leaning out. He's shooting at the people in the boats.'

Cabot paused, considering his orders, before muttering, 'What the hell. Take her up XO, man the forward gun. It's time we lent a hand.'

Al-Adil stood in shock as the lifeboats began to be lowered down the side of the liner. He hesitated for a few seconds only. With a snarl of rage he reached into his pocket. Withdrawing a small electronic device, he extended its aerial and pressed the button at its centre. Nothing. He pressed again. Still nothing. No explosion ripping out the hull and sending the ship to a watery grave, along with its passengers and crew. If the transmitter wouldn't work then they must set off the charges individually. He screamed instructions at his brother, Akmir, who nodded nervously. With a second hijacker, he rushed down the stairs, heading for the engine room.

Akmir was terrified out of his wits. Whatever he had expected it hadn't been this. Glorious martyrdom was one thing, ignominious death was another. He was a coward, he realised, something he had not been prepared to admit even to himself, never mind his heroic brother, Abu.

On the pretext of tying his shoelace he paused and gestured the other man ahead. He rushed around the corner straight into the arms of Matt Dunston. As the two men collided, Dunston recovered quickest. He rammed the palm of his left hand into the

Arab's nose. The upward blow broke the cartilage at the base of the nose and sent it with devastating effect into the man's brain. The hijacker's scream was cut off abruptly as he staggered backwards, almost knocking into Akmir. The youngster didn't wait to see what was wrong. He turned on his heels and fled as fast as he could, back the way he had come.

Pausing at the stairs to the bridge he was suddenly terrified of facing his brother. What could he say? They had been heavily outnumbered? He shook his head in despair. Abu could always tell when he was lying. He didn't know how long he stood there, in an agony of indecision. Another noise startled him and he fled once more. Amidst the mannequins of a luxury boutique he found a small cupboard. He crawled inside, closing the door behind him. He sat in the darkness, ashamed yet so thankful to be alive.

Hunter was hard pressed. Heavily outnumbered, he and Badonovitch were trying to hold back heavily armed fanatics who didn't care if they lived or died. The hijackers' objective now thwarted, all that was left to them was to kill as many of the passengers and crew as possible before they escaped. Already two of the passengers who had stayed to help had died.

Al-Adil was cowering by the bridge wing screaming orders to his men, directing their efforts.

Matt Dunston radioed Hunter and Badonovitch. 'I'm working my way along the main corridor, back towards the dining room. I've got the engineers with me. We've taken out one hijacker but a second escaped. We'll attack from below. Try and distract them.'

'Roger that. But hurry, Matt, things are getting hot up here.' That was an understatement. The hijackers were becoming desperate as the lifeboats began to appear at the stern of the ship and move slowly away to safety.

Hunter, Badonovitch and four of the passengers were concealed behind protective barriers, waiting for an opportunity to return fire. The hijackers were moving slowly but steadily towards them. Soon there would be no hiding place.

'We need to move, boss,' said Badonovitch, crouching behind one of the lifeboats' davits.

'I know. Count of three. I'll use the last flash-bang and then we attack.' Hunter paused, 'One, two . . .'

'Boss! To starboard . . . Do you see what I see?'

Hunter glanced quickly over his right shoulder and a broad grin broke out. 'The US Navy to the rescue. Flash-bang now. Keep them distracted.' He snatched the pin from the grenade and lobbed it along the deck. It erupted with a loud bang and a blinding magnesium light that gave Hunter and the others the opportunity to return fire. Out of the corner of his eye Hunter saw men appear in the submarine's conning tower. A heavy machine gun was placed in its bracket before firing commenced.

Al-Adil continued to rant, screaming at his men to press the attack, his attention focused on the stern of the ship. He was watching the lifeboats slipping away. The sun was now just below the horizon and the sea was an early morning, undulating grey. The wind was gusting 15 to 20 knots and intermittent rain squalls were passing over every few minutes. He was on the port side of the bridge wing and couldn't see the submarine to starboard. When the sub's machine gun began shooting his men were caught in a cross-fire and they were forced to retreat towards the bridge. Al-Adil saw three of his men virtually cut in half. Another two were badly wounded as they broke cover and ran for the relative safety of the bridge.

The terrorist leader screamed at them to attack but it was to no avail. They were brave men but not totally foolhardy. They reached the bridge and Al-Adil rallied them with a mixture of haranguing and threats. There were still eight of them unscathed while two were wounded.

'Remember the words of the prophet. Peace be to you who persevered. Worship the Lord until the certain end comes to you. Which is better – this Hell or the Garden of Immortality?' After a few seconds he stopped and said softly, 'Let us die doing God's work.'

He looked at their unshaven, bleary-eyed faces. 'We have

nowhere left to go, my brothers. We charge down the port side, hidden from the submarine. Achmed, you and Abdullah lead. I will see you and your descendants in Al-Janna!'

The two men nodded, knowing that they would be the first to die.

The submarine, left without targets, had stopped firing. Unknown to the hijackers, Hunter and his men had closed to within a dozen metres of the bridge while Matt Dunston and the engineers were walking quietly up the stairs behind them.

Forgotten in the mêlée was Ericksen the master of the *Silver Beech*. He was hidden in the chartroom, holding a heavy, metal rollerruler in his right hand. Old-fashioned and little used, it helped to train officers in the basics of navigation. It weighed around half a kilo and felt good in his hand.

Al-Adil yelled and his men leapt to their feet. Achmed and Abdullah reached the deck outside the port bridge door before being shot to pieces by Hunter's party. Urged on by Al-Adil the rest began to advance. One of the passengers was hit, giving heart to the Arab gunmen. The terrorists knew they had to end it soon and so began to close on their enemy.

Matt Dunston and the engineers, reaching the bridge, opened fire into the backs of the hijackers. Al-Adil, having dived for cover, worked his way around the front of the bridge and came in behind Dunston. He shot dead the third engineer before Ericksen rose and smashed the ruler across Al-Adil's arm, breaking the ulna and radius with a loud snap. Al-Adil's scream could be clearly heard above the noise of the guns. Even so, he flung his gun at the master's head, catching it a glancing blow. Grabbing the container of nerve gas, he knelt on the deck with it between his legs, snatched a knife from a sheath at his side and plunged it into the plastic.

Outside the firing ceased, as the last of the hijackers was killed. The door was slammed in Dunston's face by Ericksen. His words left them numb.

'He's let the nerve gas loose. Don't come in.' The master darted across the bridge to the other door and slammed it shut. They were watertight doors and the seal was complete. The gas would slowly permeate the ship. But before it escaped to the outside he hoped the authorities would have time to deal with it.

He looked at Al-Adil with contempt. 'You lose.'

Even over the sound of the rising wind outside, both men could hear the faint hiss of the escaping gas. Ericksen was consumed by fear but he was damned if he was going to show it to Al-Adil. This had been his last cruise. With no family, and after a lifetime at sea, he had been dreading old age.

Al-Adil had been chanting prayers, holding his injured arm and rocking rhythmically back and forth. His eyes locked on Ericksen's, projecting all the hatred and intolerance of his warped beliefs. Suddenly he arched his back and let out a piercing scream of pain. His eyes watered and mucous erupted from his nose. The tears turned red as small blood vessels around his eyes began to burst.

Ericksen, a few metres away, looked on in horror. Al-Adil's death throes continued, the Arab thrashing around in unspeakable agony. Unable to watch his suffering any longer, Ericksen moved towards the terrorist. Grabbing the hijacker's gun he checked the safety, saw it was off and blew Al-Adil's head apart. He looked out the window as the sun burst over the horizon, showing a cloudy sky and a rainbow stretching across the heavens. Feeling nauseous and disorientated, he placed the barrel in his mouth and pressed the trigger.

Hunter had immediately understood the implications of the master's warning and had despatched the surviving men to close all outside, watertight doors. They ran around the ship, in a hurry to complete the job and get off, but aware of their duty. If the gas could be contained, even for a few hours, they would do it.

Once they were finished they took to a lifeboat, moving away from the ship's side, heading up wind, towards the submarine.

They were helped on board by the crew. Within minutes Hunter was reporting to Cabot.

'So the nerve gas has escaped?'

'Yes, sir. We watched it killing one of the hijackers. The ship's master shot himself, knowing he too was contaminated. He was a brave man. He saved our lives by closing the bridge doors.'

'Indeed. All right, Lt Cdr Hunter, I'll signal Washington for instructions.'

'May I suggest a flash message, sir? We also need coastguard help around here to keep other boats and ships away.'

'Thank you, mister, I do know my job. For your information the US Coastguard is on its way to pick up the survivors in the lifeboats.'

Chastened, Hunter merely nodded.

'Your men are up forward if you'd like to be reunited with them.'

Recognising a dismissal when he heard it, Hunter nodded and went forward to find the remainder of the team. He would signal Macnair later.

Less than ten minutes went by before the Captain made his announcement. 'Do you hear there, all hands. We have been ordered to sink the liner as quickly as possible. We will fire four mark forty-eights in two minutes.'

This time there was no stopping the torpedoes. The warheads slammed into the liner's hull at one and a half second intervals. The bottom blew out of the luxury ship and it sank within three minutes in water only eighty metres deep.

Akmir Al-Adil felt the huge explosions and wept. For long seconds fear held him in its grip and he was unable to move. He prayed fervently to Allah. Water seeping into his hiding place broke the paralysing grip of his cowardice and he pushed open the door. Crawling out, he ran for the stairs to the bridge. He stumbled as he reached the top and fell to the deck. His eyes took in the sight of his dead brother and the ship's Captain. Suddenly he arched his back with a gasp and collapsed in agony. For Akmir, there was no considerate non-believer to put him out of his agony.

Hunter and his team made their farewells and were flown by helicopter to Houston in Texas before flying back to the UK.

Thirty-six hours after the *Silver Beech* sank they found themselves back in Scotland at TIFAT Headquarters, Rosyth.

Expecting to see Ruth, Hunter asked where she was.

'She's being flown to Tel-Aviv,' said General Macnair.

Whatever he had been expecting it wasn't that and the surprise showed in his voice. 'Why there, sir?'

'It was at her own request, apparently. The Israelis do have about the finest trauma surgeons in the world. Her father arranged it.'

Hunter nodded gloomily. Ruth's father, David Golightly, was now opposition spokesman for defence. He was a critic of the current right wing in power and unpopular, particularly with orthodox Jews. But he still had a great deal of influence and would use every ounce of his power to get the best help for Ruth, his only daughter.

'I'll try and phone her later.'

'It's the middle of the night,' said Macnair kindly. 'Leave it until the morning, afternoon her time. It'll be the best time to speak to her.'

Hunter nodded agreement, though some instinct was setting off warning bells.

Macnair interrupted his thoughts. 'We saw some of what went on from the PACER SKY pictures. I've also read your report. I think congratulations are in order.'

Hunter shrugged. 'It was a pity those passengers had to die.'

'It couldn't have been helped, Nick,' said the General. 'As it was, deaths were at a minimum.'

'Have the hijackers been identified yet, sir?'

'We're still working on that. The boffins have declared the area safe and salvage will begin soon so we might learn more, but I doubt it, somehow. If we can't ID them from photographs we may have luck with the pathologist reports.'

'How can a pathologist help to identify the men?'

Macnair lifted his hands in a show of uncertainty. 'I asked the same question. I was quoted the maxim, we are what we eat. They'll be able to tell which part of the world they're from and even their countries of birth from things like the fillings in their teeth and the constitution of their innards.'

'Who do you think we're dealing with, sir? The Iraqis? Saudi fundamentalists? The Palestinians?'

'None of the above. Isobel is working on something right now and we've information from the FBI which may or may not be useful. Only time will tell. In the meantime I suggest you go home and get some sleep.'

Hunter nodded, weary to the bone. The emotional roller-coaster of the last few days, followed by twenty-four hours of travelling had taken their toll. His inclination was to bunk down in the cabin he had at the complex, but he also wanted to see his father and talk with him over a stiff drink.

It was a fine September evening, an unusually wet few months having given way to a warm and pleasant Indian summer. Collecting his grip, he slung it into the boot of his old MGB, then spent a few minutes folding down the roof and stowing it away before climbing in. On this occasion, the deep, throaty growl of the engine failed to give him any pleasure.

At the main gate he returned the salute of the sentry and pulled away, driving up past HMS *Caledonia* and through the narrow winding lanes. Fiddling with his radio, he found BBC Radio 4. A heavyweight interviewer was giving a British politician, whose name he didn't catch, the third degree. It was the usual waffle. Bombs were exploding across Europe, people were being killed and injured and hundreds of millions of euros of damage were being sustained. Yet all the politicians could manage was a plea for calm.

The wind ruffled his dark hair as he arrived at the main road and headed for Kincardine Bridge. Once over the River Forth he hit the motorway and put his foot down. Knowing Ruth was so far away in Israel left him feeling unsettled. He hadn't had the opportunity to talk to her since her injury. What was she thinking? Feeling?

In spite of his gloomy thoughts and overriding concern for Ruth, he couldn't help but enjoy the feel of the sun on his face as he turned off the motorway and headed towards Loch Lomond. He adjusted the sun shade and ambled along behind a string of vehicles, slowed down by a heavily laden tractor and trailer carrying round bales of hay.

It was nearly 18.30 when he arrived at Balfron. The pretty village nestled amongst farmland near the Campsie Hills, which formed a rugged backdrop to the surrounding area. Near the bottom of the hill he turned into the drive of the white house belonging to his parents. The rear garden stretched back an acre and was well tended. His parents were sitting outside enjoying the evening sun, glasses of wine on the table in front of them. Seeing him pull in they both smiled and rose, hiding their worry behind their effusive greetings.

Being home was somehow enough to reassure him that the forced separation from Ruth was no insurmountable obstacle. Hunter, seeing his parents, was struck not for the first time by how contented they seemed together. Sian and Tim Hunter had met when Tim was writing the story of the Griffiths family at the end of the sixties. He had been a reporter with *Time* magazine and commissioned to write a book about Sian's dynastic family who had influenced European politics for so long. The book, *A Million Tears*, had been short-listed for the Pulitzer, missing it by a very narrow margin. Now retired, Tim was still passionately interested in world politics and liked nothing more than a healthy debate with his son over a dram or two.

While his mother fussed over him, getting him a glass of wine, Hunter sat at the table, smiling wanly at his father.

'You look all in, son. It must have been a tough trip. How's Ruth?'

'I don't know. She's been taken to a hospital in Tel Aviv. I'll phone David in the morning and get the number to call her.'

'Be sure to give her our love,' said his mother. Sian Hunter was still an attractive woman, despite the grey streaks in her black curly hair.

Tim Hunter nodded, his blue eyes sombre in his lean face. 'So what have you been up to?' his mother asked.

Hunter hesitated for a second. He had known he would be asked and had been thinking about his reply. He kept few secrets from his parents, but he didn't want to worry his mother too much. His father was different. Over a late whisky he often filled in the bits he had omitted earlier.

He began his tale. It continued while they barbecued marinated pieces of chicken which they ate with baked potatoes and salad.

His story finished with the meal. His parents sat in shocked silence, absorbing what they had just learnt.

Typically, Tim Hunter's grasp of the situation was immediate and incisive. 'If they are using weapons of mass destruction,' began his father, 'you need to find out who's behind it and fast. The world-wide ramifications are enormous. Where did the gas come from? North Korea? China? The Middle East? Each one means a possible scenario with horrific consequences. America is not going to stand idly by and let a rogue state threaten them with WMDs.'

Hunter took a gulp of wine and refilled his glass. 'We know. But so far we haven't identified a target to go after.'

10

They were walking alongside the River Endrick. Hunter's dog, a golden Labrador named Winston, was eagerly rushing back and forth, torn between tantalising smells and his desire to spend time with his master. Hunter whistled and the dog stopped by his side to have his ears stroked.

'Something tells me,' said his father, 'that you're putting on a brave face about Ruth's injury. How bad is it really?'

'I didn't want to worry Mum too much, but it's pretty serious. Ruth's crippled but we don't know to what extent. Certainly she won't he able to operate at TIFAT any longer, unless it was in some sort of admin job and I can't see her settling for that.'

'Nor me. There is a bright side.'

'Tell me, please. I've been looking for one since it happened.'

'If you still love her . . .'

'Of course I do,' Hunter interrupted. 'The accident hasn't changed my feelings for her.'

'I'm glad to hear it as she's a wonderful girl. There's absolutely nothing stopping you marrying her. She can live here, while you continue working for Macnair. You could even go back to general service.'

'After TIFAT I doubt I could settle for general service. I think fighting terrorism is a worthwhile job while being another seaman officer in the Royal Navy won't amount to much.'

'You could leave.'

'And do what?'

'Whatever you put your mind to.'

'Nice try, Dad, but I think I'll stay with Macnair for a while longer.'

They walked a short distance in companionable silence, before Hunter senior continued. 'You know I've stayed friends with my old cronies at *Time* magazine? Apparently they've had a tip-off. They're working on a story that suggests the trouble erupting all over Europe like a plague of boils is being orchestrated by a group of right-wingers.'

Hunter nodded non-committally.

'You knew?'

'General Macnair is working on the same theory. How did *Time* find out?'

'You know journalists. Nothing's safe from their prying eyes and inquisitive tongues. Hell, nearly all intelligence gathering these days amounts to nothing more than a bunch of analysts reading foreign newspapers from across the world. By piecing together snippets of information our security services can usually discover what's going on. Good news magazines work in the same way.'

'I'll pass it on to the general.'

The two men began to retrace their steps, slowly, enjoying their time together. Back at the house they had a final night-cap before Hunter retired. He had a restless night, in spite of his tiredness. When he left the following morning he felt jaded and out of sorts.

There was no sign announcing TIFAT's Rosyth base as The International Force Against Terrorism. Instead, it was still known as HMS *Cochrane*, anonymity being the order of the day. Hunter, dressed in the naval uniform of a lieutenant commander, a rank he'd held for two years, was thinking about his conversation with his father. If he hoped to be promoted to commander, he would need to return to the navy proper, a prospect he didn't relish. He knew he had several options – some very tempting ones. His mother's family were rich beyond avarice, owning and operating many businesses world-wide. They would find him a senior manager's job, somewhere, one that suited his organising talents. After all, his training as an officer in the RN would stand him in good stead, regardless. But would it be enough? Only, he realised, if he had Ruth by his side.

In his office, he spent the first hour going through paperwork. File after file he annotated with his initials and dropped into an out-tray. He was bored with it long before he was finished but he persevered. Nowadays, a modern fighting force lived by its paperwork.

He made four attempts to phone David Golightly in Israel but without luck. Each time he left a message and his number. At 10.00 he went to the wardroom for stand-easy. Being a weekend there were few officers around. He was helping himself to coffee when Isobel and General Macnair arrived.

'Any news on Ruth?' Isobel immediately asked.

Hunter shook his head. 'But I've had an interesting conversation with my father.' He related the theory of the *Time* journalists. 'He gave me copies of e-mails he's received. It's all circumstantial so far.'

'We've acquired information in myriad ways. By combining data drawn from bank accounts, credit cards and other sources, we've pinpointed certain individuals who fit the profile. Now the FBI report on the submarine survivor confirms it. We think a man by the name of Charles Gustav is behind it,' said Macnair. 'Did you catch the news this morning? About the rallies in America protesting about their troops being in Europe.'

Hunter nodded.

The general went on, 'I can't say I blame the Americans. Stopping the liner was a close call. We might not be so lucky next time. Now the Cold War is well and truly a thing of the past there is no reason why Europe shouldn't police its own borders.'

'We've relied on the USA for too long, sir,' said Hunter.

Macnair sipped his coffee before replying. 'I think those times are passing fast. The storm being whipped up in the States right now could turn ugly and the Americans could pull out before we're ready.'

'But that'll make them more isolationist than ever,' Hunter argued. 'They already have enough trouble taking the international community along with them as it is.'

'Be that as it may, the majority of Americans believe we aren't pulling our weight in Europe and the rest of the world – and they're right. If Europe needs to take military action on a big scale, can it?'

'No. Not without the States.'

'Precisely. And if they left us to our own devices can we expect them to come to our aid?'

'It would be highly embarrassing even to ask.'

'Right again. So we have to keep them with us. The West must have a united front at all costs. Never mind the reality. The *perception* is all-important.' Macnair paused and then added, 'We need to confirm who's responsible for the attacks in Europe and the attempted attack on America and deal with him. In accordance with our mandate.'

'I thought the finger of blame was pointing squarely at Charles Gustav.'

'Unfortunately we've no definite proof. Isobel is working on the problem right now. The woman they pulled out of the sea, Chantelle Suchard, has given us some information to work with. But she's holding back.'

'Why would she be doing that?' Hunter asked.

'There's no doubt she's lying about her involvement. If she's to escape a long jail sentence she needs to cut a deal. I believe that's what they're discussing right now. In the meantime we carry on as usual.'

By lunchtime Hunter had caught up with his paperwork and had still failed to contact Israel. He was beginning to wonder if Ruth was deliberately trying to avoid speaking to him. *But why*? He decided to work out his frustration in hard physical exercise. In his cabin he changed into running gear and set off at a steady, mile-eating pace around the perimeter fence of the base. His speed would have placed him as a contender in the London marathon. He was about ten minutes into his run when a figure fell in alongside him, matching him stride for stride.

'Hullo, Matt,' Hunter grunted.

'Save your breath, Nick, you'll need it.'

147

Hunter grinned in spite of himself and imperceptibly increased his speed. Dunston matched him easily. They kept going, working up a sweat, stretching themselves. Hunter marvelled at the older man – at his stamina and toughness. Matt's friendship was a constant in his otherwise turbulent life. Not only was he one of the fittest men that Hunter knew, he was also one of the toughest. Although he was an ordained minister, and the base's Chaplain, Matt had started life as an officer with an infantry unit and then transferred to the Special Air Service. He had seen action all over the world – and had medals to show for it. He had taken Holy Orders in his thirties and rejoined the military after completing his studies. Evil, Dunston argued, could not be battled by turning the other cheek. Anyone who argued that Jesus was gentle, meek and mild had mis-read their bible.

After approximately twenty miles they came to a panting halt. They limbered up some more and then began a series of fighting katas, mixing different styles from different disciplines, looking for the advantage. Their movements were fast, each strike deadly, pulled at the last nano-second, avoiding damage. One or two blows were mis-timed and reached their targets, bruising flesh. After fifteen minutes they called a halt, exhausted.

'I needed that,' gasped Hunter, bent over, his hands on his knees, sucking in air.

Dunston, in a similar pose, looked up, smiled and said, 'Me too. There's nothing like it for clearing the cobwebs.'

The two men made their way back to the wardroom and their cabins to shower and change. What little activity there had been around the base had died away to nothing now the afternoon was so advanced. Those who were duty watch would be glued to a football game on TV or in their cabins with their heads down, catching up on their sleep.

Hunter chose to doze for a while and as dusk was falling snapped awake, thinking immediately of Ruth. He showered and dressed before going to his office and phoning David Golightly. This time there was an answer. 'David? It's Nick. How's Ruth?'

Was it his imagination or had there been a moment's hesitation?

'What can I tell you, Nick? They've got her resting. The knee appears to be knitting together but she's in a good deal of discomfort. She's on heavy sedation and has been ordered to remain still. Our doctors are amazed by what the surgical team who operated on her have managed. And as you know, we have some of the best surgeons in the world.'

'When can I speak to her?'

Again a pause. 'I don't know, Nick. It'll be at least a few days. Perhaps longer. The knee has to be kept absolutely still to give it time to heal sufficiently so that small movements won't matter. She is literally tied down and heavily sedated. Look, as soon as she is able, I'll get her to call you. Deal?'

'Thanks, David, I appreciate it.'

They exchanged a few more platitudes and hung up. Hunter had planned to return to his parent's home that evening but was tempted to make his excuses and stay in the mess. He was in no mood for small talk. The thought made him feel guilty as he had seen very little of them over the last few months. Reluctantly he decided to make the journey back to Balfron.

The following morning he returned to TIFAT and, for the first time in a long time, he went to Sunday Service.

It was conducted by Matt Dunston, and, as usual, was well attended. After the service, which included a prayer for Ruth's full and speedy recovery, the officers adjourned to the wardroom and the other ranks to the bar in their mess.

Hunter stood with a dry sherry in his hand making small talk with some of the others when General Macnair joined them. With him was a member of the European Parliament, Christine Woolford, the General's 'other half', as she was delicately referred to by the members of the wardroom. An attractive woman of medium height, Christine's best features were shrewd eyes and a wide smile.

On this occasion however she wasn't smiling. 'Nick, I'm so sorry about Ruth. I hope she recovers fully.'

'Thanks, Christine.' Hunter quickly changed the subject, feeling strangely ill-at-ease. 'How long are you staying with us?'

'A few days. Malcolm and I intend getting in a round or two of

149

golf before I have to return to the bear pit of Strasbourg. Do you play?'

Hunter shook his head. 'Afraid not. I've tried but somehow the game does nothing for me. I'd rather be on the rugby field.'

Christine chuckled. 'Dear Nick, you can't do that all your life. Golf you can play to a ripe old age.'

Hunter smiled back. 'In that case I'll take it up when I'm a ripe old age. You know the General is supposed to be a good player?'

Christine cast a quick glance at Macnair's back and made sure he couldn't overhear. 'I know,' she said in a quiet voice. 'He told me. Warned me, more like. What he doesn't know is that I'm off scratch. I played professionally when I was in my twenties. Before politics enticed me into its embrace. I think Malcolm is in for a wee surprise.'

Hunter chuckled. 'I love it. Where are you playing?'

'Banchory. A course called Inchmarlo. One of the directors used to be in the RAF. He's sent a standing invitation to all members of TIFAT to play there.'

The General joined them and asked if either wanted a refill. They both declined.

'I gather you're away for a few days, sir,' said Hunter.

'Until Wednesday.'

'Playing golf, I understand.'

'Yes, I'm looking forward to it. It's been a while. I used to have a single figure handicap but I expect it's more like fifteen or sixteen nowadays.' He frowned. 'I did ask, but you never told me. What's your handicap?' He was looking speculatively at Christine but Hunter answered for her.

'Christine was just telling me, sir, that's she's very rusty. It's been an age since she played. She was hoping you'd go easy with her.'

Macnair chuckled. 'Of course I will. Ah, Hiram, a word.' Macnair moved away to talk to his second-in-command.

Christine winked at Hunter.

The Sunday took its usual quiet course. This time Hunter did decide to stay at the base. In the bar before dinner he met a glum faced Lieutenant Napier, wearing his mess undress.

'You on duty?' Hunter asked him.

The Special Boats Service officer nodded. 'Worse luck. I had a hot date in Dunfermline, as well.'

'I wouldn't have thought it possible. Not in Dunfermline.'

'You'd be surprised,' said Napier, darkly.

'I'll take the weight, if you like,' Hunter offered.

'Are you sure?'

Hunter nodded. 'I'm staying on board anyway, so I may as well. You go while I get changed.'

Napier turned to the barman, 'Put Mr Hunter's bar bill on my tab, please, and I'll sign for it in the morning.'

'You'd better go before I change my mind.'

'Thanks, Nick. I owe you one.'

Hunter went back to his cabin and changed into his mess undress. He phoned the duty senior rating and the guardroom at the gate to let them know he was now the duty officer, then wandered back to the wardroom bar.

There were only half a dozen officers present. After dinner Hunter and Dunston whiled away the evening playing snooker. Dunston thrashed him soundly. The ten o'clock news bulletin depressed both men. It seemed unending. Atrocity after atrocity was being committed Europe-wide and each time the finger of blame was being pointed firmly at Muslim fundamentalists. Analysis by the TV pundits blamed immigrants and Islam. Inflammatory rhetoric was being used which only a short while earlier would have been considered racist and quickly stamped upon. Matters were becoming uglier by the hour.

Over a nightcap in the bar, Dunston said, 'The sad fact is, even moderate people who recognise the benefits of a multicultural society are becoming Islamaphobic. The growth of fascism in Europe is terrifying.'

Hunter nodded gloomily. 'It's so well orchestrated. We *have* to find out who's behind it. According to the latest intelligence signal there have been another fifty-eight incidents resulting in eighteen deaths, dozens injured and millions of euros of damage and all this weekend. There are marches planned next week in every European capital.'

'Pro or anti-Muslim?'

'Both,' was the chilling reply.

'They can't be allowed to go ahead,' said the Chaplain.

'They can't be stopped,' said Hunter. 'It's their right. And any government trying to stop one or the other would be in political trouble. If they ban *both* it could be the fuse to a powder keg.'

'With what result?'

'Virtually all-out war, I should think. Whites against blacks and coloureds.

'Is it al-Qaeda?' Dunston asked.

'They're certainly doing the damage. But are they behind it? Not according to Isobel and the General.'

'So you go with the Gustav theory?'

'I think I do. But how on earth did he get the Muslims to do his bidding?'

'Maybe they don't realise exactly what his agenda is. AlQaeda and the other fanatics don't see beyond being anti-West and pro-Islam. They don't discuss the implications of their actions. They're destroyers, not builders. Look at the ravages people such as the Taliban inflicted on Afghanistan. And Gustav, if he's the man we're after, will ensure he's kept himself at arms length from the atrocities.'

Gustav closed the folder of newspaper articles with satisfaction. Everything was working as planned. His country of birth, Sweden, was at last talking about stopping immigration. Repatriation was high on the agenda of all the mainstream political parties in Europe. Furthermore, a change in European law was at last being contemplated. Controversial in the extreme, but for Gustav long overdue – collective responsibility for a criminal act by a non-European. On the release of a convicted felon, the whole family was to be deported back to their country of ethnic origin. Algerian-Dutch? Back to North Africa. Pakistani-British? Back to Pakistan. Draconian in the extreme, there was furore in the European Parliament about the measure. He still had some persuading to do with a few of the MEPs but he was sanguine the law would pass. The dossiers he had been compiling for years were now proving invaluable. Blackmail, bribery and coercion were wonderful tools. Once the law reached the statute books the bloodshed in the streets would be as great as anything he could hope for. He would have a whites-only continent if it was the last thing he achieved. Enlargement of the European Union might have been on the agenda but the idea was fading fast. Story after story about the West being swamped with immigrants, particularly Muslims, was being spread. They were hitting the newspaper headlines and the television news broadcasts practically all day and every day. Public opinion was now firmly on Gustav's side as to where the ills of Europe lay – at the doors of illegal immigrants, asylum seekers and economic migrants. His hands clenched tightly, crumpling the papers he was holding. Unwashed, uneducated, *filth*!

There was a discreet knock on the door. 'Come in! Ah, Duval, any news?'

'Not yet, sir,' replied his secretary. 'The assassination,' he glanced at his watch, 'is scheduled for just over an hour's time.'

The raised eyebrow spoke volumes and Duval nodded. 'Relevant details have been taken care of, sir. Evidence of his affiliation will be found in his hotel room.'

'Excellent. It's a pity such a popular politician with strong right-wing views has to be sacrificed. But he will benefit the cause so much more by his martyrdom.'

Duval placed sheets of A4 paper on the desk by his employer's elbow. 'These reports relate to incidents that have taken place in the last hour. You may like the third item in particular.'

Gustav glanced down the paper and then read with evident enjoyment. A mosque on the south side of Glasgow had been torched. Burnt to the ground. Neither the fire brigade nor the police had arrived in time to be of any assistance. Initial reports suggested five, perhaps six, people killed, all Muslim, all elderly, all with children and grandchildren born in Scotland. Excellent.

General Macnair and Christine Woolford had arrived in Banchory the previous evening, too late even for a quick round of the nine hole course. Instead, after a leisurely breakfast, mid-morning found them in the clubhouse discussing the championship course with the club's professional. Local rules about out of bounds, water hazards and obstructions were discussed. Some of the idiosyncrasies of a few of the holes were mentioned and then it was time to start. The course wasn't busy and Macnair and Christine wandered out to the first tee.

Macnair breathed in deeply. 'Perfect. This has to be one of the most picturesque views in the country. An ideal spot for a golf club.'

'I couldn't agree with you more. Is that the first green?' Christine pointed into the distance.

The first hole was known as Queens Drive and was a par four. The distance for the men was 284 yards, for the women 251 yards.

They had tossed a coin to see who played first and Christine had won. Much to Macnair's surprise she placed her tee in the man's position.

'My dear,' he said, 'you tee off from down there.' He pointed.

Christine nodded and smiled. 'Indulge me. I just thought it would be better fun to play together.'

Macnair looked at her appraisingly and suddenly laughed. 'You never did tell me your handicap.'

Christine took her stance and addressed the ball. Her club swung in a perfect arc. The ball sailed straight down the fairway. She turned to him and smiled sweetly. 'It's scratch.'

'Somehow,' Macnair said, bending to place a wooden tee in the ground, 'I thought you were going to say that.'

Macnair's superior strength was, in the long run, no substitute for Christine's greater skill. By the time they had played the fourth hole, known as Loch Hope, Macnair was two down. They had halved the first and second. He had lost the third to a birdie and Christine took the fourth, sinking a thirty-foot putt. She had smiled sweetly when she'd done so. With two such committed and driven people the game had become one of noholds-barred, each playing to the utmost of their ability. Macnair's rustiness was fading fast, and he was regaining some of the ruthless skill he'd honed years earlier. Christine played with the concentrated passion which in the past had taken her so close to the highest echelons of the game. While they were starting at the ninth hole, known as Glencommon, Macnair's telephone rang.

'Blast!' The warbling note distracted him and he hooked the ball to the left, into the rough, close to the trees. He answered in a bad humour, eager to be rid of the intrusion. 'Macnair.'

'Sorry to disturb you, sir' said Hunter, 'but we have a situation developing and I needed to talk to you.'

'What is it?' he asked testily.

'A group of Muslims have taken Glasgow Cathedral and are threatening to blow it up.'

'That's a police affair. Nothing to do with us.'

'Normally, sir, I agree. But in view of recent events on the continent I thought you might want us involved.'

Macnair was deep in thought. There had been over two dozen similar situations and the outcome had been the same every time. Historic buildings had been destroyed and many of the police involved had been killed. Even negotiators who had approached to talk to the terrorists had been shot. Hostages had been used to prolong the incidents – in order, it seemed, to ensure maximum publicity. All the hostages had been killed. He remembered the incident in Rheims. A group of children sent out of a church were gunned down as they approached the police barrier. All the children and several bystanders had died. They had never been negotiable situations.

Christine caught his attention and pointed. Others were waiting to tee-off, their impatience becoming evident. Macnair grimaced and waved them through.

'Have we been asked for?'

'Not as such, sir.'

'Meaning?'

'We've been told by the Chief Constable of Strathclyde to keep away. Quote, "he doesn't need gung-ho types like us queering his pitch and causing needless death and destruction".'

'What's your analysis?'

'We've discussed this situation in detail. There's no doubt in our minds what the outcome will be. If we don't go in those hostages are as good as dead already.'

Macnair sighed. The devil of it was, Hunter was right. 'How soon can you move?'

'In ten, sir. We've been getting prepped. I have a team of six ready to go. The helo is cranked up and ready for take-off. But the CC was adamant when I spoke to him. He was in no mood to listen to me.'

'Have you a number for him?'

'Yes, sir. His mobile.' Hunter relayed the information which Macnair jotted down on the back of his score card.

'Get going. Leave this to me. You know what you have to do.'
'Yes, sir.'

Christine was looking at him quizzically and Macnair explained the situation as he dialled the Chief Constable's number.

'Blackwater.'

'Ah, Chief Constable, this is General Malcolm Macnair. I'm . . .'

'I know who you are.' The tone was abrupt and angry. 'I already told your people that this is a police matter and we don't want your help.'

'Be that as it may, you're getting it.' Macnair kept his own temper in check. 'I am giving you the courtesy of this phone call to allow you to change your mind.'

'Listen to me, General. This is a police action. We don't need your cowboys charging in and causing the deaths of innocent people. This takes time. We negotiate and do our damnedest to protect lives and property. In that order. And these people, whoever they are, deserve a fair trial. We don't need your lot judging and passing sentence with a bullet.'

'Now listen, Mr Blackwater, under normal circumstances I'd agree with you. But you know that there have been similar incidents all over Europe resulting in innocent deaths and destroyed buildings . . .'

Interrupting again, the Chief Constable said, 'I'm aware of that. We had a similar situation last year and negotiated a peaceful outcome. And I can do it again.'

'I remember the incident, Blackwater, and it was expertly handled. But this is entirely different. Then you were dealing with criminals. These are fanatics who *are ready to die*.'

'What utter nonsense. Not on my patch, Macnair. I can end this peacefully or by sending in my own ARU.'

Macnair knew that the Armed Response Unit was highly trained and effective in normal policing incidents. But he also knew that this wasn't normal. The man was a fool.

'Now I'm saying this only once, Macnair. Stay away and don't bother me. I have work to do.' *Click*.

Christine had heard Macnair's side of the conversation. 'I take it he doesn't want to play ball? What are you going to do?'

'Fire my big guns, call up a helicopter and finish the round while we wait to be picked up. Would you mind packing our cases and driving back to Rosyth? I'm going to Glasgow. Sorry our break is cut short.'

Christine smiled wryly. 'Duty is a concept I understand.'

11

Hunter, Dunston and four others were airborne. There were no other operatives to spare. Burg Schwarzkopf was flying a modified Lynx helicopter. As soon as they were in the air he called Air Traffic Control at Glasgow.

'Glasgow this is Tango India Foxtrot Alpha Two, over.'

'This is Glasgow, authenticate, over.' Authentication codes changed according to the date and time of day.

'I authenticate Charlie Mike Bravo Sierra.' Schwarzkopf folded away the secret tables and slipped them into a side-pocket.

'This is Glasgow, what are your requirements, over?'

'Priority to land near the Royal Infirmary, over.'

'Approved. All aircraft are being routed clear of the area. Good luck. Out.'

'We'll be there in twenty minutes,' Schwarzkopf announced over his communications system.

Hunter radioed Isobel at headquarters. 'Has the General taken off yet?'

'Two minutes ago. Not best pleased. He lost the game. Am patching you through now.'

'Sir? Hunter.'

'Nick, the Assistant Chief Constable is now in charge. I've briefed him precisely on what's required. He appeared relieved that we're taking over responsibility.'

Though he was itching to know how Macnair had side-stepped Blackwater, Hunter knew it was wisest not to ask. 'Any special instructions, sir?'

'None at present. Don't go in until we get a clear picture of what's going on. Did you get a plan of the building?'

'Affirmative. Isobel got it for us. Even as cathedrals go, it's a very large and beautiful building.'

'Which is why it must be saved.'

'What's the priority, sir?'

'Your ears only, Nick. My instructions are the building. There are twelve hostages and an unknown number of terrorists. More people are killed on our roads every two days than are at risk in the cathedral. The building has been there for over nine hundred years. It is irreplaceable. The site itself has been held sacred for over fifteen hundred years. It's no contest I'm afraid.'

'Roger that, sir. Have there been any messages from the terrorists yet?'

'Not so far. We're still waiting to hear their demands. Waste of time, of course. We won't negotiate with them under any circumstances, as they well know. This is revenge for the mosque which was torched in Glasgow yesterday. Wait, Nick. I'll be right back.'

Hunter's earphones went dead and he sat pensively. Who, he wondered, had given the order to save the building at the possible cost of innocent lives? Well, he was the man on the ground. As far as he was concerned he'd save lives and damn the consequences.

'Nick? Macnair. Where are you?'

Hunter looked down. 'Coatbridge is on our right, sir. Ten minutes out at the most.'

'Don't go in. Go high and stay high while I try and sort out a few problems. The terrorists have made contact. They've said that if they see the slightest sign of military personnel they will kill three of the hostages.'

'They won't know we've arrived, sir.'

'Unless they have somebody on the outside watching events. Which is most likely.'

'Roger that, sir. How is the evacuation progressing?'

'It's going on apace. But there are thousands of people to move out, a whole hospital to empty. That takes time. Seriously ill patients need a great deal of surgical support and nursing.'

'If this incident follows the pattern of the others, the terrorists must intend to demolish the cathedral. I've studied the plans. It will take a lot of plastic to destroy it completely.'

'We have to assume they can do just that.'

'I agree, sir. But the amount of explosives needed means that the peripheral damage could also be huge.'

'I'm aware of that. So?'

'If the terrorists are aiming for maximum publicity then the sooner they detonate their explosives the more people will die. Particularly if evacuations are still going on.'

'Then why haven't they done so already?'

'Maybe they intend to milk more publicity out of it first. The more television and radio reports the better, as far as they are concerned.'

There was a few seconds silence. 'I agree. That makes sense. The journalists will howl like stuffed pigs but I'm pulling the plug on them right now. I'll talk to the Assistant Chief Constable.'

'What about freedom of the press, sir?'

Macnair's reply made Hunter grin. He tapped Schwarzkopf on the shoulder. 'Burg, go high, stay high. We need to get a better picture of what's going on.' He changed frequency. 'Isobel? How are the satellite pictures coming?'

'Not good, Nick. I don't understand it. There's a definite huddle of people in the Chapter House – the hostages I suspect, but I can't trace anybody else.'

'What? That's not possible!'

'I've checked the equipment and it's working perfectly.'

'Could the terrorists be hiding amongst the hostages?'

'Not according to my count.'

The solution hit them both simultaneously. Hunter voiced the thought. 'Aluminium.'

Terrorists world-wide were becoming wise to the ways of governments and the bag of tricks they had developed in counter-terrorism. Heat-seeking satellites read the ambient temperature and that of any object or living body in the locale. It was so effective that the shape and size of the body, and any movements, could be measured and followed. One way to counteract the system was to wear clothes impregnated with aluminium. Older style prototypes were uncomfortable and rustled but the new outfits coming into use had overcome these drawbacks. So far, to the best of the West's intelligence services' knowledge, no one outside government organisations had the new design.

Macnair called back. 'The police have been warned. If anyone looks or smells like special forces or army they'll detonate the bomb and kill the hostages. They must have someone on the *outside* who would tip them off. I've got the ACC working on that right now.'

'What should we do, sir?'

'Do you have the portable heat-detector with you?'

'Yes, sir.'

'We can't risk you being recognised for who or what you are. And we don't know yet who the mole is on the outside. I have an idea.' The General gave his instructions. All operations of this sort were developed in three separate stages. The decision to go was made at the highest level and ordered by the senior officer. Then planners debated, argued, plotted and finally issued the outlines and guidelines for the operation. The third stage was okayed by the man in command on the ground. He had the right to veto a plan or an operation at anytime if he thought it was unworkable or too dangerous. Such a veto was a decision he would make perhaps once, at the most twice, in his career. After that he could look for a new occupation. Hunter's acquiescence to the General's idea was paramount.

The Assistant Chief Constable was named Graham Baldock. Unlike Blackwater his high-flying and younger superior – who had just been called to the Home Office at a moment's notice – he was an old fashioned cop. He had come up the hard way, through the ranks, serving his time. He was due to retire shortly from what was, by any yardstick, a highly successful career. Shrewd, hard-working, in his middle fifties, Baldock's neatly cut grey hair was hidden beneath an old-fashioned fedora hat. Despite a bulbous, drinker's nose, Baldock was teetotal and had been all his life. Drink had killed his father at an early age and the son had sworn an oath to his mother that he would never imbibe. He still kept his word even after she, too, had died. As far as he was concerned Blackwater's removal was a godsend. The pompous ass saw this as an opportunity to further his career, disregarding the safety of his men, the prisoners and the possible destruction of the cathedral. With great difficulty he had somehow managed to keep a straight face when his superior was called to London. The possibility of an outsider watching what they were doing had occurred to him and he was already combing the area for possible suspects when Macnair had called. The ACC liked what he was told.

A control vehicle had been placed next to the statue of the missionary David Livingstone. Baldock knew he and his officers were too close to the cathedral. If it blew up the falling masonry would probably kill everybody in a wide radius. The M8 motorway was closed in both directions, and barriers had been set up as far as a thousand yards from the area.

Looking moodily at the large scale map pinned to one wall Baldock pondered the problems they were facing. The biggest was the Royal Infirmary Hospital, right next door. There were operations taking place which could not be interrupted, as well as critically ill patients who needed to be moved to other hospitals. Those who could be discharged were being sent home, while alternative beds were being arranged all across Scotland. Anger erupted in the ACC's stomach like acid. Nothing on earth justified this sort of atrocity.

Around him, senior officers were busy giving orders and relaying information. As each building was cleared it was marked with a yellow highlighter. Baldock sighed. There were too few coloured yellow.

Turning to Chief Superintendent Douglas Matthews he said, 'Doug, I want the press moved right back. They have to go behind the barriers as well. The concession to film is now withdrawn.'

He and Matthews had joined the force together and had been friends all their adult life. 'Is that wise, Graham? They're going to howl like . . .'

It was an indication of the pressure the ACC was under that Baldock snapped, 'Just do it, all right?' He was immediately contrite. 'Sorry. This is the biggest incident we've ever faced. Tell the press it's for safety reasons.'

'But it isn't?'

'No. It makes good sense operationally. I'll fill you in later.' He was about to say something else when he thought better of it. Instead he took his assistant to one side, out of hearing of the busy control van, 'We've a helo coming in, TIFAT. I want them taken into the hospital nice and quiet. They'll be in civvies, not combat gear. They're setting up an observation point on the top floor of the Royal, overlooking St Mungo's. There's going to be a news blackout imposed ASAP. We must isolate this incident as far as possible. It may buy us time.'

Matthews nodded. To him it made little sense but he would follow out his instructions to the letter. 'Where do we want the helo to land, sir?'

'As far away as possible and still get the passengers here double quick. What the . . .' Both men heard the unmistakable thwacking noise made by a helicopter in flight and dashed outside. Baldock felt a surge of anger as the helo came in to land close by. The bloody fools! Perhaps Blackwater had been right. Maybe they were just a bunch of cowboys. Then the helo turned and the unmistakable sign of the red cross was displayed. The Lynx continued turning as it came into land, ensuring, with a three hundred and sixty degree sweep, that its insignia was plainly visible.

Schwarzkopf had landed in a field to the east of the city where the TIFAT team had quickly decorated the sides of the helicopter with a white banner and red cross. They had changed out of combat gear and into jeans and tee-shirts, before pulling on white medical coats and hanging stethoscopes around their necks. The disguise was Isobel's idea. The hospital was the logical place to set up an observation post. The equipment the team would be using was contained in white boxes marked with a red cross, the paint still drying. If there was somebody on the outside watching, an open approach was better than a clandestine one. To add to the subterfuge, the helicopter was to be used to ferry the seriously ill to other hospitals, a refinement Hunter had dreamt up only minutes earlier. Isobel was already informing the hospital authorities that the helo was available and patients were ready to move. Six stretcher cases plus six staff could fly out. The same information was being relayed to the police control caravan, as well as to the radio and television stations. It was the last piece of news that was to be broadcast on the siege. After that the news blackout would be enforced.

With satisfaction Hunter saw the police moving away the hordes of press, live TV cameras and still photographers. After a good deal of angry argument from the brave but bloody-minded reporters, they gave ground. The policemen and women had been given their instructions. They were not to take no for an answer. If anyone refused to go they were to be arrested. Just for a few hours, freedom of the press and civil liberties were to be suspended. Those refusing to move out of their homes were also to be removed, for their own safety. They could kick up a fuss afterwards. Those fitting a certain profile were to be arrested and their property searched. The criteria? Muslim or foreign nationals in properties over-looking the area. As for search warrants, a state of emergency had been declared and different laws were in force.

So far nobody had been arrested.

Hunter ignored the uniformed ACC beyond a brief nod. Already stretchers bearing seriously ill patients were being wheeled out. Hunter and the rest of the team helped them into the helicopter. At the same time they moved their equipment onto empty stretchers and began walking towards the hospital's main entrance. The team quickly disappeared into the throng of evacuees now milling around Castle Street.

The team were met at the entrance by a worried-looking man who introduced himself as the Director of Administration.

'You understand our requirements?' Hunter asked.

'Yes, yes, certainly. Please, follow me.'

A lift took them up three floors. They soon found themselves in a small ward with six empty beds. The ward's windows overlooked the Cathedral of St Mungo's, a glorious sight in the sunlight.

They began to assemble their equipment. Priority was given to a high-powered heat-seeker that resembled a TV camera. While it was being fixed to a tripod and aimed at the cathedral a second device was placed on a table and switched on. It looked like a normal radio but was in fact an eavesdropping device of amazing complexity. Every frequency within five miles was being sucked up and transmitted back to Isobel at Rosyth. There, computers were listening to every conversation currently taking place on a telephone, mobile phone or radio within that radius. Leo had programmed the software to identify certain words, certain languages and foreign accents. The system was hampered by the fact that foreign correspondents were reporting on events even though they couldn't see what was going on. It was hoped that the news blackout would quickly change all that.

Hunter stood at the window, powerful binoculars to his eyes, scanning the ancient cathedral. It was, he realised, quite stunning in its majesty.

'Claude, you got anything on that monitor yet?'

'Yes, boss. I think the hostages are in the furthest corner. I'm just comparing it to the map.' He pointed. 'Here. They're in the Chapter House.'

'Just as Isobel said. Found the perps yet?'

'I've focused the sight all along the building at maximum power. Faint heat spots are showing up and we're comparing them to other possible sources.'

Frowning, Hunter stared at the monitor and then pointed. 'That looks like a head.'

'I agree,' said Lt Napier.

Matt Dunston looked intently at the tiny points. 'I think you're right. So they're definitely wearing aluminium suits.'

'Seems like it,' said Hunter. 'Jan, how are you getting on with the ex-torch?'

'The light is flickering green to amber. That's because we're so far away. We need to get a lot closer,' the Spetsnaz replied.

'It can wait,' said Hunter. 'At least we know there are explosives, we just don't know where or how much.'

Hunter's phone rang.

'Nick? Isobel. We've got a possible contact. A conversation has just been intercepted in the five mile radius – in Arabic. From the readouts I would say that one of the people speaking was in the cathedral and the other very close by.'

'How close?'

'I can't tell exactly. It's a little bit odd, to tell the truth. This isn't an exact science for locating message transmissions but I'd expect the target to be within, say ten yards.'

'And?'

'The signal appears to have been sent from the clear ground to the east of St Mungo's. But that's been evacuated.'

'Could it be somebody in one of the flats behind, watching?'

'It's possible,' Isobel sounded doubtful.

'But you don't think so?'

'No, to be honest, I don't. Could someone be hiding in the cathedral grounds?'

'Possibly. But it's not a location I'd choose. Is it a radio or phone signal?'

'Mobile telephone. We've tried tracing it but no luck. It was reported stolen a week ago.'

'Stolen? Where from?'

'Somewhere in Glasgow.'

'Which police station was the report made to?'

'Let me see.' There was a pause while Isobel checked her computer. 'Maryhill.'

'Okay, thanks.' He broke the connection and relayed the information to the others.

'Matt, can you nip down and have a quiet word with the ACC? Ask him to come and talk to me. Make sure he knows it's a request.'

Dunston, dressed in a grey suit and dog-collar, nodded. 'Leave it to me.'

While he was away the others continued examining the faint thermal images on the monitor. Each one was marked on the large scale map they had of the cathedral. They double checked.

None of the images appeared to have moved very far. That was the good news. The bad news was there appeared to be eleven terrorists in all.

Hunter reported to Macnair.

'Okay, Nick. I'll be with you in fifteen minutes. We're landing at Port Dundas. I'll walk from there. Tell ACC Baldock to expect me. I don't want to be held up by some over-zealous PC Plod.'

'Will do, sir. In fact, he's just walked in.' Hunter broke the connection and smiled to the ACC, his hand outstretched. The men shook hands, each assessing the other.

The ACC, apparently satisfied, smiled. 'This gentleman in the vicar's costume politely asked me to come and speak to you.'

'Thank you, sir,' said Hunter. 'The dog-collar is real, though. He knows the cathedral pretty well but he's also one of us.'

The ACC looked as surprised as he felt and re-appraised his initial opinion of Dunston who had seemed to be such a tough son-of-a-bitch when they'd met.

Hunter explained about the intercepted phone signal and Baldock looked suitably shocked.

'You realise what this probably means?' The ACC asked.

Hunter shrugged. 'It could be a bent policeman.'

Baldock nodded. 'Leave him to us. If it is, whoever he is, I'll have his balls.'

Hunter shook his head. 'I've a better idea. We need to buy time. It's now eighteen hundred and darkness is still three hours away. If these terrorists follow the usual pattern they'll balance killing hostages against the maximum publicity achievable. Which means that sometime in the next hour or so they'll set off the explosives. Loads of media coverage and lots of bodies. How long will the evacuation take to finish?'

'Hours yet. We have to search every building. The hospital is a nightmare. You just can't rush so many people, especially if they're bed-bound. The staff are doing their damnedest but there are only so many lifts and so few volunteers to push the beds, trolleys and wheelchairs.'

'I suggest we find this bent copper and feed him some misinformation,' said Hunter.

'What do you propose?'

'Tell him the evacuation is taking a great deal longer than expected. That there are still many hundreds of people in the surrounding buildings. Tell him it will take until well after midnight to make a dent in the numbers.'

'That won't stop them detonating the explosives,' said Baldock. 'Hell, it may even encourage them to set them off now for maximum effect.'

'Here's the clincher,' said Hunter. 'You also say that the news blackout imposed under section eleven of the Official Secrets Act is already being questioned by the newspapers. A special court is sitting in Edinburgh right now to discuss the pros and cons. Say you think we're going to lose. That the press will be swarming around the cathedral before the night is out. Emphasise it will be world-wide coverage and that you're bloody angry about it. That may hold the terrorists for a few hours.'

'I need to find the traitor first,' said the ACC.

'Broadcast it to all your force as a sitrep. He's bound to transmit the info to those in the cathedral. Now we know which frequency he's on and where to look we can listen in.'

'He may not tell the terrorists what's going on,' said Baldock.

'True,' said Hunter. 'But the mis-information is too important not to pass on as it means the perps are guaranteed world-wide coverage. If he doesn't, contact Maryhill and find out if they have any Muslim or Islamic personnel. Match them with whoever is in the grounds. Oh, and see if there are any Arabic speakers.'

'He or she will probably have moved by now. The sweep of the open spaces is complete and everybody is now working at emptying the buildings.'

'It's definitely a man. That was confirmed.'

'Nick,' said Dunston. 'I've just thought of something. As far as the terrorists are concerned, what would be the worst case scenario?'

'They get taken out before they can set off the explosives,' said Hunter.

'And how do you guard against that? You have a man on the outside with a transmitter as well, just in case. If it all goes pear-shaped he presses the button and up it all goes. That's what I would do. Either way the cathedral is destroyed.'

Hunter nodded gloomily. 'Is it likely to be the same man?'

'I should think so. They can't have that many assets on the ground in Glasgow.'

'Don't you believe it,' said the ACC. 'We've had a huge influx of immigrants from all over the Middle East in the last two years. Any number of them could be al-Qaeda supporters. And probably are.'

'In that case search anybody who looks of Arab extraction,' said Hunter. 'If he has anything on him that could possibly send a signal arrest him and hold him incommunicado until this is over. But my bet is, it'll be the man who telephoned.'

'How do you intend to infiltrate the cathedral?' asked the ACC.

'We've found a way in. One thing, sir,' said Hunter, 'we may not be taking prisoners. Does that present you with a problem?'

'No. I hate paperwork,' came the response. 'Now, if you gentlemen will excuse me, I have a lot to do. I'll speak to you later.'

'One more thing,' said Hunter. 'My boss, General Macnair, is arriving soon.'

'I'll see he gets straight through.' On that note the ACC departed.

'Think it'll work?' asked Doug Tanner, a frown on his normally cheerful face.

'We can only pray,' said Dunston.

The American SEAL grinned, his white teeth shining in his black face. 'That's your part-of-ship, Matt. We leave all the hallelujah stuff to you.'

'With you lot that's a full time job.'

The ACC went downstairs, sucking an antacid drop. Yet again his anger had erupted in bile. That one of his men could be helping these scum was beyond his comprehension. Well, he knew just the man to finger the likely culprit. But first of all he would update his men.

Back in the control van he said to Superintendent Douglas

Matthews, 'The media barons are up in arms. A special court is sitting right now in Edinburgh challenging our exclusion of the press. We'll try and keep them at bay for a few hours but I've been told we're going to lose.'

'Damn,' Matthews said with feeling. 'The last thing we want are reporters and cameras all over the place.'

The ACC sighed theatrically, 'That's the price of freedom and democracy.'

The Superintendent looked at his boss in surprise. He knew Baldock's position on civil liberties – the rights of the guilty at the expense of the innocent he called it.

'I want to tell everyone what's happening. Put me through on the universal channel, will you?'

A few moments later the ACC was speaking to hundreds of officers who were busy in the area. 'The evacuation is taking a lot longer than expected. I've been speaking to the hospital authorities. We don't expect the building to be emptied before tomorrow morning. The evacuation of patients cannot be rushed. So just keep things moving along at the present pace. Secondly, I have news regarding the press blackout. I'm not happy about this but we can expect the cameras back here around twenty-three hundred or shortly afterwards. Unfortunately, this will play into the terrorists hands, giving them global media coverage. Be that as it may, I want a peaceful resolution to this affair. We will co-operate with the media and at the same time try and establish contact with the men in St Mungo's. I want no precipitate action unless they start killing hostages. If they kill even one person we go in and we go in hard. As long as the prisoners live we'll try and talk to the terrorists and establish their demands. Oh, one more thing. Well done, all of you. I'm proud of what you've achieved to date. That is all.'

Baldock broke the connection and looked into the frowning face of his friend and colleague. The ACC placed a finger to his lips and gestured to the door. Outside he casually looked around to make sure nobody could overhear him. 'There's a mole and we think it's a copper.'

'What!' Matthews was scandalised. 'Are you sure?'

'As sure as we can be. Find Ali for me. He knows all the Muslim coppers – maybe he can suggest which scumbag is to blame.'

Ali al-Faruq was Glasgow born and bred. His father had emigrated to the West from Saudi Arabia in the 1960s. With a medical degree from Oxford, al-Faruq senior had gone on to become one of Glasgow's most respected and eminent plastic surgeons. Ali had shown no desire to follow in his father's footsteps and instead had taken a law degree. Being a lawyer hadn't suited his temperament and eight years earlier he had joined the police force. Fast-tracked because of his education and special skills – he spoke four languages including Arabic – he had quickly made Inspector. He was tipped for the top and was widely expected to be the UK's first ethnic minority Chief Constable. He was the type of man that an old-fashioned copper like Baldock would normally heartily dislike. But in this case Baldock had the highest regard for the man, respected his beliefs and thought him a good policeman. He was a devout Muslim, although he never paraded his beliefs in the other coppers' faces. There had been a lot of comment about his rise through the ranks but it had been richly deserved. Lesser men had talked about quotas and ethnic minorities getting the best jobs and political correctness leading the way. Only Baldock had known better. Al-Faruq had proven to be a superior police officer in every way.

'Ali is over by the barriers in Duke Street,' said Matthews.

'I'll find him myself.'

The ACC walked out of Cathedral Square and along John Knox Street, deep in thought. If the cathedral was destroyed it could never be replaced. The expense alone was one thing, but there were no longer craftsmen capable of re-building such a magnificent edifice.

He spotted al-Faruq on his mobile telephone a short distance from the barriers, one hand against his ear, talking softly. The Inspector was in uniform and looked up when the ACC approached. He said something in what the ACC assumed was Arabic and broke the connection.

'Important call?'

Al-Faruq was a good-looking man in his early thirties. Tall, slim, black-haired, brown-eyed and still a bachelor, the ACC knew that many of the policewomen in the force would have gone to bed with the man if he had given the slightest hint. But he had played it straight. He never mixed pleasure with business. His girlfriends had all been from outside the force.

'My mother. I was explaining I would be home late.'

Years of training told Baldock that al-Faruq was lying. The ACC's nose was twitching and he had learnt to trust his nose in cases like this. Realisation hit him like a thunderbolt but he knew instinctively. Al-Faruq was based at Maryhill.

Was the man a traitor? Baldock thrust his hands into his jacket pockets, his fists clenched tightly as he fought down an almost overwhelming desire to smash the answers out of the handsome face before him.

'Everything all right?' Baldock managed to ask without betraying the emotions coursing through him. He checked his watch, to give his expression a chance to settle.

'Ah, yes, sir. Everything is fine. I em . . . heard your broadcast.'

The ACC pulled a face. 'Can't be helped I'm afraid. It's going to take even longer than I said but I didn't want to dishearten the troops too much. But I meant it when I said if they kill one hostage then we go in hard. Immediately. There'll be no waiting for the cameras to arrive. In many ways I'm hoping they'll give me the excuse. I would have liked this over before the media got back, one way or another.'

'Do you know when the press will get back here, sir?'

Baldock nodded. 'I've been speaking to our people at the court in Edinburgh. They think they'll manage to delay matters until around midnight, but definitely no longer. So anytime after that.'

'I see, thank you, sir.'

'I'll speak to you later. I'm just going to have a word with the armed response unit.'

Armed policemen surrounded the cathedral. It would be their task to storm the building if they were ordered in. Or so they thought. Baldock had no intention of enlightening them. He spoke briefly to the Chief Inspector in charge and returned towards the control van. Once he was out of sight he hurried instead to the hospital entrance. Within minutes he was with Hunter and his men.

He was introduced to General Macnair who had just arrived and was being brought up to speed with events.

Baldock asked, 'Have there been any more phone calls?'

'Yes,' replied Hunter. 'One.'

'At what time?' The time given confirmed his suspicions. Although his gut instinct was proven correct, Baldock was devastated – who *could* be trusted? 'The man we want is Inspector Ali al-Faruq. He was using his phone then and I didn't believe his story. Damnation! His involvement makes matters even worse.'

'Why?' Hunter frowned. 'The strategy appears to have worked. We've bought time and . . .' He held up his hand. A phone was ringing and, glancing at the display, he said, 'That's Isobel at HQ.'

'He's used the phone again,' prophesied Baldock.

Hunter listened to Isobel and hung up. 'You're right.'

'He told the perps that the press are away until midnight?' Baldock hazarded.

Nodding, Hunter asked, 'How did you know?'

The ACC repeated his conversation with al-Faruq.

'Good,' said Macnair. 'In that case it's time to go over the battle plan.'

12

It was dark at last. Or as dark as any city becomes once the sun has set. At 22.30 the city was plunged into total darkness as an electricity blackout hit the whole conurbation of Glasgow.

Hunter and the team had changed into grey attack gear. They moved like ghosts out of a rear entrance of the Royal Infirmary and into the grounds of the cathedral. Each member was in contact by personal radio, both with Macnair and back to Isobel at H.Q. Satellites were passing overhead, focusing on the cathedral, recording silently. The heat-seeking camera installed by the team displayed an almost static image. Eleven faint shapes scattered around St Mungo's Cathedral.

Each team member carried an ex-torch and was working his way around the building, holding the torch close to the walls, looking for the slightest indication of plastic explosives. Here, even through the great walls of the cathedral, the torches worked effectively. The indicator lights were firmly on amber and flickering to red. By cross-referencing the angles of the beams they identified eight locations. The information was relayed back to H.Q. A few minutes later Isobel called back.

'There are explosives in the eastern arm, in the Presbytery and Feretory.' The former, Hunter knew, had been the ecclesiastical and spiritual court, while the latter housed the portable shrine for relics of saints.

'Roger that,' acknowledged Hunter.

'A second lot is in the Chapter House, in the north-east corner. The remainder are fixed to the four main pillars opposite the

174

Blackadder Aisle and to two of the lesser pillars in the centre. We've tried to estimate how much explosives there are and it must be hundreds of pounds.'

'Easily enough to raze the cathedral to the ground.'

'The cathedral, the hospital and every building in about a half mile radius I should think,' said Isobel.

'Agreed. Thanks.'

On the north side of the building, protruding like a small arm, lay the Sacristy and Treasury. Near its ancient wall was a metal plate, a metre square, leading down to the main drains. With oxygen masks and night-vision goggles in place, the team quickly prised up the plate and vanished, one by one.

Their entry was watched by a dark-haired man standing on the far side of the grounds. He reached for his mobile. *They had been lied to! Special Forces were going in.*

Assistant Chief Constable Baldock stood in the shadows with Superintendent Matthews. They too had watched the team vanish into the ground. Normally they would have seemed like dark ghosts against the grey stone cathedral walls but the two senior officers were wearing NVGs borrowed from their own force. Inspector Ali al-Faruq was equally plain to see. He had just removed the phone from his pocket when Baldock approached him.

'Ah, Ali, there you are,' said the ACC. 'We need you back at the control van straightaway. Something has come up.'

'Yes, sir. I'll be right with you. I just have this call to make.' Al-Faruq knew he could make the call in front of his superiors as he would be speaking Arabic. He almost laughed out loud at the irony of it. His anger though, was making him tremble. If his companions didn't stop them and delay matters until the press arrived he would set off the explosives himself, as soon as he was at a safe distance.

Baldock was standing near the Inspector. For a big man he could move extremely quickly when he needed to. Even as alFaruq began pressing buttons on the phone the ACC sprang forward. The small cosh he held in his hands was illegal but it had saved him on a number of occasions when facing down some of Glasgow's hard men. The blow to the upper forearm was hard and numbing. His hand paralysed, al-Faruq yelped in shocked outrage and dropped the mobile.

Chief Superintendent Douglas Matthews wrestled al-Faruq to the ground, twisted his arms behind his back and quickly fitted handcuffs. He ensured they were just tight enough to cut off his prisoner's circulation. 'Not bad for a couple of old men,' he said to the ACC.

Baldock chuckled. 'You're right there, Doug. Read the bastard his rights and take him away. Get him out of my sight before I do him some real damage.'

'This is an outrage . . .' al-Faruq began but got no further.

The ACC kicked him in his ribs. 'Shut up, you traitor. You're a disgrace to your uniform and your family. You've betrayed your people to the scum in there,' he gestured to the cathedral.

Making no attempt to deny it, al-Faruq said, 'And what of the greater betrayal to Allah and Islam? The obscenity of policemen standing by and watching my mosque being burnt to the ground by ignorant savages who are not fit to clean the shoes of Muslims? That is a far greater betrayal. There is only one true faith. And it will prevail over all the earth . . .'

'Search him,' said Baldock.

In al-Faruq's pocket they found a small radio transmitter with a switch and a button.

'It looks like that chap from TIFAT was right. He does have the transmitter.' Baldock bent down and grabbed the supine Inspector by the scruff of his collar. Rage gave him strength and he jerked the man to his feet. 'You're going down for the rest of your life, al-Faruq, you bastard!'

His prisoner laughed. 'You've nothing on me, Baldock. Nothing that will convict in a court of law. If you do get to court it'll be circumstantial. I found that transmitter lying in the grass and was about to bring it to you when you attacked me without provocation. You two are the ones going to jail.'

'Shall I tell him or you?' Baldock asked his friend.

'Let me, please, Graham. But not until I can see his face.'

Matthews was looking forward to watching al-Faruq listen to his own voice on tape. The case they had was watertight and al-Faruq would be lucky ever to leave prison alive. His fellow prisoners would see to that.

Gustav had been watching his own channels on TV – nine screens in a phalanx filling an entire wall. Every channel shared footage of the cathedral in Glasgow. His TV companies across Europe and beyond were 'on message', communicating live, describing events of the latest outrage in Norwegian, French, German, Swedish, English, Walloon . . . the polyglot babble filled Gustav with deep satisfaction. Immigrants were blatantly destroying European culture as evidenced by the atrocities already committed and epitomised by the outrage in Glasgow. Once the cathedral was destroyed there would be no turning back. The acts of terrorism would continue until the right-wing were in power across Europe. Then they would pounce. Draft legislation, conceived by him over the decades, honed and polished, the finest details thoroughly researched, would come into force. Islam would be outlawed. All mosques would be shut down forthwith. Muslims would be forced to leave Europe and return to the land they claimed as their country of origin. If a third generation German could describe him or herself as Algerian/German then so be it. They could return to Algeria. Let them, he thought, eat sand.

There was a knock on the door and Duval entered.

'Anything new on the Glasgow affair?' Gustav asked.

'No, sir. We can expect something to happen at any time.' He looked at his watch. 'It is half past eleven now, so it is half past ten their time. It can't be much longer.'

'Are the press releases ready?'

'Yes, sir.'

'The politicians and commentators' comments?'

'Of course. This will be the most savage attack to date. We've doubled and in some cases trebled the tallies of dead and injured and highly exaggerated the cost of the damage. The vitriol against the Muslims will be so great that no politician in his right mind will speak up on their behalf. The news from America is also good. The populace is baying for the repatriation of its troops from Europe. They are demanding that their own shores be protected, saying its time we Europeans stood up for ourselves. Our press release will be saying the same thing. With a concerted orchestration of public opinion on both sides of the Atlantic the present administration will have little choice.'

'Is everything in place to disengage our connections with the followers of Islam?'

'Yes, sir. I have only to send the orders down the computers. The electronic walls and cut-offs we designed will slot into place. No one will be able to trace anything back to us.'

'In that case we will send the instructions after the destruction of the cathedral.' Gustav chuckled. As political structures disintegrated and alliances shifted, now was the time to make the break, before the pressures of secrecy multiplied out of control. With current technology it was almost impossible to work out who the real enemy was. How easy to cast suspicion elsewhere. Black holes, viruses, trap doors . . . child's play. 'This is indeed excellent news. I think a little celebration is called for.'

'Herbal tea, sir?'

'No. Open that bottle of one-hundred-year-old brandy.'

If he was surprised, the ever faithful secretary didn't show it.

The team had walked, bent double, underneath the cathedral all the way to the Blackadder Aisle. The drain cover inside yielded to a slim jemmy forced in from one side and slowly pulled down. According to the infra-red information supplied by the general there was nobody in the area. But they moved silently and cautiously nevertheless. A fibre optic camera lens was slipped through the minute crack. The picture and sensors confirmed the room was empty.

Badonovitch lifted the cover clear and Tanner hoisted himself into the cathedral. He took the cover out of the Russian's hands and held it while the rest of the team quickly followed. Replacing the cover he followed the others to the stairs that led to the half landing and the crypt. The cathedral was in pitch darkness. Without their NVGs they would have been working blind. At the back of their minds the question was, did the terrorists have the benefit of goggles too? A clock chimed a soft ding-dong twice. Hunter checked his watch, 23.30 precisely.

The team were awed by the cathedral's interior. It was worse than sacrilege to think that its immense beauty, its serenity, could be destroyed at any moment. It was so silent that nobody dared to use their personal radios. All they could do was listen for Macnair who was watching the infra-red, heat seeking monitor.

Hunter pressed the send button twice. Macnair immediately responded. 'They haven't moved. From their positions they would be able to smash a window and shoot at anybody approaching the cathedral. They're relying on being warned from the outside. It's still as we thought. If we attack the whole building goes up.'

Hunter clicked twice again. From supposition and information from previous attacks, they knew the terrorists would leave no one alive. Prior to detonation, the prisoners would be shot. Probably just as they were exiting the main door. That would bring the police down on them like a ton of bricks and the resulting explosion would kill as many of the force as possible. It was a clever plan, if you didn't intend living.

The indicator light on the ex-torches glowed red when briefly flashed on in the stygian darkness. Dunston slid across the floor to the Crypt. From there he could see along the Nave and back to the Choir, Presbytery and Feretory.

The least damaging explosives were those in the Chapter House. If they went off they would kill the hostages but probably not destroy the cathedral. The four pillars underpinning the crypt were the priority. If they were destroyed the damage would be total and irreparable. Masson, Napier, Badonovitch and Tanner followed Dunston while Hunter went into the Nave. Four catchments of explosives, two either side of the Nave, were Hunter's responsibility. His dilemma was that the explosives were out in the open – and there was a terrorist between him and the target.

The outer door was solid oak but was approached through a vestibule with a glass door either side. Hunter stood at the side entrance normally used by visitors. A terrorist was kneeling on a prayer mat, facing east, preparing himself spiritually for the conflict ahead.

Hunter moved very slowly and very carefully. He knew the location of the other terrorists. In theory only one other man was in a position to see him. He eased behind a pillar, out of sight of the kneeling man and looked to his right. There he was! At the north wall, also on his knees – praying! He was wearing old-fashioned NVGs, which temporarily blinded you if a bright light were shone upon them. Nonetheless effective under normal conditions. Hunter watched the terrorists preparing their souls for departing this world, ready to greet the majesty of the Prophet. This was the edge they could only have dreamed of. Hunter grinned mirthlessly. Prayed for.

Suddenly he was aware of a presence alongside him and found Dunston by his side. Hunter pointed to the two kneeling men. The chaplain pointed at himself, then at the man on the north side. Hunter nodded and moved further along the Nave, intending to come around behind his target. Using the pillars as cover, he flitted across the stone floor. At the main entrance he stopped. There were two terrorists on the floor above the door, one on either side, but he was in their blind spot.

He approached his target. The aluminium in the man's clothing rustled loudly as he lifted his body and prostrated himself once more. Hunter inched closer and was only feet away when the man began to arch back up. At the top of his movement, Hunter stepped forward, clamped a gloved hand over the terrorist's mouth and slid a blackened blade under the man's ribs and into his heart. He died without a sound. Hunter eased the body back to the supplicant's position. He sent three clicks down his transmitter.

Macnair immediately responded. 'Nick, one dead terrorist?'

Click.

'Good. The explosives in the Crypt have been dealt with. Jan

went back into the aisle to speak to me. It's semtex. Three detonators, each wired to a receiver. No booby traps. They're going
after the others on the upper floors. Matt has just called in. He's
dealt with his target. You're clear to go after the other explosives
in the Nave.'

One click. Hunter moved silently to the nearest pillar fitted
with plastic explosive. A brief glance told him all he needed to
know. He even recognised the detonators. New Mark 10s, supplied
courtesy of the Ministry of Defence to anybody willing to pay the
price. Short lengths of electrical wire connected the dets to a
receiver. He cut the wires and pushed the ends into the PE. To a
casual glance, the explosives still appeared ready to go. Looking
across at Dunston he received the OK sign and nodded. He made
four clicks to Macnair.

'You and Matt have dealt with your explosives?'

One click.

'Excellent. The two terrorists on the floor over the main door
are down. I'm watching the screen now. Two of our men are
approaching their targets. The one in the upper part of the Sacristy
and the other in the Central Tower.' There was a few seconds
delay. 'Both men have been shot.'

Neither Hunter nor Dunston had heard anything. Hunter
acknowledged the information.

Macnair continued. 'That leaves the five we have on screen.
Two are still either side of the stairs leading to the Chapter House
and two are behind the main pillars either side of the Presbytery.
The fifth man is moving. He's now approaching the Crypt. I think
he's going to check on the others.'

Hunter sent a click. The man was walking towards him. He
would pass within feet of the pillar Hunter was hiding behind.
The distinctive rustling of the aluminium clothing came to
Hunter's ears, virtually drowning out any other sound.

Maybe it was instinct. Something warned the man and as
Hunter stepped forward the terrorist turned to look straight at
him. He was opening his mouth to yell a warning when Hunter
dived forward and slammed a shoulder into his midriff. Hunter
had been expecting a vicious fight. Instead the terrorist collapsed

under him. Hunter had no difficulty slamming the haft of the knife into his temple, knocking him out. He reversed his action and was about to ram the knife into the man's throat when he realised how slight the body was. Pulling off the unconscious terrorist's goggles he saw it was a young girl. Hesitating, he knew he couldn't do it. He pressed a finger to her carotid artery for a few seconds and induced a deeper unconsciousness. She should still be there when he came back for her.

The noise had caused consternation in the Presbytery. A voice called out. 'Fatima, are you all right?' No reply. 'Fatima, answer me.'

'Flash-bangs,' ordered Hunter softly into his throat microphone. 'On two. One . . . two.'

The silence of the cathedral was abruptly shattered as the heavy grenades clattered amongst the pillars surrounding the Presbytery and Feretory. The team cowered down and closed their eyes as wild shooting began. As the grenades exploded, the bangs and bright lights were overpowering in the quiet darkness of St Mungo's.

The team moved fast, Hunter and Dunston along the southern wall, Masson and Napier along the north. Badonovitch and Tanner went straight through the Choir. The two terrorists were firing blindly, screaming at the tops of their voices. The bullets from their machine guns splattered against stone and ricocheted around the walls. The team took aim and fired silenced shots. Two taps each. Six bullets into each terrorist, any one a killing shot. The firing ceased abruptly.

Screams were heard from the Chapter House and already Hunter was diving over the floor, bullets flying above his head. Just as suddenly they stopped. Now the screams were mixed with voices begging for their lives. The terrorists were turning the guns onto the prisoners.

A harsh voice called in Arabic. A second replied. Hunter reached the steps, saw two terrorists on his right, behind a supporting pillar. Both carried transmitters.

'God is great!' One of them screamed as Hunter shot him twice in the head.

The other man dropped to his knees and looked up at Hunter. 'Too late.'

Hunter felt a presence at his shoulder and dropped to one knee, thinking one of the team was with him. He saw the terrorist press the button on the transmitter. Nothing happened. The man pressed again. And again. He looked up at Hunter, snarling his hatred. Hunter was inwardly calm, a feeling unlike anything he had ever had before. He shot the man in the neck. The terrorist flew backwards, blood pumping from his wound, the transmitter dropping from his hand.

Hunter leapt into the room and picked up the transmitter, placing it in his pocket for safe keeping. As the prisoners realised they were unharmed, one by one, they stopped screaming. Many had been temporarily blinded and deafened by the flashbangs.

'You're safe,' said Hunter. 'Just rest for a while. Your sight will return to normal – along with your hearing. Stay where you are and we'll try and get you out of here as soon as possible.'

He looked up as Dunston appeared in the doorway. There was nobody else there. Hunter shrugged. He could have sworn somebody had been right behind him.

Hunter radioed Macnair with a sitrep. 'Excellent. Are all the terrorists accounted for?'

'Yes, sir. One is still alive. A young girl. Sorry, I couldn't bring myself to kill her.'

Macnair was silent for a few seconds. 'That's all right, Nick, I understand.'

'I'll apologise to the ACC.'

'What for?'

'Leaving him with paperwork to do. It's pitch dark in here, so we'll lead out the people we've rescued. I think it will be best if we remove the PE and the other gear.'

'Is there much?'

'I'd say ten or twelve kilos in each pile, tamped down like a collar around the base of the pillars. Luckily we had a mis-fire. The devastation would have been beyond belief.'

183

'What happened?'

'We didn't make it to the Chapter House in time. Somehow it didn't go off. None of the detonators worked, otherwise we'd have a different tale to tell. Certainly all hostages would have been killed or seriously injured.'

'It was a high-risk strategy Nick, but one we had to take.'

'I know that, sir. We were lucky, that's all I'm saying.'

'Well, we need and deserve luck sometimes. Leave the girl to the local police.'

'Will do, sir.'

Dunston was already organising the evacuation of the cathedral. When the door opened the ACC was waiting to greet them. Hunter showed him around St Mungo's.

'We'll take the explosives,' said Hunter, 'and let you have a report. I'll estimate the amount of devastation I think would have occurred had the terrorists been successful. The evidence will be presented in written format with no court appearance. You know that, sir, don't you?'

'Yes, I do,' said Baldock. 'And thanks. The City of Glasgow owes a debt it cannot repay.'

Hunter nodded and smiled. 'The girl is over here.' Leading the way to the south wall he showed him the unconscious figure.

'She's only a wee chit of a thing.'

'That may be, but she can pull the trigger of a machine gun with the best of them.'

'Any ID?'

'No idea. We haven't looked. They're all yours now. Sorry about the paperwork.'

Baldock's Glaswegian roots showed when he was either under stress or happy with his lot. 'Laddie, think nothing of it. It's been a pleasure to know you.'

At that moment General Macnair joined them. 'We'll bag up and get out of here. Burg is on his way back from Ninewells Hospital in Dundee and will be here soon.'

The clock over the main door chimed ding-dong three times. Exactly fifteen minutes had elapsed since they had entered the building.

The semtex was placed in separate bin bags, the receivers were tagged to each detonator and placed separately. All other equipment was collected. As they stood in the Cathedral Square waiting for the helicopter, the lights came on all over Glasgow, revealing a lot of grinning faces.

From his plinth, David Livingstone looked down as serenely as ever.

When they arrived back at TIFAT HQ they found the wardroom bar open, food ready and bottles of whisky and beer laid out. They needed to unwind, to let the adrenaline work its way out of their systems. The debrief would come in the morning.

Dunston found Hunter nursing a large whisky and in philosophical mood. A couple of whiskies later, the reason for his ruminations emerged.

'You know, Matt, I envy you.'

'You surprise me. You have more than most men, Nick – surely you're the one to be envied?'

'Material things, the career, yes. But you have an inner peace, a contentment that comes directly from your belief. Everything is so clear to you. Sorry if I'm not making much sense but I've had three, or is it four, of these?' Hunter waved his glass.

'As with anything else, Nick, faith is something you have to work for.' Dunston sat opposite his friend, a low table between them, and leaned forward. 'I think hard and I pray even harder. Others will tell you about Jesus extolling us to turn the other cheek, to forgive our enemies. But the bible also tells us of a vengeful God who makes demands on us and expects us to obey. Otherwise we can expect retribution. If not in this world, then certainly the next.' Dunston took a gulp of his own single malt and continued. 'I have as many doubts as the next man but I work at it. I want to believe and so I do. I have a deep conviction that I have an important role to fulfil here at TIFAT. I don't hate or even dislike Moslems. But I do hate the corruption of a great religion for earthly ends. Hell, enough moralising. It shows I've had too much to drink. Time, old boy, to hit the sack.'

The following morning the whole team were at their desks at the usual time, following morning prayers. If anybody was suffering a hangover nobody was admitting to it. Hangovers were for wimps.

'Nick,' Napier put his head around Hunter's door, 'we're off to Barry Buddon. Coming?'

Hunter looked at his in-tray of paperwork. 'Getting rid of last night's PE haul?'

'Yes – we've taken the serial numbers and Isobel is trying to trace where the dets, receivers and transmitters came from. Burg's taking us.'

'Okay. The fresh air will do me good. Give me ten minutes.' Barry Buddon was a point of land between Carnoustie and Monifieth that defined the north east of the Firth of Tay. It was a firing and explosives range consisting of sandy hillocks and salt-laden earth. The helicopter landed mid-morning and the team were soon engaged in setting off the semtex and the detonators. The PE in each firing ring had been weighed and indeed found to be 12 kilos. They used a small amount to light a fire and boil water for coffee while the PE was split into 4 kilo piles and exploded by a single detonator.

It was time consuming work. Four kilograms still made for a loud bang and they didn't want to disturb too many of the locals. By the time coffee was ready they had set off seven explosions. By lunch time only the PE from the Chapter House was left.

'I've brought extra dets and a firing circuit,' said Hunter, 'since this lot didn't go off in the cathedral.'

'I'll try it first, boss,' said Badonovitch, 'otherwise we'll have to blow the dets as well.'

Hunter nodded.

The first four kilos went off as normal. As did the second and the third. As each explosion erupted Hunter found his mouth becoming drier. He remembered the presence he had felt at his shoulder – but there had been nobody there. He remembered the terrorist pushing repeatedly at his transmitter button, calling out to Allah. He also remembered the overwhelming feeling of calm and peace that had descended on him and he wondered.

13

Jerry Stapizki straightened his tie, ran his fingers through his hair and entered the room in the hospital. Chantelle Suchard was sitting in a wheel chair, a book unheeded on her lap. Her hair was lank and she had lost a good deal of weight.

'How are you feeling?'

In a bitter voice she asked, 'How do you think I feel? I'll be stuck in this wheelchair for the rest of my life. I hope,' she added, 'your jails are cripple friendly.'

Stapizki shook his head. 'Nope. I'm afraid not. But we've no shortage of murderesses to help you up and down the iron stairs. I can just see them, carefully tucking a blanket around your legs, putting you on the toilet, helping you into bed . . .'

'Bastard!' Tears sprung to Chantelle's eyes.

'What do you expect?' The FBI agent leant against the wall and crossed his arms.

'I've co-operated fully. Told you everything I know. Charles Gustav is the brains behind the unrest in Europe. He planned the attack so that American hysteria would force your troops to be withdrawn and brought back here. And it's happening! He was right!'

Stapizki nodded. 'I fear my fellow countrymen are nothing but predictable. Which is why we have to move fast with the information you've given us. Here, you'd better read this.'

Taking an envelope from his pocket he thrust it into Chantelle's hands and stepped back Tentatively she opened the legal sized envelope and withdrew a single sheet of paper. Unfolding it, she read slowly, with obvious trepidation. Finally she looked up at him with confusion in her eyes.

'What does it mean?'

'It's pretty clear. There's to be no trial because of your cooperation. Cognisance has been taken of the fact that you're crippled from the waist down, but the return of feeling in your upper body was entirely down to the treatment you received here at the hospital. You should consider yourself lucky under the circumstances. Many felt you hadn't deserved the help you received in view of your role in Gustav's plans. However, you are to be kept in a safe place while we continue to debrief you.'

'How long?'

Stapizki shrugged. 'Until we're satisfied you've nothing left to tell us. It won't be pleasant, I assure you.'

'And after that?'

'You'll be deported. You'll never be allowed back into the United States again.'

Tears trailed down her cheeks and she awkwardly wiped them away with the back of her hands.'

Stapizki reached for a box of tissues and placed them in her lap. 'It's out of my hands now. You'll be moved in a few hours. Don't worry, there'll be medical assistance available if it's needed.'

She nodded. 'I've been racking my brains for anything else I can tell you about Gustav but he operates strictly on a need-toknow basis. His homes, the ones I've mentioned already, are all I know about.'

'What the hell does a man want with seven houses?'

Chantelle shrugged. 'He needs a base in the countries he visits most regularly. The house in Palermo is new.'

'Why Sicily? I'd have thought he'd get too much attention from the Mafia.'

Chantelle smiled. 'There's sense in Charles' madness. Think about it, the Mafia want a whites-only Europe more than anybody. All black and Asian criminal gangs taken out at one stroke? Europe for Europeans affects more than just legitimate businesses. The white crime cartels will clean up, big time. He's there to get that message across to them. After all, the Italian government is in the pockets of organised crime.'

The FBI agent nodded. She wasn't telling him anything new on that score. But the Gustav slant was interesting. It made sense. The crime cartels wielded a great deal of power in many parts of the world, including the good old US of A.

Chantelle had obviously been using his silence to think too. She had one trump card to play and as a gesture of goodwill she decided to deal it. 'He's got a boat. A small ship really. Called the *Stockholm*.'

'Where does he keep it?'

Chantelle shrugged. 'All over. It cruises between Scandinavia and the Med with a professional crew. It's big enough for a helicopter pad.'

'What does he do for fun? To enjoy himself?'

Chantelle looked startled. 'I . . . I hadn't thought of that. I've never seen Gustav enjoying himself. Never relaxing with anybody. And I have never seen him drink alcohol. He's . . . obsessed.' She halted then began again. 'He's totally driven by his ideology, fanatical about a whites-only Europe. He'll stop at nothing.' She frowned and then added, 'It's almost as if for Gustav the world ceases beyond Europe. He sucks in assets, money, raw materials and gives back as little as he can. He was . . .' again she paused, searching for the right words, 'uncomfortable when he was in America. He couldn't wait to get back to Europe. It was most peculiar to see such a sophisticated man so ill at ease outside what he considers his environment. I've never known anyone else like him.'

'Any women in his life?'

'No, I don't think so.'

'Any sexual liaisons of any kind?'

'He's not homosexual. And if you mean boys and girls, the answer is no. Charles thinks paedophiles should be hanged or castrated.'

'Finally, one redeeming characteristic. Okay, you rest now. You're looking tired. I'll be back later.'

She nodded, too dispirited to care.

* * *

Macnair read the FBI report with interest. Chantelle Suchard's information confirmed all the research Isobel had done on Gustav. The tip-off about the ship was new though. It was probably owned by a series of companies, all offshore and virtually untraceable. He would need to find the *Stockholm*.

The list of houses tallied with what they already knew. But currently Gustav wasn't located at any of them. Macnair allowed himself to play Devil's Advocate for a moment. Even if Gustav was killed, would it be too late to stop the backlash against nonwhite Europeans and immigrants? Macnair knew there was a critical mass element. At some point it would become unstoppable, no matter what they did. Gustav and his news media had to be destroyed. To do so he needed over-whelming evidence that the atrocities being committed through-out Europe were actually being perpetrated by the very people who were denouncing Islam and the immigrants. Evidence that stood up in court. It had to be in-your-face, irrefutable, shocking, strong enough to force right-wing newspapers, television and radio stations to come down firmly on the side of the non-white Europeans. To admit that they were an asset to whichever country they were settled in.

Of course he had an ally in the European Parliament. The only trouble was, if Christine stood up and made any accusations, no matter how well founded, her life wouldn't be worth a wooden euro. He balked at the idea of using her. Yet time was of the essence.

Elections were due in Germany, and soon in France. A shift to the right in either country would prompt the same in other democracies. And although Italy and Spain weren't due to vote until next year, anything could happen to force an election. Italy was on a knife edge as it was. If her government lost any more parliamentary motions they would *have* to have a General Election.

Was there time to get a man on the inside of Gustav's organ-isation? To steal as much information about Gustav's main supporters as possible? With that knowledge Macnair could decapitate the right-wing hydra. Knowledge at that level could divert an international tragedy. Shaking his head, Macnair lifted the red phone on his desk which connected him directly to the Prime Minister. He was aware of the limit of his mandate.

The Prime Minister knew immediately that the call would be the harbinger of bad news. Malcolm Macnair only rang when it was serious.

'Prime Minister, sorry to trouble you.'

'I've just been reading your report on the operation at St Mungo's. Good work.'

'Luck played a significant role, Prime Minister.'

'I didn't like to say so, but you're right. What's particularly gratifying is that TIFAT has been kept out of it. The ACC is claiming that his police team did the work.'

'Yes. It's better that way. Thanks for getting the Chief Constable off our backs.'

The PM chuckled. 'Think nothing of it. We called him to a COBRA meeting as a matter of great urgency. The pompous ass was full of it. He was extremely upset at the success of your operation. It was almost as if he had wished you'd failed and St Mungo's *had* been destroyed.'

'It would have been if we hadn't made our move.'

'Agreed.' The Prime Minister sighed. 'The galling fact is, we appointed Blackwater. So I can't even blame the Tories.'

Macnair chuckled. 'That's what comes of being in office for so long. Eventually the buck does stop with you.'

'On that note, why have you called?'

Macnair brought the Prime Minister fully up to date. He listened attentively. His lawyer's training stood him in good stead at times like this. When Macnair had finished he was silent for a few moments.

'I don't know if I can sanction that. I'd never get it past the Cabinet. My own party is already leaping up and down in agita-tion as it is. They still haven't learnt the lessons of the past. Immigration, crime and perceived inequalities are making the working class rebel. That's why the Home Sec must get tough on bogus asylum seekers. And we must stop the atrocities being committed. Even if they are being orchestrated by Gustav and his men, the Muslims are being seen to carry out the acts. And in politics it's people's perceptions that count.'

'I'll leave the politics to you, sir. I can't think of a better idea than the one I've put to you.'

'Oh, the idea is first class – but I won't be able to sanction it.' The PM's words were clear.

'What about your blessing?'

'That you have – unofficially.'

'It's probably for the best. This way we can keep a lid on matters for as long as possible. The fewer people who know the better.'

'Why, General, you aren't suggesting my Cabinet leaks are you?' There was humour in the question.

'No more than a colander, sir. Even if we don't have your sanction, you can help ease matters considerably. There is one important factor. At the right time you will need to make a great deal of political noise across the world. We need to muster every pundit who will come down on our side. Have every talk show in Europe decrying the fascists, while supporting Europe's non-whites. I can't stress how important public opinion will be. Already I think it's too close for comfort. Gustav is winning hands down unless we do something drastic – and quickly.'

'Leave that to me. When you're ready, I'll get Alastair to push all the right buttons, he's good at that.'

Macnair chuckled. The Prime Minister's Press Secretary was *very* good at pressing buttons.

Hunter was sitting in the church in Balfron, his home village. He slouched down in the front pew, his feet outstretched. He was alone and deep in thought. His experience in the cathedral had shaken him. Not the action and the violence. He was used to that. But that feeling he'd had. And the fact that the transmitter hadn't worked. The experience had caused him to seriously question his faith, or lack of it. He knew he was trying to find a rational explanation where none existed. Intellect alone couldn't unravel mysteries pondered for centuries by greater men than he.

He didn't expect an answer to his musings and he wasn't surprised when he didn't get one, though he felt the benefit of time spent in contemplation. He stood up and walked out the front door, taking a little of the peace and solitude he had found with him. Maybe, he thought cynically, I'd better start behaving as if there really *is* a God.

Walking down the hill he enjoyed his stroll back to the house. His parents were out at some dinner party or other. He'd been invited but had cried off. He badly needed some time to think. And plan. Macnair's latest idea was so crazy it might just work. But the ruse was exceedingly dangerous, before, during and after. Who would be the best people to trust for this one? The decision was quickly made. Matt, Jan, Doug Tanner and Douglas Napier. Tanner would be perfect, being black.

His parents' house had been extended out from the kitchen and Hunter effectively had his own quarters. He sat at a desk, a whisky near at hand, a synopsis of the operation in front of him. He considered the different options available to them. Three of Gustav's houses were no use. They were too isolated. After the operation there had to be a way of removing the bodies. So that left four other possibilities. Another factor was actually locating Gustav. Well, that wasn't his problem, it was Isobel's, and he had the utmost faith in her.

The four houses which seemed best suited to their purpose were Munich, Oslo, Fontainebleu and Spiez. Isobel had found architects drawings and had satellite photos of all the properties. The operation in each case would be almost identical, differing only in the detail.

His glass of whisky was sitting untouched by his elbow and he raised it to his lips to take a sip. At that moment his sat-nav phone rang. With a curse he placed it to his ear. 'Hunter.'

'Nick, Isobel. Gustav will be spending the next two days at Spiez.'

'When does he arrive?'

'As near as I can tell, about midnight tonight their time. One hour ahead of us.'

'I'll be back in an hour. Do we have any contacts in Switzerland?'

'A bit of luck, really. We have someone MI6 used twice a few years ago. His father was a Royal Naval officer, his mother Swiss. He lives in a small suburb of Thun known as Uetendorf. In Altelsweg Strasse.'

'How reliable is he?'

'For what we want, we think he'll do. He's a bit of a playboy but the sort you can rely on in a difficult situation. He's proven that on more than one occasion. He took a bottle in the eye a few years ago in a fight involving one of Six's men. He was trying to calm the situation. I'd say, reading his record, tough enough when required.'

Hunter wasn't convinced. 'And do we definitely need him?'

'He's on the spot. He's also got a speed boat licensed for the Thunersee. More importantly he's got a house you can hole up in. Saves using hotels. Nick, think it through. It's your op. Over to you.'

'Thanks, Isobel. I'll see you soon. What's his name?'

'Oliver Michael. There's a note here in his record. Known as Olikins.'

Hunter replaced the receiver in disgust. *Olikins! What sort of a stupid name was that?*

He poured the whisky down the sink, wrote a brief note to his parents and climbed into his MGB. He broke the speed limit all the way back to Rosyth.

In the briefing room he found the General, Isobel and his team. Macnair stood in front of his hand-picked audience and said, 'This is probably the most difficult and ultimately dangerous job you can possibly undertake. Lieutenant Commander Hunter will have briefed you on the outline. No doubt he can now fill in the detail. Nick?'

'Thank you, sir.' Hunter got to his feet and stood with his hands behind his back. 'We've got all the props we need. It will come down to your acting ability. You've all seen enough people killed in your time, so you know how to react. Just go with it. You know the difference with the mags. Don't mix them up.'

That earned him a chuckle, though they were all aware of the deadly earnest behind Hunter's words.

'Where are we kipping when we get there?' Doug Tanner asked.

Isobel looked at Hunter who shrugged. 'With some toss-pot called Olikins.' His expression earned some real laughter.

They continued discussing their options until there was no more to say.

The briefing over, the men left. Hunter was already at the door when Macnair called to him. 'Nick.'

'Sir?' Hunter paused in the doorway and looked back.

'You know the priority. It is absolutely vital we get the information. No matter what the cost.'

'Yes, sir.'

'Be careful. Other agencies will be after the same thing. We've a big enough problem as it is, with inter-agency fighting still going on, in spite of the fine rhetorical speeches following 9/11. There's a lot of resentment from our American cousins, especially the CIA, because of the funding that's being redirected to us. Five and Six are watching us like hawks. You can't rely on them. Not for this one.'

Hunter nodded and left. He was only too well aware of what was at stake.

The next flight out of Scotland to Zurich the following morning was British Airways. In the hold was a diplomatic bag, though to call it a bag was a serious misnomer as it was in reality a large, well-packed trunk. Its contents had little to do with the world of diplomacy either. The team drank the coffee offered by the stewardess but ignored the disgusting excuse for breakfast. They dozed most of the way. Like all soldiers they had learned to sleep whenever the opportunity presented itself. You never knew when you would next get the chance.

Their journey through Zurich customs was quick and effort-less. They were met by a lackey from the British Embassy who took charge of their gear and transport. Soon after arrival they were in a Mercedes People Carrier on the autobahn, heading for Bern and then Thun. There was little talk. Their driver wasn't cleared to hear anything they had to say.

Two hours later they pulled off the autobahn and found themselves in a small mixed industrial and residential area. They stopped alongside an Audi S6.

Their driver pointed at the house door, handed over the car keys and walked away. He was, they decided, a man of few words. Another diplomatic car had followed them to pick him up.

There was no need to ring a bell as the door opened within seconds of their arrival.

Oliver Michael was late twenties or early thirties, blond-haired, clean shaven, about six feet two. His appearance certainly wouldn't hurt his playboy reputation any, Hunter conceded. He had broad shoulders, narrow hips, a square jaw and brown eyes. His handshake was firm.

They went up two flights of stairs and into a spacious living room. 'I've two bedrooms upstairs, a room next to this and the space here. I hope that's okay?' Michael smiled. 'And the coffee maker is over there.'

'Thanks,' said Hunter. 'Can I ask what you've been told so far?'

'Enough, I think. I have been out on the lake this morning looking at the target.' Seeing the team's concerned glances he hastened to reassure them. 'I had a skier behind me and a camera locked onto the house. Will that suit you?'

'Thanks,' said Hunter. 'We aren't used to working with non-combatants. Sorry.'

'That's okay. I learnt a great deal from my father.'

'He was Special Forces?' Dunston asked.

'No. Merely paranoid.' The quip earned Michael a few smiles. 'I think we should take a recce this afternoon. In the meantime I've got my people asking questions in Spiez.'

'Is that wise?' Napier queried.

Oliver Michael grinned. 'Is any of this wise?'

Nobody answered.

'Why are you called Olikins?' Tanner asked.

The grin on Michael's face was quickly replaced by a scowl. 'Let's get this straight. That's a pet name, used only by my mother. The guy from MI6 overheard her and started calling me that to rile me.'

There was more to the story and Napier asked. 'What happened?'

'He returned to England with a few loose teeth. Call me Oliver or Oli.'

'Oli,' said Hunter, 'I have to ask. What's the smell?'

Tanner laughed and answered for their host. 'That, boss, is the all-pervading smell of cannabis. Lot's of it, if I'm any judge.'

'I have an industrial-sized growing room under here. All perfectly legal, so don't look so worried.'

Charles Gustav had landed by sea-plane on the Thunersee. He was in a foul mood. He hadn't been fooled by the police reports. The whole affair at the cathedral had TIFAT written all over it. Well, they'd interfered once too often. He would up the stakes, bring forward every operation he had in the pipeline by at least two weeks. His original idea to control the organisation had evaporated. TIFAT would be history as soon as political power was where it belonged.

In the meantime, en route to his yacht in the Mediterranean, he was forced to spend a couple of days at Spiez. He hated the place. He had bought it only because he needed a legitimate address in Switzerland The house was built on stilts, between the shore and the lake. Underneath was a boat pen, holding two speedboats, each capable of speeds up to 100kph. Not so fast when you considered there was no speed limit on the lake and that the police patrol could reach over 130kph.

He was there to transfer money into dozens of different bank accounts all over the world. Funding terrorism was an expensive business. Normally the transactions were done via computer and passwords, but he was becoming more concerned daily about his personal safety and the security of his operations.

Rumours were beginning to circulate. Soon he would have to instigate a full-scale propaganda offensive of misinformation and denial. Not a problem to a man in his position. He was still vulnerable if the wrong people snooped too closely, in spite of the safeguards he had in place. Because of the debacle in Glasgow his intention to break all ties with the Muslim terrorists he was using had been put on hold.

It was lunchtime, the day was warm and sunny. The view was breathtaking but Gustav was oblivious to the natural beauty around him. He was sitting on the balcony, a cup of coffee cooling at his elbow, carefully studying a flip-pad on his lap. Each page contained meticulous details of a new operation. As he worked through them he marked the corner of the page with a tick or a cross. A tick indicated that the attack could be brought forward. So far he had made almost two dozen ticks although he was less than a third of the way through.

The sound of a speed boat caught his attention. He scowled across the water at the source of the intrusion. Less than a hundred metres away he saw a boat with three men and one skier. They were all laughing, joking and yelling in German. They appeared the worse for drink but it could just as easily have been mere high spirits. It was too early in the day even for a German to get drunk.

Turning his head he addressed the man in dark glasses standing behind him. 'If they get any closer go and warn them off. Explain that the first hundred metres of water is private.'

'Yes, sir.' There was no inflection, and almost no discernible accent. René Faubert was six feet six inches tall, blond haired, broad shouldered and without a trace of fat on him. He spoke seven languages fluently and until recently had been a Captain in the fabled Vatican Guard. More money and limitless travel had persuaded him to join Gustav. That and his deep hatred of foreigners, Muslims in particular. His guard detail consisted of himself plus five others. All tough, utterly ruthless and completely committed to Gustav and his cause. When Gustav was in Europe he always travelled with them, their task was to protect him. In the words of the American Secret Service, to take the bullet if necessary. It was what they were paid to do.

Faubert spoke into his lapel microphone. A few seconds later the deep throated roar of a powerful engine could be heard under their feet and one of the speed boats nosed into the open.

The boat with the skier was now less than fifty metres away, paralleling the shore and taking no notice of either the house or the boat approaching rapidly from the shore.

'*Sie da! Hier ist Privateigentum – scheren Sie sich weg!*' On board the speedboat the man next to the driver stood up and waved at Hunter and the others.

'*Ich verstehe Sie nicht!*'

The pantomime of not hearing or not understanding lasted a few more exchanges, by which time the boats had drifted to within thirty metres of the house. Gustav was now standing by the rail watching, bristling with anger. He turned to Faubert and said angrily, 'Get rid of those clowns.'

The message was relayed and this time things changed out on the water. The man had stopped yelling and drawn a gun. He ostentatiously drew back the bolt. The gesture was enough to cause the other boat to speed away, Hunter and Napier making rude gestures at Gustav's men, playing their role of obnoxious tourists to the full.

'Did you see Gustav?' Hunter asked.

'Yes,' said Napier. 'And I've got some excellent pictures of the layout. As well as close ups of his men. I'll get them off to Isobel and see if we can match their identities.'

'Thanks, Oli,' Hunter said to the boat's driver.

He was rewarded with a grin and then a sober observation. 'If I had known guns were going to be involved I'd have doubled my fee.' He was silent for a few seconds, 'But then twice nothing is still nothing. Ah, well.'

'You aren't getting paid?' Hunter asked in surprise.

The Swiss shook his head. 'The General asked for a favour and I was happy to oblige, this time.'

'You know Macnair?'

'Sure. Have done for a few years. I've helped him out once or twice before as well as your lot at MI6.'

'Still – no fee . . . Isn't that taking altruism too far?'

'I don't believe in what Gustav is up to. Where does it end? You can't chuck people out of their homes and countries because you don't like the colour of their skin.' Shaking his head he looked keenly at Hunter. 'Are you going to tell me what's really going on or do I just tag along for the ride and hope for the best?'

Hunter pursed his lips, thought for a few seconds and then said, 'We're going to need you tonight so it's only fair you know what's going down.'

Above the roar of the engine he briefed Michael. If he was surprised he didn't show it.

Tanner skied all the way back to the small marina where the boat was kept. They tied up, piled into Michael's black Audi, and drove back to Uetendorf.

That afternoon snippets of information came through from Michael's informants around the picturesque village of Spiez. As far as they could tell, the household consisted of a married local couple, a cook and factotum, plus eight male visitors – Gustav, a secretary and six tall, apparently armed bodyguards. This was only the third time the house had been used in two years.

'Okay, that'll do us,' said Hunter. 'Call off your people, Oli. We don't want to warn Gustav.'

Michael nodded and made a call, speaking heavily accented *Schwiezerdeutsch*, practically unintelligible, even to fluent German speakers like Hunter and Dunston. They went over their plans once more and carefully selected the equipment they would require. All that was left was to wait until the early hours of the morning. Hunter tried telephoning Ruth but had no joy in getting through to Israel. He gave up after his fifth attempt and like the rest of the team settled down to sleep. For once sleep evaded him for some time.

It was 01.00 when they quit the apartment. They were dressed in dark civilian clothing, their combat jackets stowed in the trunk of Michael's Audi. Hunter, Dunston and Michael went to the marina to take the boat while the rest travelled in the Mercedes to Spiez. It would be a two-pronged attack.

14

Hunter sat next to Michael as he eased the boat along the shore. He was in direct contact with the team and Isobel back in Rosyth. Satellite infra-red pictures were being relayed to a small monitor on board. The whereabouts of the house's occupants were clear. One couple asleep in a small annex to the main house were, they guessed, the cook and handyman.

Identification had been received on three of the images sent to Isobel – Gustav, Duval and the ex-Vatican Swiss Guard, Faubert. Two of the others could be ex-SF, one a French Legionnaire, the other from the Royal Marines Special Boats Service. Of the others there was no inkling.

Three of the guards were patrolling the area, two indoors and one on the balcony. The remainder were asleep in different bedrooms. The lake house was as silent as the grave.

Michael's boat puttered to a stop before the noise of the engine reached the shore. Hunter and Dunston sat with their oxygen rebreathers on, purging their bodies of carbon dioxide. After two minutes they cleared the black bag that sat across their chests and slipped into the water. They quickly left the surface and swam around the shore, only a few metres under the water. The depth was sufficient to ensure that any cameras, infra-red and light-enhancing equipment didn't see or sense them.

The two men surfaced under the boat shed. Silently they clambered onto the nearest speedboat and stripped off their diving gear and dry suits. They checked the silencers on their weapons and went up the solid concrete steps to the balcony above. Hunter led the way. A guard was standing with his back to the house, looking out across the lake, diligently using binoculars, sweeping the area and then glancing at the TV size monitor on a table next to him. The combined light-enhancing and infra-red camera showed nothing moving on the water.

The distance to the guard was too great. The monitoring equipment was state-of-the-art, so it was safe to assume that the man carried a quick-response alarm on him that he could reach instantly. The night was so still that the man's movements, cloth on cloth, could be heard faintly. To cross the open space undetected was nigh on impossible. Hunter decided to try it. Stepping onto the wooden balcony from the shadows of the stairwell, Hunter was ready to shoot if necessary. The single pace he took was enough. The guard was already turning to see what had caused the intrusion when Hunter shot him. Two rounds, one into the heart, the other into the head. The gun made a sound like a sheep coughing on a faraway hillside but the guard's body fell with a clatter that was heart-thumpingly loud in the night.

Hunter contacted Napier. 'Are you ready?'

'Negative, boss. We're still checking the alarm system. We've placed the plastic. And we've glued the door and windows of the annex shut.'

'Roger that.' Hunter didn't waste his breath telling Napier to hurry. They each knew their job and what was expected.

Ten minutes elapsed before Napier confirmed, 'Ready.'

'Okay. Hit it and drive them this way.'

Gustav had paid a handsome price for his privacy. The house stood in splendid isolation far from other houses in the area. The shaped charge that blew open the front door and took out a downstairs side window was barely heard a hundred metres away.

Hunter and Dunston entered the house by the simple expedient of opening the balcony door and stepping inside. Over their radios Isobel's voice came clearly to all the team. 'Everybody's awake and moving. The two guards are hurrying towards the break-ins. One will pass the main stairway any second now.'

Hunter stood on the third stair and waited. The guard appeared and Hunter shot him twice, both head taps. He fell dead, his blood a black pool reflecting in the moonlight streaming through the window.

The second guard, the only other person sufficiently awake to react fast enough, was approaching the blown door cautiously, his gun held straight out in a two-handed grip. Napier was in the doorway, crouching, his NVGs showing the man as clearly as daylight. Two shots dealt with him. Europe was heading towards the most appalling bloodshed and violence and it had to be stopped. The men guarding Gustav were well-trained professionals. They were the sort you didn't give a second chance to. By now the remaining three guards would be wide awake, fully alert, armed and dangerous. Isobel was able to tell them the location of each individual. Two of the images were static, the other three were on the move. It was safe to assume they were the remaining guards.

Badonovitch and Tanner appeared in the door and followed Napier into the house. The corridor was long, with rooms opening off on both sides. The house layout was, in effect, upside down, with the living quarters built on the upper floor to take advantage of the views. The bedrooms were downstairs. A door was opening cautiously on the left.

Napier let loose a hail of gunfire from his silenced BXP South African sub-machine gun. The bullets thudded into the door and wall and hit the guard along the arm and in the side of the head. He flew backwards across the room.

One down. Two to go. It was vital to leave Gustav and Duval without protection.

Isobel's voice was heard once more. 'Two of them are at the end of the corridor, by the door leading to the basement. They've split up. One is going up the back stairs while the other is crouching in the doorway to what I'm fairly certain is the basement.'

The time for finesse was past. Napier hurled a flash-bang along the corridor and as it exploded he pulled the trigger on his gun back two stops to fully automatic. Twenty rounds of 9mm Parabellum bullets followed the searing white light and loud bang. The guard was hit in the arm and leg, blinded by the while light and deafened. But like the professional he was, he attacked back. Tanner killed Faubert, shooting another hail of bullets across the prone figure of Napier, who had thrown himself to the floor.

Badonovitch took off up the back stairs. Dunston had already turned around and rushed back to meet the last remaining guard. He was caught in a trap between the two TIFAT men and died quickly.

Reports were made on their personal radios. The way was clear to Gustav and Duval.

Hunter stood to one side and tapped on the door of one of the bedrooms. 'Come out with your hands up or we shoot,' he said loudly in German.

The door was practically blown apart as a machine-gun, unsilenced, opened fire. Taking a grenade from a pouch, Hunter threw it through the shattered wood. It was still in the air when it exploded. There was a loud scream and Hunter followed the flash-bang into the room. Gustav was on the floor, his eyes screwed tightly shut, in obvious distress.

Hunter hauled him to his feet and sat him on the bed. The two men were alone for a few moments.

'Who are you?' Gustav demanded. The white spots in front of his eyes were fading and the ringing in his ears was easing. If he was afraid he wasn't showing it. Over the decades he had been in many tight spots – a man of his convictions attracted enemies. But this time he realised he would need more than luck to emerge with his skin in tact. 'More to the point, what are you? Special Services?'

'*Das ist unwichtig,*' said Hunter.

'Speak English. I can hear the faint accent. But of course, you people are all multi-lingual now, aren't you? Who do you work for? TIFAT? Are you Macnair's bunch?'

'Very good, Mr Gustav.'

Gustav squinted up at the soldier standing in front of him. His vision was clearing and he could make Hunter out. Just as he thought, all brawn and no brains. What would it take to get him out of the situation he was in? Time was running out! 'What do they pay you, eh? What's it worth to risk life and limb for an ungrateful government?' There was no response so he decided to try the Islamic card. 'Lost any comrades in the war against the Muslims?' Still no reaction. 'I will pay you ten million pounds sterling to let us go.' Now he got a reaction.

'That's a great deal of money, Mr Gustav. Two million for each of us.'

'Enough so that you can vanish and live a very happy life.'

'It does sound like it. And it's very tempting.' There was doubt in Hunter's voice and Gustav allowed himself a small smile. It never failed. Greed was a very powerful motivating factor.

'The problem is,' said Hunter in a heavy voice, 'that my men have principles.'

'Every man has his price.'

'Some men cannot be bought, Mr Gustav, no matter how much you offer.'

'Perhaps,' said Gustav, hearing the hesitation in Hunter's voice.

'Let's go, Mr Gustav,' said Hunter, keeping his voice deadpan.

The rest of the team were inside the house, ostensibly searching it. The couple who looked after the house were safely glued up in the annex.

Hunter used his radio to call the team back to the balcony. When they trooped up they stood with their backs to the low balcony railing.

Hunter untwisted the silencer off his machine gun and changed the magazine. He said in a loud and harsh voice, 'Drop your weapons. All of you.'

'Nick! You can't be serious,' said Dunston. 'What on earth are you up to?'

'I've just been given ten million reasons to let Mr Gustav go.'

'If you do this we'll hunt you down wherever you go. You'll never enjoy the money,' said Napier.

'Nick,' there was pleading in Dunston's voice, 'I know you've had your last warning from Macnair. But you can go back to general service.'

207

'And you know if I do,' Hunter replied brusquely, 'that my career is over. There's nothing left. A few years at sea and then early retirement. I'll be washed up with nowhere to go.'

Gustav and Duval were following the exchange in some confusion, hope coursing through their veins.

'But this isn't the way,' said Dunston.

'I'll take my chances,' said Hunter in a calm voice. He knew that Duval's and Gustav's eyesight would be fully clear so this was the moment. Hunter opened fire. The stream of bullets hit his comrades across the chest. Blood flew everywhere. All four flew backwards over the railing and into the water beneath. The chatter of the gun had been loud in the night.

'My God!' Duval spoke in awe.

'Ten million, I think you said, Mr Gustav?' Hunter casually walked to the railing and looked down, as did Gustav. They were in time to see the bodies sink beneath the water, the weight of their clothes taking them down.

Below the surface each member of the team slipped a hand to the cord they wore around their necks. From the cord hung a steel device shaped like a pen. It incorporated a small mouthpiece that they could grip between their teeth and seal with their lips. Twisting one end opened the oxygen flow and in the warm, dark water of the lake they swam silently away, hugging the bottom, leaving no tell-tale signs.

Gustav, suspicious as ever, stood and watched the water for some minutes. By now, in the moonlight, he could see the lake's surface. Instinctive caution and years of watching his back made him wary. He suspected that all was not as it seemed. Minutes later, however, none of the bodies had resurfaced and his doubts began to dissipate.

Hunter stood dispassionately by his side. 'Their clothes and equipment will have dragged them down. It'll be days until they come back up, depending on how bloated their bodies become.'

'What was that about your career?' Duval asked.

'You heard the man. I'm washed up as far as the navy and

TIFAT are concerned.' Hunter paused for a few seconds before adding, 'I may as well tell you. I was overheard saying that I believed Europe should be for white people. That all immigrants should be deported and all blacks sent back to their country of origin. If their great grandparents came from Nigeria that's where they should go. I said it to the wrong person. I was reprimanded for my views. Since then Macnair has been picking on me all the time. So I knew I had to find a way to get out. As soon as we knew you were behind the unrest in Europe I knew I had my solution. Those men I just killed were, shall we say, the more liberal minded amongst us? Hell, you saw for yourself, one of them was black. But you should know, Mr Gustav, that many of my colleagues think like I do. Or, I should say former colleagues.'

'How do I know you're telling the truth?'

'How do you know?' Hunter allowed incredulity to sound in his voice. 'I just killed four men, for God's sake. How much more proof do you need?'

Gustav nodded thoughtfully. 'So it would seem.'

Hunter thought for a second and said, 'Get one of your men to hack into the Ministry of Defence computer and look me up. It'll all be there.'

'I may do that. What's your name?'

'We need to get away before the police get here,' Hunter said.

'We? Where do you fit into all this, Mr Hunter?'

'You've no bodyguards and nobody to help you until you get away from here. You arrived by sea-plane didn't you?'

'You're particularly well informed.'

'That's our job. We plan every operation carefully and to the nth degree. We always know what's happening.'

'And what about your HQ?'

'They'll think I'm dead along with the others. And as long as they think so, at least until we have the right governments in power, I'm safe. Do you want my help or not? I'm happy to just wait until morning, collect my money, preferably in a banker's draft, and get the hell out of here. Or we leave together.'

Gustav hesitated. He could certainly use somebody as ruthless and with as much apparent ability as Hunter, but on the other hand, could he really trust him? Time was wasting as Gustav pondered the question. Either he was as he seemed and therefore an ally or he could help them escape and Gustav could deal with him later. A dead Hunter would have no use for ten million pounds. The faint sound of sirens coming along the lakeside road from the direction of Interlaken stopped him in his tracks. They could see the flashing lights of a string of police cars.

'With what's happened here the police will hold you long enough for TIFAT to find you. Then it'll be too late.'

Gustav nodded. 'All right. It's time to go. What do you suggest?'

'We take one of the boats into Thun. I have a car parked in a marina near there.' Hunter could see him hesitate.

'That's very fortuitous,' said Gustav.

'No, it's not,' Hunter replied. 'It's simply a well-conceived plan. I'll get the boat flashed up while you and Mr Duval get your clothes and any bags you need.' He looked at the fast approaching cars. 'And I suggest you hurry.'

With the three of them in the speedboat they took off straight across the lake, leaving a wide wake behind them. Neither Gustav nor Duval noticed the TIFAT team sitting quietly in their boat, watching. Gustav had apparently swallowed the bait.

Dunston reported back to Rosyth. There was no need to give chase as they knew exactly where Nick was going. What was more, the car had a tracking device fitted in the trunk which was easily read by satellite. Hunter also had a similar but smaller device fitted in each of his shoes. Unfortunately, the car was Michael's Audi, and his pride and joy. However, he had been promised a replacement – with all the gadgets he seemed to like so much – if the car wasn't recovered.

They were soon at the marina and Hunter put the boat in Michael's empty berth. At the car, Hunter stripped off his combat gear and put on a white shirt and charcoal grey suit. The tie he took from his pocket was dark red with a faint stripe. He took his time tying it. Gustav became impatient.

'Please hurry, Mr Hunter.'

'We can't fight our way out of Switzerland, Mr Gustav, but we *can* bluff it if we're stopped. We'll dump all the military gear here and drive away normally. You've got your passports? Good, then let's go.'

Hunter opened the driver's door and settled behind the wheel. To his surprise Duval sat next to him, with Gustav in the back. Considering what the two men had been through, Hunter was further surprised by how relaxed they seemed. If their *sang froid* was a sham, they were extremely good actors.

'Which way do you propose we go?' Gustav asked.

'Bern, Neuchâtel, Pontarlier. That's where we cross the border into France. The border's manned but cars are very rarely stopped. If an alert goes out, I think we can expect things to be different. The customs are good, well trained and armed. Will the police be able to connect you to the house on the lake?'

Gustav's reply was short and to the point. 'No.'

'What about the staff?'

'They know me only as Mr Steinway. They *believe* that's my name. The house cannot be traced back to me, Mr Hunter.'

The car moved onto the autobahn and accelerated towards Bern about twenty minutes away. The first roadblock they hit was on the outskirts of the capital. There were two cars ahead of them and they pulled up behind. The cars were quickly allowed through and the Audi drew up beside an unthreatening and unarmed policeman. Hunter wasn't fooled. The armed police were there, watching, careful, unobtrusive.

'*Guten Tag.*' The policeman touched the peak of his hat.

'*Grüss Gott*,' replied Hunter, not to be outdone with the courtesies.

Their conversation was in German. Papers and passports were presented, due respect was shown to Charles Gustav, his secretary and their chauffeur and they were waved through.

Hunter pulled sedately away, staying within the speed limit, bearing right onto the E25 minutes later. To reach Neuchâtel they pulled off the autobahn and onto a two-lane highway. In the early morning the roads were deserted and they continued to make good time. Dawn was breaking when they arrived at the customs post five kilometres before Pontarlier.

Already a long line of lorries had built up. Trade between Switzerland and France was prolific. Many trucks from Italy and Austria used Swiss roads to avoid the high tariffs on French motorways. Extra hours of driving were often considered well worth the price. Normally the lorries went through without any delay. Customs were cursory unless they were looking for something specific and acting on a tip-off. What they *did* check was that the vehicle was displaying this year's badge showing the driver had paid the one-off fee for the licence to drive on Swiss motorways.

Hunter patiently switched off the engine and settled down to wait. Looking over his shoulder he said, 'You can go back to the restaurant if you wish and eat breakfast. This is going to take a long time.'

Gustav looked at Hunter and said, 'I am not a man used to being kept waiting. Duval.' He nodded to his secretary who immediately climbed out of the car and walked the hundred metres or so to the customs post. He was back within minutes.

'Pull out and go ahead.'

In truth, Hunter had expected little else, but he managed to plaster an impressed look on his face. Gustav merely stared back at him.

The car was waved straight through.

'We'll stop at Pontarlier for breakfast,' Hunter announced.

'We keep going,' said Gustav.

Hunter looked at his new employer in the rear-view mirror and said, 'I've been going all night. I need sustenance. I need carbohydrates, protein and caffeine. And not necessarily in that order. You need me fit and alert. You've got TIFAT after you, Mr Gustav, and they won't give up until they get you. It may take them a while to learn that you've survived the attack. But when they do and when they find the team they sent after you is missing, presumed dead, then there isn't a rock you can hide under where they won't find you.'

Gustav blanched. Fear was a wonderful motivator and an even

212

better clouder of judgement. It would help to keep the initiative with Hunter, at least until Gustav felt safe again. The Swede nodded as the car pulled up outside a large alpine hotel and restaurant. Although it was early there were already several cars and lorries parked outside.

Locking the car and pocketing the key, Hunter led the way inside. The layout was typical of the region. Heavy tables and high-backed bench seats were in serried rows. The air was thick with smoke and the aroma of freshly cooked food. There was nothing as politically correct as a 'No Smoking' area in this French stop-over. The middle-aged, and somewhat frumpish waitress quickly took their order. The coffee was served in moments. 'Where are we heading?' Hunter asked, after an appreciative sip of his drink.

Gustav sat pondering the question for some moments before replying. 'I'm still not entirely sure I trust you Mr Hunter.'

Hunter broke a bread roll, added butter and took a mouthful with relish. 'That's up to you. We'll wait here. The banks open around nine. I want you to arrange a banker's draft for the ten mill. I know you can do it. After all, a deal is a deal. Then I'm out of here. You make your own arrangements. A taxi will take you to Besançon. You can get a train from there to anywhere you wish.'

'That's a great deal of money, Mr Hunter.'

'I'll need every penny of it, if I'm to hide from TIFAT. They take a dim view of betrayal, Mr Gustav. And particularly the murder of their own people. You, on the other hand, can never hide. Your only hope is to get your people to power. To break TIFAT before they come after you. But you'll have to move fast. Their mandate is world-wide. And they are the best force ever conceived. They have enormous resources and backing from governments all over the world. General Macnair has access to Presidents and Prime Ministers, although to the best of my knowledge he has never abused the privilege. They know they can trust him and rely on him. His men will follow him to the ends of the earth. He has a natural gift for leadership.'

'Except with you.'

Hunter pulled a sardonic face and shrugged. 'The exception that proves the rule. You don't have to believe me. Quite frankly, I don't care. I did what I did because I believe in your cause. I'll happily take the money, then let you battle it out and decide what I do depending on the outcome. You win and I settle back in Europe. You lose, I sail the high seas and settle in a land far enough away that TIFAT won't know where I am.'

'Is there such a place?' It was Duval who asked the question and for a second it took Hunter by surprise. Then he realised the significance of the question. Duval wanted to know if there was a bolt hole he, too, could use.

'New Zealand would be a safe bet. Japan, if you've got enough money. Although it would have to be Tokyo. You'd easily get lost in the crowds. A small town in the mid-west of America is an equally good bet, especially if you've got the right passport and a green card. I have both.'

'You seem to have planned your options very well, Mr Hunter,' said Gustav thoughtfully.

'I'm a careful man. It's why I've lived so long in a very dangerous job.' He allowed some bitterness to creep into his voice. 'I've risked my life dozens of times for my country and for what? Forty thousand a year and a silver gong they pin on me every now and then! There's a good lad, go and save us yet again. And if you live we'll give you a crappy pension. But if you die! Great news! We'll give you a wonderful funeral with all your friends and colleagues there to say goodbye. If you're unmarried your pension dies with you. A wife? That's different. We'll give her half.' In his anger Hunter crushed a bread roll to pieces, scattering crumbs across the white tablecloth. *A nice touch*, he thought.

The waitress returned with their meals and Duval, without prompting, instructed her to clean up the bread crumbs. Hunter's apparent anger faded as quickly as it had materialised and he settled to eating the scrambled eggs and bacon while it was still hot.

214

Gustav watched Hunter closely for a few seconds then made up his mind. 'Which would you prefer? To be on my payroll or to accept the ten million?'

'How big is the payroll?'

'Half a million euros a year.'

Hunter stopped chewing, took a sip of coffee and said, 'I'll take the ten million. If it's all the same to you.'

Gustav threw back his head and laughed. 'Excellent. The right response. I would never trust a man who gave up the chance of so much money for a cause. Duval, arrange for a banker's draft in Mr Hunter's name – to be ready when we arrive in Palermo. The job is still yours if you want it.'

'What job, exactly?'

'Head of my personal security.' Gustav smiled. 'You were responsible for permanently retiring the last man who held the post.'

'You mean René Faubert?'

'You knew his name?' Gustav's surprise was evident.

'TIFAT found out within seconds of us transmitting his photo-graph to HQ.'

Gustav nodded. 'Of course, the boat, yesterday. Your idea?'

Hunter tried to look modest but failed, miserably. After a few seconds of apparent thought he nodded. 'You've got yourself a deal, Mr Gustav. This way,' he allowed himself a tight smile, 'I get the best of both worlds.'

At Gustav's shark-like smile Hunter felt a shiver go along his spine. He knew he couldn't trust the man an inch. Reaching into his pocket, Hunter took out a small-scale map of Europe. He pointed at the map.

'We're here. Palermo is all the way down there. It's a long drive.'

'And one I don't intend taking,' said Gustav. 'The sea-plane was a charter. It was due to pick us up tomorrow. We can easily arrange for it to meet us somewhere else.'

Hunter nodded. 'I presume you were in Switzerland for a purpose. What business do you still have here?'

Gustav stared at him. 'That's a very astute question, Mr Hunter.

All I need is a major bank in a city or large town. Switzerland was merely convenient. I like their banking laws.'

'Lyon is two hours away. It's still early so the traffic won't be too bad. Even rush hour in this part of France is hardly more than a tractor and an over-laden lorry or two. Will that do?'

'It will be perfect.'

'How long will you need in Lyon?'

'Duval?'

'I'll have everything encrypted and ready to go. I can use the bank's computer, so not more than ten minutes. I'll have it all on a memory stick.'

This time Hunter really was impressed. 'You can get a bank to let you do that? To download information into their system without first checking what's in it?'

Duval frowned as though the question was beneath his understanding. 'Of course. We have established routes through the banking system which we use regularly. We pay a hefty premium for it but it is invaluable. Especially when you consider the sums of money involved. All major banks have the same facilities for large customers. It's like . . . like tentacles that weave across the world, one leading to another, smaller tentacle that eventually gets to the end user. Highly sophisticated and highly effective.'

'That will do,' Gustav snapped. Duval had the good grace to blush.

'If I'm to look after your personal safety then I need to know what's going on. I can be of more use to you then.'

'In theory, you are correct, Mr Hunter. But we will proceed slowly. One task at a time. Your first task is to get me to my destination safely.'

Hunter nodded. 'Fair enough. In that case we had better go. We'll fill up with petrol and while I drive I'll think about getting you safely to Sicily.'

Duval dropped a hundred euro note on the table and the three men departed. This time Gustav sat in the front while Duval occupied the back seat. He was soon busy using his lap-top computer, filling the quiet, high-powered car with an irritating, irregular tapping. By the time Hunter had filled up with petrol,

Gustav had found a radio station playing light classical music which helped to drown out the sounds from the back.

Hunter settled down to enjoy the drive. *So far, so good.*

15

At Lyon Hunter drove around until he found what he was looking for. Less than a block from an international bank he pulled into a multi-storey car park.

When they got out of the car, Hunter said, 'I'll be a few paces behind. When we get to the bank I'll see you inside. From there on you're on your own. I'll be sitting opposite the bank at the café I pointed out. I'll have a newspaper. If it's open in front of me then it's safe to come out. If you can't see the paper then stay in the bank until I'm quite certain there are no problems.'

'What sort of problems are you expecting?' Gustav asked, frowning.

Hunter shrugged. 'I'm just being careful. We have no idea what TIFAT knows right now. It may be everything or nothing. By assuming it's everything we'll live a lot longer. Trust me, I know what I'm talking about.'

Gustav nodded. This time there was a hint less arrogance about the man. Hunter's continual drip-feed of TIFAT's omnipotence was beginning to wear him down.

'And if there are any problems?' Duval asked, licking his lips. The thought of TIFAT close at hand was also beginning to get on his nerves.

'We'll have to cross that bridge when we get to it. I've no weapon and, quite frankly, don't relish the idea of a gun battle in the middle of Lyon. We wouldn't get very far. One of the reasons I picked this bank is the car-park. More importantly, the back entrance leads directly onto a side-street. If I'm not here then go out the back door and wait for me. I'll get to you as soon as I can with the car. When you go through the rear entrance, directly opposite you'll see a bar with a plate glass window. Stand in the window and watch for me. I'll only be gone if I'm seriously unhappy about what I see. And one more thing . . .' He paused and looked at each man in turn. 'I'm alive today because I take precautions. Extra precautions. I will always err on the side of caution. Faubert didn't, which is why he's dead. Better to *look* stupid than to *be* dead. I hope you both understand that.'

Reassured, they both nodded. It made good sense to them.

'While you're in the bank please inform the aircraft hire company that we will require the plane in southern France somewhere. You'll pass to them exactly where no later than close of business today. In the meantime, you wish the plane to be prelocated at Port-de-Bouc on the south coast.'

'Why there?' Gustav asked.

'It's a safe place to land and in easy reach of Montpellier to Monaco. That's where we'll spend the night. Somewhere on the south coast.'

'That's a long way to travel,' Gustav protested, though only half-heartedly. Hunter's thinking intrigued him.

'First of all we'll be on the move, therefore a more difficult target. Secondly, we need to stop for the night and there are so many large and anonymous hotels right along the coast we'll be virtually invisible. Thirdly we can go in-land by car or steal a boat and head out to sea. Which means the plane can come for us and land without any restrictions.'

Gustav nodded, further reassured. He liked what he was hearing.

They walked purposefully along the pavement towards the bank. The streets of Lyon were packed with people going to their work. Early shoppers filled the wide pavements. At the bank, Hunter watched as Gustav and Duval were immediately greeted by what looked like a senior member of staff. So, thought Hunter, Duval's computer also incorporated a mobile phone system. He grinned. Why wasn't he surprised?

He picked up a *Figaro* from a street kiosk and went across the road to the café. The outside tables were only half full and he selected one next to the pavement, with a clear view of the bank. Across the street Duval put his head outside the door and looked over to him. Hunter ignored him. He ordered a large *café au lait* and a croissant and settled down to enjoy both with his paper. Ten minutes later he had finished eating and drinking. He had already paid his bill and so he stood up and walked away. Gustav seemed relaxed now, happy to go along with Hunter's plan. Now it was time to apply pressure. Emotional roller-coasters were ideal for keeping a man off balance. They helped to prevent clear thought.

Back at the car park he paid for the exit ticket at an automatic dispenser. Next to it was a telephone. He was through to Scotland within seconds and reporting events to date, along with his plans. There were no specific instructions for him. The tracking devices in both the car and his shoes were working correctly.

He drove out of the multi-storey and around the city. Lyon had a complicated one-way system and it took him several minutes to get to the street he wanted. Gustav should have finished the transactions by now, and have realised he wasn't at his position in the café. Hunter was in no hurry – let them stew for a while. Cars were parked on both sides of the road, half on the pavement. Driving slowly, he approached the bar behind the bank. He braked and the door flew open. Gustav and Duval hurried out. They piled in and Hunter drove away, tensed over the wheel, his eyes flicking everywhere.

'What happened? Where were you?' Gustav asked.

'I suggest you get down. I had to leave fast. I saw two men I recognised along the street from the bank.'

'Who were they?' Duval asked as both men slid down in their seats.

Hunter suppressed a grin. 'They were both from TIFAT. A Captain Clements and a Sergeant Masters.'

'I'll check the names on the Ministry of Defence computer later,' said Duval.

'Did you look me up?'

'Yes. It made interesting reading. There was a recommendation you be given SNLR, whatever that means.'

Hunter laughed. 'Services no longer required. It looks like I jumped before I was pushed.'

'You didn't tell us you'd hit a senior officer.'

'Nothing to tell. The man was getting on my nerves. Let's leave it at that.'

'How did TIFAT get on to us so quickly?' Gustav asked.

'As I've told you, their resources are incredible. I can guess, though.'

'Then guess,' the Swede ordered.

'They will have blanketed Switzerland with satellite coverage. Every phone call and radio transmission will have been listened to. Certain words will have triggered an automatic response. If the police or customs had reported that you had passed through, which is highly likely, then they'd know about it immediately.'

'But how did they get those men here so quickly?'

'Easily. We have a number of operations going down in this part of the world, mainly to do with anti-Muslim unrest. It would be a piece of cake for Macnair to move operatives into the major cities. After all, where else would we be? He'll also have the local gendarmerie looking for us. We have to be more careful. I think we had better get rid of this car. It's too conspicuous.' Hunter was on thin ice and he measured his words carefully. 'They were doing exactly what I'd expect them to do. Searching for somebody, without firm knowledge of where they are, is a hit or miss affair. Usually the latter. But you'd be surprised how often a chance sighting happens. And I for one won't take a risk. Ever. Please remember that, Mr Gustav and you'll live to a ripe old age. I think you can get up now, gentlemen. We're clear of the city.'

'What now?' Duval asked.

'We stay off the motorways. The pay booths can be alerted and we could easily get caught. We'll stop at Vienne thirty kilometres away. There I suggest you use cash and buy new clothes and toilet gear. It'll be safer if we split up. It will look peculiar, three men together shopping. I'll dump the car and buy us train tickets for Marseilles.'

Gustav was quiet for a few minutes and then he said, 'I'd like you to stay with me, Mr Hunter. Duval can shop alone.'

'Fair enough.' Hunter settled behind the wheel a little more comfortably, satisfied with his progress to date.

Vienne was relatively quiet after the bustle of Lyon. Hunter parked the car in a side-street and the three men walked away from it without a backward glance. Hunter and Gustav went to find a men's clothing shop while Duval located the railway station.

Shopping didn't take long. Much to his chagrin, the small town didn't boast the *haute couture* garments Gustav preferred. He finally settled on a sports jacket and trousers. He also bought two sets of shirts, underclothes and socks. His hand rasping on his chin convinced him of the need for a razor and shaving cream.

Hunter bought shaving gear, boxer shorts and a couple of white shirts. He also found himself a blue tie with a tasteful motif. The suit he was wearing was new and still looked immaculate. Gustav bought a small suitcase, Hunter a leather holdall. Outside the shop they were joined by Duval. He told them that the express south was due in forty minutes. They arranged to meet at the station buffet inside the terminal and Duval went inside the shop.

As they walked along the street Hunter dropped the red tie into a waste bin. Gustav looked at him with a raised eyebrow.

'Ties are a give away for a description.' Hunter didn't elaborate and Gustav didn't ask.

The train departed on time. They sat in a first class compartment, Duval and Gustav side by side, Hunter opposite. They were in the end carriage, next to the engine. Hunter sat facing the length of the train, so no one could approach without being seen. To his travelling companions, Hunter's vigilance was entirely convincing.

'Why don't we take it in turns to wash and brush up?' Hunter suggested. 'There are facilities directly behind us.'

Gustav heaved himself to his feet and Duval moved to let him out.

Once he was away Hunter said, 'Would you like a coffee or something stronger?'

'What did you have in mind?'

'A couple of aperitifs from the restaurant car. What does Mr Gustav drink?'

Duval shook his head. 'Nothing. He's teetotal. Usually. Occasionally, a very special brandy, but I have only ever seen him drink it twice in ten years.'

Hunter nodded. 'In that case I'll forego any alcohol. I don't want to upset the boss. I'm going to walk the train. Take a look at the other passengers. Now we're moving we should be safe enough but as I keep saying, you can't be too careful. I'll be back in ten minutes. All right?'

Duval was tired and merely nodded. 'You know your job,' he said, accepting that Hunter was now part of the team.

Moving effortlessly along the speeding train Hunter arrived at the restaurant car. Using a credit card he telephoned Scotland and reported where he had left Michael's Audi.

'We've got it located. I take it you're on the train?' Isobel said.

'That's right. Did you track the transactions at the bank?'

'Doing so now. Take care, Nick.'

Hunter broke the connection and continued his meandering along the swaying carriages. Turning round he picked up three coffees at the restaurant car and returned to find Gustav back in his seat and Duval away.

'Everything all right?'

Hunter nodded. 'If there's anybody on board, I didn't recognise them. More importantly, no one appeared to take the slightest notice of me. I think we can relax until Marseilles. If you can, I suggest you get some sleep.'

Gustav nodded. 'Not a bad idea. I won't bother with the coffee.' He reclined his seat and closed his eyes. Fairly soon a gentle snore suggested he was in a comfortable doze.

Duval returned. Seeing his boss asleep he downed his coffee and settled back to do the same.

Hunter sat quietly for a few moments thinking about Ruth. Then he stood up and went for a shave and wash. Back in his seat he closed his eyes. He was beginning to feel bone weary. But the closer he got to Gustav's lair the more alert he needed to be. Then sleep would become more problematical – and possibly more dangerous.

The call for the first sitting at lunch woke all three of them.

Back in Scotland, Leo and Gareth, Isobel's 'right and left hands', were doing a superb job. The instructions given to the computer at the bank in Lyon were easily identified by means of a time selection program. Breaking the code was child's play – it only took twenty minutes. Following the paths the money and orders took was relatively simple. Doors in the paths were either circumvented or opened – and always closed behind them.

Isobel updated Macnair continuously. Knocking on his door she handed him another report. 'Thank God Nick made contact – the bank transfer in Lyon has highlighted several new tricks Gustav has up his sleeve. Although everywhere's operating on a state of heightened alert, the intelligence agencies would never have learned of these attacks until it was too late. Another two identified. That makes thirty-three in all.'

'Is the time-scale still the same?'

'Yes, General. The attacks are scheduled to take place within the next five days. And all across Europe. The usual targets – churches, three banks, a cathedral in Spain, four aircraft bombings and seven hijackings.' Isobel shrugged. 'You've got the list. One thing I find very significant; the money to fund the violence is all passing through Saudi banks. The program is closing down right behind the transactions once they arrive in Saudi. If we weren't so close we'd lose them. But then the track becomes very interesting indeed.'

Macnair sat back in his chair and waited patiently.

'The paths become so obvious it's child's play to follow them.'

'Hardly that,' argued Macnair, 'but I take your point.'

'It's like the computer equivalent of a three lane motorway straight back to the Arabs.'

'Neat,' said Macnair. 'Presumably providing enough proof that Arab fundamentalists are behind everything.'

'You've got it, sir. The evidence would convince anybody. Gustav has covered his tracks extremely well. There's a good deal of nascent anger mixed with ancient hatreds out there right now and it'll get a lot worse. The havoc these fresh attacks will cause beggars belief. A lot of innocent people are going to die unless we do something.'

Macnair placed his hands behind his head and said. 'It's our job to stop the attacks. But we'll need a lot of help.'

'Who?'

'Nato. I'll contact Brussels and speak to George.'

'You've always maintained that Nato isn't equipped for work like this. The requirements are too specialised.'

'I know. We'll put some of our men with each Nato detachment.'

'Sir, *nobody* is going to like that. Not Nato and certainly not our people.'

'I don't have any choice, do I? We're stretched about as thin as possible if we're still to function. We're down to a skeleton staff here and right now I'm having to recall troops who are long overdue for leave. Every Nato country from Belgium to Turkey is involved with the exception of Canada. There are three operations alone in the United States.'

'America can look after itself.' Isobel sounded callous but both of them knew what she meant. It was the one Western country that took its security seriously. 'They have the resources and the manpower to do it.'

'Where are our weakest links?'

'I'd have to say Belgium, Greece and Portugal. And not necessarily in that order. Of the rest, I don't see the Icelanders or the police in Luxembourg being much use. Apart from that, we ought to be able to contain what happens because of the detailed information we have. We know where, what, who and when. It can't get much better in intelligence terms.'

'That's what I thought. What's the latest on Hunter?'

'He's on a train heading for Marseilles. Gustav and Duval are with him. He's now Gustav's new head of security.'

Macnair summoned up a grin. 'Good for Nick. Let's hope he

gets us what we want. Okay. Leave this with me. I've got calls to make.'

Lunch was superb, considering they were on a fast moving train. Nobody drank anything other than water followed by coffee. Hunter's steak was the best Aberdeen Angus, once more available now that France had lifted it's illegal embargo on UK beef imports into the country.

'When we get to the next stop,' Gustav instructed Duval, 'buy as many newspapers as you can find.'

'I can download from the internet,' he offered. 'The world's an electronic village square.'

Gustav waved his hand. 'You know I don't like reading off the screen. Get me the hard copy. Which town is next?'

'Valence,' Hunter replied. 'And this looks like it.'

Duval hurried to the door and was waiting for the train to stop. He alighted quickly and rushed to the kiosk selling newspapers. He grabbed one of each, threw a fifty euros note to the man behind the counter and hurried away.

The Algerian nodded his thanks and pocketed the money. He would say a special thank you to Allah at evening prayers.

The doors were already closing when Duval climbed back onto the train.

Hunter was speaking to Gustav. 'The plane can wait for us at Port-de-Bouc. We'll spend the night in Marseilles – it's big and anonymous. I want to hire a car. Something powerful, just in case.'

'Then do so,' Gustav frowned. He hated being bombarded with petty detail.

'They will want credit card and passport details. The passport is no problem. I have a false one. The credit card, unfortunately, is in my real name. The instant I use it TIFAT will find out.'

Gustav looked up from yesterday's Washington Post in some surprise. 'I thought you had all this planned?'

Hunter scowled. 'To have a false credit card you need money, big money. When I get my ten million, I'll have sufficient credit cards to satisfy me. More importantly, ones that will match my new passport.'

'What do you suggest?'

'Duval can hire the car. A big Citröen or Peugeot. We also find a hotel. Not too big and not a flea-pit either. Near the harbour where the pleasure craft are berthed. We'll also take a twenty-four hour hire on a fast speed boat.'

'Why?'

'To give us options. A car along the coast or a boat if we need it. A car can be followed, a boat less so, especially if they aren't ready for it.'

'You sound as though you expect somebody to be waiting for us,' said Gustav. The feeling of safety he had been enjoying after the good lunch was fading fast.

'I don't expect anything,' Hunter corrected him. 'But I plan for all eventualities. It's the only way. Believe me.'

'Oh, I believe you, Mr Hunter. And I like your thoroughness. Now if you will excuse me, I would like to get back to my newspapers.'

Hunter nodded and sat back in his seat. Gustav and Duval read the news. Both men appeared satisfied by the stories they were reading. Hunter read the English and German papers.

One item came as a shock and was in all the newspapers. In France a new draconian law had just been passed. In order to claim citizenship you had to prove that at least one great-grandparent was French born. Without it you were no longer considered *vraiment Français*. And your passport was to be amended accordingly. Many immigrants, first, second and even third generation, were beginning to panic. If they didn't leave now would they be able to get away later with their money and possessions? Political unrest was mounting. Acts of violence against innocent people were becoming commonplace. More and more often, if the victims involved were non-white or non-European, the police stood by and watched. Europe was fast becoming a powderkeg.

Tapping the paper in front of him, Hunter asked, 'Did you know about these new French citizenship laws?'

Gustav looked at him in some surprise. 'Yes. I helped draft them. They are merely the start. We will tighten the screws at

227

every opportunity until all non-white foreigners leave. Do you have a problem with that?'

Hunter forced a smile. 'Not at all. I hope to see the rest of Europe following France's lead soon.'

'You will, Mr Hunter. Believe me, you will.'

Hunter nodded his satisfaction and continued reading, seething with anger. He decided to interrupt their evident enjoyment. 'I need some cash for expenses,' Hunter said to Gustav, who nodded to Duval. The latter reached into his briefcase and extracted a wad of notes, counting out five thousand euros in mixed bills. Hunter pocketed the money.

The train pulled under the huge canopy of Marseilles railway station and glided to a smooth and silent halt. The three men stood, stretched cramped limbs and prepared to disembark. Hunter went first, paused in the doorway and glanced along the platform. The main concourse was only a few metres away and was teeming with people of various shapes, colours and dress. Marseilles was one of the most cosmopolitan cities in Europe and had, by far, one of the most diverse populations. Many of her inhabitants were from North Africa, stretching from Morocco to Egypt. But vast numbers came from former French colonies south of the Sahara.

Hunter cast a glance at Gustav as they forced their way through the throng. The Swede was having to work hard to keep the distaste off his face. When a black woman, in native dress, bumped into him and turned to apologise, his look of venom caused her to back away with fright. Gustav actually shuddered at the contact.

Hunter walked around the suitcases and boxes of goods piled up at the travellers' feet, deliberately weaving a complex path to the main entrance.

Half way Gustav caught him by the arm. 'Can't we go straight outside? The smell of these . . . these cattle disgusts me.'

Much to Hunter's amusement Gustav was looking ill. He was pasty white and sweating. Hunter wondered what had caused such a deep-rooted xenophobia. 'It makes it more difficult for a man with a rifle to predict our path and shoot you.'

'I'll risk it. Just get me out of here.'

Next to the huge entrance Hunter paused at a kiosk and bought a guide book, this being his first visit to Marseilles.

Within moments they were in the warm, humid air of the bustling city. Even here there was little respite. Beggars approached with hands held out, others offered trinkets for cash, still more had oranges and slices of melon for sale. The one thing they all had in common was their dark complexion. Gustav looked like he wanted to be sick.

Deciding it was time he earned his money, Hunter went to the front of the taxi queue and pushed aside the man about to climb in. As the man turned to protest Hunter thrust a hundred euros note into his hand. He looked at it in astonishment before nodding his thanks. By this time Gustav and Duval were in the car and Hunter climbed into the front passenger seat.

The driver turned to protest at the rough treatment of his potential fare but thought better of it. Hunter didn't look like a man to argue with. Besides, he had also seen the money exchanging hands.

'*Ou partir, messieurs?*'

'Drive,' Hunter said in English. He looked back over his shoulder as the car pulled away, his eyes scanning the train station.

The driver was a scrawny African, with grey curly hair. He had his window open and was smoking. A torrid mouthful of French from Gustav caused the man to go rigid with tension before contemptuously flicking the cigarette away. '*Comme vous voulez, monsieur.*'

The Gare St Charles gave way to the Place Victor Hugo. It was packed with cars apparently heading aimlessly in different directions. The driver got them through by the judicious use of his horn and middle finger. He paused on the Boulevard Charles Nédelec and looked over his shoulder.

Duval waved a hand indicating straight on. Gustav looked fixedly out of the window. Hunter suppressed a smile. He was flicking through the pages of the guide book and said, 'Quai Des Belges.'

The journey continued in silence. It was only a few kilometres to the Vieux Port. They could probably have walked it as quickly. The streets were packed with people, all carrying suitcases and boxes, all going towards the port. It reminded Hunter of the stories he had read about the Jews leaving Germany in the late thirties. Some had had the sense to get out before it was too late. Most hadn't and had perished.

The taxi deposited the three men at the edge of the old basin. The previously run-down dock area in the decaying city had been transformed during the past decade with European aid. Now fashionable bars and restaurants stood side-by-side with *avant-garde* theatres, small clothing boutiques and ships' chandlers. Looking along the basin from where they stood, they could see the picturesque forts guarding the entrance to the port, Fort St-Jean on the north bank and Fort St-Nicholas opposite.

By now it was early evening and the sun was setting on a warm and humid day. Down both sides of the Vieux Port many tramp steamers were berthed. Filing up the gangways were families – men, women and children, people of all ages – none were white. The bright colours of the Africans contrasted sharply with the white robes and black chadors of Arab men and women.

'Good riddance,' said Gustav with satisfaction. 'Like animals into the ark.' He looked at his secretary, 'We will need to find a way to speed up the process.'

Hunter found the thought chilling.

'Where now, Mr Hunter?'

'The Hotel de Ville. Three star, central, anonymous. Around the corner on the Quai de la Tourette are a number of boat-hire places and over there,' he pointed to the other side of the road, 'is a car-hire.'

The hotel was only a few hundred metres away on the Quai du Port but the pavements and streets were completely packed with people. Climbing out of the taxi, they left it stranded in a sea of humanity. They had to fight their way through the throngs, piles of baggage in their paths. Children were crying, their parents subdued in the oppressive atmosphere. *They're scared*, thought Hunter. *Terrified*. For the first time Hunter felt the fear at grass roots level. After the deaths and destruction of recent weeks, terrorism was no longer a vague concept. It had forced its way into people's lives. He listened to them. They were nearly all speaking French. Idiomatic French. Hunter felt rage surging through him at the injustice of it. If he needed more proof that Gustav had to be stopped, then this was it. These people were abandoning their homes, their livelihoods, their friends, even, for many, their culture. Their French culture. Many talented people were leaving. Doctors and teachers, writers and singers. And many were hard workers prepared to do menial tasks for a pittance, tasks many whites refused to soil their hands with. It was a long-term disaster in the making.

They finally reached the hotel. The foyer was packed and Hunter had to shoulder his way to the desk. The harassed staff ignored him until he took a fifty euro note from his pocket and held it flat with his forefinger. Within seconds a man appeared in front of him.

'*Monsieur*? *Vous désirez*?'

'Three rooms for one night,' Hunter said.

The man switched smoothly to English. 'I am sorry, sir, there are no vacancies. You can see. Many people are waiting to take ships away from France. The city is virtually full.'

'How much for your best rooms?'

'*Desolé*, monsieur, sir, I must repeat. They are taken.'

'I will pay ten times the normal rate for one night.' Hunter pushed the note across the desk where it was expertly palmed.

'Excuse me for one moment, sir.' He turned away and hurried into a back office. A few seconds later another, older man came out and crossed the reception area to Hunter.

'You said ten times?'

'Cash.'

'Alphonse.' He spoke in a loud voice, 'You have made a mistake. Get the rooms ready immediately. *Voilà, enfin*! Sir, I am very sorry. If you and your companions would take a seat in the bar I shall arrange to have the three best suites made ready immediately.'

'Thank you.' This time Hunter slid a thousand euro note over and it too vanished as though in the hands of a magician. Cynically he wondered if palming money was one of the skills you learned when working in a hotel. 'This is a token of my thanks. The bill will be paid separately.'

The man beamed his appreciation.

The bar was also crowded and they stood in a huddle just inside the door. Hunter heard a phone ring and looked up in time to see the barman answer it and glance in their direction. He hung up the receiver and waved to them and pointed.

A small corner table with a reserved sign suddenly had three chairs placed around it. A dish of olives and an ashtray magically appeared. Hunter led the way, shouldering his way past protesting men who took one look at him and decided not to protest too much.

A ten euro note took care of the waiter. Drinks were ordered. A pastis for Duval, coffee for Gustav and sparkling water for Hunter. He sat with his back to the wall, playing at being a body-guard.

'Once we have our rooms, we pay the bill and you, Duval, go and see about a car. I'll see about a boat. Incidentally, the room is ten times its normal price.'

'What!' Gustav was infuriated. 'You should have cleared . . .'

'Mr Gustav, take a look around you. These people, or some of them at least, have money. They will already have tried bribing their way to a room. I'm told the city hotels are full with so many people leaving France. I don't fancy a park bench because I suspect they'll all be full too. What's it to be? Pay or go?'

Gustav scowled and then nodded. 'You did the right thing. I must learn to trust your judgement more.'

Hunter nodded in satisfaction. 'One more thing. The banks are open late. I would like my ten mill before close of play today.'

Gustav emphatically shook his head. 'That is not possible. Truly. It will be arranged in Palermo.'

'Not good enough. Fix it for first thing in the morning. Okay?' He directed the question at Duval who looked at Gustav. Gustav nodded imperceptibly.

'Yes. It will be done,' said Duval.

Hunter found it interesting that Gustav was prepared to part with ten million pounds yet protested about the cost of a hotel room. Perhaps he didn't believe Hunter would have the chance to cash the cheque.

16

Walking towards the Quai de la Tourette was a nightmare. The streets and pavements were jammed solid with people and cars. The air was filled with noise and above the strangely dehumanised mass, there came the occasional loud shriek of a ship's whistle as yet another over-laden vessel left the quayside. As soon as the space was empty another came in. Many of the luxury yachts and boats that were normally berthed there had left for safer harbours. Too many had already been stolen.

In a small boutique Hunter bought a pair of shoes. He ditched his old pair in a rubbish bin after removing the location transmitters from the heels. The shoes were clearly visible for some lucky tramp to find. The transmitters he crushed beneath his heel. Walking along the road he carefully scuffed the soles and uppers of his new shoes.

Hunter had to walk a good kilometre until he found what he was looking for. The small office had a plate-glass window festooned with pictures of boats for hire and sale. The shop was due to close shortly but Hunter took no notice of the scowl that greeted him from its only occupant.

In passable French he said, 'I see you have boats for hire?'

The man's English was home-grown. 'Yeah, mate. What're you looking for?'

'Scouse?'

'Near enough. What can I do for you?'

'I'd like to hire a speedboat.'

'We're closing. Come back tomorrow.'

Hunter settled himself more comfortably into the chair he wasn't offered and said, 'I need it for tonight. I'm planning a moonlight ride with a very attractive woman, and I want something fast and smooth.'

The man was in his early twenties, casually dressed, with long fair hair and a deep tan. He spread his hands in an apology and lifted his shoulders. 'I'm sorry, mate, I can't help you.'

He sounded genuine enough but Hunter persisted. 'Money's no object. Name your price. How about five times the normal fee?'

The man blew out his cheeks and shook his head. 'She must be a hot date but it ain't the money. We don't have anything for hire.'

'But the signs in the window . . .'

'Just for show. Don't mean nothing. They pull the punters in and we persuade them to take something they may not really want. You know how it is.'

Hunter nodded. He knew. 'What would you normally charge for a good speedboat with a small cabin?'

'It depends. Top-of-the-range, about twenty euros an hour. Plus petrol and a deposit.'

Hunter guessed that was well at the top end but said, 'I'll pay fifty euros an hour and pay for a full twelve hours. Cash.' He enjoyed spending Gustav's money.

That made the young man sit up and take notice. 'How long do you want the boat?'

'Not that long.' Hunter managed a smirk.

'Okay, leave it with me. I'll make some calls. You'll have to leave a deposit. Same again. Non-refundable.'

'Nice one, sonny, but no. I'm giving you a good deal as it is.'

His reply was greeted with a grin. 'You can't blame a man for trying. Two doors along is a bar. I'll join you there as soon as I can. Name's Steve.'

'Nick.'

Hunter nodded and left. The bar was packed and Hunter had to elbow his way to the counter. He was in need of a drink but he settled for a small beer. He went to the window and looked out.

The streets were still thronged with people, the ships filling up and leaving. The air of desperation sickened him. Hunter's fist clenched tighter around the glass handle as he took another sip of beer. He'd just drained the glass when Steve entered.

'Got one!' he grinned. 'Want to see?'

Hunter nodded and placed his empty glass on a nearby table. Outside they made their way along the street and past the huge cathedral that dominated the skyline.

'Down here.'

Hunter was led into a side street and down some steps. A solid looking metal gate blocked their path. Steve took out a bundle of keys and selected a heavy brass one. He pushed open the gate and said, theatrically, '*Voila!*' The path led down to a small stone lined inlet, about three metres wide and six long, in which sat two boats.

Steve pointed to the nearest boat, low and sleek, painted a glistening maroon with white go-faster stripes down the sides. There was no cabin, but Steve said, 'The seats fold down and the mattresses fit for a perfect union. If you get my meaning. Want me to show you the controls?'

'Please.'

It only took a few minutes. With another key Steve unlocked a special clamp on the fuel leads and used a third key to start the engine. It burst into life with a deep-seated roar.

'She'll do a hundred and forty kilometres an hour. But I'd go a lot slower than that. In any sort of weather she's an unstable bitch. But there's a cove about ten minutes down the coast, full of buoys. You can tie up to one of them. It's usually deserted at night. Most of the boats go back to their marinas after dark. You unlock that grill when you want to leave. Close it behind you afterwards, will you? They're a light-fingered, thieving lot around here.'

'Of course. This is fine. We'll leave the boat here. On the way back to my hotel, I'll drop the keys through your letterbox. Fair enough?'

'Sure.' Steve unthreaded the keys and held them in his hand. 'Mullah?'

Hunter reached into his pocket and extracted the notes. He counted them into Steve's hand and added another hundred euros. 'For your trouble.'

'Hey, thanks, man. You're all right.'

Hunter doubted he would feel the same when neither the boat nor the keys were returned in the morning.

They switched off the engine and returned to the street above.

'I go this way,' said Steve and set off with a jaunty swagger, waving goodbye as he did so.

Once Steve was out of sight Hunter returned to the boat. There were too many locks hindering the boat's passage for his liking.

All Hunter had to do now was to panic Gustav and Duval into taking the boat. It all, he thought, added to the melodrama. But first things first. He found a telephone and rang Scotland. He was soon explaining the situation to Isobel.

Returning to the hotel he found both Gustav and Duval in Gustav's suite. It was pleasant enough, a large en-suite bedroom with a comfortable sitting area.

Hunter sat on a hardback chair. 'Did you get a car?'

Duval nodded. 'A Ford Taunus.'

'I'd have preferred a French model. Can I have the keys? I'll check it out and park it properly.'

'Properly?' Duval frowned at him.

Hunter asked, 'How easy is the car to get away? Is there room to manoeuvre? Or is it hemmed in, like practically every other car on the street?'

Duval tossed the keys to Hunter with bad grace. Gustav nodded his approval.

'I've got us a boat.' Hunter explained exactly where it was. 'If anything happens and we split up make for it. I'll meet you there.' He stood up. 'I'll be back soon. Where's the car parked?'

Hunter found the Taunus near the Avis car park. As he'd suspected, there was a vehicle parked hard against the rear bumper and a second too close to the front. If he had to drive away in a hurry he wouldn't get very far. Unbeknown to Gustav the need would become a certainty in the next twelve hours. Unlocking the door, he climbed in and started moving the car back and forth, opening the gap front and back, inch by inch. He was careful not to set off the alarm in either of the other vehicles. Eventually he managed to pull away and drove around until he found what he was looking for. An empty space on the corner of a one-way street. Nothing could park behind him. He noted the street name and wandered back to the hotel. On the way he stopped for another watery beer, one of the few alcoholic drinks the French made badly.

In the hotel he explained where the car was parked and the quickest way to it.

'I'm going to get some sleep,' he announced. 'If you need me, you know which room I'm in. However, I'll be out some of the time.'

'Doing what exactly?' Duval asked.

'Checking. Walking the hotel and the streets. I've left enough money at the desk to buy their loyalty in case someone comes in asking for us. But you never know. TIFAT may come and offer them something more.'

'More money, you mean?'

'No. Their lives. Breakfast at eight, I think.' Hunter bade the men goodnight and left, enjoying the melodrama.

'He's very efficient,' said Gustav to his secretary.

Duval nodded. 'Then why don't I trust him?'

Gustav smiled. 'For the same reason I don't. I can't quite put my finger on it, but he doesn't ring true.'

'You saw his record.'

'Even so, it's all too smooth. Once we get to Sicily we'll have to take another look at our friend Hunter. Have you made the arrangements with the bank?'

'Yes. He can have his cheque.'

'Let's ensure he doesn't get the chance to spend it. The message is sent?'

'Yes. The fun will start later tonight.'

Hunter lay with his hands behind his head for a few seconds. Everything he could do had been done. Now he needed to panic

Gustav some more. Keep him off balance. Stop him thinking. Use fear.

He was soon asleep but came wide awake just after midnight. Sliding out from his bed he made his way to the balcony that overlooked the Old Port. Opening the doors he stepped outside. The screams and yells he had heard, muffled by the glass, now came clearly to his ears. People were running along the street in panic. The slowest were being trampled by those behind. The bravest were jumping into the water to avoid being hurt, while others tried to take refuge behind cars and in doorways.

Looking up the street Hunter saw a gang of men, waving what looked like baseball bats, coming in line abreast, two deep. Hunter almost expected skin-heads sporting nazi insignia and steelcapped boots. But from the street lights he could see that they were dressed in civilian clothes, jeans and tee-shirts for the most part, but there was no doubt that these were trained men. Either soldiers or riot police. Hunter suspected the latter from the way they were using their bats. Heads and bodies were being broken before his eyes and there was nothing Hunter could do but stand and watch.

He was aware of a presence on the balcony next door and he turned to see Gustav and Duval step out. Both men had wide smiles on their faces. Gustav noticed Hunter and said, 'An inspiring sight, don't you think, Mr Hunter? Soon, French soil – no, European soil, will be free of these parasites.'

Hunter managed to sound normal when he said, cheerfully, 'It does my soul good to see it. Well, goodnight again.' Going indoors Hunter sat on his bed, his head in his hands. *Bastards*! He knew, somehow, that Gustav was behind the riot. How had he organised it right under his very nose? He shouldn't underestimate Gustav's power – it could prove fatal. Climbing back into bed he lay for a while listening to the fading sounds of the attack. Finally he drifted into an uneasy sleep. At 04.00 he snapped awake.

Shaving and showering took only minutes. He put on a clean white shirt, the blue tie and the charcoal grey suit. Cautiously he opened the door and peered out. The corridor was as quiet as a crypt.

Paul Henke

He went down the back stairs to the basement and out the tradesman's entrance. The streets appeared deserted but in almost every doorway he passed he heard muffled sobbing, the groans of children and adults in pain. He was glad he didn't have far to go. The Opéra was less than a kilometre away.

He went the long way around. After a while he knew he was being followed. He took different turnings but there was always somebody there. Just hidden, a ghost almost. He grinned and ducked into an alleyway. He didn't have long to wait.

'Nice one, Jan.'

'Hullo, boss. We thought we'd try and surprise you.'

'You almost did. Good try though. Where are the rest?'

'Nearby. Follow us.' Badonovitch and Doug Tanner led the way.

In a back street they found the rest of the team from Switzerland. They had been joined by Claude Masson and Peter Weir.

Dunston shook Hunter's hand.

Hunter gave them the information they needed, including the numbers of the rooms in the hotel.

'What time do you want us?' Napier asked.

'Come into the hotel at eight o'clock. We'll be in the restaurant having breakfast. I'll see you. Let us escape out the back entrance. We'll go through the kitchen. The car is parked here.' He pointed to his street map of Marseilles. 'And the boat is here.' He continued the briefing. 'You all got that?'

'Sure, boss,' said Badonovitch, 'only I can't remember which magazine to use.'

There were a few chuckles and Hunter said, 'In that case, Jan, aim high.'

Hunter telephoned Gustav's hotel room at 07.00. 'I suggest we go down for breakfast in forty-five minutes. We're due at the bank at nine o'clock. Bring your briefcases in case we have to move fast.'

'You fuss too much, Mr Hunter. It is beginning to annoy me.'

'Suit yourself. But I learned I live longer that way.' He hung up with a wide grin on his face.

They sat at a table in the far corner of the dining-room. Neither man had brought his briefcase. They were already becoming blasé – which suited him. He sat facing the door that led to the foyer. He ordered a cooked breakfast, wondering if he would have time to eat it. The orange juice was freshly squeezed and the coffee freshly filtered. He enjoyed both.

Duval and Gustav sat with their backs to the room and the foyer. Gustav leant forward and said, 'Mr Hunter, why are we sitting at this disgusting table? Everytime the door swings we hear the noises from the kitchen. The waiters push through and cause a draught. It is most unpleasant.'

'Look, Mr Gustav, if you want to sit somewhere else then please do so. Only this is the safest table in the room. I can sit with my back to the wall, the door to the foyer is across what will shortly be a crowded room and we have an escape route. I would rather suffer a little discomfort than a bullet.'

'You talk such arrant nonsense. If they were going to find us, they would have done so by now. Nobody is going . . .'

'You're wrong.' Hunter ducked his head. 'The men at the window are from TIFAT.'

The only members of the team that Gustav and Duval hadn't come face to face with were Masson and Weir. They were now looking through the door and straight at the three men.

'Rubbish!' Gustav said with anger, looking over his shoulder. 'They are just two ordinary . . .'

He got no further. A bullet hit the wall above his head, fired by Olympic Gold medallist, Peter Weir. Other bullets were fired but none came near them, a fact altogether missed by Gustav and Duval in their panic to follow Hunter into the kitchen. Shoving staff out of the way, knocking over pots and pans, Hunter caused as much confusion as possible in his attempts to delay their pursuers. The yells and screams merely added to the chaos, although nobody tried to hinder their passage.

'Out! Out! Out!' Hunter yelled at the two men, hustling them through the back door. As he followed, a gun fired and he ducked, the bullet clipping the wood next to his ear.

Gustav and Duval were now in a funk. With no weapons, all they could do was flee.

'Come on, this way.' Hunter led and they followed on his heels. He took them straight towards the car, a five minutes mad dash along the side of the road, missing the pedestrians, avoiding the traffic. Angry motorists beeped their horns and used the entire panoply of Gallic gestures which the fleeing men ignored. Approaching their car, Hunter was aiming the electronic key when another bullet hit empty ground just in front of them. Diving into the driver's seat, he had the engine started and in reverse before the other two had closed their doors. Another bullet hit the bonnet and ploughed a furrow along the gleaming paintwork. To the uninformed the impact seemed highly dangerous. Hunter knew the bullets had only fifteen percent of explosives in them. They lost their power as soon as they hit the slightest of objects. Nobody wanted innocent people killed.

The car turned onto the main road, backing into another vehicle, smashing its grill and bonnet, stopping it in its tracks. More bullets flew. Hunter swerved across the road and drove up it the wrong way. He flashed the lights, the hazard indicators were working and he kept his hand pressed firmly on the horn. Swerving around car after car they ran out of luck about halfway along. An overloaded lorry careered across their path and smashed into them, bringing them to a halt.

Hunter threw open his door. 'Move it!' he said loudly over his shoulder.

The two men needed no urging. They fell out of the car and lurched after him. Although not young Duval and Gustav were reasonably fit but in no way trained and so they shambled along behind Hunter as he lengthened his stride. People were standing and staring as they ran down the middle of the street, in between the traffic which had come to a halt following the accident. It had taken skilful driving to hit the lorry as Hunter had, making it appear that the other driver was to blame.

'Not far now,' he encouraged them.

Both of them were gasping, sweating, Duval most of all,

although he was a good ten years younger than Gustav. A bullet hit the tarmac and both of them began to run faster.

Hunter had the keys to the metal gate in his hands by the time they arrived at the small boat pen. He fumbled with the lock as a bullet hit above his head. He managed to get it open and tore down the steps.

Inserting a key into the ignition the engine burst into life as the other two fell into the boat. Hunter slipped the berthing ropes and pushed the lever into forward. The boat surged ahead, hit the grill, unlocked by Hunter the previous night, and smashed it open. The grill bounced back and scraped a deep gash along the port side, right down to the white fibre-glass hull.

The powerful engine was already picking up speed and the boat was beginning to lift onto the plane. Hunter ignored the 10kph speed limit.

Where the narrow, stone-lined inlet turned north to the open sea, men wearing balaclavas appeared behind them and opened fire with automatic weapons. Bullets hit the side and stern of the boat but did no real damage other than to the paint work. Already the boat was moving out of range. It shot into the main channel under the bows of a departing coastal vessel and Hunter threw the wheel hard to starboard, just missing the over-laden ship. In impotent anger the ship's master sounded a series of short blasts on its horn.

They flew past the old forts as the boat edged its way up to 100kph. Although the water was flat there were small ripples across the surface and the boat skimmed over them, a faint judder passing through the hull. As in all ports, departing ships had the right of way and just outside the entrance there was a long line of old and not-so-old coastal vessels waiting to enter. These ships were there to take the dispossessed away from Europe. Even in times of misery and hardship there were those who would make money. In this case, a fortune.

Gustav and Duval lay in the stern, on the deck, leaning against the rear seat, their legs outstretched. Slowly they were beginning to recover their breath and their strength, the sweat drying on their faces.

Hunter was concentrating on driving the boat. At such a fast speed it was easy to turn too hard and overturn, a problem less experienced helmsmen had encountered many times – often with fatal results. He throttled back to a more sedate 50kph. After a few minutes Gustav struggled to his feet and clambered into the seat alongside Hunter.

'How did they find us?' he called loudly.

Hunter shook his head. 'TIFAT operates on a need-to-know basis, Mr Gustav. Some things are way beyond my pay-scale.'

'We got away.'

Hunter turned his head and gave Gustav a penetrating look. 'We were lucky. I wouldn't have placed odds on us escaping. Would you?'

Gustav returned the gaze for a few seconds and then shook his head. 'No. You were right. We have to be very, very careful.' He didn't elaborate.

'Mr Gustav, humour me. You are so close to achieving your objectives for the good of all white Europeans,' the words stuck in his throat but he persevered, 'just go along with what I tell you. Your ideas will soon shape the reality of a new Europe. I'm determined to make sure your interests are looked after and to ensure your safety.'

Gustav looked ahead at the unfolding scene of a pleasant Mediterranean morning and licked dry lips. If it hadn't been for Hunter, he and Duval would be dead by now.

The team vanished into the backstreets of Marseilles. They removed balaclavas and placed their weapons into the trunks of their cars which were parked on the top floor of a multi-story car park and still empty at that time in the morning. Like all good commuters, the French filled up from the bottom first.

They were in high spirits when they drove away. Dunston and Napier got out at the Hotel de Ville and went inside. Dressed in smart business suits they looked as though they belonged.

They didn't bother with Hunter's room. The corridor was empty and neither man bothered with finesse. A heavy shoulder to each door of Gustav's and Duval's rooms and they were in. They quickly collected together the men's few belongings, including Duval's laptop, and met in the corridor once again. Unhurriedly they walked down the stairs and out of the front entrance. As before, the quayside was packed with people and they had to elbow their way to where the cars were waiting.

Roads all across the city were closed. Police cars were speeding in all directions with their lights flashing and sirens blaring. The team were stopped at one roadblock but their diplomatic passports saw them waved through. Soon after they were at the British Consulate, 24 Avenue de Prado.

A Queen's Messenger took charge of the bags they had lifted from the hotel. Within minutes, the same official was taken in a consulate car to the airport. He was booked on an Air France flight to Paris and on to Edinburgh, where he would be met by a member of TIFAT. Isobel and her team were waiting ready to unravel the secrets held in Duval's computer.

In the meantime, the team left the city for a small private airfield about twenty kilometres inland. Schwarzkopf was waiting for them with the helicopter. They were due in Réggio Di Calabria at the toe of Italy later that day.

The Port-de-Bouc was a natural harbour adjacent to the Regional National Park of the Camargue. Gustav's hired sea-plane, a twin-engined Griffin Land-Water II, was the only one there, tied to a buoy about fifty metres from the shore. They approached the plane but it was empty. They had not been due to leave until 10am.

'What now?' Gustav asked.

Hunter felt a good deal of satisfaction that the question was directed at him. He raised an eyebrow. 'Now we finish our interrupted breakfast. We can't do anything else.' Easing forward on the throttle he took them in towards the sandy, gently sloping beach.

The bow of the boat grated onto the sand, still a few metres from the water's edge. Hunter took off his shoes and socks and threw them onto the beach. Duval and Gustav followed his lead and removed theirs as well. While they did so, Hunter climbed into the warm water and took hold of the small anchor and chain kept in the bow. The others joined him and they dragged the boat well up the beach. He left the keys hidden in a small compartment under the driver's seat just in case the boat was returned to Steve. Somehow, Hunter doubted it.

Picking up their shoes and socks they trundled through the sand and onto the pavement. Sitting on a nearby bench they dried their feet and replaced their footwear. There were quite a few pedestrians walking along the promenade, many with small dogs on leashes, out for their morning constitutional. The dogs fouled the pavements and gutters, the mess ignored by their owners. It was all so normal.

'We'll head over there,' said Hunter, indicating a restaurant with tables and chairs outside, where a small clientele was already beginning to gather.

Hunter ordered breakfast and ate with gusto. The other two picked at their freshly baked croissants, but drank copious amounts of orange juice and coffee.

When they had finished, Hunter said, 'Let's take a stroll. We'll wander the town. You two go together while I follow. We'll be less conspicuous than three men walking together. I'll be right behind but you may not see me. Before we leave, I should ask. What about your briefcases? If they're handed in, is there anything incriminating in the contents?'

Duval managed a grin. 'If anyone tampers with the laptops, a program cleans the soft and hard drives completely and utterly. Unlike most systems mine really works.'

'Excellent! TIFAT know too much as it is.' Standing up Hunter indicated for the men to go ahead. He followed, keeping them in sight for the most part, allowing them out of his sight from time to time. The ruse permitted him to access a payphone in a *Tabac*. He was quickly through to Scotland. Having warned Isobel about the computer system, he was back on the street within two minutes.

Gustav and Duval were clearly unhappy and nervous. Hunter on the other hand enjoyed his stroll. At ten minutes to the hour he indicated that they should head back to the beach. There a small, yellow inflatable dinghy was now tied to a strut on the aircraft.

Duval waved to the plane and was instantly rewarded by an arm appearing through the cockpit window and waving back. A few seconds later the inflatable was heading for shore.

The co-pilot made two trips, first with Gustav and Hunter and then with Duval. Hunter insisted on the arrangement. He had no intention of being left behind. By the time Duval reached the plane the engines had been started and pre-flight checks finished. The co-pilot let go the buoy and puttered around to the door. With a practised movement he climbed aboard and pulled open a dump valve in the side of the boat. The boat collapsed and he dragged it inside where it was neatly stowed.

The Griffin was luxuriously fitted. With only eight seats it was possible to recline them fully and sleep almost as comfortably as in a bed. An attentive blonde stewardess offered them light refreshments, which they declined. Having ascertained that the distance to fly was 350 miles and would take approximately one hour and forty minutes, Hunter wondered briefly what lay ahead before falling asleep.

17

The sea-plane landed to the north-west of Palermo. It taxied across the calm water to within a few metres of the hull of a luxury ship. It was, Hunter realised, the *Stockholm*. She was about 200ft long. Details flashed through his mind from the information garnered by Isobel. Dead weight 2,000 tonnes. Widest beam 65ft. Cruising speed 25 knots and a possible top speed in excess of 36 knots. Helicopter deck. Twenty state rooms. Crew of thirty. Beautiful and very expensive.

The hull was a deep blue with a white stripe along the plimsoll line matched by a second line just under the lower deckedge. This deck held the helicopter pad and hangar. A further two decks tiered upwards, the top one starting from halfway along from the stern. All three decks ended in a sheer wall, topped by the bridge, thirty feet from the bow.

There was no need for the inflatable. They were met by a sleek launch manned by two sailors wearing pristine white teeshirts and trousers.

A short while later Hunter found himself in a starboard state-room. Its opulence was awesome. A four-poster bed dominated the room, set against the aft bulkhead. The room was en-suite and boasted a balcony big enough to take a table and four chairs. A teak cabinet held a well-stocked bar, which would do a world cruise-liner justice. As he stood there contemplating his surroundings there came a knock on the door. A steward appeared. He carried a complete set of fresh clothing over his arm.

'Mr Gustav's compliments, sir, but I've come for your clothes.'

'May I ask why?' If he was surprised, he didn't show it.

'Orders, sir,' was the enigmatic reply.

Hunter nodded and stripped to his underpants. He threw his clothes onto the bed and slipped his shoes back on while he reached for a bathrobe.

'Your shoes and pants, too, sir.'

Hunter decided it was time to get angry. 'What the hell for?'

'I don't know, sir. I was told to get your clothing as soon as you came on board.'

Hunter fully understood the reasoning behind the request but he intended to play the injured party for a bit longer. 'Tell Mr Gustav I want to see him right away.'

'Oh, I can't do that, sir.' The steward reached behind his back and brought out a gun which he now pointed at Hunter's midriff. 'Please be sensible, sir.'

Shrugging, Hunter tied the belt of the robe tighter, slipped off his boxer shorts, shoes and socks and held out the shoes to the man. When the steward reached for the shoes, Hunter hit the gun arm aside and quickly disarmed him. 'Pick up that lot and get out. And don't wave a gun in my face again.'

Sheepishly the steward did as he was told. When he got to the door Hunter called to him, 'Here.' He lobbed the gun, causing the man to fumble with the clothes and drop a shoe. Hunter watched him leave before going for a shower. They'd find nothing.

Wearing white trousers, a white open-necked shirt and loafers on his bare feet, Hunter left the cabin. The corridor ran fore and aft and was heavily carpeted. His was the end cabin and to his left he could see a gleaming open deck with a swimming pool and separate jacuzzi. He went right, towards the bows. Hanging between each door was a painting, modern art of the kind which Hunter disliked but knew to be expensive. He assumed correctly that they were originals. At the end of the corridor he stepped out onto a large balcony that overlooked the bow where passengers could stand and watch as they entered harbour or ploughed their way through the seas. A circular set of stairs led to the lower deck. A notice on the gate said it was for the use of the crew only. Looking behind him, Hunter saw separate stairs which led to a balcony above. He knew the owner's suite was to be found there. Looking up further and leaning out, he could make out the bridge windows and bridge wings. An officer was standing on the port wing looking down at him. He didn't respond to Hunter's cheery wave.

He went down the stairs to the bow and looked into the clear blue water. The white anchor chain led into the depths and vanished in a shimmering haze. A few dark shadows darted around the chain and further down he could make out rocks on the bottom, stark against the barren sand. He had an overwhelming desire to put on a diving set and plunge into the crystal clear waters. To forget the danger he was in if only for a little while.

He continued around the deck, along the port side and as far as the helicopter pad, where he loitered at the stern and looked towards Sicily. The sea was fairly dotted with boats, sailing vessels and powered craft of different shapes and sizes.

Apart from two sailors who watched him as he went past, ignoring his friendly nod, he saw nobody. Halfway along the starboard side he found a doorway that again said 'Crew Only'. He went in. Although not nearly as opulently decorated as the guests' quarters it still looked well appointed.

Moving along the corridor he came to a door marked 'Crews Mess' and entered. Half a dozen men sat at a table littered with Styrofoam cups, smoking, drinking and talking. Along one wall stood a cafeteria-style, stainless steel counter with clear plastic shelves, holding plated food. Aware of the men watching him, Hunter walked over to take a look. He helped himself to lobster salad and cold water from a cooler. Nodding to the men he took a seat at another table.

One of the crew stood up and approached him. 'What are you doing here?' The question was asked truculently. About Hunter's height, blonde and muscled, his accent suggested he was Swedish or possibly German. Hunter decided it was the former.

'What's it to you?'

'I ask the questions. I'll ask you again . . .'

He didn't get any further. It was time, Hunter decided, to stamp some authority on the crew. The man was standing next to Hunter's chair. Hunter drove his fist hard between the man's legs, practically lifting him off his feet. He gurgled, clasped his hands in front of him and sank to the floor with a loud gasp. His face had turned a mottled green and yellow.

Hunter pointed at the two nearest men. 'You and you, carry him to his cabin.' When nobody moved, Hunter hit the table with the flat of his hand and yelled, 'Now! And listen up! I'm in charge of Mr Gustav's personal security. From now on what I say goes around here. I go where I like, when I like. Do I make myself clear?'

One or two nodded nervously. The two men he had pointed to stood up and went to help their moaning companion. They too were blonde and muscled. From the few words Hunter heard them exchange it was clear that they were Swedish.

'You,' he pointed at another man, 'where will I find the Captain?'

'On the bridge.' The words were uttered between clenched teeth.

'You have a problem?' Hunter stood up nonchalantly and stepped to one side of the table.

The other man did likewise. 'Yes. That was a cowardly attack. You gave Kurt no chance.'

'I'm giving you one.'

The man was in his middle twenties, an inch or two shorter than Hunter but broader in the shoulders. From his toned muscles he obviously pumped a lot of iron. He glanced at the men still at the table before launching his attack. It was no contest. Hunter moved as hard and as fast as he had ever done in his life. The man stood stock still for a second or two and then keeled over with a loud crash, smashing his head on the deck. Hunter wasn't even breathing hard.

'I repeat, I'm in charge of Mr Gustav's personal security. When I say jump you ask how high. Got it?' This time he didn't raise his voice and had the satisfaction of seeing them nod nervously. 'When I ask a question or want information it will be for a good reason. My only concern is our leader's well-being.'

He left, perfectly satisfied with the little encounter he had just engineered. They would not be so quick to question him from now on. All he had to do now was deal with the ship's Captain. He would have to be tackled in an entirely different way.

Along the corridor near the bow he found a set of stairs. He ran up them and found himself on the bridge. A man in white uniform with gold stripes on his shoulders looked up when he walked in.

'Captain?'

The man was leaning over a desk, a pencil in his hand, a ship's log book lying open.

'*Ja*. I am the Captain.'

Hunter stepped forward with his hand outstretched. 'My name is Hunter, Nick Hunter. I am in charge of Mr Gustav's personal security.'

The Captain ignored the hand and turned back to what he was doing. 'I know who you are.'

'Captain, I don't care if we get on or not. I have only one concern and that is the safety of Mr Gustav. Your concern is the safety of the ship. Mine takes priority. I hope you clearly understand that.'

'I take my orders from Mr Gustav only. No one else.'

'Captain, I had hoped we could resolve any differences or difficulties amicably. If need be I can speak to Mr Gustav.'

The man tensed and then straightened up slowly. He looked at Hunter. He was about forty-five, tanned, fit looking with brown hair and grey sideburns reaching to his lobes. His was the fitness of the tennis courts and the ski resorts, though a small belly was beginning to fight against his muscle-tone.

He seemed to be thinking over Hunter's words. After a few seconds he nodded. 'That won't be necessary. Mr Gustav's safety is also my main concern. Followed by the ship and her passengers.' He held out his hand. '*Kapitän zur See* Jürgen Novak.'

'Good,' Hunter smiled. 'Then we'll get on famously together.' Hunter shook the captain's hand. There was no answering smile.

General Macnair replaced the receiver on his desk and sat looking at it for a few moments, as though there was something more to learn from staring at it. Leaning forward he pressed a button on his internal intercom. 'Jim, can you spare a minute?' The request was the equivalent of a senior officer's command. Carter would give Macnair as long as the General wished.

'Take a seat. I've spoken to Nato. They've been co-operating fully, or at least, as fully as we can expect. Until now.'

'What do you mean, sir?'

'I just had Hiram on the phone. He's in the Netherlands. In Rotterdam.'

'Yes, sir. Staking out a police station.'

Macnair had no need to tell Carter why the police station was a target. A week earlier there had been an attack on a supermarket in the Dutch city. It was in the centre of the Muslim enclave and catered primarily for local people who worshipped Islam. It sold mainly foods which were specially prepared or imported from Muslim countries. Such strict adherence to Islam had led to trouble in the past, and the supermarket had become the focus for hatred by gangs of the city's skinheads and neonazis. Now the shop had been attacked and torched to the ground. Three Muslims had lost their lives and many more had been hurt. The Dutch police had been late in responding. When they had arrived at the scene they had done little apart from make a half-hearted attempt to stop the violence. There had been no arrests.

Since that night there had been sporadic unrest in the city and more people had been killed, mainly Muslims, but also a white Dutch couple and their baby. The blame had been laid at the door of Islamic extremists. According to the information Isobel had collected, the police station was now a target and due to be attacked that night.

'Hiram met with a Nato major, a Dutchman, which is appropriate under the circumstances. He promised a contingent of troops to help contain the problem and back up the men in the police station.'

'Sounds reasonable.'

'Except none of the troops have appeared. The attack is in three hours and Hiram can't find the officer.'

Carter allowed the surprise to show on his face. 'What gives?'

'We know Gustav *needs* Muslim success. He needs white people killed and injured to prove that everything he's saying is true. He needs death and destruction in Europe on a scale great enough to convince Europeans of his goal. I hadn't realised how far Gustav's influence had already extended. If he can pull Nato troops out of action what else can he do?'

'What are you proposing to do about it, sir?'

'Our best bet of holding the lid down – until we get the information we need from Hunter – is to stop any Muslim success. Once we can show that the real mastermind behind the attacks is Gustav and his right-wing cohorts we can swing back public opinion. But if we lose the battle in the next few days then it could be too late. No matter what we say and do the hatred will be too deep and too raw.'

'Not to mention the hatred the Muslims will have for us, sir.'

Macnair spoke fervently. 'The hatred has been there for centuries, Jim. I'm only interested in today. We keep the peace, or what passes for peace, across Europe. Whilst we do, our politicians will have to work harder at appeasing the fears of the majority. Whether they like it or not. Re-deploy Dunston and his team.'

'But, sir, that'll leave Nick without any back-up!'

Macnair nodded. 'I'm aware of that. But they are wanted elsewhere. I need every man I can trust. Hunter will be on his own for a short while. Hopefully, it won't be long enough for him to get into any serious trouble.'

Dunston and his men flew to Rome airport, 300 miles away. From there they were dispersed, to assist at forthcoming attacks. Isobel was downloading information even as they were in the air. Dunston was lucky. His destination was Fiumicino, Rome's international airport. There he met David Hughes in deep discussion with the airport's chief of security.

'Matt, meet Sylvestre diSilvio.'

The two men shook hands. DiSilvio was short and fat and smelt strongly of expensive aftershave.

'I am very pleased to have you here,' were diSilvio's opening words. 'I have been given much details and I am very worried. What should we do? The General Manager wants to close the airport.'

'I don't see how that will help,' Dunston frowned.

'He say that if the airport closure is on the radio and television then the attackers won't come.'

'That's wishful thinking,' said Hughes, 'and highly unlikely. Mr diSilvio, it doesn't work like that. These men are coming here to attack the airport. We know that their primary target is the American Delta flight due in at nine o'clock. They want to kill Americans but they will also kill anybody else who gets in their way. This is a suicide attack intended to cause maximum death and destruction. Closing the airport is not an option.'

Nodding his round head, diSilvio said, '*Si, si, si*. But my manager . . .'

'I'll talk to him,' said Dunston, soothingly.

The door opposite burst open and the General Manager bustled in followed by a retinue of staff. There followed a heated argument between him and diSilvio. The Chief of Security appeared to be getting the worst of it. While this was going on, the two men from TIFAT stood to one side, completely ignored. After a short while Dunston telephoned Macnair and explained the situation. He replaced the receiver. The phone rang a few minutes later while the two Italians were still arguing.

Dunston answered and then held the receiver towards the General Manager. It took three attempts to attract his attention.

'I am too busy now,' he said angrily.

'Prime Minister? He says that he is too busy to talk to . . .' He got no further.

The GM tore the phone from his grasp. There were a series of *Si's*, a lot of gulping and no further arguments. The General Manager replaced the receiver, looking older than his sixty-three years by about a decade. 'What do we do?'

'Ask your staff to leave while I brief you. Just you and Mr diSilvio, please.' The GM's entourage left the room. 'This is an operation of containment,' said Dunston. 'The biggest risk is to innocent bystanders, either other travellers or their families and friends. So we have to isolate the terrorists.'

'How?' asked diSilvio.

'That's what we're here to work out. We know the attackers are coming in on a train from Rome . . .'

'How do you know this thing?' diSilvio interrupted.

'From our intelligence sources. We even know which train the terrorists will be on. If we wait until they arrive at the terminal then they will be able to disperse across the railway station, into the adjacent multi-story car parks and even get into any of the three terminal buildings. A lot of people could be killed and a vast amount of damage done. How many planes are usually at the terminals?'

'Eighteen, possibly twenty,' diSilvio answered.

'Some will be embarking passengers, others disembarking. Some planes will be ready to leave and others arriving on the hard-standing. A concerted attack by the terrorists could be enough for one of them to get to a window overlooking the area. One man with a grenade launcher is all it takes to create a vast amount of damage and loss of life.'

'You are painting a bleak picture,' said the General Manager.

Dunston raised his hand. 'The only place that we can contain them is on the train.'

The relief on the General Manager's face would have been comic if the discussion hadn't been so deadly.

DiSilvio said, 'It is an express, direct from Roma. It will not stop until it reaches here.'

'Then we stop it . . . where?' Dunston asked.

'Acilia,' diSilvio replied. 'What do we do then?'

'These people have to be stopped permanently,' said Hughes. 'Otherwise they'll regroup and come again. And next time we may not have the advance intelligence to stop them. We know that they are members of al-Qaeda, and are fanatics. So we have no choice.'

Dunston nodded. 'My colleague's right. We also need to enter the train with overwhelming force. It's the only way. These people will be travelling alone or in pairs. We know that they will *look*

Middle Eastern. They will have bags nearby, either above their heads or on their laps, or next to them. We go in with a lot of noise and we contain each carriage. What's the situation with manpower?'

DiSilvio looked sheepish and shrugged.

'What about police or army help?' Hughes asked.

'I swear I had it arranged but they have been called off,' said diSilvio. 'An hour ago.'

'There's nothing we can do about that now.' If he was dismayed, Dunston didn't show it. 'How many men do you have here?'

'We need them to protect the airport,' protested the General Manager.

'Why?' Hughes asked in his quiet Welsh voice.

The ludicrousness of his statement was apparent even to the GM and he lapsed into silence.

'Luckily we have a shift change coming up,' said diSilvio. 'I can gather thirty, perhaps thirty-two armed men and a few women.'

'How many carriages will there be?' Dunston asked.

'Usually fifteen,' answered diSilvio.

'How busy will they be at this time of the evening?' Dunston asked.

'Half full, I should say.'

Dunston looked at his watch. 'The train departs in just over an hour.' He looked at the General Manager, 'Sir, can you get the railway authority to cut the train in half?'

'I don't know. Why?'

'These are modern open carriages, yes?'

'Of course. The best in Europe,' the Italian boasted.

'With only two people for each carriage anybody in the middle would be able to draw a weapon before we get to them. I want to avoid a bloodbath if I can help it. We need at least four men to rush in and to quarter each carriage. If we can manage even more then all the better. Any questions?'

There were none.

'One more thing. We do *not* tell anyone else what the operation is about,' said Dunston.

257

'I not understand,' said diSilvio.

'Get your men in position but don't tell them why we're there until it's time to go. We can't afford any word of the operation being leaked to the terrorists.'

The General Manager stood straighter and was about to remonstrate with Dunston at the idea that there could be a traitor in their midst when he thought better of it.

Colonel Hiram B. Walsh, late of Delta Force and now second-in-command at TIFAT was not a happy man. He was in a meeting with a senior police officer in Rotterdam's main police station. The officer was not happy either. The antipathy between the American and the Dutchman was almost palpable. They came from diametrically opposite viewpoints to the same conclusion – the other man was a fool.

Inspector Paul Schroder was Dutch, tall and thickset with a spreading waistline held in by a residual fitness from when he played professional football. He had learnt only an hour earlier that his station was to be attacked by Muslims. He knew and understood the reason for it and had expected back-up from either the army or other police units. None was forthcoming. Indeed, Schroder had been looking forward to catching the Islamic scum, as he put it, in a trap. Now there wasn't going to be one. The building they were in was practically Gothic. It would be a nightmare to defend against armed men, particularly if the reports on their opposition proved true.

'We need to evacuate,' said Schroder. 'Let them come and destroy the building. At least my men will be alive.'

Walsh couldn't argue with that. It was precisely what he would do and so he nodded. However, 'There's one problem with that.'

Schroder raised an inquisitive eyebrow.

'They won't stop with torching this place. We know that twenty plus, fully armed men, are going to hit this building. They have automatic guns, grenades and probably a missile or two. If they meet no resistance what will happen? They'll go on the rampage. This area is predominantly white and middle class. It would trigger a killing orgy and it's your task to stop it.'

'But why have I no support?'

Walsh was aware that Schroder was not the brightest policeman he had ever met but such stupidity was breathtaking. 'Normally, you would have had no prior knowledge of the attack, would you?'

'True. The only intelligence we have been given is from TIFAT.'

'Would you have been ready for an attack?'

The man looked uncomfortable for a second before having the grace to admit, 'No. But we would have responded very quickly. With the tension around nowadays we are better prepared than ever.'

'You'd have been too late,' Walsh said quietly. 'The likelihood is you'd have been wiped out. You still could be. How would you describe this station? Pro-fascist? Anti-immigrant?'

'You can call us what you like. The men I've got here are all true Europeans. We believe this is a white continent for Christians. Muslims should go back to where they come from.'

Walsh didn't bother replying. 'You've been set up, my friend. Your men stood by and watched the supermarket being burnt to the ground while Muslims and non-whites were killed. Well, the situation is about to be reversed. The deaths of white policemen will ensure a frenzy of anti-Islamic, racist feelings.' Walsh stood up and stretched cramped muscles. 'The trouble is, you don't realise who you're dealing with.'

Schroder was about to protest but thought better of it. He needed Walsh right then.

'Believe me, Schroder, the men who are responsible want the deliberately engineered deaths of Dutch citizens. Particularly the deaths of white, Christian folk. Right now there are millions of Europeans who think like you do. When your deaths and those of others like you hit the TV screens, people will flock to the cause. Europe could easily become a whites-only continent. Except *you* won't be alive to see it. Do you live locally, Schroder?'

'What?' The policeman was looking dazed but he replied. 'About two streets from here.'

'If this station is attacked and destroyed, do you think it'll stop there? With your police officers dead who's to stop them rioting? Killing more innocent white people?'

Schroder's bleak gaze was answer enough.

'We need to be ready for them. How many men do you have on duty?'

'Eight, at this time of the night. I only came in because of you.'

'Weapons?'

'Sticks, CS gas and side-arms.'

'Not much against a heavily-armed and fanatical terrorist group three times stronger. That map,' he pointed at the wall, 'is your jurisdiction, I take it?'

'Yes. We are in the corner, here.' Schroder pointed with a stubby forefinger at the map behind his head. 'This is our normal patrol area, except when we are in hot pursuit. But any robberies or murders that take place within the red lines are dealt with from here.'

'How do you get on with the other stations? The other senior officers?'

Schroder shrugged. 'All right, I guess. We have different opinions, we sometimes argue when we meet. On the whole we agree that our problems are caused in great part by the immigrants. Some want a radical change, others think . . . differently.' There was no need to ask Schroder which option he preferred.

'Could they help you? Send men?'

Schroder thought about it for a few seconds before he reluctantly shook his head. 'They are already stretched too thinly. Crime has gone up in the last few years to such an extent that there are never enough officers available.'

'What about off-duty officers?'

'Yes. That is a good idea.'

'It's just after nine now. According to our information we can expect an attack any time after one o'clock. Get me somebody I can trust to come outside with me. I want to take a look around. In the meantime, round up as many of your officers as you can. And don't let any go off on some crime bust. Tonight, the criminals can have it their own way around here.'

* * *

The plan they settled on was not ideal but it was the best that Dunston and Hughes could come up with under the circumstances.

The train, half its normal length, left Rome station ten minutes late. The carriages, seven of them, were between half and three-quarters full. Profuse apologies were broadcast to the passengers about the delay and the cramped conditions. Trouble on the line ahead was blamed. The train travelled more slowly than usual. After a few minutes another broadcast informed those on board that there would be a delay at Acilia because of a power failure. But the delay would not be too great. Many, many apologies.

There was indeed a power failure at the station. All the lights had been extinguished. The train stopped and the doors hissed open. There was a silence as nobody got on and nobody got off. After all, this was not a scheduled stop.

Then it erupted.

Clad in full riot gear, two airport security guards, wearing flack-jackets and carrying Beretta Model 12S Italian sub-machine guns, issued after 9/11, stepped quickly through the doors.

Some of the men yelled in English, 'Don't move! Police! Don't move!' Other officers screamed the same in Italian. They rushed along the carriages, pointing their guns and yelling.

There were no obvious targets. The people sitting in their seats looked suitably shocked and frightened. A quick search showed nobody carried weapons. The people with Middle Eastern or North African passports were few. They were searched and questioned closely but to no avail.

Hughes took Dunston to one side. 'Matt, something's wrong. Our intelligence is too good. You know that.'

Dunston nodded, frowning. He caught a look. A smirk. Whose was it? He looked around but saw nobody acting oddly. But there *had* been something.

'The airport! Let's go! I hope we're not too late. Mr diSilvio, warn the airport. They can expect an attack at any time.'

The men ran from the station and bundled into cars. With screaming tyres and over-revving engines the cars sped towards the airport only a few kilometres away.

The vehicles screeched to a halt outside the main terminal and the men ran into the concourse. Armed and dressed as they were, they made a frightening sight, sending the passengers screaming and panic stricken towards the exits. As Dunston stopped indecisively, near the moving stairway, shots were heard coming from the upper level. He and Hughes bounded up the steps as more panicked people streamed down. Hughes was at Dunston's left shoulder, each man covering the other. A grenade went off and the screams turned into the high-pitched sound of the injured.

They were on the viewing floor. On the other side of the room a plate glass window blew out as an automatic weapon opened fire. Around a pillar, the TIFAT operatives saw a masked man shooting out the glass of a window while next to him a second man was raising a rifle to his shoulder. On the end of the barrel was the unmistakable lump of a grenade.

Dunston and Hughes opened fire simultaneously. They cut the terrorists down before the grenade was fired. More shots came from their left and they ran towards the noise. By now the area was clear of innocent bystanders but the floor was littered with the bodies of the dead and wounded. Blood was everywhere.

More firing and glass smashing came from around the next corner. The two men slowed down and approached carefully. It was a repeat of the scene they had just witnessed. They fired their guns. Dunston's shot hit the man with the grenade launcher in the shoulder, deflecting his aim just as the terrorist pulled the trigger. The grenade missed the wing of the Airbus it was aimed at and hit the tail. As it went off, pieces of shrapnel smashed into the plane's tail. If it had hit the wing, the aviation gas-filled conflagration could have resulted in many deaths.

Dunston fired again, killing the man. Hughes' first shot had been lethal. More firing was heard in the distance. It tailed off to sporadic shots and then silence.

Dunston turned to Hughes and said, 'We failed, Dave.'

An hour later Dunston contacted TIFAT HQ and reported to Macnair. It was a sorry tale. Thirty-three innocent people killed, a further forty-two injured. Six terrorists had died and two were wounded. The wounded men were in custody.

'What went wrong?' Macnair asked.

'They were warned, sir. I don't know how or by who but I'm sure of it.

Hiram Walsh had fifteen Dutch officers. Two others had turned up, but were either drunk or on drugs and had been sent away again. The officers bore only side-arms, Belgian Browning BDA 380s specially manufactured for the police forces of Western Europe. The magazine held thirteen, 9mm Shorts, and was useful at close quarters. Walsh knew they were completely inadequate for what he envisaged was ahead that night.

'You know the situation,' he addressed the police officers. 'They will be coming and they'll be coming in hard. This is a suicide mission as far as these men are concerned. They are here to cause maximum damage and the maximum number of deaths. Once the station is taken care of they'll attack the civilians in the area. You'll see grenades, automatic weapons and petrol bombs. They must be stopped at all costs.'

The officers sitting in front of him nodded with varying degrees of enthusiasm. This was *not* what they had signed up for.

'Sergeant Baedecker and I have scouted the area.' Baedecker was an ex-military policeman, who had proven to be a useful man to have around. 'And we have a strategy of sorts. It's vital we capture some of their weapons. It's possible they have Stingers, but they will have grenades and at least one, maybe two, launchers. The men with those weapons are our priority. The area will be lit-up as much as possible. They may have Night Vision Goggles; we certainly don't. All the lights will be on in the station but nobody will be inside. We'll be hiding in the streets. Sergeant?'

Walsh handed over to the burly Dutchman. Baedecker had spent fifteen years with Nato and knew his stuff. Of all the men in the room, he was the one Walsh could rely on.

Midnight found the officers deployed around the area. The police station sat in a square, surrounded by shops with residential apartments above. The streets were one-way and ran north to south, east to west, cutting off the station like an island. Cars were parked alongside the pavements and would remain there until the morning when a no-parking ban came into force. Around the station, cars could park only if they were there on police business. Currently there were two in front of the building and two behind. The station could be approached from any direction, by anyone. This was, after all, one of the freest societies in the world. It also had one of the biggest proportion of immigrants in the Western hemisphere.

The police sat in nondescript vans or crouched hidden in doorways. They had the four streets leading to the square under surveillance and were in constant touch by personal radios. And they were very, very nervous. Walsh noted again the difference between TIFAT operatives and even well trained men.

The attack began around 02.00.

18

Aboard the *Stockholm* Hunter had feasted with Gustav and Duval in a splendid dining-room off the main salon and bar. Bisque was followed by fresh skate, vegetables and three different potato dishes. Cheese and fruit followed. A superb white wine had been offered. Hunter and Gustav drank water.

'I am so sorry about your clothes,' said Gustav over coffee. 'An accident with the drier, I believe. We've had to destroy them.'

Hunter waved a nonchalant hand and said, 'It doesn't matter. Somehow I never expected to see them again.'

'Good. Then we understand each other perfectly.'

'I think we do, Mr Gustav. However, I am still waiting for my cheque.'

'Ah, yes, the ten million. Duval?'

The secretary reached inside his shirt pocket and withdrew a folded piece of paper. He handed it across to Hunter.

Opening it, Hunter saw that it was made out in euros and was near enough to ten million sterling as to make no difference. 'Thank you.'

'My pleasure,' said Gustav. 'After all you did save my life. Twice.'

'The second time was on the house. I was looking after, shall we say, my investment?'

Gustav chuckled. 'Very good, Mr Hunter. I gather you've been introducing yourself to the crew?'

'I take your safety very seriously, Mr Gustav. When I give an order I expect it to be obeyed. That way you'll have a better chance of survival. Trust me, I know what I'm doing.'

Gustav smiled. 'Of that I have no doubt.'

'Sir, I need to know your movements. I have arrangements to make for each destination. I also need to see about recruiting more help.'

'All in good time, Mr Hunter. All in good time. For now, be assured that I am staying here. I have everything I need. Worldwide communications, every comfort conceivable and perfect safety. Come, let us go and see the good news.'

The room on the other side of the bar was a fully-fitted cinema. The ship could receive every television station in the world that broadcast via satellite and Gustav was soon flicking through the channels. Whatever he was looking for he didn't appear to find. 'Duval, try the BBC and Reuters.'

'Yes, sir.' Duval left the room.

Hunter walked over to one wall which was lined with the very latest DVDs of films only just out on general release. 'You have an eclectic selection.'

'My guests have very different tastes.'

Gustav went back to flicking through the channels while Hunter sat down again and watched. Duval returned ten minutes later. 'There have been a dozen episodes so far. Mainly in the east, Greece. An Orthodox Church and a museum destroyed. A number of other killings and attacks. Nothing of major importance.'

'Anything on Rome or Rotterdam?'

'No, sir.'

'Paris? Stockholm? Madrid?'

'No, sir. It's still too early.'

'All right. As soon as you get something, let me know.' Gustav went back to channel hopping, ignoring the other two men.

Hunter stood up. 'I'm going to take a look outside. I want to get a better feel for your security. Mr Duval, may I have a word?' Duval followed him outside, closing the door. Hunter asked,

'Where's the armoury?'

'What?'

'The armoury. You must have one. Right now if we came

under attack I can improvise one or two weapons but they'll be about as much use as a chocolate teapot. You must have some real armaments stowed away somewhere. Somewhere a cursory customs examination won't turn up.'

Duval hesitated for a second before nodding. 'We do. But I need Mr Gustav's permission to show you.'

'Then get it. I can't emphasise enough how much danger he and by extension you and I are in. If TIFAT come after us we're in deep trouble. Believe me. I'll be on the upper deck. I want to recce the ship and anchorage and work out a plan of action. Meet me on the bridge in ten minutes.'

Before Duval could argue Hunter walked away. It was a small, almost imperceptible victory, but he had established that he took orders only from Gustav, not from his lackey.

Walking around the deck it was obvious that nothing could save Gustav in the event of an attack even by the most amateurish troops. Hunter bounded up the outside ladder to the bridge wing and stood admiring the view of the island, now directly ahead of the ship. Duval found him there a few seconds later.

'I'm to show you the armoury,' he said without preamble.

'Good. In the meantime we should flash up and get out of here. I cannot protect Mr Gustav if we are at anchor. If special forces came in now there would be nothing I could do to stop them, Duval. Nothing.'

'But they have no idea where we are.'

'Do you want to bet your *life* on it? We need to keep moving. I can talk to the Captain and work out a racetrack.'

'A racetrack?' Duval shook his head, confused.

'A course we can follow all night. Keep moving. Stay safe. I need to know how much fuel we have and what speed we can maintain and for how long. The higher the speed the better.'

Duval nodded. 'I'll speak to Mr Gustav.'

'You also need to talk to the Captain. He won't listen to me.'

Duval led the way onto the bridge where Novak sat in his captain's chair. 'I would like you to give Mr Hunter all the information he requires. Then prepare to get under way. Mr Hunter will tell you where we are going.'

'Yes, sir.' If Novak resented his orders he gave no indication. Duval left the two men. Hunter bent over the chart table and studied the local Admiralty chart for a few seconds. 'We want to be away from these shipping lanes. Out of sight of land and moving at a reasonable speed. How much fuel do we carry?'

'We're pretty much topped off. I filled the tanks in Palermo before coming to anchor.'

'What range does that give us?'

'Three thousand miles at fifteen knots. Less at higher speeds. Fifteen is our optimum cruising speed.'

Taking a pair of dividers Hunter measured off distances. 'If we establish a racetrack twenty miles south of Sicily we'll be out of sight of almost all the shipping lanes. Say fifty miles in each direction. Better yet, three hours in each direction.'

'Why? We're only wasting fuel.'

Hunter was about to explain as he would have done normally but decided it was time to exert a little authority. 'Does that present a problem? Endanger the ship in any way?'

'No. Of course not, but . . .'

'No buts, Captain. If I give another order, I don't expect you to ask questions. You're responsibility is clear, as is mine. So you do as I tell you provided it doesn't hazard the ship.'

The Captain had been bending over the chart but now he straightened up, bristling with anger. 'I do not care for your tone, Herr Hunter. As the Captain, if I ask a question, then I expect an answer.'

Hunter too straightened up and looked at the Captain squarely. 'You'll get one if I think you merit it. This once I will tell you. But only this once. A moving target is much harder to hit. Right now special services divers could be arriving under our keel and we'd know nothing about it. Or they could be parachuting in for all we know and the first indication we'd get is when they start shooting. At least if we are under sail they'll find it a damn sight more difficult. Is that understood?'

'*Ja. Ich verstehe.*' The Captain had lapsed into German.

Hunter was about to reply in the same language then thought better of it. 'Speak English, man.'

Struggling to hide his contempt, Novak said, 'I understand.' Quickly he added, 'I also agree. I can get us underway in thirty minutes.'

'Make it fifteen and we'll get on a lot better. I need to see the armoury. Get somebody to take me there.'

'We have a lookout on the upper bridge. He can show you.'

Hunter shook his head. 'I'll go and speak to him. Get two more men as sentries. They can accompany me to the armoury. It's time we sharpened the crew up around here.'

The armoury was deep in the ship, on the starboard side. Hunter entered through a door in the engine room. It was long and narrow, with room to walk past cage after cage of weapons. It was almost as well stocked as TIFAT's.

Hunter carried a bunch of keys in one hand, each one colourcoded to match a locked cage. One of the crewmen pointed ahead. 'Behind that door is where we keep the plastic.'

'Let's take a look.' Hunter unlocked the door and went inside a storage locker big enough to stand upright in. On the starboard side were racks of slabs of plastic explosive, while on the port side were different types of boxed detonators. Each was individually held in a round, padded slot, ten dets to each box. 'I've seen enough. Let's get topside.'

They had arrived at the engine room and Hunter was locking the door when the four big diesels began to burst into life. The men hurried. The noise level was nerve shredding. By the time they closed the engine room door behind them all four diesels were operating. Through the soles of their feet they could feel the chain rattling as it was shortened, prior to being raised.

Back on the bridge, Hunter found Duval as well as the Captain. 'Is Mr Gustav still in the cinema?'

'Yes. He's watching the news. He agrees with your strategy.'

'One more thing. We need to have the men fully armed at all times. The guns, if they remain locked in the armoury, give us about as much chance as a snowball in hell.'

'The sentry we have on watch is carrying a sidearm,' Duval argued.

Hunter snorted in derision. 'Useless. They need to have some thing with real stopping power. And they need to be ready at all times. From now on the men sleep with their guns. Leave it to me. I'll make all the arrangements, but first answer me this. How often has Mr Gustav been on board?'

'This is the first time in nearly a year.'

Hunter nodded. That explained a lot. The Swede obviously felt safe on the ship and his security man, Faubert, hadn't had an opportunity to implement the most commonsense of precautions. Hunter knew that what he was suggesting would have occurred to either Duval or Gustav at some point. Better to come from him as he continued to establish his *bona fides*.

The anchor was raised and the ship got underway. It was past 02.00 when they reached the area Hunter had suggested they patrol. On the way, he had taken members of the crew down to the armoury to find suitable guns. The choice was staggering. Hunter decided to issue Austrian Steyr TMPs. It was a close-quarter gun and had been in production for less than ten years. For himself, Hunter chose a Steyr AUG Para, an assault rifle. Three times heavier than the TMP, it held a magazine of 32 rounds and was far more accurate with a much longer range. He slung the gun over his shoulder, barrel pointing down, cocked and primed. He only needed to flick the safety to be able to fire the weapon. He had all the men, except the crew on watch, assembled in the crew's dining room. 'From now on you keep your guns with you at all times. Raise your hands if you've used this type of gun before.' He wasn't surprised to see every man raise a hand. 'Have you all served in the armed forces?' They all nodded. A few smirks were exchanged.

Hunter nodded and smiled. 'Good. That makes my life a lot easier. From now on the ship will operate in two watches. You'll either be on watch and alert or eating or sleeping. As far as we know nobody knows where Mr Gustav is and hopefully we'll keep it that way. But just in case . . .' Hunter continued his briefing. 'One last thing. Keep your guns safe. Don't have one up the spout and make sure the safety is on at all times.' It would give Hunter a half-second advantage. He hoped it would be enough.

Down in the cinema, Hunter found Gustav watching CNN, glued to what was happening on the screen. It looked like the aftermath of a street battle.

Gustav glanced over at Hunter and said, 'A police station in Rotterdam. Terrorists attacked it twenty minutes ago. Eight policemen have been killed.'

'And the terrorists?'

'Wiped out.' Gustav spoke with a degree of bitterness in his voice. 'I had hoped for a great deal more damage by the Arabs. And a lot more Dutch fatalities. But they were stopped at the police station.'

Hunter kept the anger out of his voice. 'Are there any details?'

'Rotterdam's Chief of Police has been speaking. The fool! All he had to do was follow orders. I wanted the station isolated and wiped out. Our Muslim puppets would have then gone on a killing spree in the area before being taken out by other police units. But they were stopped too soon. It is unbelievable.'

'Who stopped them?' Hunter asked.

'I don't know. But I will learn the answer soon.' The phone interrupted him. 'This is probably my source now.'

Gustav answered and held a short conversation in Dutch. The language was close enough to German for Hunter to be able to follow it. Gustav made it clear that he was angry with the low death rate among the police. He hung up, scowling at Hunter. 'It seems your former colleagues have interfered once more. A man named Walsh. Do you know him?'

'Of course. Colonel from the American Delta force. Second in command. Tough as hell.'

'He won't be bothering us again.'

'What do you mean?' Hunter asked. 'He's dead?' Somehow he managed to keep his voice steady.

'No. Merely wounded. A bullet in the leg and arm. He organised the policemen outside the station. When the Muslims attacked they were surprised from the rear and sides. The Chief of Police has had no option but to praise the action. A classic way of defending against greater odds, so I understand.'

Hunter nodded. 'Makes sense. That's what I would have done.

Take out the terrorists and then take their guns. No police force in the world is equipped to deal with heavily armed terrorists. I take it the Arabs were heavily armed?'

Gustav grunted. 'The best money can buy. It should have been a walk over. The stupid swine cannot be trusted to do the simplest of tasks.'

Hunter refrained from answering. It was a ludicrous and unjustified comment born of ignorance of urban guerrilla warfare. Knowing Col Hyram B. Walsh as he did, Hunter suspected it had been one hell of a fight. He only hoped Walsh would survive. Leaving Gustav to his browsing of TV channels, Hunter decided it was time to properly explore the ship. He had hopefully proven beyond a shadow of a doubt that he only had Gustav's safety at heart. The arming of the crew, the movement of the ship, all pointed clearly where his loyalties lay – the well-being of their leader.

He found what he was searching for on the top deck, directly below the bridge; the communications room. He tried the door. It opened at his touch and he went in. There were two men sitting there. One had on earphones, the other sat at a desk. A heavy calibre Colt Anaconda revolver lay on its wooden surface. A second after he had entered, the gun was pointing in the region of Hunter's belly button. The hand holding the gun was as steady as a rock.

'What's the latest?' Macnair asked as Isobel entered his office, obviously exhausted.

Isobel poured herself a cup of coffee and took a mouthful. 'Ugh! It's like tar.'

'I'll make some fresh,' Macnair spoke impatiently, 'but tell me the news first.'

'It looks like Gustav has only been playing with us up till now. He has really upped the ante in recent days. There have been twenty-eight incidents. In all of them we managed to take out the terrorists but we've suffered a lot of casualties. So far the totals are one hundred and ninety-eight terrorists dead, eighteen wounded and seven captured. On our side we've had thirty-eight civilians killed, nineteen policemen, seven soldiers and four – as you know – of our men.'

Macnair nodded. Four good men, each killed in separate incidents. Sergeants Maguire and Estephan, Corporals Hanson and Jarvis – Irish, Portuguese, Canadian and American. Good men. Hard to replace. They would be sorely missed.

'What about the nerve gas aboard the *Silver Beech*? If there are Weapons of Mass Destruction out there we need to know who's producing them and where they're coming from.'

Isobel shook her head. 'General, we've been everywhere. About the only place left is North Korea and I don't see it somehow. The Americans have been leaning very hard on anybody and everybody who could even remotely have supplied Gustav with the biotoxin. Nothing.'

'Do we yet know what the gas is?

Isobel shook her head. 'From the description of the deaths of Al-Adil and the liner's master we surmise that sarin is one constituent. But there is something else which we are unable to identify.'

'Okay. Back to the big question. Who? North Korea?'

'It doesn't make any sense. They want back into the international fold. And they have no love of Islam. No money in the world would be sufficient compensation if the Americans find out they were involved.'

Macnair sat back and put his hands behind his head. He was groggy from lack of sleep. He rested his eyes for a second and then snapped wide awake, sitting bolt upright. 'What if he manufactured the stuff *himself*? Start re-examining all Gustav's companies. Holdings within holdings. Doesn't he own a chemical manufacturer or something?'

Reaching for the file on his desk he flicked it open, running his finger down a list of names. 'Here. A chemical company. And here. An ecological company. What the hell does an ecological company do?'

Isobel shrugged. 'God knows. May I?' She took the file and checked what was written against the names. 'He sold them . . . oh, a year ago.'

273

'Did he indeed? Or did he just go underground with them? Check it out as soon as you can, please. And try and find out what it was the companies produced.'

'Yes, sir.' Isobel stood up, the coffee forgotten. 'Any news on Hiram?'

'He's going to be okay. One bullet went through his thigh and a second caused a flesh wound in the upper arm. Lost a lot of blood. Looked worse than it was. The hospital said, and I quote, "We'll discharge him in a few hours to protect our nurses".'

Isobel smiled. 'That sounds like Hiram.'

'What about the ship?'

'It's ploughing a furrow in a piece of the Med about twenty miles south of Sicily.'

'At speed?'

'Fifteen knots or so.'

'Figures. Hunter protecting Gustav. I just hope it's enough to keep him safe as well, till we get him some back-up. Check out those companies.' Where on earth could Gustav have got that gas from? And which was worse? A rogue state selling the stuff to him or Gustav making it? It was really no contest. If Gustav control over its manufacture and hence had unlimited access, then the threat he posed was mind-numbing.

19

'Point that gun the other way or I'll ram it up your . . .' Hunter didn't get any further as the hammer of the gun was cocked back with a loud click.

'You were saying?' The man was mid-thirties, blonde, muscle-bound and by his standards, tough. His hooked nose had obviously been broken at least once. He spoke English with an accent that sounded vaguely Scandinavian.

Hunter did the unexpected. He raised his arms, put his hands behind his head and said, 'You've got me.'

The man obviously felt in control. He stood up from behind his desk and walked around, a grin on his face. He knew who Hunter was and what Hunter had done but liked the feeling of control he was experiencing with a gun in his fist. He wondered how Hunter would react to a hard poke in the belly with the barrel. His curiosity made him step too close.

Hunter brought his hand down hard, jamming his thumb between the gun's hammer and the breech. Clasping his hand around the man's fist, Hunter twisted the gun through 180 degrees so that it was pointing at the man's stomach. The trigger guard had torn the skin off the man's finger and blood dripped steadily onto the deck.

Hunter smiled. 'If I take my hand away the hammer will strike the cartridge. It may or may not be sufficient to set it off. What do you think?'

The man stood stock still, sweat appearing on his brow while Hunter continued to smile at him.

'What I suggest,' Hunter spoke conversationally, 'is that you gently let go the gun and give it to me. This takes a Magnum point four-four cartridge and is one of the most formidable closequarter guns in the world.'

The man let go. Without breaking eye contact, Hunter felt the cylinder latch on the left side of the frame and pulled it to the rear. Swinging out the cylinder he pushed the ejector rod and dropped the bullets into the palm of his hand. He swung the cylinder shut and dropped the weapon onto the desk. As it was a trigger retracted hammer block, there was no safety catch.

'You're bleeding all over the deck.' Hunter's voice was still as measured. 'I suggest you clean it up.'

The man nodded nervously. He still didn't know how it had happened. One second he had the English bastard at the end of his gun and the next he was looking down its barrel. Putting his skinned finger into his mouth he took out a spotlessly clean handkerchief and knelt to wipe up the few drops of blood. He looked up nervously at Hunter, expecting a kick in the teeth at any time. Instead all he got was a smile.

'Good,' said Hunter. 'We're on the same side. Please don't point any more guns at me, the next time I may not be so understanding.'

'Nobody is allowed in here without Mr Gustav's express permission,' the man with the headphones said. He licked his dry lips. He had witnessed the move but couldn't believe it either.

'I suggest,' said Hunter, 'you add my name to the list. Please make sure your reliefs know it. Otherwise I won't be so gentle. You're the operator and you, I take it, are the guard.'

By now the guard had regained his seat behind his desk, feeling safer with a barrier between him and Hunter. He looked longingly at the stainless steel revolver and wished he could start again. Only this time he'd shoot the swine and ask questions after.

'The Colt is a good choice,' said Hunter. 'It's ideal for close work. Real stopping power. But if you are going to point it at somebody make damn sure you are able and willing to use it.'

The guard nodded. Hunter handed him back the bullets. 'Load

it. It's useless without them.' Turning to the operator, Hunter said, 'I want to know about our communications set-up. I assume they're world-wide and can be encrypted?'

Hunter spent the next ten minutes with the operator, making it clear that he knew what he was talking about, building up a rapport with the man. Once the operator's nerves had eased, they joked about being able to send Morse even in this day and age. Now almost anybody who understood computers could use the equipment in the room. It required only a bit of time with the instruction manual to learn what to do.

Even so, Hunter ensured he received a quick lesson on one or two pieces of gear.

'Do you carry an emergency transponder?' Hunter asked.

'Sure. It's operated by this button, and fires out the side of the hull. If we're sinking it'll stay attached down to a few thousand metres. The emergency signal covers all the usual frequencies from UHF to VLF so it reaches near and far.'

'Good. Let's hope we never need to use it.'

'Amen to that, sir.'

Good, thought Hunter. He had the man's respect; the 'sir' proved it. So he would have his obedience. Hopefully.

He had done what he had come to do, established a right to be in the comms centre. Now it was time to leave before any awkward questions were asked. Or he was found there by Gustav or Duval and had his right of entry immediately rescinded.

'Good night to you both.'

The men returned the salutation as Hunter went back into the corridor. He spent the next twenty minutes roaming the vessel, ostensibly checking the disposition of guards around the ship and who was on watch. He quickly sized up the operation. There was no engineer. The officer of the watch monitored the engines from the bridge. Any problems and alarms rang on the bridge, in the engineer's cabin and in the main mess. Engines could be shut down using controls on the starboard side of the bridge. Fire sprinklers worked automatically, water or inert gas, depending on the location of the conflagration. The *Stockholm* was fully automated and needed only a very small crew to run effectively. In two watches, the ship had many spare hands to act as guards. In fact there were ten of them, scattered throughout the top decks.

Hunter had a word with each man. His message was always the same. 'They'll come from the sea. Fast inflatables. Very vulnerable. They won't have a chance. Trust me.'

By the time he had finished his pep talks the guards were jumpy, just as he had intended. Peering at the sea, imagining what wasn't there, they were tense and on edge. TIFAT wouldn't come from the sea, when they *did* come. Or so Hunter hoped.

There was nothing more he could do for an hour or two. It was time to get his head down.

At 04.30 he was up again and prowling the ship. All was quiet and nobody saw him passing. The cinema was empty so he supposed Gustav had gone to bed. A quick search convinced him that the information he was looking for was not to be found. There was only one thing for it – a detour to the engine room.

The corridor outside Gustav's quarters was brightly lit. Hunter used a screwdriver to unscrew the light fixing and gingerly took out the bulb. It was hot. A quick shake and he heard the filament break. He replaced the bulb and the fixing, leaving that part of the corridor in shadow. Gently he tried the door handle. He moved it so slowly it took a full minute to twist all the way back. Using his other hand he eased the door open, millimetre by millimetre. The room was dark but he still took his time. It was minutes before the door was wide enough for him to slip through. Equally gently he closed it behind him. Standing for a few moments to let his eyes become accustomed to the deeper gloom, he gradually began to make out the hard edges of the furniture.

The opposite side of the cabin had a door to Gustav's sleeping quarters. The room Hunter was in was luxuriously furnished with a huge desk in one corner. Using a masked torch, lifted from the engine room, Hunter rapidly went through the drawers but found nothing of use. He found a lap-top computer and was about to switch it on when he had second thoughts. If it was properly secure then as soon as Gustav switched it on himself he would know somebody had tried to get into the machine. And it wouldn't take a genius to guess who that somebody was.

Behind a painting he found a locked safe. It had a combination lock and key. He had no skills to open it so he left it alone. Twenty minutes later he was back in his room, lying on his bed, hands behind his head, deep in thought. There had to be another way.

He slept until 05.50. After a shower and shave he dressed, armed himself with a cup of coffee and went up to the bridge. There were three seamen officers who were qualified to keep watch, including the Captain. As he knew, the First Officer was on watch.

'My name is Hunter,' he introduced himself.

The man nodded warily. He wore two gold stripes on his shoulders. Hunter guessed he was mid-twenties, European but not British. He was stocky, black haired, fit looking. Sitting in the captain's chair, he watched Hunter with a mixture of trepidation and interest. 'My name is Jacob Hernstein.'

'Jacob, I'm a qualified watchkeeper. If you'd like to take a break I'll relieve you for an hour. The cook's up and making breakfast.'

Shaking his head, the officer said, 'I think not. The *Kapitän* would have me hanged.'

Hunter wasn't surprised but he'd thought he'd try. 'Okay. I'll be in the chartroom. I need to work out where we're going and discuss our options with Mr Gustav.' The words were meaningless but the officer, used to obeying, merely accepted them at face value.

The chartroom was accessed via a door at the back of the bridge. It contained a full portfolio of charts covering the world, a rack of used ship's logs and a bookcase of maritime publications. It also had a navigation computer that Hunter was very familiar with. It only took seconds to instruct the machine to print out every port of call the ship had made during the previous two years and to give the date and duration of each stay. The laser printer spewed out the information and Hunter quickly pocketed the A4 sheets. Lifting an atlas from the rack he tucked it under his arm before returning to the bridge.

A magnificent dawn was breaking and he stood for a few seconds next to Hernstein, awed by the sight. He could see from the other man's face that he too was enthralled.

'There's nothing like it, is there?' said Hunter.

'Mmm?' Hernstein glanced at Hunter before returning his attention to the sunrise.

'This time of morning, at sea, watching another day breaking. People who have never been to sea have no idea how truly beautiful it is.'

The officer nodded his head. 'I agree, it is magnificent.'

'I'm going below to get another coffee and look through this atlas before speaking to Mr Gustav.' Hunter left with a smile. It wasn't much but he had connected with Hernstein and begun to build a little rapport based on a mutual passion for the sea. It could make the man hesitate at the wrong moment. *Would it be enough*?

Back in his cabin, Hunter quickly scanned the printed lists. Most of the names were of major ports around Europe. There was one he didn't recognise. Pozzallo. It took only seconds to find in the atlas. The southern end of Sicily. One visit. Three weeks before the attack on the liner. Interesting, thought Hunter, but was it the answer he was looking for?

Isobel found Macnair in the briefing room with many of the teams just back from their operations across Europe. They were all agreed on what had gone right and, more importantly, what had gone wrong. Across the continent TIFAT operatives had been fighting desperately to contain the damage Gustav's attacks could have wrought. The deaths of four of their number cast a pall but they had been lucky. Many more could so easily have died.

Seeing Isobel enter the room and gesturing, Macnair excused himself and left the debriefing to Jim Carter.

'Fresh coffee, this time,' the General greeted her.

In his office he put on the coffee maker. 'Hiram will be back in a few hours. Burg is picking him up at Edinburgh airport.'

'Good. Thanks.' She took the proffered mug. It was black,

strong and sugarless, just as she liked it. 'We tracked down those companies you were interested in. They were both closed down about a year ago after Gustav ostensibly sold them. One was definitely involved in some sort of genetic engineering but exactly what we don't know.'

'What about previous employees?'

'Ah!' Isobel smiled. 'We thought of that. So we looked up the tax records of the companies. They were both UK based which made it marginally easier. We identified twenty-five former employees from the more likely of the two companies – Genotech Laboratories.'

Macnair, his own coffee in hand, sat behind his desk and waited patiently for Isobel to continue.

'What we found is very interesting. And statistically impossible on two accounts. After the company closed, seventeen employees left the UK. But,' Isobel paused significantly, 'the remaining eight employees, within a period of less than six weeks, were all dead.'

'What!' Macnair jerked upright, spilling coffee onto the floor. He ignored the rapidly expanding stain and asked, 'Are you sure?'

'Positive. One died in a house fire, four perished in separate car crashes where no other vehicle was involved, two were mugged and one was shot. The muggings and shooting are still open files with the police forces involved. It can't be a co-incidence. Somebody had those people killed.'

'Gustav.' The general screwed up his face, concentrating hard. 'What jobs did they do?'

'Drivers, lab-technicians, a secretary . . . No major players. They ranged in ages from late twenties to early fifties. There's nothing connecting them apart from their work with Genotech. The other peculiar fact which cannot be coincidence is that none of the men were married. They don't appear to have any families or close relatives.'

'Any idea where they went?'

Isobel smiled. 'An inspired piece of work by Leo. He compiled a list of those who had emigrated and went into every social-security computer in Europe to see if they were to be found.'

'And?'

'They work for a new company in Italy. Sicily, to be precise. We are trying to trace ownership right now but I'll bet a pound to a penny it'll be Gustav's. He has a house there on the north side of the island.'

'I won't take your bet. Do we know where in Sicily?'

'A little place called Íspica. It's seven or eight kilometres from the southern most tip of the island.'

Macnair was busy with his computer, calling up Sicily, typing in the name of the place. He pointed at the screen. 'There it is. Just to the north of a small port called Pozzallo. Get the satellites on it, will you?'

'I've issued instructions already.'

Hunter needed to get the information on Pozzallo to TIFAT HQ. The bridge's state-of-the-art radio system would suffice. But how to gain access without alerting the officer of the watch? The goons in the communications centre meant it was a no-go. But this was absolutely vital information. He wasn't one hundred percent certain, but it might let Isobel look in the right direction. Was it worth the risk of exposure to tell her? Possibly. The trouble was, looking at Sicily on the chart, Gustav could have chosen any of a hundred places to manufacture the deadly nerve gas. Anywhere from Catánia in the east to Caltanissetta in the west. But that made no sense. The ship could have gone into a closer port. He stared down at the chart. No, it would be somewhere local. Ragusta, Módica, Íspica, Rosolini . . . But which one? There was only one thing for it. He would have to find an excuse to get ashore and take a look.

Isobel walked into Macnair's office pushing a wheelchair. 'General, look who I've found.'

Macnair bounded to his feet. 'Hiram, my dear fellow, but it's good to have you back.' The two men shook hands. 'Can I get you anything?'

'No, sir. I'm fine. The wound in my arm is nothing and the bullet went straight through the top of my thigh. It missed the bone, thankfully. And it was a steel tipped bullet so the entry wound and exit wound are the same size. About as big as a dime.'

'You were lucky,' said Macnair. 'By the way, I've spoken to Bragg.'

Walsh's detachment of Delta Force was headquartered at Fort Bragg. 'Thanks, sir.'

'It seems they're going to put you up for a Purple Heart.'

Walsh groaned. 'God, how embarrassing.'

Macnair grinned. 'That's what I told them you'd say. Can't be helped though. Wounded in action and all that. Now,' Macnair became serious, 'are you ready to get back to work?'

'Sir!' Isobel began to protest, 'Hiram needs proper rest. I only brought him in to say hullo.'

'Thanks, Isobel, but I'm okay. I'm ready, sir. I learnt a lot in Rotterdam. The rot in the police force is widespread. They talked only because Gustav hung them out to dry. They lost half their men in the fight and won't support him any longer. Quite the reverse. We ought to be able to take advantage of the fact.'

Macnair nodded. 'Will they testify?'

Walsh grinned. 'You bet your life they will. In exchange for immunity.'

'From prosecution?' Isobel asked, puzzled. 'But they haven't done anything wrong. Not in the legal sense.'

'Isobel's right,' said Macnair. 'The only criminals are the Islamic terrorists. And Gustav for financing them. But technically the police forces and armed services who agree with Gustav are not guilty of any crime.'

Walsh nodded. 'All along they've been counting on the rightwing coming to power in Europe. If that happens then they would definitely be safe. But if we stop Gustav then who's to say laws won't be changed to punish those same men for supporting the idea of a whites-only Europe? They don't trust the politicians. And who can blame them? It's because of Europe's politicians you're in this mess.'

Macnair nodded gloomily. What the Delta Colonel was saying not only made sense but was, without doubt, the case. Damn all politicians! Europe was a complete quagmire with its immigration policy. No wonder there was a backlash.

'We've contained Gustav for now,' said Macnair. 'The blood-bath he'd envisaged hasn't happened. I don't know how many more fundamentalists he has on his pay-roll but he must be hurting by now. Especially in light of the number that have been killed or arrested.'

'Which means he might try to do something desperate,' said Isobel.

'Precisely,' agreed Macnair. 'Like let loose with more WMDs. Any news about the factory on Sicily?'

Isobel shook her head. 'Nothing. I've learnt that they closed down the original business because of the level of animal rights protesters the company was attracting. Italy doesn't have the same problem. Besides which, it seems the local Mafia has given the place its blessing and support. A lot of money has gone into the area, thanks to the company. We don't know who the ultimate owner is but my money is still on Gustav. We've no proof of the WMD manufacture. As far as the public is concerned they do genetic experiments, looking for cures for certain ailments. Stem cell work and all that. It's highly controversial but with huge potential.'

'Is it possible that's what the place is really being used for and we're making complete asses of ourselves?' Walsh asked the question the other two had also been considering.

'Anything's possible,' replied Macnair. Glancing at his watch he added, 'Tea is being served in the wardroom. Let's go across and I'll bring you up to date on a few facts. The bottom line is, we can't be certain. And we can't go ahead without proof.'

Finally, Hunter had an ideal excuse to go ashore in Sicily and he wasted no time in speaking to Duval about it. If he could convince the secretary then Gustav would be all the easier to persuade. He found the man in the upper salon, standing at a window, staring out to sea.

'I've been giving more thought to a possible attack while we're at sea,' said Hunter without preamble.

Duval appeared to snap out of a trance. 'What did you say?' he frowned.

'I think it is all too possible for special forces to attack the ship using fast raiders. Now, we'd give a good account of ourselves but it would be a good idea to get some real fire-power. Heat seeking missiles and heavy machine-guns would be useful.'

'And what do you suggest?' There was no hiding the sarcasm in Duval's voice, 'That we call in at our local supermarket and buy some?'

'No. I suggest we go ashore in Sicily and ask your friends in the Mafia. They can get us what we need.'

Duval looked dubiously at Hunter for a few seconds, then said, 'We're already headed for Sicily. I'll see what I can do. Though I doubt we'll have the time to meet them.'

Hunter frowned. 'When was it decided that we were going to Sicily and why wasn't I informed?'

'Mr Gustav doesn't consult his bodyguard about his movements. He issues instructions. We carry them out. He only made the decision a few minutes ago. I'd stay out of his way for now, if I were you. He's absolutely furious about the reports we've received from Europe. The attacks we orchestrated have, to a large degree, been foiled by your ex-colleagues. Mr Hunter, we have lost many of our,' here Duval managed to crack a smile, 'shall we say, friends? The useless swine. Many of them have been killed and others arrested. Thanks to Mr Gustav's foresight, the cells operate in isolation; none of the attacks can be traced back to us. However, insufficient damage has been done to sway public opinion to the extent we hoped. So we have to go to Sicily.'

'What's on Sicily?'

'That, Mr Hunter, is not for you to know. Meet me on the bridge in half an hour. I need to speak to Mr Gustav.'

Recognising a dismissal when he heard one, and not prepared to make an issue of it just then, Hunter left the room. He went quickly along to the bridge where he found the Captain sitting in his chair. A glance at the chart told him all he wanted to know. The pencilled course headed straight to Pozzallo.

'Can we get alongside?'

Novak looked at Hunter with irritation. 'Yes.'

'It would be safer if we stayed offshore, steaming.'

Novak looked at Hunter for a second or two before replying. 'Believe me, Mr Hunter, we will be perfectly safe alongside. If anyone came within a hundred metres of the ship they wouldn't live longer than a minute or two.'

'How can you be so certain?'

'Trust me, I know.' The Captain turned his head to look back out to sea, binoculars in hand, scanning ahead of the ship.

Another glance at the chart showed that they would be near Pozzallo in about ninety minutes, alongside shortly after that. If he was right, then Hunter guessed that they were going to pick up more nerve gas. Gustav had to be stopped, no matter what.

Hunter offered to take the watch, but was curtly refused. Nevertheless, he stayed on the bridge until Duval arrived.

'Care to tell me what's going on?'

'We are going into Pozzallo. There we will be met by some friends, who will escort us to our destination. We will be away from the ship for less than an hour. When we return we will put to sea immediately. Captain, please arrange to take on fresh provisions. Mr Hunter, you will escort us. Please select three other men to accompany us.'

'And my recommendation that we need heavier weapons? Missiles?'

'Mr Gustav feels it won't be necessary. That we have all we need.'

Hunter was about to argue then thought better of it. What the hell. He'd only suggested it as an excuse to get ashore on Sicily. And here he was, being handed the perfect opportunity.

'I'd say,' said Leo, looking at the picture, 'that the ship is heading for Sicily. More accurately, Pozzallo.'

Isobel stood at her assistant's shoulder and watched the screen. 'It looks like it. And that's right next to Íspica where we think Gustav's factory is located. Of course, he could just as easily be going to any one of a dozen or more ports once the ship has neared land.'

'It's not likely,' replied Leo. 'Otherwise they'd go straight there. What's that?' He pointed at the screen. 'There's another and another.'

'Looks like small craft to me,' said Isobel. 'And they're heading fast towards the ship. See if you can get better pictures.'

Leo's fingers flew across the keyboard, hammering it, issuing instructions to the satellite orbiting hundreds of miles above the Mediterranean Sea. Slowly the picture zoomed in on the smaller targets about ten miles ahead of the ship. The small boats were closing fast.

'They're carrying armed men. Looks like soldiers. They're either reinforcements for Gustav or they intend to attack him.'

'There's nothing we can do about the former,' Isobel said. 'But if they are on the attack, where did they come from?'

Leo plotted a hypothetical course backwards. All three tracks converged on a civilian ship steaming south and currently just off the south-eastern corner of Sicily.

'Doesn't tell us anything. They could be anybody.' Isobel frowned at the screen.

Hunter spotted them on the radar first. Grabbing binoculars he scanned the sea. Rigid raiders and coming in fast. Where the hell had they come from? And who were they? One thing was certain. They weren't TIFAT. The primary objective had not yet been achieved. It was vital they learn where the WMDs were sourced. Killing Gustav might not be enough to stop his organisation; not if they retained access to Weapons of Mass Destruction.

Nobody else had noticed what was happening until Hunter grabbed the microphone to the ship's tannoy system. 'Do you hear there? Stand-by to repel boarders. We are under attack by three fast boats coming in from ahead. All off-watch men muster on the upperdeck. Do not, I repeat, do not show yourselves until the boats are close in.'

'What the hell!' *Kapitän zur See* Novak looked at Hunter in shock.

Duval, too, stood frozen to the spot, unable to move.

'Take a look,' said Hunter. 'You can see them without glasses now.'

Three black spots were approaching on the horizon, taking shape, hardening in the late afternoon sun. Each boat held half a dozen men. They were well armed and opening out in a pincer movement.

'Are they guests of yours?' Hunter asked Duval.

'No, of course not.'

'I don't care who they are. They have to be stopped,' said Gustav appearing on the bridge. 'Mr Hunter, annihilate them!'

20

'Hold your fire until I tell you,' Hunter shouted. 'Stay down and out of sight. When I give the word open up with everything you've got. Remember your weapons are short range and don't waste any rounds. Shoot at the engines. Try not to kill anybody.' Now, he thought, I'd better try and save a few lives.

His Steyr AUG Para was three times as long as the weapons carried by the crew and far more accurate. He slung the gun across his front and went out onto the starboard bridge wing. One boat was at about green four-five, one right on the bows and a third at red four-five. The shot he was attempting was extraordinarily difficult because of the rate of change of the target's relative position. A glance through his binoculars confirmed one motor. A big one.

Settling his elbows on the top of the safety rail he squinted along the barrel. He had set the sight for 200 metres. A second later the bow of the boat came into his sight, then the engine, and he fired. The gun was on single shot. He missed. He readjusted his aim and waited for the boat to appear in his sight again. It was now at 150 metres. Bow – motor – fire. The bullet smashed into the engine and it stopped almost instantly. The men in the boat opened fire with a withering blast. Bullets struck against the sides of the ship and shattered glass on the bridge.

'Hard aport and increase to full ahead,' Hunter yelled.

The Captain did as ordered and the ship began to pick up speed. By now one of the boats was within 100 metres and thirty degrees on the starboard bow, turning to keep track. Because of its speed and the way it was bouncing across the water, its occupants couldn't open fire. The men in the inflatable Hunter had stopped were still shooting but now they were being hampered by the second rigid raider edging into their sights. Their fire was tailing off.

Hunter fired three times in succession and saw the top of the second boat's engine blown away. The boat surged to a halt, giving its occupants a more stable platform and they opened fire. The *Stockholm* was still turning, its speed increasing, and she was now stern on so that the bullets struck harmlessly at the hull.

Looking at the wake, Hunter guessed they were approaching 25 knots or more. The third boat was almost alongside, its occupants throwing grappling hooks upwards at the starboard rails. The ship's crew didn't wait for orders. They leant out and opened fire from close range. It was a turkey shoot. The men in the boat didn't stand a chance. Hunter shot out the third engine and the boat floundered but not before many of the eight men on board were wounded or killed.

'Stop firing! Stop firing!' Hunter yelled. Though some of the crew did as ordered others continued shooting until the boat was out of range.

One man was still taking pot shots when Hunter stalked up to him. He grabbed the gun, tore it from his hands and swiped him across the side of the head with it. 'When I say stop, I mean stop,' he snarled. 'You bloody fool! We don't want to make enemies of special forces or whoever the hell they are. They have long memories and a longer reach. They'll hunt us down one by one to get revenge for what you stupid swine just did. This is a short term situation. Once Mr Gustav's people come to power we will have to work with these men. We don't want them to resist us any more than necessary.' He gave up. He could see from the man's obdurate look that his message wasn't getting home. Instead he stalked back to the bridge to have it out with Gustav.

By now the ship had turned again, giving the stopped raiders a wide berth, before continuing its journey towards Sicily. On the bridge he found Gustav, looking deadly serious. Novak was trying hard not to smile.

'Of all the stupid . . .' Hunter began but Gustav raised a hand to stop him.

'I wish an explanation, Mr Hunter. Why did you not just kill those men?'

Hunter understood the Captain's smirk and had difficulty controlling his temper. 'You really are the biggest bunch of moronic thugs and dickheads that walk,' Hunter began.

'How dare you speak to me like that,' Gustav began but Hunter interrupted him by prodding his finger into the other man's chest.

'I dare, *Mr* Gustav, because your thugs have just endangered all our lives. I couldn't care less about their lives. *Your* life I'm paid to care about and *my* life I care about very much. We don't know who those men are. Suppose they are CIA or MI6? Or Special Forces from one of a dozen countries? They harbour grudges. They'll come after you no matter what. And it won't be a big splashy death. It'll be quiet and subtle and the headlines in your own papers will be that you died of a heart attack or an accident. And why? Because you killed their mates. Interservice rivalry is one thing, support for your oppo is another. Word has got out that you're behind the troubles and they know where you are.'

Gustav stared at Hunter, weighing his words. 'You may be right, Mr Hunter. I appear to have underestimated you again.'

'Well make it the last time! Now, tell your crew and this idiot of a Captain that from now on they do what I tell them. That way you may just live long enough to enjoy the fruits of your labours.'

Gustav nodded. 'Duval. Issue the orders.'

From the expression on Duval's face, Hunter didn't think he'd have any more trouble with the American.

'Now, will you kindly tell me what's going on?' Hunter spoke in a reasonable voice. 'So that I can plan what we do?'

'I have to visit one of my companies on Sicily. It is near to where we are berthing.'

'Where?'

'That doesn't matter,' Gustav shot back with a flash of his former haughtiness. 'Suffice to say that I will not be there for long.'

'Total time?'

'No more than an hour.'

'Make it less. Captain, I want to see a chart of the harbour. You go alongside and drop us off but be ready to leave fast. Those troops came from somewhere and that could be anything from a tramp steamer to a nuclear submarine. Or even an aircraft carrier.'

'An aircraft carrier?' Gustav queried.

'Yes. Part of the American Sixth Fleet, which operates almost continuously in this area, keeping an eye on the Middle East. Those men we just stopped could even now be whistling up reinforcements. And I don't mean another raiding party but aircraft that'll blow us to kingdom come.'

The other three men looked nervously out of the window as if expecting an attack at any second.

'You won't see them,' said Hunter, 'until the rockets start landing. Captain, our only chance is full speed for Sicily. Even the Americans won't open fire on an unarmed ship in a port belonging to one of its allies.'

Kapitän zur See Novak pushed open the throttles of all four diesels as far as he could, trying for every fraction of a knot of speed. What Hunter had just said made eminent sense.

Macnair, alerted by Isobel to the attack, was already on the telephone demanding explanations. He was getting nowhere. The Secretary-General was apologetic but he had no more intelligence than TIFAT. Of course, he agreed with Macnair, until the source of the nerve gas was found Gustav had to remain unharmed. He also agreed to try and find out what had happened.

Isobel rushed back into his office, uncharacteristically without knocking. Macnair had just replaced the receiver and greeted her with a raised eyebrow.

'It was a combined Op, General, CIA and the French.'

'How do you know?'

'We intercepted some signal traffic. They're spitting blood.

Five of their men have been killed and two seriously wounded. They want Gustav dead.'

'The fools! Okay, Isobel, leave it to me. I've more calls to make.'

The CIA at Langley wouldn't or couldn't put him through to the Director and so he had to go via the Pentagon. He finally managed to track down General Colin Stafford.

'Macnair? What can I do for you?'

Hearing the formal tone in the senior officer's voice Macnair modified what he had wished to say. 'Sir, you heard about the attack on Gustav's ship?'

'Yes. I have just received a request to blow the bastard out of the water. We're considering sending in a couple of F14s.'

Macnair tightened his grip on the receiver as though he was trying to crush it. 'Sir, you can't do that.'

'Don't tell me what I can and cannot do, General.'

'Listen to me, Colin,' Macnair changed tack. 'We have to find out from where Gustav got the nerve gas and to destroy the source at all costs.'

'I hear you, Malcolm,' Stafford said more reasonably, 'but the CIA and the French are screaming blue murder.'

'They shouldn't have gone in. This is our job. TIFAT's. Not theirs.'

'Well, as they see it you aren't doing very much. And they saw an opportunity to stop Gustav.'

'What will that achieve?' Macnair's tone was icy. 'This isn't about one man any longer. He may have funded the Islamic fundamentalists initially but now half of Europe is backing him. Tens, maybe hundreds of millions of ordinary people think he's right. Many are political leaders. The bandwagon is rolling so hard and fast it's almost unstoppable. If Gustav dies now what will we say? That the French and Americans killed him? That'll go down well with his supporters. Or how about more disinformation and we blame the Muslims? Or Europe's right wing? Whichever way you play it we'll lose and the tidal wave of change that Gustav has created will be unstoppable. What's more the WMDs would still be in their hands.'

'So what is it you're suggesting?'

'His control of the print and TV media has been almost total. In effect, we're fighting a propaganda war. We need absolute proof that Gustav has created WMDs for use in Europe. We have to discredit him and his followers with an overwhelming blitz in newspapers, on radio and television. When the silent majority learn how they've been duped and to what length Gustav and his cohorts were prepared to go, they'll turn away in revulsion. But we need time to prepare. And we need Gustav alive for a while longer yet.'

Stafford was silent for a few seconds, pondering Macnair's words. 'I hope,' he said finally, 'you know what you're doing.'

'So do I, Colin. So do I. Now please, call off the dogs.'

The sun was setting as the SS *Stockholm* entered the small port. There was plenty of water under her keel and sufficient room for her to dock – just. Normally Pozzallo would have been full of fishing boats and a few private yachts but, unknown to Hunter, the local Mafia had arranged for the harbour to be emptied.

Standing on the port side, watching the land slip close by, Hunter could appreciate the Captain's delicate handling of the ship. When the first heaving line was thrown, the ship's bow and stern thrusters were already pushing the hull towards the wall. Men with guns helped to tie up the ship alongside.

Three large, black saloon cars with tinted windows waited on the quay. There were no sightseers, nobody out strolling or sitting in either of the two small cafés. He looked around the port. There was just enough room to turn the large vessel.

Entering the bridge, Hunter said, 'Captain, I take it that normally you'd make a sternboard and turn once you were in the open sea?'

'*Ja*. That is correct.'

'Can you turn here? That way we can save a few minutes.'

The Captain pondered the question before nodding. 'If we use ropes to warp the ship around. With the thrusters it should be possible.'

'Good. Then please do so while we are away.'

Minutes later Hunter, Gustav and Duval were in one of the cars, three of the crew followed behind. In the lead car four armed Mafiosi led the way. The driver of Hunter's car was an ill-smelling oaf who reeked of stale wine and cigarette smoke. His grin showed broken and discoloured teeth. Nothing was said as the cars accelerated away from the tiny village.

At the edge of the buildings the road branched right along the coast and left inland. They veered left towards the mountains. Ten minutes later they were approaching a main road that circumnavigated Sicily. On the other side of the road was the small town of Íspica. The cars swept right towards Rosolini and, a kilometre along the highway, turned off the road. They halted in front of a locked gate with a guardroom to one side. The driver in the first car spoke to the armed guard and the gate opened electronically. The perimeter fence was brightly lit with arc-lamps placed every fifty metres. Running along the top of the fence and leaning outwards were strands of wickedly sharp-looking barbed wire. A patrol of two armed guards with large, brutish dogs walked briskly along the fence. It was, Hunter concluded, well protected.

'What about staff security?' Hunter asked. 'How do they get in and out?'

If he noticed the exchange of glances between Gustav and Duval he showed no sign.

Gustav shrugged. 'There is no harm in you knowing. The staff live on the premises, in an underground complex. It is extremely well equipped.'

Hunter was surprised. 'And they put up with that? What about recreation?'

Gustav smiled with satisfaction. 'These people are extremely well paid. The job lasts a year. We bus in, what shall we call it, entertainment? Yes, just the word. Every Saturday.'

'What about the female staff?'

'They're all men,' came the blunt reply.

There had been no sign announcing the company and there was no name on the building's façade. When he alighted from the car Hunter could see that it was a brand new, single story

295

edifice, about a hundred metres wide. What was most discon-
certing from his point of view was that there were no windows.
Even the door was solid.

'Mr Gustav and I will go in alone,' said Duval.

As Hunter made a move to follow them, Gustav put a hand on
his arm. 'You will stay here too, Mr Hunter,' said Gustav. 'I will
be perfectly safe inside. And we will be less than ten minutes.'

Knowing when not to argue, Hunter nodded. 'Spread out and
keep your eyes open,' he told the other bodyguards. 'If the men
who attacked us knew we were on the ship then they might be
tracking us and know about this place.' He turned back to Gustav.
'Please hurry.'

His words galvanised Gustav and he hurried towards the door,
casting nervous looks around him. Duval followed, equally
perturbed. The fact was, Hunter *was* concerned. Whoever had
attacked the ship could come after them again. If so, a firefight
would be most unwelcome, he thought, with complete understatement.

Gustav and Duval were back within five minutes. Duval carried
a holdall which appeared full though not heavy.

'Open the trunk,' Hunter ordered the driver and stood at the
back of the car. He took the bag from Duval and placed it inside
the car. Quickly running his hand over the simulated leather he
felt three round shapes each about the size of a football. His blood
ran cold. Any lingering doubts disappeared.

'Let's go, let's go,' Hunter chivvied them as they piled in and
took off with a squeal of tyres.

The return journey to the ship was uneventful and less than
thirty minutes after leaving Pozzallo they were back in the port.
The ship had been turned and was pointing towards the open sea.
Only a bow line and stern line held her alongside.

Hunter had taken a step towards the gangway when a gun was
shoved into his side. He stopped in bewilderment. 'What the
hell . . . ?'

Gustav turned to him with a smile. 'I am sorry, Mr Hunter,
but I'm forced to terminate your employment. Forthwith and
with immediate effect. You won't be coming with us.'

'But . . .'

The blow was hard and he didn't see it coming. As he sank to his knees he was engulfed by blackness.

'Take him away,' said Gustav. 'I want to learn everything he knows. About me, our organisation and about TIFAT.'

Hunter came to slowly. His head hurt like hell and when he tried to move shooting pains flashed from his skull down his shoulders and arms. Nausea washed over him and he fought hard to keep it down. He lay still, collecting his thoughts and his strength. What was niggling at him? That was it . . . why was he still alive? Information! Gustav needed to know what he carried in his head.

Gustav must have planned it all along. The nerve gas! Christ, the man was a maniac.

Slowly Hunter became aware of his surroundings. He knew that a blow to the head was a lot more dangerous than shown in film stunts. You didn't just get up and walk away, fully functional. Permanent brain damage could be sustained which could result in epilepsy, tunnel vision or a host of other problems, even paralysis. He realised that he was lying on his back, on something soft. There was a smell of earth and fish. An odd combination. Perhaps the blow had affected his olfactory nerves? He was on some sort of rough cloth. His fingers moved, gripping the fabric. His brain suggested he was on a pile of sacks and he didn't question it.

Tentatively he moved his legs and his arms. He touched the side of his head. It felt sticky. With a great effort and a stifled moan he sat up. He placed his head between his hands and threw up all over his feet. They appeared to have taken his shoes. He sat still and tried to open his eyes. He couldn't and panic welled up in him, threatening to engulf him, but he fought it down. Blood, he thought. Slowly he collected saliva in his mouth and spat into his hand. He wiped his right eye and the lid flickered open. He pulled the left lids apart and blinked owlishly around him.

It was dark. Not pitch black but it was obviously night time.

He was in a shed of some description. Images and thoughts tumbled through his mind. Yes, he was on a pile of sacks. Over in a corner there appeared to be a pile of lobster pots. One window cast pale, white light from a full moon. There was utter silence and then a cat meowed faintly.

Standing up with difficulty, Hunter felt the room spin and collapsed back onto the sacks. He felt sick again but controlled the urge to vomit. His mouth tasted like the bottom of a bird cage. This time when he stood he stayed on his feet. He shuffled across the packed earth floor.

The outline of a door was clearly discernible. He heard running water and followed the sound. The hut was large, maybe ten metres by seven or eight. About three metres high. The roof was pitched and what looked like tanks lined one wall. The sound of water was coming from one end of the tanks. When he got to them, his eyes now accustomed to the gloom, Hunter saw they were open topped and full of water. He reached in and wet his hand. It was cool. He tasted it. Salty! Gingerly he leaned forward and washed his face and then his head. The side of his head stung like hell. Taking a deep breath he ducked his face into the water. The cold reduced the pain and cleared his mind. He saw something moving in the tank and in alarm lifted his face. Tentatively he reached in and, with his sleeve rolled back and the water up to his elbow, felt the hard body of a lobster. He lifted it out and saw that its claws were tied shut. Dropping it back into the water he continued searching.

By the door he found a tap and turned it on, slowly, careful not to make too much noise. He washed out his mouth and drank copious amounts of fresh water. He was beginning to feel like the living again. The side of his head had a bump the size of a small egg. When he touched around it, it felt painful but hard. Thank God. If it had been even the slightest bit soft he knew he would have been in serious trouble. Though he was in agony, he didn't think his skull was cracked.

His next priority was to get out of there. He went to the window and stared out but could see nothing. Realising the panes of glass were grimy with dust, he rubbed a spot clean. He had assumed he was near the coast and sure enough, in the distance, he could see the sea, shifting restlessly in the moonlight. It was maybe a kilometre away. Perhaps two.

There didn't appear to be any guards outside. The building was in a clearing, surrounded by trees. Not high but widespread, bushy. Olive trees, he guessed. He tried the door, opening it very, very slowly. It took an age but eventually the gap was wide enough to put his head through. Cautiously he looked out. Nothing stirred. Nobody yelled and no one shot at him. He stepped outside, straining his ears, listening to the sound of the night, trying to distinguish between the breeze in the leaves and any alien sounds. He heard nothing untoward.

He was surprised there was no guard. Maybe, he thought, they believed they'd hit him so hard he'd stay unconscious.

The ground outside the hut was scrub – stony but predominantly sand. Packed earth showed where vehicles regularly came and went. He walked around the hut. The olive trees were set about fifty metres away. They surrounded the area, except where a track led towards the sea. He went down the track, picking his way carefully, the ground uncomfortable on his shoeless feet. About two hundred metres from the hut he saw a gate, three or four metres high. Then he saw the glinting of moonlight on a high, wire-linked fence. When he got closer he saw it was topped with barbed wire, similar to the wire he had seen around Gustav's factory. *Curiouser and curiouser.*

A clink followed by what could have been a footfall sounded close by. Hunter ducked down behind a small bush. He could smell tobacco smoke. He heard someone walking slowly with a measured step, only a few metres away. Was this the guard?

A man appeared, on the other side of the fence, a rifle slung over his shoulder, a cigarette cupped in his hand. Pausing beside the gate he looked along the track, towards the hut and away from the sea. Then he continued walking. After a few seconds, Hunter heard a second guard. This time he had stopped and the unmistakable sound of a man urinating came to Hunter's ears. Every thirty seconds or so an armed man walked past where he hid. He was sure the sixth man was the same person he had seen the first time. He watched them go round again. There was no doubt. Five guards! But that made no sense! No sense at all!

Why have five men guarding him when two would have been more than enough? Then it hit him. They weren't guarding him. They were guarding the premises. But that was equally nonsensical. Whoever heard of guards on a lobster farm? And armed guards at that.

When the coast was clear for a few seconds he retreated the way he had come. He needed to think. Nobody guarded lobsters. Not on Sicily. Not with guns. But they did guard drugs. He was suddenly alert. That was it! Drugs! What better method of distribution? The heroin could be smuggled across Europe in tanks containing lobsters stuffed with packets of heroin. It was callous and cruel but highly effective.

Back in the hut, he ripped strips off the sacks and wrapped them around his feet like bandages. Tying them around his ankles, he tried walking. They were uncomfortable but adequate. Hunter searched the place. He needed a diversion. There must have been room for hundreds of lobsters and he quickly ascertained that the tanks were full. What was the situation? Were the lobsters full of heroin and ready to go? Or had the heroin still to arrive? Or was the heroin in-situ and yet to be put into the lobsters?

It had to be the first or third. Otherwise why have such a heavily armed guard? Apart from the tanks and the sacks there was nothing else in the hut. Except the lobster pots! They were piled high in the furthest corner. He went across to examine them. There were dozens. He pulled them away from the wall. At the back he found a packing case with hasp and lock. It was a flimsy looking affair. Even so, as he tore at the lid, Hunter felt shooting pains stabbing through his skull. Reaching in, he dragged out a handful of small, clear plastic bags. He took them across to the window and examined them. They were filled with a white, crystalline powder. It didn't take a genius to work out it was heroin.

Feeling in his pockets he looked for something to use. They had been emptied of everything, including his passport. In the lining of his jacket he felt the crinkling of the paper he had hidden there but it was no use to him in this situation. He searched the hut more thoroughly. What he needed was a fire. In a corner he found a broken blade from what he guessed was a scythe. It was about half a metre long, rusty, blunt.

Taking the steel blade he went outside into the moonlight. He found a flat stone and dragged it along the blade, clearing away the rust. He rubbed hard and soon saw clean metal shine through. Hitting the steel, a small spark flared briefly.

Hunter returned to the hut and made his way to the container of heroin. He dragged it across to the pile of sacks. Tearing off a piece of the cloth, he shredded it finely. He placed the rusty blade amongst the threads and struck it with the rock, using a sweeping motion, down the blade, rapid but not too hard. The sparks flew and fell amongst the hessian threads. He could smell smoke, faint but there. Bending down he blew gently on the sack while still striking the blade. The threads burst into flame and he fed more pieces onto the fire. The sacking smouldered, billowing thick smoke into the air before bursting into flame.

He lifted the heroin and placed it in the middle of the sacks. The wood of the container began to catch fire and he left the hut, satisfied he had done all he could. Taking two of the empty hessian sacks, he hurried along the track towards the gate until he came to the only bend. There he found a thick bush, behind which he scraped a shallow hollow using the broken blade. He worked frantically, expecting a yell from one of the guards at any moment.

He lay down with the hessian sacks covering him and waited. The yell wasn't long in coming. He heard a chain rattling and the gate being thrown open. Running footsteps thundered past him and he looked at the retreating backs, silhouetted against the flames that had spread to the wooden walls. He counted five of them.

Hunter rose to his feet, the sudden movement causing him to stagger, pain shooting across his head. He tried running towards the gate but each step caused a thudding in his temple and he was forced to walk quickly instead. He lengthened his stride, reached the gate and was about to hurry away when he paused. The padlock and key were still hanging from the chain, forgotten in the guards' haste to save the heroin. Pulling the gate to, Hunter locked the padlock through the chain and threw the key into the bushes. It wouldn't stop them but it might slow them down for a few minutes.

There were no houses to be seen and the track meandered down a steep hill towards the coast. He looked around for a few seconds but couldn't see a vehicle. He decided to cut straight down the slope instead of following the track. In the moonlight it was easy to see where he was treading.

The ground was reasonably smooth going, stony and scrubby with small bushes and an occasional olive tree. The sacking around his right foot came loose and he stopped to retie it. While he did so, he looked back. Flames and sparks were shooting into the sky as the roof collapsed. He would have grinned if he didn't hurt so badly.

He was halfway down the hill when he tripped and fell headlong. He lay there for a few seconds, too dazed to get up. The world was spinning, his head throbbing and he just wanted to shut his eyes and go to sleep.

Get a grip, damn you, he told himself. *Get up! Now!* Groaning he pushed himself to his knees and then staggered to his feet. His vision was blurred and he waited until he could see again to walk straight. The dizzy spell passed and his vision cleared. He carried on downhill, crossing the track from time to time, getting nearer to the sea. Suddenly the land flattened just as he walked out from behind some low bushes. To the right lay a two-lane highway. He stopped to take stock. The road was at a cliff edge and he looked down at the endlessly undulating water of the Mediterranean. To the left was darkness while to the right he could see the glow of street lights. They looked to be a long way away but he knew he had no choice. He started in their direction.

After staggering along for a few minutes he became aware of the sound of an engine over-revving. Looking ahead and behind, he couldn't see any sign of a car or other vehicle. Then he looked up the hill. Headlights were cutting a swathe of white along the hill, following the track. The guards were on the move. Hesitating for only a second he made up his mind. He wanted the car.

Hunter hurried back to the track. On either side of the road there was a ditch, to drain away surface water during thunderstorms and flash floods. He found two rocks, both fist sized and scrambled down into the dry ditch. He was only just in time as the car's lights suddenly lit up the scene.

In his haste, the driver was driving erratically. Even so, he had the presence of mind to stop at the road. He was close enough for Hunter to see that he was alone. The guards must have split up to search for him. He looked right, away from Hunter, the car moving slowly. Hunter lobbed the rock in his left hand onto the bonnet of the car. It struck with a loud clang. The driver instinctively hit the brakes hard. The engine stalled, Hunter grabbed the door handle, ripped the door open and smashed the other rock into the side of the man's head. It was hard and effective. The sickening crunch of the blow was loud in the still night.

Hunter dragged the guard out and laid him on the ground. Quickly he rifled his pockets. He found a fistful of euros and a credit card. Pocketing both, he was about to roll the body into the ditch when he caught sight of the watch on the man's wrist. With delight he realised it was his old Rolex and he unclasped the metal hinge, sliding it off. Putting it on his own wrist he glanced at the time – 03.38.

The man was still breathing and Hunter decided to leave him where he was. If he was found he may yet live. If he hid him in the ditch it was less likely. I must, he thought, be getting soft in my old age.

Straightening up, a wave of dizziness and nausea washed over him and he held onto the roof of the car for a few seconds until it had passed. With a huge feeling of relief he climbed into the car and sank onto the seat, fumbling for the keys. The car was an old Fiat that had seen better days but it was a godsend. Turning the key, the starter motor whirred and then jammed. He tried again. This time the engine started.

He was putting the car into gear when he saw the barrel of a rifle resting on the floor, against the passenger's seat. Picking it up he quickly checked it over. It was the ubiquitous Russian AK47, easily recognisable by its banana-shaped magazine. He checked the safety, found it was on and slid it two positions to single shot. Pulling back the cocking handle he ensured a round was in the chamber before placing the rifle on the seat, the butt facing him.

Engaging first gear with a loud grating noise he set out along the highway towards the loom of lights in the distance. He was feeling light-headed but at least the throbbing pain had subsided to a dull ache. With his foot on the floor, the car increased speed, the needle flickering between 50 and 90kph. The oil pressure gauge was equally as erratic but at least the engine temperature needle was steady. Regrettably it was in the red.

21

The signpost said *Agrigento 8kms*. The name meant nothing to him. The only thing he was sure of was that he was on the south side of Sicily, but where exactly? A few minutes later he came to another signpost pointing inland to Agrigento, now only 4kms away. He ignored it and stayed on the main highway. The more distance he put between himself and the guards the better. He checked the fuel gauge and frowned. It was showing full. That wasn't possible and so he surmised it, too, was broken.

The next big town was Sciacca, 80kms away. He'd hole up there and contact Scotland.

He had travelled halfway when wisps of steam began to emanate from under the bonnet. With a curse he pulled over. By a process of elimination he found the bonnet release under the passenger's side of the car. Once he had the bonnet open he took a look. By now the moon had set. The sky was brightening as another day dawned and Hunter could just see the cap on the radiator. Tentatively he touched it. It was red hot. Opening the boot, he searched for a water bottle but found only the jack and a worn-looking spare wheel.

The car was a rust bucket, held together by its paint. Hunter found a rock and used it to smash apart the hinges holding the bonnet in place. He dumped the bonnet over the cliff. The road was on a slight decline and he released the handbrake, gave the car a shove and jumped behind the wheel. The car moved slowly, picking up speed as the decline increased. The cold air sweeping over the open engine helped to cool it more quickly as the car free-wheeled slowly downhill. The momentum lasted for ten minutes before the road levelled and then began to rise again.

Hunter stopped and got out. The radiator cap was much cooler and Hunter unscrewed it. There was no eruption of water and no steam. Stretching on his toes, Hunter urinated into the radiator, grateful he had drunk so much water while in the shed. He replaced the cap, climbed into the car, started the engine and drove away. Without a bonnet, the noise of the engine was about twice as loud as it had been.

Each time he crested a hill he switched off the engine and coasted. The sign *Rio Plátani* warned him that a river crossing lay ahead. He slowed down and pulled over to the side. The fast moving river was only a few metres away down a gentle incline. Driving to the water's edge, he stopped, letting the engine cool for a few minutes. Leaning his head back against the seat he shut his eyes and promptly fell asleep.

It was a combination of a heavy truck roaring past and the rising sun that finally brought him around. With a jerk he was wide awake, groaning at the uncontrolled movement of his injured head. Climbing out of the car he went down to the river. The water looked clean enough but he didn't dare drink it. Instead he washed out his mouth, ducked his head into the freezing water and held it there for a few seconds. When he looked up, dripping water, he felt better.

He had made two journeys with water cupped in his hands to put into the radiator before he saw a rusty tin. The cola can speeded up the process. Climbing into the car he started the engine, drove up onto the road and continued his journey in the strengthening daylight. Although he felt better for his short nap he was angry with himself. He didn't have time to sleep.

The town of Sciacca was off to the left and less than a kilometre away when the radiator erupted. Hunter kept going. Steam hissed out for a minute or two before it evaporated completely. The car began to jerk as bearings over-heated. *Just a few seconds, that's all I ask*, he prayed. Ahead he could see a large hoarding advertising a new time-share complex being built on the site.

By now the car had developed a serious case of the judders and he put the gear lever into neutral and let it coast. It stopped a few metres short of the sign and he clambered out. He pushed the car behind the hoarding and out of sight. Briefly, he thought about taking the AK47 with him but realised it was impractical. There was no way he could carry it without it being seen. Reluctantly he stripped it and walked away from the car, distributing pieces of the gun as he went. The last thing he wanted was for some Sicilian child to find the weapon.

Macnair was in the operations room. 'Where's the ship?' he barked at Isobel, his weariness evident in the abruptness of his manner.

'Continuing towards the western end of the island.'

'Are we sure it docked in Pozzallo?'

'Yes, General, according to the satellite pictures.'

'So Íspica looks a good bet?'

'It does but we still can't be absolutely certain.'

Macnair sighed. 'I know. But do we have any choice?'

It was a rhetorical question. The buck stopped with Macnair and it was his decision alone to make. He had compromised. A TIFAT team was in the air in a Hercules C130 and heading for Italy. It was fully equipped and ready to go as soon as the General could confirm the target. The team was led by Matt Dunston who had only arrived back a few hours earlier. All the men had barely been debriefed before they were on their way again. They could, Macnair had told them, sleep on the plane.

It had sounded callous but in fact campbeds had been taken on board and the team were soon fast asleep.

Macnair's mobile rang and he answered. 'Nick! Where are you?' The General listened to what Hunter had to say. 'Excellent. Good work. Stay where you are. I'll have Matt with you ASAP. I have to go. I've work to do.'

Breaking the connection he looked into Isobel's enquiring eyes. 'Hunter confirms the factory is in Íspica. He also witnessed Gustav leave with three spheres of the biotoxin.'

'Where is Nick?'

'Hiding in a hotel in a resort known as Sciacca.' As he spoke,

Macnair was busy with his computer. A map of Sicily appeared on the wall screen in front of them. 'There it is. On the south coast. Nearest airport is on the west coast near Paceco. We'll divert the Hercules there. I need to speak to Nato and see if we have any liaison officers with the Italian army on the island.'

'Why, General?' Isobel asked.

'The Mafia are probably after Hunter from what he told me. We can't trust the police and even some elements of the Italian armed forces are suspect. But if we can get a Nato officer to baby-sit him, he should be all right.'

'Nick needing a baby sitter?' Isobel couldn't keep the surprise out of her voice.

'He's hurt, Isobel. He's fallen unconscious twice in the past hour.'

Hunter had telephoned from the railway station. His original idea had been to find a small hotel but he realised that the Mafia, if they were looking for him, would easily track him down. Instead he had gone down to the still deserted beach. He had sat in the shade, on a sun-lounger, for a few minutes, to regain his strength and promptly passed out. Whether it had been the effect of his head wound or sheer exhaustion, he had slept for an hour. When he had awoken the sun was well above the horizon and people were about. At a nearby stand-pipe he had washed his head and drunk some water before going back into town. He had bought shoes and some fresh clothes in a shop on the sea-front before returning to the beach. In a Gents toilet he had changed, and had dumped his old clothes in a waste bin. He had remembered to remove the piece of paper from his jacket lining. Gustav's cheque – well, he was certainly earning his money now.

In a chemist's he had bought toiletries and Aspirin – downing four. After he had freshened up he felt almost human again. He had returned to the nearby sun-lounger for a few minutes rest. He had lain back, telling himself it would only be for a few seconds and had promptly fallen fast asleep. This time he had been woken by somebody shaking his shoulder.

With a start he had looked into the swarthy face bending over him. Before he knew it, he had the man on his back, in the sand. He was leaning over him with his arm drawn back, before he realised the man was gibbering with terror. He had merely wanted to collect the rent for the bed.

Hunter had apologised profusely, paid him, added a tip and left the beach. He went shopping again. This time he bought stationary, drafted a quick note and posted the ten million pounds cheque to his off-shore bank account in Jersey. It was a subsidiary of the family's bank, Griffiths Buchanan Plc. He wondered idly if the cheque would clear. He walked to a different part of the beach, where sun-worshippers were already gathering, and paid for a day's hire of a lounger. In the shade of an umbrella he settled down and slept again, this time until half the morning had wasted.

A beach-side café provided excellent coffee and pizza. The coffee helped to wash down another two Aspirin. Back on his lounger he slept until the middle of the afternoon. When he awoke his head was no longer throbbing. The pain had faded to a dull ache. That disappeared within a few minutes of swallowing more pills. The bump was definitely going down and was less painful to touch. A scab had formed over the cut.

More coffee and food left him feeling more alert than he'd been all day. He was sitting at a table outside the café. Two similar establishments were to his left. To his right was the entrance to a small port and marina. Masts swayed in the swell and rigging and bunting flapped in the breeze. People were scattered across the sandy beach, some in the sun, others under the shade. Hunter noticed two men walking up and down the beach, looking at the sun-worshippers. These were no holiday-makers. For a start they wore suits. But they were also interested only in the men rather than the topless women and they were moving quickly.

Hunter nonchalantly walked back to his lounger, the men were still around fifty metres away. Discretion being the better part of valour he headed for the beach toilets. Opening a cubicle, he locked the door behind him. He had just sat down when he heard somebody slam open the first cubicle door. Then the second. His door was hit hard. A voice called something in Italian. He didn't reply. Instead he straddled the toilet and stood back from the door. There was an almighty crash and the door flew open. If he had been sitting down it would have smashed into his right knee.

They weren't really expecting any trouble. They were after a man who was badly hurt or so they had been told. He was unarmed while they carried guns. They were Mafiosi while he was a stranger. And this was *their* island, *their* town. Nobody dared stop them. Or even try.

Hunter kicked hard. Not between the man's legs but all the way up to his chin. A bone shattered and the man collapsed with a scream, his hands to his face. The second man had already moved past Hunter's cubicle and was pushing open the end door. As his friend hit the wall he turned with his jaw open, his hands by his side.

Hunter was already out of the cubicle and stepping towards him. The man stood still in utter astonishment, unable to believe what he was seeing. Too late he reached for his gun. Hunter's palm swept upwards and took the man in the nose, breaking the cartilage, thrusting it into the front lobes of the brain. The man collapsed, his arms and legs moving like jitterbugs. They stopped when he drew his last breath.

Reaching under the man's jacket, Hunter removed a revolver and slipped it into his belt, pulling out his tee-shirt to cover the gun. He removed the Sicilian's wallet and dumped it in the holdall. Grabbing the man by his belt and jacket lapel, he put him into the nearest cubicle. The door didn't go all the way to the floor and he reached under, grabbed the man's leg and pulled it against the door, jamming it closed.

The first man had drowned in his own blood. Hunter took the Sicilian's gun and dumped it in the holdall before disposing of the second body in the same way. A wave of dizziness washed over him and he rested for a few moments before he went back out into the sunshine. The irony of sudden death and a beautiful day wasn't lost on him.

There was a small veranda and wooden platform outside the

door and he paused in the shade to look around the beach. No one else appeared to be other than they seemed – holidaymakers enjoying themselves.

Macnair had told him to stay where he was. That the team would come for him. But it was too dangerous. It would only be a matter of time before the bodies were found. But where could he go? The Mafia were obviously looking for him and next time he might not be so lucky. It was only the incongruity of men in suits walking up and down the beach in the heat of the day that had alerted him so quickly. Another dizzy spell came on and he put a hand out to support himself. When it had passed he was aware that his head was hurting again and he took more Aspirin, swallowing them dry. He wandered slowly back to the café for a drink for all the world like a tourist without a care. Ice-cold fresh orange never tasted so good.

Gustav and Duval were the sole passengers on the craft speeding away from the side of the *Stockholm*. Marsala on the western tip of Sicily was less than one nautical mile away. The ship had slowed but not stopped for the launch. It continued on its way as soon as the boat left the side, quickly returning to its cruising speed of 15 knots.

Only one man accompanied them. He steered the boat expertly into the port and alongside the wall. A large limousine was waiting and the three of them disappeared into it, hidden behind its tinted windows. They carried no luggage, except for the holdall containing the three plastic spheres filled with the nerve gas.

Macnair wished Hunter would phone again so that he could bring him up to date on events. He was unable to find a Nato officer and had decided not to trust anybody in authority on Sicily. So the operation would be hard and fast. The one piece of useful information he'd received was that Nato was staging an exercise in the Mediterranean. Under the control of the American Sixth Fleet, units from seven Nato countries were taking part. They would be invading a deserted piece of Greece, using amphibious forces and landing craft. Thousands of

311

personnel were involved in a simulated invasion of another country. There were two reasons for the exercise. The first was self-evident – to train the armed forces of the world's democracies. The second was a not-so-subtle reminder to the rest of the world that the West still had the power to project its will should it be necessary.

On Macnair's wall map, now focused on Sicily, the Hercules was shown lining up to land. The SS *Stockholm* was shown but here was a slight anomaly. She was a few miles short of where he expected her to be.

Time was of the essence. At present it didn't look as though she was heading for any particular port, unless it was out of the Med. That was always a possibility. On no account could the spheres with their deadly contents be taken ashore. God alone knew where they could end up.

Isobel phoned his office. 'I've had Porton Down on the line.' Macnair recognised the significance of the location – it was the home of Britain's Defence Science and Technology Laboratory. 'They are suggesting the gas used on the liner is a mixture of sarin and ricin. If it is, there is no known antidote.'

Macnair sighed, thanked her and hung up. He telephoned the PM and they agreed. They would meet in the Cabinet Office Briefing Room in four hours. He next phoned the Director at Porton Down.

Was there anything else he could do at this stage? Under the guise of taking part in the Nato exercise, the team was being picked up at the airport by a Sea King helicopter from the task force. It was waiting for them and would be in the air only minutes after the Hercules landed. Customs had already been alerted to ignore the plane. Immigration didn't warrant an alert. Travel across the borders of Europe was virtually unrestricted, even for the military. Or perhaps, especially for the military.

Macnair stood lost in thought, staring at the projected wall map. He'd dealt with everything. Had he missed anything? It was an uncomfortable thought with so much at stake. Not just the lives of thousands if Gustav used the gas, but the future of

Europe as a multi-cultural, multi-ethnic mix of people. Indeed the very future of democracy hung in the balance.

Hunter sat in the café and kept a close eye on the beach. He saw no other suspicious characters. So far three people had gone in to use the toilets but none had re-emerged, panic-stricken and hysterical. There was a public phone in the café but it had an out of order notice on it and Hunter didn't want to draw attention to himself by asking to use the café's phone. But time was passing and he needed to talk to Macnair. He had already checked the other two bars for a public phone but without success. He could, he supposed, walk towards the town and find the nearest phone booth. The sudden appearance of two black sedans, driving fast, racing down towards the beach made his mind up for him.

Hunter stepped into a doorway. As the cars passed him, he saw the ominous black rods of gun barrels appearing in the windows. Each car held four men. The cars screeched to a halt and the men emerged, fanning out over the beach. Within seconds a gunman entered the Gents toilets. He rushed out excitedly, yelling. It seemed to galvanise the others and they moved quickly, one man to each of the cafés, the others along the beach.

Unnoticed, in the distance, a small dot appeared on the horizon, rapidly growing larger. It stopped, out of noise range and hovered low down, the roundels of the Royal Air Force indiscernible from the beach. None of the gunmen even looked in its direction.

Hunter, looking towards the sea, had seen the helo and had known instantly who it was. His problem was that between it and him were the Mafia. Already the shops' shutters were coming down and doors were being locked. He saw the waiter who had served him earlier come out and point along the road in the direction he had taken, speaking and gesticulating excitedly.

The man he was speaking to said something in a loud voice and the other gunmen converged on the road, guns at the ready.

Hunter was about sixty metres away and had his back to a glass door. As he tried the handle a woman's face appeared and she locked it. He gestured at the door to let him in but she shook her head and angrily indicated that he leave.

Looking cautiously out he saw it was too late to make a run for it. The men were strung out across the road and advancing steadily towards him. Hunter knelt down and opened his holdall. For the first time he took a closer look at the guns. One was a Spanish Llama Comanche, not very old, holding six rounds of .357 Magnum bullets. The other was a battered and worn looking French Manurhin MR73, also holding six rounds of the same ammunition. The longer barrel of the Spanish gun convinced him it was the one to use first. It was probably more accurate at the longer range while the French gun's unique roller-bearing trigger system made for a smoother and faster action.

Gunfight, he thought, *at the OK Corral*. They still had no idea where he was, which was evident from the way they were looking into the doorways. What surprised him was the total arrogance they displayed walking down the street. But then, he figured, the police had probably been told to stay away from that part of town. And one man alone wasn't going to frighten them. Especially if he was unarmed or armed only with a couple of revolvers. They had automatic weapons.

A man appeared on the other side of the road, to Hunter's left, and started pulling down the metal shutter to his shop. One of the gunmen yelled something. The shopkeeper turned with a startled look on his face and scuttled inside. More like *High Noon*, thought Hunter.

He lay on the ground in the doorway. Luckily the glass windows of the shop front sat on solid stone about half a metre high. Out at the edge of the pavement a metal lamp post stood tall, shielding him slightly from the gunmen across the street. Cars were parked on the other side but on Hunter's side there were no vehicles. By now the pavements and street were completely deserted.

With his eye at ground level Hunter took a quick look. Forty metres. Close enough. It was time to discourage them. To buy some time until reinforcements arrived. A glance at the sky wasn't encouraging. The helicopter had vanished.

One gunman was walking the pavement directly towards

Hunter and another was a few metres to his right. The remainder were strung across the street. He knew that left-handed his chances of hitting either target was a lot less than if he used his right. To use his right hand he had to show more of himself than he liked. So be it. Two double taps and back in. Resist the temptation to continue firing. Two seconds maximum. By which time the remaining men would have collected their wits and opened fire with automatic weapons. Then he'd retreat through the glass door which, he was sure, would be smashed to pieces in the hailstorm of bullets. One bullet was all it would take to finish him. It was now or never.

He rolled out, the gun in his right hand, cocked and ready to fire. His left hand immediately cupping his right fist, he came up on his elbows and aimed. His sudden appearance shocked the man he was aiming at into immobility. Hunter was pulling the trigger when the man threw his hands in the air with an anguished cry and fell forwards. Hunter hadn't heard the shot being fired. His own gun stayed silent as he watched the eight Mafiosi fall. Hunter's shock turned to pleased surprise when he saw a man appear along the road. The unmistakable figure of Dunston strolled towards him.

Lowering his hands he dropped his head onto his arms with relief. A feeling of dizziness swept over him and he had difficulty getting to his feet.

As though from a distance he heard Matt Dunston ask, 'Are you all right, Nick?'

Hunter nodded. 'Thanks, Matt, you arrived just in time.'

'We were waiting for you to make your move. We saw the play going down from the chopper so figured what you'd do. We rappelled down and took up position. It was, as the Yanks say, a turkey shoot. Let's get you out of here. We've a lot to do.'

The helicopter landed on the still-deserted street and Hunter climbed aboard, followed by the team. He was not surprised to find that the original RAF pilot had been replaced by Burg Schwarzkopf. For such a covert operation TIFAT used its own men.

Schwarzkopf was gently raising the collective as the last man climbed through the door. He pushed forward the cyclic and the helicopter took its characteristic nose-down aspect and surged out to sea. The remainder of the team were pulling off their skimasks, grins on their faces.

'Good job you've got a hard head, boss,' shouted Lt Napier.

Dunston was already checking Hunter over, feeling for the tell-tale sign of a slightly soft feel to the bone around the skull. If he was hurting, Hunter didn't show it.

'It should have had stitches but it's healed over,' announced Dunston. 'Does it hurt?'

'A bit,' Hunter admitted. 'I've taken a few Aspirin.'

'I'll give you a local anaesthetic. That'll hold it for a few hours. You up to coming on this jaunt?'

'Sure. Have you got kit for me?'

'In the corner.'

In the team were Claude Masson, Doug Tanner, Don Masters, Jan Badonovitch and Josh Clements. The Delta captain handed a holdall to Hunter.

Over the internal headphones they heard Schwarzkopf say, 'The General's on line one, Nick.'

Hunter flicked his communications switch to one. 'Sir? It's Hunter.'

'Nick, glad you're in one piece. Matt will brief you. We're shadowing the *Stockholm* and won't go in until you've taken out the factory. It must be razed to the ground.'

'Yes, sir. What about the personnel?'

'Hold them until the Americans get there. They're spiriting them away. It'll be up to them whether the scientists stand trial for crimes against humanity.'

'Roger that, sir. I'll let you know how we get on. Out.'

Macnair was flying into Heathrow when he spoke to Hunter. Landing, he was met by the police. A car, alarms and lights flashing, whisked him into London and deposited him at No 10 Downing Street. There he was introduced to Dr John Williams, a scientist from Porton Down, a tall, distinguished looking man of about fifty. Along with the Prime Minister were the Defence

Secretary, Home Secretary, Deputy PM and Chancellor of the Exchequer. All had sombre looks on their faces.

Williams sat at the end of the table. He had no props, no papers. 'Shall I begin?'

The PM nodded.

'It's important to understand that this is all guess work. Do you know anything about ricin?'

The men shook their heads. The Home Secretary stroked his beard and said, 'Only that we've found traces of it recently in London and that we think there is a quantity out there somewhere.'

Williams nodded. 'Ricin is a natural toxin found in castor bean husks. A million tons of the beans are processed every year for oil used as an industrial lubricant. About seven percent of the residue is ricin. So it's easily obtainable. The husks need only be ground into powder, dissolved and then dried into crystalline form to be deadly. Death from pure ricin takes thirty-six to forty-eight hours and is caused by circulatory and respiratory failure. It's not contagious and by itself makes a lousy WMD. However,' the doctor paused, 'mixed with a nerve agent such as sarin and with whatever else is in the gas then it becomes far more deadly. What we suspect,' again he paused and added, 'and this is *pure* speculation, is that the third gas is relatively heavy. So when released the mixture will stay at ground level.'

'Why is that?' asked the DPM.

'Maximum fatalities,' was the stark reply.

'What sort of numbers are we talking about?' Macnair asked.

The scientist shrugged. 'Impossible to tell. We've programmed various scenarios into our computers,' he paused again, licking dry lips.

'Well, man,' the DPM asked impatiently, his strong Yorkshire accent grating in the quiet room.

'If released in an underground station it would kill everyone there and then infect other places as it drifts with the draughts through the network, ultimately causing thousands of deaths. If released in the open the breeze could disperse it over a wide region. We've done some "what ifs" on the computer.' He looked down at the sheet in front of him and paused. 'With average weather and winds for this time of year a city the size of Manchester would experience ninety-five percent fatalities within twenty-four hours.'

The helicopter landed on a deserted spot, away from prying eyes. It was too early to attack. A guard was posted and the remaining team sat over hot drinks, exchanging stories of the last couple of days. When it was time to go, they dressed in their Nuclear, Bacteriological and Chemical Warfare Suits. Fully enclosed from head to foot, refined gas masks hung from their necks. The masks could be used in the conventional way, filtering the outside air, or by turning a handle, they could be used in a closed-circuit mode. Then the wearer would breathe pure oxygen carried in a small cylinder strapped on the back. Thanks to a unique scrubbing system, the oxygen was reused until it was fully depleted. This meant that the bottles had an endurance of about twenty minutes for an ordinary person. For the physically fit that time span was extended to around thirty minutes. The team could squeeze out at least forty minutes thanks to the controlled breathing techniques they had learned as divers.

With the helicopter four thousand feet up and two miles out they bailed out. Their wings deployed and they swooped down like huge bats, hardly noticeable against the moonless sky. It was barely 21.00 and moonrise was at least three hours away.

Their NVGs showed them the way and they deployed in accordance with the plan of attack. Dunston landed behind the guardhouse. The man inside was looking out, down the road. Unaware. Dunston wrapped up his wing and approached the glass door in the back wall. Gently he tried the handle. The door opened and was only slightly ajar when the guard looked over his shoulder. His jaw dropped in shock as Dunston threw caution to the wind and smashed the door wide. He gestured with a Glock 19 in his hand for the man to raise his hands. The guard did as he was told. Dunston didn't see him lean against a red button protruding from the side of a table. A low but intense two-tone hooter sounded. The guard grinned.

Dunston wiped the smile off the man's face with an open edged stroke of his hand into the guard's neck. He collapsed, unconscious.

'Sorry, lads. I didn't see that one.'

'Never mind. Hit it!' Hunter ordered.

Explosives kneaded along the sides of the front doors blew the hinges. Badonovitch pushed the middle of the doors with his shoulder and they smashed to the ground with a loud bang. They stormed in. A short corridor faced them. At the far end glass doors were already more than half covered by a metal shutter, rolling down.

The plans Isobel had lifted from central records in Rome had been pored over by Dunston and the team prior to departure. The building above ground was less than twenty percent of the total and consisted of the foyer and storage rooms. The remaining structure was underground. The first subterranean floor was made up of public rooms, the second of combined bedrooms and sitting rooms and the third held the laboratories. Eighteen servants worked at the establishment, one per scientist. How many of them were armed guards?

They knew that every door and internal window had steel shutters which closed at the press of a button. They also knew that the steel shutters were much tougher than the walls. The team had brought with them round, metal mines, packed with explosives, eight inches in diameter and two inches thick. The flat base of the charge was surrounded with thick soft rubber, one inch wide. When pressed against a reasonably smooth surface, like a wall or a door, a small thumb-operated pump quickly sucked the air out and made a seal. The mine stuck to the surface like a limpet. It could be exploded by timer or remote detonator, the preferred method for this operation. The explosive was shaped to go into the surface, creating a jagged, circular hole, about three feet in diameter. Two were used, either side of the door, to devastating effect, the explosive power smashing into the wall.

A flash-bang grenade was thrown through each of the holes. Hunter dived through the one to the right, Napier dived left. Both men had guns ready, on full automatic.

In their NBC suits and respirators they looked like beings from outer-space. Aliens invading an antiseptic and tranquil haven of peace. Two men stood in shock, disorientated by the grenades. Both were fit looking and armed. Two taps each took them out.

They had entered a large foyer, carpeted and plush enough to be found in a five star hotel. To the left of the reception desk was a corridor. Again a shutter was rolling down, rapidly sealing off the door. It was like being encased in a tomb.

There were doors around the foyer leading into toilets and storerooms that were quickly checked. Nobody and nothing of interest was found. A lift was situated in one corner, the indicator showing it was on the lowest floor. They called it up, ready for any nasty surprises. When it arrived they found a man huddled in the corner, away from the door. He was about fifty, scholarly looking. He wore black-framed glasses, his grey, receding hair swept back. He was shaking with fear.

'Don't shoot! Don't shoot!' He held up his hands. The fear wasn't an act.

'On your feet and move outside,' ordered Clements.

'American? You're an American?' The relief was clear in the man's voice. 'Oh, thank God.'

'Shift it.' Clements prodded the man outside and into the waiting arms of Dunston. There the chaplain handcuffed the man with plasti-cuffs and made him sit on the ground. Two minutes of conversation had Dunston on the radio to the others.

'Listen up. According to the man I've got here, the scientists are being held under coercion. Promises made by Gustav haven't been kept. The guards are there to keep them in line. The laboratories are numbered one to four and are confirmed as being on the lowest floor. Number three contains the gas. Number two is where the antidote is being created. From what this guy is telling me, I think it would pay to get as many of the scientists out alive as possible.'

'Why?' Hunter asked.

'Because the antidote hasn't been perfected yet. And Gustav has definitely left with three containers of the virus.'

'Do we know what's in it?' Hunter asked.

'A mixture of sarin and ricin plus a new super toxin. They call the mixture SRX. I'll let the General know.'

'How many guards and how many servants are there?'

There was a pause before Dunston came back on. 'Bad news, I'm afraid. Even the servants are armed. There are eighteen of them in total and eleven scientists.'

'Does he know where they all are?'

'Negative. Although some of the scientists will be in the labs.'

'Roger that,' Hunter acknowledged.

'There are fewer scientists than we expected, boss,' said Masters.

'Yeah. I was thinking that. Matt? Ask your guy where the other scientists are.'

'I can answer that, Nick,' said Dunston heavily. 'Six of them have been killed. By the guards. As an incentive to the others to give Gustav what he wanted.'

'Whatever happened to old fashioned bonuses?' Napier asked.

The door past the desk was the main entrance to the complex and mines were placed either side, blowing holes in the wall. In the confined space they paused to let the dust settle. The portable thermal imager showed that the corridor beyond was empty. They climbed through the holes to find themselves in a short corridor with a stairwell leading down.

22

'SS *Stockholm,* SS *Stockholm*, this is warship. Heave to immediately and prepare for a boarding party.'

'Warship, this is the *Stockholm*. I protest. I am lawfully going about my business in international waters. You have no right to stop me.'

'This is warship. I say again. Stop your engines immediately or be prepared to be fired on. You have two minutes.'

'Warship, this is the *Stockholm*. If you do I will have you arrested and in court. The world's media will take a dim view of your actions. Are you American or English?'

'Look behind you, *Kapitän zur See* Novak.' The words were spoken with contempt. 'Perhaps you recognise the flag of the country where you are registered.'

During the exchange the *Stockholm*'s engines had been put to full ahead and the ship was gathering speed. Through his binoculars Novak focused on the stern of the frigate that was a mile astern and coming up on his quarter. He knew that in a straight race, the *Stockholm* could outrun the naval vessel. The blue and yellow cross of the Swedish flag came into sight.

Even as his brain registered the colours, the captain experienced palpitations of shock. Screaming blue murder at the Americans or the British for human-rights violations was one thing. Sweden, famous for its neutrality, was another. It had been pure inspiration by Macnair to suggest using the Swedish frigate to the Secretary-General of Nato. The Swedes, for the first time in history, had been exercising with the fleet. It was part of a political softening up process to persuade the Swedish people to come into the fold at long last. Their neutrality meant that for too long Sweden hadn't been pulling its weight in the world. Especially now with the all-too present dangers faced by Western democracies.

Novak had his orders. Keeping to international waters, the *Stockholm* turned away from the frigate. Gustav had said that the likelihood of even the Americans firing on them were slim. The Swedes? Forget it. There was not a dog's chance in hell. It was therefore all the more shocking when a solid shot, 4.5 inch round, slammed into the midships section of the ship. If it had been a high-explosive shell or a missile the devastation would have been horrendous. As it was, the shot went through the port side of the ship, hit number two diesel and smashed it to pulp.

The Captain's shock and torment were so great that he stood still for a second, unable to take it in. He launched himself at the radio and began sending a Mayday signal saying the ship was under attack. Unknown to Novak, a blanket jamming was in force from an American stealth bomber, ten miles above the ship.

The next two shells hit the bows. Both at the waterline. The sea began to flood in and the ship slowed down. However, the *Stockholm* didn't slow fast enough. She drove the water into her hull and began flooding, settling with a forward momentum that would take her a full nautical mile before reaching the seabed. Before giving the order to abandon ship the last thing Novak did was to let loose the emergency beacon.

When the ship finally settled, on her side, in a rocky region of the Mediterranean, the beacon was floating on the surface, forty metres above the seabed.

Dunston came back on the radio. 'Listen up. More bad news. I've just been told that an alarm connects to somewhere else on the island. It will bring the Mafiosi in hordes, according to my friend here.'

'Can you whistle up reinforcements?' Hunter asked.

'I've already done so. Two stealth fighters are inbound to ride shotgun plus a contingent of marines will be arriving by helo. The fighters will be here shortly. The ETA for the marines is one hour at best.'

'Okay folks,' Hunter said, 'let's shift it. I don't want another firefight with the Mafia if we can help it.'

At the bottom of the stairwell they found another shutter, fitted across the whole width of the corridor. Close examination showed that the shutter was embedded into the wall either side. They would have to go through the metal. They moulded plastic explosives into a long, thin shape and tamped it down around the steel shutter. The explosion was not clean and the circle of metal was still held in place by tiny bridges of steel. A hefty kick pushed it clear.

The thermal imager showed two men were somewhere on the other side. Hiding behind the shutter, Hunter fed in an optic fibre camera and checked the area. He was looking at a short corridor leading to a T-junction. A shadow moved on the floor.

'Come out and you won't get hurt,' Hunter called. 'This is a Nato contingent of special services. Come out with your hands in the air.' Nothing happened.

If the people inside expected a flash-bang then they would know what to do. By sitting in a foetal position with heads bowed, eyes shut and hands over the ears it was possible to avoid most of the damage inflicted by the grenade. Hunter had no intention of risking any of the lives of his team if he could help it. He threw in a high-explosive grenade that detonated as it passed the junction. Badonovitch and Weir went through the hole like rats up a drainpipe. They reported two armed guards, both dead.

Quickly they checked the corridor was clear while the rest of the team followed them through. There were five doors either side of the corridor, each signed clearly, indicating the room's function. The thermal imager found four people in the room marked cinema. According to the sensor, two were in the furthest left hand corner, lying on the floor. A third was cowering in the near left hand corner and a fourth was kneeling opposite the door, partially protected by something. The team placed a mine either side of the shuttered door and blew two holes. Gunfire erupted from inside the room and sprayed the first hole with bullets. Through the second, Tanner saw the gunman kneeling behind a stuffed armchair. With his Glock 19 on automatic he fired six shots, killing the man.

'Come out with your hands up,' said Hunter in a loud voice.

Three men appeared. They varied in age and physique but one thing was sure, they weren't guards. They clambered through the holes.

One of the men stood erect and with a certain dignity asked, 'Who's in charge here?'

'I am.' Hunter replied.

'You can take your ridiculous gas masks off, there is no danger.'

With relief the team took off their masks. Sweat covered their faces and streaked down their cheeks. The masks were uncomfortable at the best of times and in action they were a downright nuisance. In the right circumstances however, they could save your life.

'Who are you?' Hunter asked.

'My name is Joachim Dietrich. I am in charge of the research scientists. We have been held prisoner by Charles Gustav for nearly a year.'

'Save it,' said Hunter. 'We need to get out of here. The Mafia could be arriving any time. But first we need to find the remaining scientists, so tell us where they are and quickly.'

'I refuse to be spoken to like that.'

The team looked at the little scientist in utter astonishment. He was barely five feet, rotund almost, with a smooth, hairless face and a bald head. His innocent appearance belied such unbelievable gall. 'I insist you take us out of here now. Our rescue is of the utmost importance. Otherwise your superiors will hear about this and I warn you . . .'

He got no further. Josh Clements had the man by the throat and lifted him up on his toes. 'Listen you little slime ball, we know you've created germ warfare here intended for use in Europe. If any innocent people die you'll be tried as an accessory to mass murder. You got that? And if you don't end up in court I'll put a bullet in you myself. Understood?'

The little man, his eyes bulging with fear, nodded vigorously.

'Now answer our questions and then you can go outside.'

More nods. Their questions were answered promptly. They learned that the doors could be opened individually from inside or from a master switch in the foyer.

'Matt? Three scientists on their way. There's a master switch for the shutters. Find out where it is and I'll let you know whether we want to use it. At present, with the men locked inside, we have better control. Oh, and cuff them,' said Hunter over the radio.

'Roger that.'

'All quiet?'

'So far. If things change I'll let you know.'

'We're left with seven scientists and fifteen uglies all on the two floors below,' said Hunter. 'Let's go.'

The next shutter yielded to the same treatment. The corridor was empty.

'Boss,' said Badonovitch, 'I think these shutters are delaying tactics while the guards pray for the cavalry in the shape of the Mafia to arrive.'

'That's what I think too, Jan. What's your point?'

'Maybe we should just seal the whole lot and get the hell topside.'

'That's occurred to me as well. Ten minutes max before we leg it. Okay? Josh, Claude and Don go straight for the next stairwell while we clear the bedrooms and sitting rooms.'

Hunter used the thermal imager to check each of the rooms. In one room they found one person and in another they found three. The rest of the rooms were empty. In both cases the images suggested the men were cowering away from the doors. Hunter used one mine on either side of the doors and blew them simultaneously. At the end of the corridor the other team's explosion was heard.

'Come out with your hands where we can see them,' he yelled.

'Don't shoot! I'm coming out.' A bespectacled man came out of the first room with his hands up. He had scientist written all over him.

'Jan, cover him while we see who's in the other room.' Raising his voice, Hunter called, 'Are you coming out or not?'

'Yes! Yes! We're coming. Only don't kill us.'

The three men crawled through the hole. They all had a number of things in common. A pallor that indicated a lack of sunshine, a soft outline that spoke of too much good food and not enough exercise and they all wore glasses.

'Get them out of here, Jan,' said Hunter.

'You're British!' one man exclaimed.

'Save it for later. Now go!'

Hurrying along the corridor they were at the stairwell when they heard firing. Cautiously they went down in time to see Clements throw a grenade through the hole they had blown in the shutter. The fragmentation grenade erupted and the firing ceased. Using the optical camera they checked to see one body lying in the corridor, the walls covered in blood.

Unlike the other rooms, the four labs had windows into the corridor which were shuttered. They also had entry-phones either side of the doors. According to the heat sensor Lab 1 held one person.

Hunter pressed the button on the entry phone. 'You in there. Open the shutter and come out with your hands up. If you don't open the shutter in ten seconds we'll come in.'

The heat-sensor showed the person inside change from a round blob in the far corner of the room to an erect figure. It came slowly towards the door and paused.

Hunter decided to give the figure a prod. 'Our sensors show you to be at the door. Open it and come out.'

There was a second's delay and then the shutter rolled slowly upwards. The man on the other side was in his thirties, wearing a white coat and spectacles. He was raising and lowering his hands in some sort of supplication when he reached under his coat for a gun. Masson had been ready and shot him between the eyes.

'He had too much tan,' the Frenchman said.

The sensors showed two occupants of Lab 2. Using the entry-phone Hunter repeated his request that they come out. The two figures remained where they were, apparently crouched behind something, on the other side of the room.

Explosives were attached to the wall either side of the door and blown. Automatic guns opened up from inside and bullets poured through both holes. Ricocheting off the wall opposite, they were a deadly danger. Two fragmentation grenades were thrown in and the shooting stopped as soon as they exploded.

That left Lab 3 where the deadly gas was concocted. Hunter used the entry-phone. There were six men inside as far from the door as possible. One of them came forward but suddenly collapsed in a heap. Tiny flecks of red light on the sensor's screen left the team in no doubt that he had been shot.

'Gas masks on,' said Hunter. 'I don't like this.'

Uncomfortable in their masks once more, Tanner said, 'Boss, I propose we go to oxygen.'

'Agreed.' The team turned on the valves isolating them from the air around them.

Explosives blew two holes through the wall. As before, gunfire erupted from inside the lab and peppered the wall behind the team with bullets. There was no time for finesse. A couple of grenades were thrown in. As they exploded, a huge scream rent the air. The firing stopped and Hunter pushed a fibre optic camera into the furthest hole. Looking at the monitor, he was trying to understand the picture he was seeing.

Two men in white coats were climbing dazedly to their feet. The younger of the two called out. 'Don't come in. The germs have been released. For the love of God get away before you're exposed.'

He suddenly arched his back and collapsed with a scream.

The men of TIFAT were amongst the bravest in the world. They had put their lives on the line often enough and proven themselves in tight spots again and again. But this was different, hideous, insidious. The gas killed in a terrible way, leaving you to die in fear and agony. And although they were suited up, wearing respirators and using their own oxygen supply, they didn't wait. Hunter paused to commit one last act of kindness, lobbing in two grenades to where the men were lying, screaming in agony. At the stairwell they each threw incendiary devices into the corridor. One floor up, Napier was already setting explosives with a two-minute delay while on the next floor Clements was doing the same.

On the ground floor they placed a third pile of PE before escaping the building. The incendiary devices went off causing a huge fireball that engulfed the laboratories, incinerating the gas and setting fire to the building, killing those left alive. The explosives sealed the stairwells.

The team herded the scientists away. They walked awkwardly because their arms were pinioned behind their backs. Dietrich protested continually while the others had the good sense to keep quiet.

'Look!' Masson pointed ahead of them.

Coming along the road were headlights. Four, maybe five sets.

'What do you think, boss?' asked Badonovitch.

'I think we've got company. Nighthawk this is Team One, over.'

'One, Nighthawk, over,' Schwarzkopf replied immediately.

'We've got company.'

'I see them. The F-117s are thirty seconds away. I'm vectoring them in now. Duck real low. Out.'

'You heard the man,' said Hunter. 'Into the ditches either side of the track.'

While the scientists cowered in trepidation the team readied for a firefight. As was the case with American stealth fighters, nobody saw or heard anything. The strike aircraft carried laser-guided bombs which could be dropped with great precision. Five car loads of Mafiosi were blown to Kingdom Come without the occupants knowing what was happening.

The F-117s circled upwards, barely noticeable except for the flickering stars in the sky.

'All quiet again,' said Hunter to Burg.

'Roger that. What now?'

'Come and get us. We need to get out of here.'

The team rested up on an American aircraft carrier, the USS *Ronald Reagan*. The ship, pennant number CVN 76, was a colossus of the sea. Its firepower was awesome, its protective screen of warships greater than the navies of most sovereign countries.

When the team landed, they were assigned beds and promptly forgotten about. The scientists were taken to the Admiral's quarters where they were treated like dignitaries. Except that their complaints about how they had been abused by their rescuers fell on deaf ears. Finally even Dietrich stopped harping on the subject. Already arrangements had been made to fly the scientists to America to continue their research. A red carpet was quietly being rolled out for them.

Macnair was awoken from a deep sleep by the ringing of his phone. Groggily he answered it. Within seconds he had snapped wide awake. 'Are you sure?'

Carter broke the bad news to his boss. 'As sure as we can be, sir. The Swedes have just signalled us. Gustav left the ship with Duval hours ago. He's on Sicily somewhere.'

'And the spheres of SRX?'

'The Captain doesn't know. Claims he's just a simple mariner going about his duties.'

'I bet. And what do the Swedes say?'

'They're back-peddling like fury, sir. You know what they're like. Big on human rights.'

Macnair grunted. 'Human rights of the criminal, not the ordinary citizens.'

'You've got it, sir. They're crapping themselves about the whole affair. Think they've gone too far. Shouldn't have done it, and so on. The usual drivel.'

'They'll hang their angst out and make themselves a laughing stock. Hunter still on the aircraft carrier?'

'Affirmative, sir. Probably having breakfast about now.'

'Okay. We need to check it out. Any chance we can get our hands on the Captain of the *Stockholm*?'

'I doubt it, sir.'

'Where is he?'

'On the frigate. The Swedes are already flying lawyers out to him.'

'What! Jesus wept! Don't they know the stakes we're playing for?'

'They do, sir. But it's no use.'

'What about holding him under some terrorism law until we can lift him?'

'I've suggested that to Downing Street. But they say if the Swedes won't play ball there's nothing we or anybody else can do about it.'

'Okay. We need to check out the ship. Do we know where it is exactly?'

'Yes, sir. An emergency transponder was sent out from the side of the hull and is floating on the surface. We have its signal loud and clear.'

'Okay. I'll get on to the Pentagon.'

Hunter didn't hear his name being announced over the tannoy system. He and Dunston were having breakfast in the wardroom. A meal only the Americans could manage – waffles, eggs, bacon, washed down with mugs of excellent coffee.

'You're up, Nick. You're wanted on the bridge,' said Schwarzkopf, walking up to the two men.

'Me?' Hunter frowned. 'Must be another man of the same name.'

'Nope, I don't think so,' said Schwarzkopf.

With a sigh Hunter arose from the table and went over to the nearest bulkhead. An internal phone was fixed to it with a list of extensions pinned alongside. He dialled the bridge.

'Second Officer of the watch.'

'My name is Lieutenant Commander Hunter. I came on board last night. Am I wanted on the bridge?'

'Just a second, sir. Let me ask.'

Another voice came down the phone. 'That you, Lieutenant Commander?'

'If you mean Hunter and am I from TIFAT, yes it is.'

'Good. This is the Captain.'

'Sorry, sir. I had no idea.'

There was a chuckle. 'That's all right. You're flying off in half an hour.'

'Yes, sir. Am I allowed to ask where I'm going?'

'Yep. You and your team are diving on that ship the Swedes sank yesterday. I've been ordered to give you all the help and equipment you need. We carry a contingent of SEALs on board as well as ordinary divers. So we've got a wide range of gear. Stay where you are and I'll send someone to find you. In the meantime, I'll get your men together.'

'Yes, sir. Sir, I recognise the hand of General Macnair behind this. Can I go to the Comms Centre and contact him?'

'Sure. Tell one of the mids to take you.'

Hunter hung up and returned to his table. 'Eat up. We're wanted.'

'What's up?' Napier asked, sitting down at the table, a tray of food in front of him.

'We're going diving on the SS *Stockholm*.'

'What for?' Clements asked.

'I don't know yet. I need to talk to the General. I'm off to the Comms Centre.' He stood up as a midshipman came through the door and approached him.

The mid saluted nervously.

Hunter glanced at the junior officer's name tag and said, 'Midshipman Hibetson, you here to show me the way to the Comms Centre?'

'Yes, sir. Captain's orders, sir. Follow me please, sir.'

They got lost twice, which was quite normal on a ship of that size. But they eventually found the right place, in the midsection and close to the bowels of the ship.

It took a call to the bridge before Hunter got the authorisation he needed to enter and use the equipment.

Macnair briefed him quickly.

'But sir, five minutes with Novak would tell us all we need to know.'

'I am aware of that, Nick, but no-can-do. The Swedes are digging their heels in. And the more we push the more obdurate they're becoming.'

'What a waste of time. Has anybody asked them what they intend to do should Gustav release one of the containers of SRX? Or, heaven forbid, all three?'

'No response other than banging on about the human rights of the individual no matter what crime they've committed.' There was no mistaking the anger in Macnair's voice.

'Where's Gustav now?'

'Gone to ground. We're pulling out every stop to find him. Our best guess is he went ashore on Sicily.'

How can you be sure, sir?'

'That's it – we can't. We were tracking the ship off Sicily when it appeared to have lost ground at one stage. With hindsight, it's likely Gustav went off by boat, and the *Stockholm* picked up speed again.'

'Good enough. Could he have already left the area?'

'With his resources? Easily. Private plane. Private ship. Nick, we're assuming he's on the loose with the SRX. But we have to make sure. Get to the *Stockholm* and check all the likely places those containers could be hidden. You're the only one who's been on board and knows where to look.'

'Okay, sir. I can check out his stateroom and the safe. After that the task is too big.'

'I agree. If the SRX isn't there and you don't see any sign of Gustav's body then we can assume he's out there somewhere with the stuff.'

'He's out there. Believe me.'

'I know, Nick. But let's make sure.' Uncharacteristically Macnair added, 'I've been ordered to make the search. Our politicians are clutching at straws. They live in hope. So just do it.'

A strange calm had descended over Gustav, a clarity of thought focused entirely on his ultimate commitment. The Swede was sitting in his house outside Bagheria, to the east of Palermo. He felt relatively safe, believing the obfuscation he had created covering its purchase to be impenetrable. Despite everything, he prided himself on his discipline and self-control. Outwardly nothing had changed. Inwardly his anger erupted like acid in his stomach. Ranting and raving would help no one. Rational consideration was required. Never in his life had he experienced so many set backs.

His contacts in the Swedish government were keeping *Kapitän zur See* Novak out of his enemy's hands but that might not last. He had to move fast. His frustration was mounting. Messages and phone calls he had been making all afternoon were going unanswered or ignored. He was almost sure that on two occasions the bastards on the other end had hung up on him. His grip on the glass of Evian water tightened imperceptibly. He'd pay them back. Once his people were in power he'd teach them the meaning of loyalty.

He could feel a momentum of resistance growing against him – TIFAT had discovered too much and time was running out. He had no idea how Macnair and his organisation had done it but he'd find out. It was now imperative that he strike the death blow. The Arabs would take delivery of the SRX shortly. The havoc its release would cause would be enough to make the white Christians of Europe rise up as one and sweep the Muslim filth into the sea.

Gustav sat back in his chair and took slow breaths to calm himself. He did so by going over the intended targets in his mind. One container was to be detonated at an American base in Germany, near a town called Paderborn. A second was to go off in the Paris Metro and a third . . . He stroked his eyebrow. The third was the one that gave him the most pleasure. It was to be detonated near the British Houses of Parliament. After all, it was from Britain that most of the opposition had come.

Duval came into the room. 'All done, Mr Gustav. The spheres are on their way.'

'The couriers?'

'As agreed. They don't know what they're carrying. They'll make the deliveries and leave immediately.'

'Excellent.'

Flying the SRX to their destinations was no longer an option. With the heightened tension of recent events and the possibility that customs were looking for them, it was too great a risk. The open borders of Europe were the perfect solution. It would take longer but was far safer.

* * *

Ursula Fritberg was an eye-catching blonde, nearly six feet tall, her features dominated by attractive blue eyes. She was a lesbian and ultra-right wing. The latter was well known in the proper circles. The former she kept a secret. She was looking forward to the train journey from the toe of Italy up to Germany. Thirty lovely hours cocooned in First Class, watching the scenery unfold. The idea was balm to her restless nature. And one never knew. There was always the possibility of a little sexual adventure.

Olaf Gustav was Charles' brother. Always in the background, content to live in the shadow of his older sibling, he was totally different in appearance. Olaf was average in every way. From his regular features, to his average height and weight. It was said of him that he would be lost in a crowd of two. Over the years this had stood him in good stead. He was a tabloid journalist of the lowest denominator. He had often been in company that literally forgot he was there. Many indiscretions therefore came to his ears. Reporting tittle-tattle, unconfirmed rumours, putting two and two together and coming up with five was his speciality. The high and not so mighty were his targets. His column was syndicated across Europe, mainly in his brother's newspapers, and often made fillers on TV and radio broadcasts. Information for potential blackmail he passed directly to Charles. Like his brother, he was a rabid right-winger. He believed fervently in a whites-only Europe and was prepared to do anything in his power to help his brother meet that goal.

He would travel by private boat to Marseilles, then by TGV to Paris. At 300kph he would be in France's capital in three hours. Time enough to enjoy a long and leisurely lunch. It was perfect. He would deliver Charles' package to the restaurant in Malmaison and then hit the hot-spots. He was looking forward to it. Damn Charles' instructions to leave immediately. Paris was just the place for his type of fun.

Clive Holmes was a disgraced civil-servant. Discovered sending British National Party propaganda over the internet from his office, he had been summarily dismissed. His guts knotted up at the memory of it. The black bitch had enjoyed telling him to clear his desk. He had appealed of course but it was no use. The government had closed ranks and he was out after fifteen years. No job. No future. No pension. Always on *their* side. The black swine. The sooner Britain returned to its Anglo-Saxon roots the better. Conveniently, he had forgotten that he had been in the civil service at the lowest grade with no hope of advancement. Holmes would tell anybody who cared to listen that the blacks, browns and Chinkies had been promoted over him because of so-called affirmative action. Well, he'd show them!

Tall, brown haired and brown eyed, he was good looking, with a dimpled chin. He kept fit by working out in the gym whenever he could. He had a boyish charm and an inane grin that women found alluring. It wasn't until they got to know him better that they realised he really was as stupid as his grin suggested. He spoke in slogans, passionate about race issues but with no substance to back his arguments.

He too was travelling by boat, but to Nice. He'd take the TGV to Paris and then change to Eurostar. He would arrive in London in the evening and make his way to Shepherd's Bush. To a particular restaurant where he would hand over the parcel. His instructions were to leave the country immediately. He always obeyed orders. It was easier than having to think for himself.

23

Two large inflatables were lowered onto the gently undulating sea. The team members were winched down. They were already kitted out in wet-suits and had only to finish pre-dive checks of their bottles to enter the water.

Badonovitch in one boat, Masters in the other, put the 120hp outboards into position on the transom and started each one. They burst into life with a deep-throated roar. In seconds they had the *Stockholm's* transponder in one craft and had lashed the inflatables together. There was a party atmosphere about the team. This was something they loved doing. Diving in clear water, from a stable platform, under a warm sun, with a job to be done. Perfect. Dunston and Masson would stay in the boats. The others would dive in pairs, secured to each other by a two-metre long rope attached to their left upper arms. Communications would be by voice from throat mikes. Hunter was buddied with Badonovitch, Masters with Tanner and Napier with Clements. They had different tasks to perform. Hunter was to look for the spheres of SRX, while the other two pairs were to set charges inside the ship's armoury and blow it to smithereens. It was too tempting a target for terrorist groups should they ever find out where the ship was and what it was carrying.

The sets they were using were state-of-the-art. The gas, heliox, was computer controlled to ensure the right mix of oxygen and helium for the appropriate depth. They had three hours, near enough, at fifty metres before they had to worry about decompression stops.

'Are you sure you're up to this?' Dunston asked Hunter, as Badonovitch helped him on with his set.

'Sure. I can't wait.'

'What about your head?'

'It's okay. Ready, Jan?'

'Yes, boss. Waiting on you.'

The two men slid over the side of the inflatable and into the warm water. Not for them the flashy back-flip with lots of show, splash and disorientation once you hit the water. They checked each other for leaks in their sets, gave the OK sign to Dunston and left surface. Once under the water they checked communications with Masson and followed the line down to the ship. Within seconds they could see its ghostly outline. Around them swam fish of all shapes and sizes that ignored them as easily as they ignored the fish. A small amount of oil or diesel was leaking from the ship. It wasn't enough to develop into a slick, and dissipated as it rose to the surface.

The *Stockholm* was at a list of about 45 degrees to starboard. Around her, curious denizens frequenting that part of the Mediterranean were congregating. Some had already found nooks and crannies to move into, intending to live there until they were either driven away or their prey no longer came near. Unerringly, Hunter led the way into the ship. It was eerie swimming in through the port side, the door latched open, fish swimming in and around the high-tech bridge. Already a thin layer of silt was beginning to form on the surfaces.

The lamps on their heads illuminated their way down to the next deck. There they were surprised to discover that the battery operated emergency lights fixed along the walls of the corridors were still operating. Water tight and with their own power supply, they were good for up to 96 hours.

In Gustav's stateroom, Hunter and Badonovitch unclipped their buddy-line and while the Spetsnaz searched the cabin Hunter set PE around the safe.

The explosion took off the hinges and Hunter was able to pull the door open. It was empty. Totally empty. He felt around, disappointed but not surprised. His fingers touched an imbedded lifting ring. Curling his finger around it he lifted a lid and inside found a locked box. He put it in the string bag he had dangling from his dive-belt.

He and Badonovitch continued searching but found nothing. Duval's room was also empty. The other staterooms were bare of everything except furniture. Not a single personal item was found.

The bridge yielded very little. Hunter took the latest log and the disc from the satellite navigation system. A safe on the bridge was opened simply by using a key hanging on a nearby shelf. Inside they found the Captain's passport and some money. Both were taken.

Throughout the search they had been reporting to the surface. They knew that the other two teams had finished and were on their way back up. Hunter acknowledged the information and told Dunston that he and Badonovitch were doing the same.

It was glorious to swim upwards, heading for the sun dappling the surface. Diving gave Hunter a sense of freedom, of entering another world. Hitting the surface the two men made the OK sign, slipped off their sets and handed them into the boat. A kick of their fins and a heave and they flopped into the bottom of the boat.

'How'd it go?' Hunter asked Clements.

'No problems. We ran the whole lot to one detonator with a back-up. It's a thirty hour delay. That'll give the clean-up vessel plenty of time to get here.'

'Good. We don't want any more pollution than is absolutely necessary.'

The clean-up vessel would literally suck up the surface of the water, filter out any oil or diesel and spit the seawater back out. It was highly effective, provided it was in the locale when the spillage was in the early stages.

'We'd better let the General know what we've learned,' said Hunter. 'Which is precisely the square-root of nothing.'

They were mid-way between Sardinia and Tunisia. While the divers had been down, Dunston and Masson had erected shades over the boats. Now the men settled down to a cold buffet, iced drinks and a short wait. Burg, who had been piloting the heli-copter, after dropping them in-situ, had flown on to Cagliari to refuel, the carrier having continued on its planned route. He was due back shortly. In fact, they heard his approach as new instructions reached them from TIFAT HQ.

Macnair had spoken to the Prime Minister in the morning. They agreed it was time to go on the offensive, the PR offensive. Press releases already agreed, written and carefully refined, were to be distributed that afternoon, in time for the evening news across the whole of Europe. A 4pm conference was called by No10.

Other European leaders were to make the same announcements. Certain facts were now clear and TIFAT's role was crucial. This was to be an orchestrated attempt to accuse the ultra-right-wing of terrorist attacks across Europe. Evidence was produced, mostly thanks to Isobel, that the attacks were paid for and planned by Charles Gustav and his associates. And the Prime Minister was as good as his word. He had given Macnair every possible support. The news release was hard-hitting, factual and shocking in the extreme. A huge propaganda machine moved into operation, led by the British and strongly supported by the European Parliament, spearheaded by Christine Woolford. She was well briefed by Macnair and in turn she had given the facts to other MEPs who now supported her. From left-wing Social Democrats to right-wing Conservatives, an awareness that they were fighting for the very existence of democracy and tolerance in Europe made them ready, willing and able to battle their corner. They were united against the ultra-right-wing and the xenophobes of every European state. Macnair clenched his fists in anger. He had to stop Gustav. *But where the hell was he*?

As if in answer to a prayer Isobel rushed in. 'General, GCHQ just traced a call from Gustav to somebody with a mobile in London.'

'Are you sure it was Gustav?'

'Positive. They did a voice match.'

'Where is he?'

'Somewhere in Bagheria in Northern Sicily. We are getting all the details now. Leo is pulling detailed maps of the place and we've re-programmed the satellites to take a look.'

'Are you absolutely sure he's there?'

'As sure as we can be. Unless he's used a land-line from somewhere else, phoned to the house and routed the call via there. But I don't see it somehow.'

'What was the gist of the call?'

'In a nutshell, to hurry up an operation. He didn't say what it was. He sounded rattled but,' she shrugged, 'still over-confident. We also received a floppy disc of information from Nick. We're working on it right now.'

In fact Gareth was working on it. He had been told to be careful, in case there was any self destruct mechanism in the program should anybody try and access the information without the right passwords. It was just as well he was prepared. As soon as the program was opened it threatened to wipe itself clean. Gareth set about constructing a mole that would break through and spit the information out of a window he would construct. He was, put simply, a genius.

The house sat in the folds of two hills, about three kilometres from the north coast of Sicily, south of Bagheria, and inland of the A20 motorway. The helicopter flew high, waiting and watching. The next part of the operation called for careful timing. A combination of satellite and infra-red pictures showed there were a number of people in a guardhouse at the main gate. Gustav's property was surrounded by a high fence and, from the information gleaned by TIFAT, it was probably electrified.

At the house, a huge sprawling hacienda, there were at least a dozen people. Some would be guards, others merely local help. Unfortunately there was too much at stake to worry about the lives of a few who may or may not be innocent. The team was going in hard and fast. But first they had to wait for the Americans.

'Two minutes,' Burg told the others. 'One minute. Tally ho.'

The helicopter swooped down out of the sky just as a stealth fighter dropped a series of smart bombs along the southern wall of the house. A second F-117A took out the guardhouse with one hit.

The dust was still mushrooming when the helicopter landed a few metres from the house. The team poured out, weapons ready, moving fast but carefully towards the smashed walls.

One, two and then a third figure staggered out, coughing, choking on the dust. Masters and Clements ran around the front of the house. Badonovitch and Napier went to the western side, Masson and Tanner went east. Hunter and Dunston approached the shattered walls. Schwarzkopf took charge of the two men and one woman who had appeared. Making them lie down, he handcuffed their hands behind their backs.

An automatic gun opened up and the team threw themselves to the ground. It had been fired from a window in the east side of the house. Masson was killed outright, while Tanner was hit in the side. He returned fire, setting down a barrage that allowed Clements to come around from the front and lob a grenade through the window. The firing was abruptly cut off.

Dunston kept low and dashed across the open ground to see what he could do for the injured men. It took only a second to confirm Masson's death. Ripping open a triangular bandage, Dunston strapped it around the entry and exit wounds in the left side of Tanner's abdomen. The blood looked healthy enough and Dunston hoped no vital organs had been hit.

'Stay put,' he ordered Tanner, who merely nodded.

Hunter was picking his way into the house. From the infrared sensors it appeared that there were people upstairs, moving around. There were others in a room in the front of the house. Schwarzkopf was at his shoulder, covering him.

In spite of the bombs the house remained standing. Practically all of the southern wall was blown away and they could see bits of bodies lying in the debris. Where were Gustav and Duval?

More shooting started from the front and Hunter and Schwarzkopf followed the sound. A door took them into a large open space from which other rooms led off. In the middle was a staircase. The infra-red sensors confirmed three people in the room ahead. Nobody was showing up in their immediate area. They darted across to the door. Hunter cracked it open and the pilot threw in two grenades in quick succession. The resulting explosions stopped the firing.

Hunter used his personal radio to check the situation with the rest of the team. They all agreed. There appeared to be only two people left alive in the house, in an upstairs room. Hunter and Schwarzkopf made for the stairs. The sensors confirmed survivors were at the end of the house, on the western side. A short corridor was faced by a solid door. Two people were hiding behind it.

Hunter tried the door handle. The door opened on silent hinges. A cautious look made him step into the room, his Glock 19 pointed at Gustav. The Swede was seated behind a desk in the corner of the room. To one side sat Duval. The secretary was nervous. Gustav, as always, was ice cold.

'Ah, Mr Hunter, I might have guessed it would be you. You keep turning up at the most inopportune moments.'

'On your feet, Gustav. You're coming with us.'

'I don't think so, somehow. I have already contacted my friend, the Chief of Police at Palermo and asked for assistance. No doubt help is on its way even as we speak. You can argue it out with him and his men.'

Hunter shook his head. 'You couldn't be more wrong, Gustav. The Italian government has warned both the Mafia and the local law enforcement agencies to stay out of this fight. Unless they want a clampdown the likes of which they have never seen before. Believe me, no one is coming to your aid.'

Gustav licked his lips. The utter confidence with which Hunter spoke rattled him. Duval looked positively sick.

'I need some information and I need it fast,' said Hunter. 'Where are the spheres of SRX?'

'I don't know what you're talking about.'

'Don't play games with me, Gustav, I haven't time.' Hunter had crossed the room and was standing in front of the desk. 'Where are they?'

'I don't . . .'

The Glock was on single shot. Gustav sat with his hands splayed on the desk in front of him. Hunter pressed the barrel of his gun onto the little finger of Gustav's left hand and fired.

Gustav screamed in pain and shock. Blood spurted across the leather desk top, leaving a red stain. 'You'll pay for that,' Gustav snarled, reaching into a pocket for a handkerchief. The white linen, wrapped around the stump of his finger was turning bloody.

'I will shoot off each of your fingers and then start on your feet,' said Hunter.

'Fool,' said Gustav with a sneer. 'Have you any idea how powerful I am? Who I control? As soon as we've taken power I'll have you, Hunter. You'll live to regret ever crossing swords with me.'

Hunter shrugged indifferently. 'It's over, Gustav. Within,' Hunter glanced at his watch, 'half an hour, a media blitz will start. Names will be spelled out. Your involvement will be clear for all the world to see.'

Gustav snorted in derision. 'Do you not realise that I would foresee such an eventuality? Anything that's said against me personally or my movement will be denied. Many men and women in high places will come out on my side, whether they wish to or not. I've ensured that. And once the Muslims have let loose the nerve gas, who will have the upper hand? Europe will panic. The people will believe what I tell them because they *want* to believe. That's the beauty of propaganda.'

'The people of Europe will believe the truth. The evidence is conclusive. After all, you are the one who hired the scientists to make the filthy stuff. Or do you deny it?'

'Of course I don't deny it,' Gustav said with scorn. 'It was the only way to ensure white Europeans will rise up and throw the coloureds and the non-Christians out.'

'Did you get all that?' Hunter asked into his throat mike.

'Yes,' said Macnair. 'Loud and clear. The picture is a little fuzzy but it will do. Isobel says she can clean it up digitally.'

'What's going on?' Duval asked, fear making him speak out.

Hunter pointed to his shoulder. 'This is a camera lens and this is a microphone. Gustav's confession has just been sent via satellite to TIFAT HQ. It will be broadcast later today.'

Gustav was shaking with hatred. 'I'll claim you made it up. Used actors to dub my voice. Synthesised my face using computers.'

'Gustav, Gustav, Gustav,' Hunter spoke in mock sorrow, shaking his head, 'you still don't get it. If you don't tell me where to find the spheres of gas I'll kill you. You won't live to see a glorious new dawn breaking over Europe. And neither will you,' he added, looking at Duval. Hunter blinked hard. A wave of dizziness was sweeping over him again. Damnation! He had thought the after-effects of the head wound had passed.

'I'll tell you all I know,' said Duval, 'in exchange for immunity.'

'Shut up, you weakling,' hissed Gustav. 'Remember which race you belong to – if you're going to die, at least die with some dignity. Tell them nothing.'

'Charles, your mind is diseased. Your obsession has become a mania. Your idea of a whites-only Europe is . . . ludicrous. Anyone with half a brain can see that. And setting off weapons as heinous as the SRX gas proves you're mad.'

'You will not speak to me like that,' Gustav hissed, standing up and leaning his weight on the desk. His eyes were bulging.

Hunter couldn't see properly but he'd heard the exchange. His eyesight was clearing when he saw the small calibre gun appear in Gustav's hand. Hunter shot him in the elbow, shattering the joint. The gun flew from Gustav's hand and he screamed in pain once more.

An image of Ruth and her damaged leg sprang to Hunter's mind. In a cold rage he fired twice more in rapid succession. He blew apart Gustav's knees. The Swede collapsed unconscious.

Duval was watching in horror. Hunter now aimed his gun at the American's left knee. 'All right, Duval, talk. Where are the containers being taken?'

'I don't know.' He saw Hunter's finger tighten on the trigger and he yelled, 'Wait! It's true! I tell you I don't know. Gustav made all the arrangements. But I do have extremely valuable information about his organisation. About the people in power who are in his pay. Hunter, for God's sake, I'm a walking data bank.'

'We'll come to that later. Right now we need to find that SRX before a humanitarian disaster happens.'

'I know who has them. I can give you their names, their descriptions.'

'But you don't know where they are going?'

'No! Gustav kept that secret. He was becoming paranoid. He was keeping more and more things to himself.'

'Or maybe he was beginning not to trust you,' said Hunter. 'Burg, check on Gustav.'

The pilot moved around the desk and knelt by the body. 'He's still alive, just.'

Gustav opened his eyes and said in a rasping whisper. 'It will be too late. *You* are too late. The uprising will start. My death will change nothing.' Blood was pooling across the floor, the metallic smell all pervading. Gustav struggled, trying to lift his head but collapsed again. Schwarzkopf checked his pulse, looked at Hunter and shook his head.

'That just leaves you, Duval,' said Hunter.

'I'll do all I can to help. But I want immunity.' Duval looked at the body and shuddered.

'What about a bullet in the brain?' Hunter aimed at the secretary.

Duval flinched but said, 'Then you'll never find the SRX.'

Hunter lowered his gun. The bloody man was right. 'I'll see what I can do.'

'Not good enough. Speak to Macnair. Tell him I can be of great help in the present situation but I want a guarantee that I won't be prosecuted.'

Hunter knew Duval's unique knowledge of Gustav's movement would be invaluable. His co-operation might well save thousands of lives. 'Show me some sign of good faith. Let me give the General something.'

'Like what?'

'Like the names and descriptions of the people carrying the SRX.'

Duval's forehead furrowed in worried indecision but then he made his mind up. 'All right. Their names are Ursula Fritberg, Olaf Gustav and Clive Holmes. I know the targets too. Ursula Fritberg's is the US army base near Paderborn. Olaf's is the Métro in Paris and Holmes' is to be set off somewhere in London.'

'Olaf Gustav? Any relation?' Hunter nodded at the body.

'His brother.'

'Did you see the three of them?'

'Yes. I handed them their instructions in an envelope. Along with some money for expenses.'

'And you don't know what those instructions were?'

'No, I told you. Charles was becoming extremely secretive with his plans. It was beginning to lead to disagreements between us.'

'Disagreements?'

Duval shrugged. 'Listen, Hunter, I've been looking for a way out for months. This makes it easier.' He cast a glance at Gustav and shuddered. Standing up, he went into a bathroom and returned with a towel. He threw it over Gustav's body. Blood began to soak into the cloth.

Hunter used his sat-phone to call Macnair. He briefly reported what had happened and what Duval had said.

'Actually, Nick, we've had some luck,' said Macnair. 'That disc you sent us has a raft of information which we can use. However, one small file contained three itineraries. Until now they made no sense. I'll phone you back in a few minutes.' The connection was broken.

The team were deployed around the house, creating a defensive perimeter. There was no telling whether the Mafia *would* stay away.

While Hunter waited for the General to phone, Schwarzkopf went downstairs to help put Masson into a body bag and stow his body in the helicopter.

Macnair phoned within five minutes. 'This all checks. The

itineraries are headed with the initials of each person. Ursula Fritberg is on the train for Paderborn and is just now crossing the German border. I've arranged for her to be picked up while the train is moving. That way she cannot escape. Unfortunately, the other two are a different problem. Olaf Gustav has already arrived in Paris. We know where he's going so we'll have him met at the restaurant. Clive Holmes is already in London. Likewise we'll pick him up at the drop.'

The arguments raged wide and deep on some TV shows. Bitter rhetoric turned into fisticuffs. It was good for ratings but dreadful for democracy.

The existence of the SRX filled containers was not disclosed. The rioting taking place was bad enough. If the populace became really terrified it would escalate out of control. Minorities in inner-cities were building barricades to protect themselves and their communities. Skinheads and other fascist groups were on the rampage, throwing petrol bombs and firing illegal guns. The police in some areas tried to control the problem. In others they stood back and watched.

There was no doubt in Macnair's mind that everything hinged on stopping the release of the nerve gas. If the spheres were found and the attacks stopped then it was possible democracy could win. If they were let loose by Islamic fundamentalists then it wouldn't matter what proof or information was shown to the public. It would be too late. Muslims would pay the price. There would be no stopping the anger flooding into the streets. The current exodus of non-whites leaving Europe, bad though it was, would become a flood. Gustav would have won.

Ursula Fritberg was feeling pleased with herself. She would be changing trains at Frankfurt in fifteen minutes. She had enjoyed her journey. The food had been very good, the wine palatable and the large brandies the night before had helped her sleep soundly. There had been a slight delay at the border but it hadn't amounted to much. A cursory look had been given to her passport but it was more for form than anything. The train had made an unscheduled stop at Darmstadt but it had only been for a few seconds. She wondered idly why they had stopped.

There were two men walking along the carriage, though not looking in her direction. Alarm bells rang in her head. Something was wrong. *What? That was it!* They *weren't* looking. Men always looked at her. She stood up with a feeling of alarm and turned away. She found herself staring into the eyes of a stranger.

He greeted her with the words, 'You are under arrest.'

She heard them as if from the end of a long tunnel as her world shattered. The SRX was found in seconds.

Olaf found the drop-point, an Algerian restaurant in a run-down part of Malmaison. The clientele were mostly non-whites and Muslim. Two tables were particularly boisterous. One white man was celebrating his divorce with three other white friends, while a black man, with three mixed-race friends, were celebrating his stag night. Both parties had obviously drunk too much before arriving at the restaurant, although the men had barely touched the wine that had been placed on their tables. They had eaten though, picking at their food, laughing too loudly, being a nuisance. The sooner they left, thought the owner, the better.

Olaf Gustav entered carrying a bag. He looked around nervously. In a corner of the restaurant sat two men. Swarthy-complexioned, Arab looking. Silent men who kept glancing towards the door.

Gustav's brother walked towards them. He was halfway across the crowded restaurant when the eight raucous customers suddenly stood up and drew guns.

'Police! Police! Stay where you are! Do not move!'

Olaf Gustav stopped in horror and looked over his shoulder. The guns were levelled at him. He couldn't help himself. Urine ran down his leg and puddled at his feet.

The two Arabs sitting in the corner had leapt to their feet and were reaching for guns they carried in holsters under their armpits. The French police didn't hesitate. The two men were gunned down even as Olaf Gustav was being thrown to the floor and handcuffed. A senior policemen grabbed the bag. Relief flooded through him when he saw the container of SRX gas.

From Sicily the team flew by helicopter to Naples. They took Duval, a laptop computer and a handful of floppy discs. Macnair had assured the American that he would do everything in his power to keep him from prison. Provided he co-operated fully. When they arrived in Naples, a Hercules aircraft met them and they changed from one plane to another in record time.

Once the team was in the air they did what they always did in these circumstances. They slept. They had been expecting to fly straight to Scotland and so it came as a complete surprise when they were diverted to Heathrow.

Hunter was informed by the pilot of the change of destination and he radioed Macnair.

'Bad news, Nick. We got two lots of the SRX but the third has gone missing. In London.'

24

Ex-civil servant Clive Holmes made a simple error. He failed to take account of the hour difference between the Continent and the UK. He arrived an hour early at the restaurant in Shepherd's Bush. Situated in a side street off Charecroft Way, its owners boasted that the food was suitable for the most observant of the Muslim faith. The two Arabs he was to meet were not yet there. In fact, the restaurant was empty. It was only just 6pm and the evening rush was yet to start.

Nervously Holmes sat down to wait at a corner table. He wasn't there for long before a kitchen door opened and two men approached his table.

'You have it?' The younger of the two asked.

'Who are you?' Holmes replied. If he was nervous he didn't show it. A total lack of imagination helped a great deal in circumstances like these.

'We know you have something for us. Hand it over.'

'How do I know . . .'

'Do not play games with us. Give me the bag.'

Holmes shrugged. He'd done what he was supposed to do. He handed the bag over.

The two men walked away, through the kitchen door. Holmes sat there for a few seconds and then got to his feet. Time to leave. He walked out the front door, bumping into a large burly man. Holmes apologised, as did the man who stepped around him. He had taken two or three paces when he heard a voice.

'Excuse me.'

Holmes looked over his shoulder.

'Aren't you Clive Homes?'

'Yes. Do I know you?'

The words were hardly out of his mouth when he was looking down the barrels of two revolvers. Armed police came pouring out of a plain white van parked next to the kerb. He was hand-cuffed and in the back of the van before he knew what was going on.

It only took a matter of minutes to get him talking. He'd had no idea what he was bringing into the country. No, he didn't know the two men he had given the bag to. He assumed they had left through the back entrance.

The police raided the restaurant but there was no sign of the SRX or the two men. Three illegal immigrants were taken into custody. At Bow Street Police Station their photographs were scanned into a computer. Two proved to have links with al-Qaeda. Their self-appointed leader, Hamad bin Thani, made clear their position. He demanded to see their lawyers and refused to talk until one was present. The offer of the duty solicitor was turned down. The Arabs had names and phone numbers of specific lawyers they wanted to represent them. The police recognised the names immediately. Apologists for terrorists under the guise of human rights, these particular solicitors would be a thorn in the sides of the police when they tried to extract information from the men arrested. The Superintendent in charge had a flash of inspiration. He telephoned Macnair.

Hunter met the police at Heathrow. The three men were handed over to the team who were kitted out in full battle dress, including black ski-masks. They looked terrifying – as indeed they were meant to. Macnair had been explicit with his instructions. A WMD was out in the streets of London somewhere and these three men had knowledge of its whereabouts. No matter what it took, they *had* to get the information.

The prisoners had been arrogant, offensive. Their attitude suddenly changed.

'What are you doing? You cannot hand us over to these men,'

screamed Hamad bin Thani. 'I demand to see my lawyer.'

Clements took hold of bin Thani by the throat and snarled into his face. 'You don't exist, scum. You're ours.' He shoved him towards the back of the Hercules which was sitting with its tail-gate open.

The other two men were herded after him.

'Superintendent,' said Hunter, 'please forget you ever saw them. And look after Mr Duval for us.'

'Saw who?' the Superintendent quipped, turned away and then suddenly walked back. 'Do whatever it takes. My family live in London. And don't worry about Duval.'

On board the plane the men were secured to their seats. Bags were placed over their heads, the feeling of claustrophobia adding to their fear.

'Where's Jan?' Hunter asked.

'On his way, boss. He'll be about five minutes. The police had a little difficulty finding what we wanted,' answered Napier.

'But he got them?'

'He did.'

A police car drew up and Badonovitch leapt out. From the trunk he took three bags, slung them over his shoulder and ran up the ramp. As soon as he was on board the door was closed and the pilot asked for permission to take-off. The Hercules was given priority but even so there was a delay of three minutes while the runway was cleared. As soon as enough height was gained the Hercules headed for the Channel before turning west.

Hunter went through the brief files the police had handed him. Two al-Qaeda men and a third unknown but definitely an illegal and probably Saudi. Did he have anything to do with the WMD? Perhaps. Certainly the al-Qaeda men would know something.

The Geneva Convention was clear on the treatment of both prisoners of war and civilians. The trouble was the enemy they were up against didn't fit into any of the categories as laid down by international law. With the images of the American treatment of Iraqi POWs fresh in his mind, Hunter hated what they were about to do. He knew the rest of the team thought likewise. But with so much at stake there was no choice.

He hoped the threat of eternal damnation would make the men talk.

Pulling the bags off their heads he watched as the men sucked in air, half-suffocated by the restricting bags. Hate and fear mixed in their faces. They were released from their seats and pulled upright. Their hands were tied to the parachute rail above them.

'Who has the nerve gas?' Hunter asked bin Thani.

'I do not know what you're talking about. You cannot do this. I demand you take us back to Heathrow and allow me to call my lawyer.'

'Let me explain something to you,' said Hunter. 'And please listen very carefully.' He hated what he was doing but knew that he had no choice. Time was of the essence. Tens even hundreds of thousands of lives were at stake. Grimly, he hit the man as hard as he could in the solar plexus. The man screamed in agony as the air erupted from his lungs. He was gasping, unable to suck air in, unable to curl over to relieve the pain.

Hunter turned to the second man. 'Your name is Omar al-Faud. Correct?'

'I tell you nothing. We demand . . .' He screamed as Hunter repeated the blow.

'Mr Ayman Zubaydah,' Hunter spoke almost conversationally, 'I hope you will be more reasonable?'

Zubaydah responded with a torrent of Arabic.

'Don't you speak English?'

The al-Qaeda man answered. 'No! I no speak English.'

'In that case we have no further use of you. No more questions to ask. Understand?'

The man nodded vigorously.

'That surprises me as you claim not to speak English. Jan!'

Badonovitch approached carrying one of the bags. He opened it and took out a dead piglet. The three Muslims looked at the pig in utter horror. Badonovitch took the suckling and hung it around the neck of Zubaydah, who was now gibbering.

'I speak. I speak English good.'

'Sorry,' said Hunter, 'you're too late.'

Badonovitch wrapped canvas around the pig and the man's

body. The other two looked on in complete shock. Chains were wrapped around Zubaydah's legs, all the way up to his chest.

'Do you see that indicator?' Hunter pointed to an altimeter over the port side door.

None of the Arabs responded. Hunter grabbed bin Thani by the hair, lifted his head and pointed. 'Do you see it?'

'Yes,' he croaked. 'I see it.'

'Do you know what it means?'

'No.'

'It means we are twenty-five thousand feet high. I can tell you we are in the middle of the English Channel, heading west-southwest.' He used his internal comms set to speak to the pilot who confirmed there was no shipping in the vicinity. Gesturing to Masters and Clements, Zubaydah was freed from the parachute rail. He was picked up and carried to the port side of the aircraft. A door was opened and he was thrown out unceremoniously and still alive.

Hunter managed to hide his emotions. He loathed what he was doing so much that he felt sick. But they had to find the SRX and there was no time. 'I don't know how long he lived,' he smiled through his mask at the other two, who were staring at him like rabbits trapped by a snake. 'But he probably didn't die until he hit the water.' He paused and then added as though it was an afterthought, 'Of course he'll never go to heaven. Never mind, he's got a pig for company for eternity.'

The faces of the two men reflected their complete devastation. Hunter stood and watched them for a few seconds, saying nothing.

Looking bin Thani straight in the eye, Hunter said, 'I want to know where the SRX is. It's a virulent form of biotoxin that will kill many, many thousands of people, indiscriminately. Christians, Hindus and Muslims alike.'

'I . . . I don't know.' The al-Qaeda terrorist was staring at the door through which Zubaydah had vanished, as though expecting him to reappear at any moment.

'If you have nothing to tell us, then you're of no use to us. You'll go the same way as your friend. Then al-Faud can answer my questions. I can promise you two things. You will scream all the way to the sea and you will have company. Jan.'

The Spetsnaz brought forward another bag and tipped the carcass of another piglet onto the deck. Both Muslims stared at it in horror.

'You won't be going to Paradise, that's for sure,' said Hunter. 'So your friends and family won't be there to greet you. Or to see you when it's their turn to die. Who will protect you then from the torments of hell-fire?'

Bin Thani dragged his eyes from the pig and looked at Hunter with hate. 'What kind of man are you,' he asked hoarsely, 'who can condemn a man's soul to eternal damnation?'

'One who finds a loathsome swine like you even breathing the same air as ordinary people an abomination. I'll do whatever it takes to save the innocent lives you are condemning to so horrific a death. I've seen the gas in action and it's a terrible way to die. In fact, your death will be pleasant by comparison. Jan,' Hunter tilted his head towards bin Thani.

The Arab screamed loudly and fainted. A mug of cold water thrown in his face revived him.

'I am running out of time and patience. Now, where is the SRX?'

'I swear I don't know,' bin Thani screamed at him.

'Jan.'

The Spetsnaz tied the hindquarters of the pig around bin Thani's neck. Screaming hysterically the Arab finally managed to say, 'He knows, not me.' He moaned and added, 'For the love of Allah, take it away.'

While Badonovitch removed the pig Hunter turned his attention to Omar al-Faud. 'You know? Is that right?'

'I know nothing! Nothing!'

Hunter appeared to be considering the man's statement and after a few seconds he sighed. 'In that case, we have no use for you. Jan . . .'

'Allah is merciful. Judgement is his alone!'

Hunter grabbed the Arab by the throat and rammed his head against the side of the plane. 'You bastard. Don't talk to us about

God's judgement. You intend to murder innocent men, women and children and for what? You perverted piece of filth. I told you I've seen the gas kill. I *know* what a horrible death it is. Now tell me where to find the SRX.'

The Arab stayed silent. Hunter nodded to Jan who picked up the pig's carcass and walked toward al-Faud.

'All right! All right, may Allah curse you. It is in a mosque in Lambeth.'

'What's the address?'

Al-Faud mustered his courage for a few more seconds but as Badonovitch placed the pig's snout against his cheek he yelled out the location.

'When is the attack going to take place?'

'Tomorrow! Tomorrow, I swear!'

'Where?'

'At the Houses of Parliament.'

Now that he had started to talk, al-Faud found it easy to continue. He gave the names of the two men who were to carry out the attack but all he knew about the timing was that it was planned for the afternoon.

Hunter radioed Macnair and told him what they had learnt.

Macnair acknowledged the information and said, 'You know what to do.'

'Yes, sir.'

Turning to the two men, he said, 'We wait and see what happens.'

The plane droned westwards, past the tip of Cornwall. An hour later, Macnair called back. 'He was telling the truth. Unfortunately, one of the men escaped with the SRX. He went through an underground passage to a house five doors along and got away. The police have picked up about twenty people who are refusing to talk. And there's no way we can get them to tell us what we need to know as their solicitors are already on the scene.'

'What now, sir?'

'Try and get more details. The Houses of Parliament cover a large area. The gas could be released anywhere at anytime. See if they know any more.'

'Roger that, sir.'

In spite of more threats they got nothing further from either man. Hunter came to the conclusion that they knew nothing more. Which made sense. Information cut-outs were the cornerstone to any terrorist act.

'You may get to heaven after all. But I doubt it.'

At Hunter's nod the two men were released from their cuffs and allowed to sit. He offered them each a drink of water which they gulped down thirstily. The poison, a derivative of curare, was fast acting and both men died within seconds.

The team wrapped chains around the bodies and threw them out of the plane. The carcasses of the pigs followed separately. Had the two men been allowed to live the uproar about their human rights would possibly have drowned out the screams of terror of the innocents killed.

Already the Hercules had banked around and was heading north, for Edinburgh. There was nothing more they could do. However, their plans were changed by a call from Macnair. The plane was being sent back to Heathrow.

When it landed they were met by the same Superintendent who had seen them off. He had already been briefed on what the team had learnt.

'So why are we needed?' Hunter asked, puzzled.

'We need sharpshooters. We've identified vantage points over-looking the square. Peter Weir and David Hughes are on their way here with four rifles. Some sort of specialist sniper guns?'

Hunter nodded. 'Probably. Weir's a superb shot and Dave Hughes is no slouch, either. The other men I can offer are Don Masters and Josh Clements.'

'Can the rest of you be in the Square?'

'No problem. What about undercover police?'

'It'll be crawling with them. Men and women. Undercover operatives are one thing. Special services quite another. And God alone knows what we'll be up against.'

The day's beauty mocked the possible horror ahead. It was warm, the sun was shining, clouds scudded across a blue sky.

Parliament Square was busy with Londoners going about their business, as well as tourists coming to wonder at and photograph one of the most famous buildings in the world. Visitors faced one disappointment. Big Ben would not be striking that day. The clock and the bells were stopped, so the press announcement said, for necessary maintenance. At that time of the day, many politicians, mostly unknown, were heading to one of the heavily subsidised restaurants or bars for lunch or a drink. It was business as usual for the vast majority of people.

It was precisely noon.

Matt Dunston and Hunter strolled around the square, to all intents and purposes in a deep discussion, enjoying the weather. Dressed in light grey, pin-stripe city suits, and wearing ties, they appeared the epitome of successful businessmen or middleranking civil servants.

About half the men and women walking in and out of the square were plain clothes police. Some, members of the armed response unit, carried concealed weapons. Others were there to look and report. They walked down the streets that led into the square and out again desperate to identify the possible terrorists before it was too late. Loiterers on Westminster Bridge stood and gossiped, watching the people walking across. One thing they knew was helpful in their search. The man or woman they were looking for would be carrying a bag big enough to hold the deadly SRX sphere.

The road had been closed to all traffic. It was causing chaos in the area but it removed one of their biggest headaches – a vehicle with the nerve gas hidden inside. The terrorists would *have* to approach on foot. But they were also gambling the attack was still taking place around Westminster.

Dunston and Hunter were leaning on the parapet of the bridge, watching, searching, aware that time was passing. With a lifetime interest and love of all things nautical, Hunter's eyes were drawn to a boat coming downstream. It was sleek and fast looking. A mean machine, he thought, capable of a hell of a turn of speed.

He turned around, his back to the river. So far five men and three women had been unceremoniously lifted, hustled into an unmarked police van and had their belongings searched. Each time the search was done quietly and efficiently. Nothing and it was fast approaching 13.00. The attack could come at any time and the afternoon was stretching far ahead of them.

There was no other way into Parliament Square apart from along the streets and over the bridge. Unless it was by boat. The thought had hardly taken hold when he looked over his left shoulder, his heart hammering. The boat was tied up next to the clock tower. Looking closely he could see the faint shimmer of the engine still running, the sunlight catching the faint stream of cooling water over the starboard quarter. The two men, non-white, Arab-looking, had just stepped ashore. One was carrying a small holdall!

They were perhaps thirty metres away, out of sight of the Square and the police.

'Matt, I've got them.'

The words were hardly out of Hunter's mouth before one of the men looked up, straight at Hunter. It was an instinctive recognition.

Hunter was reaching under his coat for his Glock while the man was reaching for his own gun. Hunter beat him to it. He drew his gun and fired twice, both shots into the man's body. Dunston had reported the sighting and police were converging on the area. The surviving terrorist threw the holdall back into the boat and jumped in after it. He let go the single rope holding the boat alongside and rammed the throttle forward. The boat took off like a Formula One racing car.

Hunter cupped the gun in his left hand and took aim. As he pulled the trigger the boat jinked to starboard and back to port. Hunter missed. He pulled the trigger again and kept firing. The boat was now passing under the bridge and in desperation Hunter leaned over and fired his last shot. The bullet missed the man but hit the steering cable just as the driver swung the wheel to port to avoid a slow moving barge. The strain snapped the wire and the boat careered out the other side heading obliquely for the left bank. Hunter took off, sprinting as fast as he could though he knew he had no hope of catching up with it. Through his earphone, he was aware of Dunston briefing Peter Weir.

The Olympic marksman was in the tower housing the bell known as Big Ben. At this point the Thames was flowing south to north. From his vantage point, Weir could see east over Westminster Bridge and north along Victoria Embankment. David Hughes was in the other quadrant of the tower and covered Parliament Square and south along Millbank.

Weir held an Accuracy International AW-AS-98, 7.62mm calibre rifle in his hands. The Arctic Warfare-Australian Special Forces model was called the most boring rifle in the world due to its accuracy. The glass he was using was a Schmitt and Bender sniper scope.

The boat flashed into sight. Weir took aim and fired at the fast moving target. The shot hit the terrorist in the left shoulder and threw him against the windscreen. He fell back and hit the throttle into reverse. The sudden change cut the engine and the boat turned a few more degrees towards the bank, out of sight of Weir. Seeing the boat slowing down gave Hunter hope.

He was running on the path alongside the river, towards the moored ship, *Tattershall Castle*. His feet pounded the concrete, resonating in a harsh throb in his skull. Pedestrians screamed as he passed. The police ran after him, though the nearest back-up was Dunston, a hundred metres behind. Hunter had changed the magazine in his Glock and fired two snap shots at the boat which was now gently bouncing against the side of the bank, still moving. They missed the driver who was frantically trying to restart the engine. Hunter's breath was coming in ragged gasps and his vision was blurring. *Damnation! Not now!*

The boat's momentum was taking it past the bow of the *Tattershall Castle* as Hunter caught up with it. Hunter didn't stop to think. He had no time. He vaulted the railings and prayed for the best just as the engine coughed and caught.

Hunter's feet hit the smooth stern and he tottered on the edge, in danger of falling into the water. With a superhuman effort he flung himself forward onto his knees and then tumbled headlong onto the backseat.

The boat was increasing speed, bouncing from the river bank to the hull of the *Tattershall Castle* when it shot past the stern of the moored ship. The driver wrenched the wheel to starboard before realising it had no effect. He let go and made a grab for the bag. It was closed and he fumbled with the zip.

The boat began to turn to starboard, following the bend in the river and headed straight for HMS *President*. The SRX container fell out of the bag and landed next to Hunter. With a snarl of triumph, the terrorist reached inside and brought out a radio transmitter.

Hunter's arm snaked out and an iron grip crushed the Arab's hand around the hard plastic box, preventing him pushing the send button. Squeezing with every ounce of strength he possessed, Hunter heard the man's fingers cracking. The terrorist screamed and reached with his other hand for the transmitter. Through a haze Hunter saw the movement and desperately hit the man in his wounded shoulder, using a clenched fist like a hammer. The Arab screamed again but his fanaticism gave him the strength to continue reaching for the box. This time Hunter aimed more carefully and brought his fist down in a smashing blow across the terrorist's shoulder, into the bullet damaged bones. There was a crunching sound as the bones parted and the Arab screamed in utter agony. The Arab's strength was fading fast as Hunter pulled the man to him, half turned and used his elbow to devastating effect, hitting him in the nose, breaking it, driving the cartilage flat across his face. The man collapsed, unconscious.

The boat, up on the plane, was now only yards away from the grey side of *President*. Hunter was on his knees in the stern and the sphere was rolling along the backseat. If the boat hit the steel hull and exploded it was possible the SRX would be released. Not that he would know anything about it, as he'd be dead from the impact.

He grabbed the sphere, curled himself around it and fell over the side, holding it tightly to his chest. He hit the water and swam down into the filthy Thames. The boat hit the side of *President* with a tremendous collision, breaking the fuel linkage at the engine, spraying petrol over the hot casing and causing an enormous fire ball. The terrorist's body was burnt to a crisp.

Hunter hit the soft mud at the bottom, the container of SRX burying up to his elbows. The current pulled him away and the smooth sphere slipped from his grasp. Swimming upwards, Hunter reached the surface, looked up at the sky and passed out. He didn't feel a boat-hook snag his collar and pull him to the side of a police launch. Nor was he aware of the hefty police constable hauling him on board. His pulse was checked along with his breathing. Mouth-to-mouth was deemed unnecessary. After a few moments he came to with a groan. Trying to sit up, he felt the world spin, gagged and brown bile vomited from his stomach.

'Are you okay?'

'Yes. At least, I think so. Christ, I hurt like hell.'

'Take it easy.'

'The SRX! I hit the river bottom with it. It's buried in the silt.'

'Don't worry. Our police divers will find it.'

Hunter nodded and passed out.

Epilogue

Duval's testimony was crucial. Details of Gustav's involvement in fomenting the right-wing backlash against Muslims convinced the majority. However, among a small percentage of the population there was still a deep simmering hatred of the minorities who had come to the West. Politicians were forced to confront the issues and tackle them properly for the first time – to be honest about the problems Europe faced. Race relations had been set back a generation and work was now needed to foster the understanding and tolerance required to live in harmony and peace. At the same time, Muslims in particular and other minorities in general, were being made to confront their own attitudes to religious tolerance and integration.

All races and creeds knew how close they had come to an utter catastrophe which would have resulted in complete polarisation. And it wouldn't have stopped in Europe. It would have spread across the world, whites forced out of Muslim countries, Christians evicted, Hindus ostracised. Where would it have ended? Thinking about it gave Macnair nightmares.

Duval escaped prosecution. He moved to the Seychelles and lived quietly in complete luxury. His book about the rise and fall of Charles Gustav bombed. He made no attempt to write anything else.

Sylvestre diSilvio took early retirement from his position as Head of Security at Rome Airport. He divorced his wife and moved into a luxury villa with his mistress with whom he'd been having an affair for nearly three years. Isobel tracked down his bank accounts and found in excess of three million euros which she quietly purloined. DiSilvio's mistress left him when she discovered he no longer had any money. Acting on a tip-off, the police raided his villa to find him dead, hanging from a rope tied to the balcony surrounding the inner courtyard. Foul play was suspected but never proven.

The cheque for ten million pounds cleared through Hunter's offshore account. The money had been paid to him by Gustav and was legally his to do with as he wished. He used it to pay the members of TIFAT a bonus. It meant that nobody had to worry about their credit cards and overdrafts, at least for a while. Only Macnair, Carter and Dunston knew where the money came from. Carter told the men it was payment from a grateful government for what they had done. They didn't really believe it, but what the hell.

Isobel, as she had done so often in the past, raided Gustav's bank accounts searching for hidden assets. There was very little there. Much of it had already been raided. Isobel guessed Duval had beaten her to it. Worse, she couldn't track where the money had gone. Some of Gustav's companies collapsed. Others survived because their infrastructure kept them going. The more unsavoury and right-wing of his publications prospered, although the readership was down.

The scientists settled in Los Alamos. There, at a top secret military establishment they continued with their work. Weapons of Mass Destruction were developed along with supposed antidotes. The antidotes provided the excuse for the research. As so often was the case, the hypocrisy of the West knew no bounds.

The crew of the SS *Stockholm* were freed. No case to answer. Damages were awarded by the Swedish government to each of the men. They could live on the proceeds without ever having to work again. It took the French Secret Service, working with the

CIA, a year to kill every one of them. Each man knew, before he died, why it was happening. The lesson, like all lessons, was only meaningful if others learned from it. The message was quietly disseminated to all those who needed to know. Sweden was invited to take part in future Nato exercises but declined.

The letter waiting for Hunter from Ruth gutted him. In naval parlance it was known as a 'Dear John'. In it she explained that it would be a long time before she could walk again, that probably she never would without aid. She didn't want to be a burden. She would always love him but it was for the best. She didn't want him to try and contact her. She was truly, very sorry.

He wasn't prepared to let it go at that. He knew she was hurting, emotionally as well as physically. Ruth valued achievement and independence over everything. Hunter had thought their love counted more and he made several attempts to contact her but she refused to accept his calls.

When he finally gave up he got exceedingly drunk. The powerful painkillers he was taking contributed a good deal to his condition. A tongue-lashing from his father left him in no doubt about what he needed to do. Macnair granted him a month's leave and Hunter left for Israel as soon as he could.

A Million Tears

by Paul Henke

1890. Murder and intrigue have forced the Griffiths family to flee their native Wales. They leave behind a village devastated by a mine disaster and the oppression of the Victorian ruling classes.

Their subsequent adventures represent the American Dream. With bravado born of necessity, Evan Griffiths builds a business empire – retail, transport, banking, real estate – in the frontier town of St. Louis. With an inherent sense of justice, and the support of his beloved Meg, he forges a political career. But on his right hip, Evan carries a gun. No one will ever hurt his family again.

In Wales, David yearned to travel, dreamed of discoveries. Shipwrecked on a coral island in the South Seas, he discovers himself.

His brother, Sion, dreams of flying, craves freedom and adventure. But will his dream – and Sion himself – die in the lawless hinterlands of the Wild West?

Through meticulous research, author Paul Henke expertly braids together fact and fiction, recreating the Frontier of America. With consummate ease, he conveys a vivid sense of life at the turn of the century, weaving the thread of history – and the lessons it can teach us – through his narrative.

The vitality of Henke's fiction is mirrored in the energy of his vibrant characters. On his vast canvas he captures their triumphs and their tragedies. In 'A Million Tears' he unveils the portrait of the remarkable Griffiths Family. A gem to be treasured.

ISBN 1-902483-00-6

The Tears of War and Peace

by Paul Henke

It is 1911 and David Griffiths is in Wales, bored and lonely. He travels to London at the behest of their family friend, John Buchanan, to start a new business in banking. There he gets caught up in the suffragette movement and falls in love with Emily. Against the backdrop of women's fight for votes and the looming First World War, the Griffiths build a vast, sprawling company encompassing banking, aircraft manufacturing, farming and whisky distilling.

The enmity of a German family follows them tragically throughout this period, leading to murder and revenge. At the end of the war, thanks to a change in the Constitution, Evan is invited to run for President of the United States. The family rally round for the most important battle of Evan's life.

With the Brown-shirts running rampage across Germany, David and Sion are soon involved in a battle for survival.

Sir David Griffiths is a colossus of a figure, striding across the world and through the century, a man of integrity and bravery, passion and dedication. Determined to win, nothing comes before the family.

The story is as compelling as ever. Historical fact woven into the fictional characters makes a breathtaking tale of adventure you will not want to put down.

ISBN 1-902483-03-0

Silent Tears

by Paul Henke

Silent Tears is full of passion and adventure. You will be captivated as three generations of the Griffiths family struggle to meet the challenges of their time.

From the depths of the depression and the rise of fascism to the abdication of Edward VIII and the Spanish Civil War, Henke's meticulous research brings the period and vibrant characters to life.

David, powerful and dynamic, at the centre of political intrigue, his love for the family is put to the ultimate test . . . Meg, his mother, stalwart and determined, guides the family with humour and devotion . . . and Susan, beautiful and tempestuous, fighting for justice. No sacrifice is too great for those she loves.

Packed with excitement, Silent Tears is a masterpiece. A novel that vibrates with sheer narrative power and relentlessly builds the emotional pressure until it explodes in a firestorm of passion and high-octane adventure. A spellbinding epic.

ISBN 1-902483-05-7

Débâcle

TIFAT File I

A Nick Hunter Adventure

Following a summit meeting in Paris an alliance of interested countries form an elite fighting force to combat terrorism throughout the world. Based in Britain and under the command of a British General, the team is made up of Western, Russian and other non-aligned countries' special forces.

Without warning the terrorists strike. A group of bankers, politicians and industrialists are taken prisoner off the coast of Scotland and the new, untried force is sent to search for them.

The Scene of Action Commander is Nick Hunter, Lieutenant Commander, Royal Navy, an underwater mine and bomb clearance expert with experience in clandestine operations.

The enemy is one of the world's most ruthless and wanted terrorists – Aziz Habib! Hunter leads the team against Habib, backed up by two computer experts: Sarah from GCHQ and Isobel, hired by the General to run the IT for the new force.

While stock markets take a pounding and exchange rates go mad, the state sponsoring the terrorism is making a fortune. It has to stop. At all costs.

This is non-stop adventure from beginning to end. A riveting story told by a master story teller. You are guaranteed not to want to put it down!

Débâcle mixes fact with fiction which will cause you to wonder, how true is this story? Did it really happen?

ISBN 1-902483-01-4

Mayhem

TIFAT File II

A Nick Hunter Adventure

Israel faces imminent destruction, nuclear Armageddon. A series of kidnaps, bombings and senseless murders have left her isolated from her allies and threatened by enemies of old. Unknown to all but a few, the situation has been orchestrated by multi-millionaire Zionist, Samuel Dayan. His vision of a Greater Israel will be carved from the charred ruins of the Middle East.

But Dayan is up against the international anti-terrorist organisation, TIFAT, and our hero Nick Hunter. To the age-old struggle of Good against Evil, author Paul Henke adds state-of-the-art communications technology and computerised warfare. In a desperate race against time, Hunter and his team of hand-picked specialists deploy satellite intelligence and high-tech weaponry to track Dayan to his lair.

The plot twists and turns in a series of setbacks, betrayals and mind-blowing developments. Myriad minor characters deserve story-lines of their own.

Relentlessly building the tension, Henke strips his hero Hunter of all resources but those within himself – knowledge born of experience and the inability to give up. Hunter simply must not fail.

ISBN 1-902483-02-2

Chaos

TIFAT File III

A Nick Hunter Adventure

Ambitious Alleysia Raduyev has inherited the family business – the largest crime cartel in Georgia. Operating on the classic theory of supply and demand, she caters for her customers every desire – narcotics, arms, prostitution, forced labour. Her payroll has extended to include lawmakers and law enforcers. No one is safe from her tyranny and oppression.

Power base secured, Alleysia moves on to her next objective – the formation of a super crime cartel, whose actions will result in global chaos. As a deterrent to those who would oppose her, she chooses the ultimate weapon – three nuclear warheads.

Desperate to prevent a new, anarchic world order, the West declares World war III against the cartels and their terror organisations. As violence escalates, the now battle-hardened troops of TIFAT are pitched against their toughest adversary yet.

Spearheading the battle is Lt. Cdr. Nick Hunter, the fearless explosives and diving specialist seconded to The International Force Against Terrorism.

The latest TIFAT novel is a clarion call to the Western world as it comes to grips with the realities of modern terrorism.

ISBN 1-902483-04-9

A Million Tears

'The summer's best holiday read . . .'
Scottish and Universal Newspapers

'An unquenchable thirst for daring and creativity . . .'
The Sunday Times

'As a literary publicist we receive over 50 books a week to eval-
uate – we knew instantly that *A Million Tears* was a classic.'
Tony Cowell, *PressGroup UK*

'Henke has written a gripping story . . .'
Corgi Books

'I smelt the coal dust in Wales and felt the dust in my eyes as
I fought alongside Evan.'
Dr Peter Claydon

'Henke tells interesting and exciting stories. He doesn't use bad
language and writes good English. A joy to read.'
The Sun

The Tears of War and Peace

'Henke isn't just talented, but versatile too. His books are very convincing. As good as Stephen King, Wilbur Smith, Tom Clancy and Bernard Cornwell.'

Burton Mail

'Read them and weep.'

The Stirling Observer

'He's one of the best new writers we've had in ten years.'
The Burton Trader

'A family saga with non-stop adventure from beginning to end.'
Tony Cowell, *PressGroup UK*

Débâcle

Mayhem

'A non-stop action adventure set in Scotland and the Middle East.'

The Edinburgh Evening News

'A fast moving tale of terror and destruction set amidst the charred ruins of the Middle East. An international force exists to fight terrorism. Terrific realism.'

The Stirling Observer

'The hero, Nick Hunter, embarks on a non-stop roller-coaster adventure from the Scottish Highlands to the Middle East. Henke is being hailed as the next Wilbur Smith.'

The Aberdeen Press and Journal

'Mayhem is a classic airport thriller. It's a veritable page turner and a cracking read.'

The Milngavie & Bearsden Herald

'A cracking good yarn. Non-stop action from beginning to end.'

Central FM radio

'Fiction becomes fact in Paul Henke's action thrillers. A superb read.'

The Northern Echo